Trisha Telep was the romance and fantasy book buyer at Murder One, the UK's premier crime and romance bookstore. She has recently re-launched this classic bookshop online at www.murderone.co.uk. Originally from Vancouver, Canada, she completed the Master of Publishing program at Simon Fraser University before moving to London. She lives in Hackney with her boyfriend, filmmaker Christopher Joseph.

THE MAMMOTH BOOK OF

TIME TRAVEL ROMANCE

Edited by Trisha Telep

ROBINSON

RUNNING PRESS
PHILADELPHIA · LONDON

Constable & Robinson Ltd
3 The Lanchesters
162 Fulham Palace Road
London W6 9ER
www.constablerobinson.com

First published in the UK by Robinson,
an imprint of Constable & Robinson, 2009

A copy of the British Library Cataloguing in Publication
Data is available from the British Library

UK ISBN 978-1-84901-042-9

1 3 5 7 9 10 8 6 4 2

First published in the United States in 2009 by Running Press Book Publishers

US Library of Congress number: 2008944139
US ISBN 978-0-7624-3781-8

Running Press Book Publishers
2300 Chestnut Street
Philadelphia, PA 19103-4371

Visit us on the web!

www.runningpress.com

Printed and bound in the EU

Contents

Acknowledgments

"The Key to Happiness" © by Gwyn Cready. First publication, original to this anthology. Printed by permission of the author.

"MacDuff's Secret" © by Sandy Blair. First publication, original to this anthology. Printed by permission of the author.

"Lost and Found" © by Maureen McGowan. First publication, original to this anthology. Printed by permission of the author.

"Stepping Back" © by Sara Mackenzie. First publication, original to this anthology. Printed by permission of the author.

"Sexual Healing" © by Margo Maguire. First publication, original to this anthology. Printed by permission of the author.

"The Wild Card" © by Sandra Patrick. First publication, original to this anthology. Printed by permission of the author.

"The Eleventh Hour" © by Michelle Rouillard. First publication, original to this anthology. Printed by permission of the author.

"Pilot's Forge" © by Patrice Sarath. First publication, original to this anthology. Printed by permission of the author.

"Saint James' Way" © by Jean Johnson. First publication, original to this anthology. Printed by permission of the author.

"The Troll Bridge" © by Patti O'Shea. First publication, original to this anthology. Printed by permission of the author.

"Iron and Hemlock" © by Autumn Dawn. First publication, original to this anthology. Printed by permission of the author.

"Last Thorsday Night" © by Holly Lisle. First publication, original to this anthology. Printed by permission of the author.

"The Gloaming Hour" © by Cindy Miles. First publication, original to this anthology. Printed by permission of the author.

"A Wish to Build a Dream On" © by Michelle Willingham. First publication, original to this anthology. Printed by permission of the author.

"Time Trails" © by Cindy Holby. First publication, original to this anthology. Printed by permission of the author.

"The Walled Garden" © by Michele Lang. First publication, original to this anthology. Printed by permission of the author.

"Catch the Lightning" © by Madeline Baker. First publication, original to this anthology. Printed by permission of the author.

"Steam" © by Jean Johnson. First publication, original to this anthology. Printed by permission of the author.

"Falling in Time" © by Allie Mackay. First publication, original to this anthology. Printed by permission of the author.

"Future Date" © by A. J. Menden. First publication, original to this anthology. Printed by permission of the author.

Introduction

Love takes its own sweet time . . . (sigh)

Have you missed your romantic destiny? Were you fated for a lover who lived 800 years before you were born? Or maybe you were meant for a mate who won't be born until 3,000 years after you're gone? Ever wondered what it would have been like to pay a visit to the Wild West and meet your perfect cowboy? Spend some quality time with a sexy Highlander? Or be romanced by a technologically enhanced lover from the far, far future? Do you ever feel like a piece of you is missing and no matter how hard you try, no matter how many frogs you kiss, you are never going to stumble upon your true love? How can you possibly meet the man of your dreams when he is living in eighteenth-century Scotland and you are stuck firmly within the confines of Earth circa 2009! It might all seem unrelentingly bleak at times, but don't despair – the heartbreakingly tragic barrier of time is no barrier at all when true love is at stake – if you read the right books, that is.

Time-travel romance has had a colourful history. But after a torrid heyday in the 1990s and early 2000s, full of Highlanders, pirates, Regency viscounts, and interplanetary hunks, it subsided into the background as edgier, fantasy-based, modern subgenres like paranormal romance and urban fantasy pushed to the fore to blossom into overnight sensations.* Suddenly there wasn't much room left for time travel. It occasionally saw fantastic flights of imagination from individual writers, but more often than not

---

* But what is time travel if not paranormal? Hurtling through space and time at the speed of light to land in a world, in a time, not your own seems pretty paranormal to me . . .

stayed on the sidelines, something of a wallflower, the plain, shy girl at the dance. But while paranormal romance swept the nation, time travel bided its time. And through the looking glass of the paranormal phenomenon, time travel began to develop some (more) paranormal elements of its own.

The Mammoth Book of Time Travel Romance is just one of many fresh, modern reassessments of time travel romance (think of the current much-hyped release of the film *The Time Traveler's Wife*, in cinemas across the stratosphere!). It's a brand-new beast, this time travel collection, yet with many, many nods to time travels origins. A massively eclectic collection of timeless romances from a diverse range of writers, some old, some new, but all playing with the conventions of genre, and with a paranormal glint in their eye. And while you'll still find an array of traditional time travel romances here – contemporary women whisked back to earlier historical periods and flung headlong into the waiting embrace of warriors, lords and lairds – this collection brings the time travel romance genre into the twenty-first century (forget simply travelling back in time, the future holds lots of surprises, too!).

From the ubiquitous Scottish glens and Victorian parlours, we incorporate a bit of the manga-influenced futuristic time travel of the fantastic, but sadly defunct, Shomi collection from Dorchester Publishing, and give a friendly nod to the new Time Raiders series from Silhouette Nocturne (created by the fabulous Merline Lovelace and Lindsay McKenna). Using a little (really little) bit of science, and a whole heck of a lot of fantasy, you'll not only find fish-out-of-water stories here, but everything in between!

The impossibility of getting a double half-caf venti low-fat mochaccino (or a decent sleep on a proper mattress, if you've been flung back into the Dark Ages) pales in comparison to the warmth of your true love's arms (believe me). New, revamped, reinvented, and reinvigorated, time travel is due its renaissance.

Isn't it about *time*?

The Key to Happiness

Gwyn Cready

The man was nondescript, Kate thought. Pleasant but entirely nondescript. Grey hair, grey eyes, medium height and as old as her parents, if not older. A face in the crowd, if this were a movie. In fact it dawned on Kate, as he leaned in to speak, that he'd probably been seated next to her for most of Van Morrison's "Moondance", though she hadn't noticed exactly when he'd slipped into the chair next to her.

"I imagine you enjoyed the cake." He spoke a little louder than necessary, to be heard over the wedding band. He re-angled his seat a degree and smiled.

The statement was unusual. Not quite a come-on – well, certainly not a come-on, not from someone old enough to have danced to "Moondance" on vinyl – but not your usual conversation starter.

"I did, yes." She took a quick glance at her plate. She'd eaten two-thirds of the slice – half the cake part and all the strawberries between the layers, but almost none of the frosting – not enough to be called out for overindulgence. She struggled with emotional overeating and had an immediate visceral reaction to any reference to her appetite.

But the man's eyes held no irony or judgment. The tweedy flecks of blue and green in the hazy irises showed only polite curiosity.

"Strawberries are my favourite," she said. "In fact, that's how Carly – the bride – and I met."

"Really?"

"We were in seventh grade, working the annual strawberry-sale fundraiser for our softball team. We ate more than we sold, I think. God, I was so sick. I threw up for three days."

He smiled. The lines that appeared around his eyes gave him a warmth she hadn't seen before. She wondered if he smiled a lot.

"That's a nice dress." He nodded towards the sateen bridesmaid skirt crinkling as she moved. "I take it the bride likes pink?"

"Oh, my God, it's a good thing Carly didn't hear you say that. This," she said, gathering a handful of fabric, "is watermelon. Not pink. Not red. *Watermelon.*"

"Clearly, I'm not as familiar with the fruit colour wheel as I should be."

"Pink is for NASCAR junkies and girls at their *quinceañera*," Kate explained. "And red is for Detroit hockey fans and sluts."

"Heavens, I see the bride has some strong opinions."

"And the only possible accent colour," Kate added, tugging at the dangling stones at her ears, "is a green you could only call, well . . ."

"Rind?"

"Exactly."

"You've been through bridesmaids' hell, I can see."

"And the seventh circle is on the horizon." She gazed at the knot of pre-teens gathering for the bouquet toss.

"I hope it goes with watermelon."

"Oh, let me correct myself." She held up a finger. "Not just 'watermelon'. Carly considers it 'frosted watermelon' because of the shiny watermark-type things swirling around in the fabric."

"Got it." He nodded uncertainly.

"Am I scaring you?"

"If I'm honest, yes."

Kate shook her head and sighed. "My wedding's going to be on the steps of the City/County Building with, like, six people watching and me wearing my friend Rema's sari."

"Your mother will never go for it."

She looked at him again. It was a comment with broad application, but there was something about the tone that suggested a specific understanding, not a mass market aside. "Do you know my mother?"

"Actually," he said, "I'm here for them." He gestured towards two men in their mid-twenties leaning back on their elbows at the bar. One was a groomsman, a broad-shouldered blond in his last year of law school at Columbia named Mark Donovan, and the other a shorter and slightly chunkier Irish-looking guy who had just elbowed his friend in the ribs and made an under-his-breath observation. Kate thought she'd been introduced to him as well, but she couldn't remember. Mark caught her eye and gave her a lopsided grin. When they were introduced by Carly's aunt before the ceremony, he'd made a joke about the likelihood of the band playing "Moondance".

"Oh?" She straightened. "You know Mark?"

The man gazed down for an instant, then nodded. "For a long time."

Mark reminded Kate of Robert Redford in *The Candidate* – a painfully handsome, world's-his-oyster sort of go-getter who would pelt effortlessly across any finish line life put in front of him, six strides ahead of his closest competition. Kate, an aide in the mayor's office, was a political junkie. She could already plot Mark's rise from assistant district attorney to whiz-kid congressman with a penchant for fiscal responsibility and green issues. She had to admit she found his quiet confidence attractive.

"He's in law school, I hear."

"He's going to make a great attorney," the man replied, nodding. "I'm Patrick McCann, by the way."

He held out a hand. Kate shook it.

"Kate Garrett." His hand was firm and dry, and it seemed like he held their clasp a moment longer than necessary. She noticed for the first time that his clothes, while well tailored, were more the uniform of a traveller than a wedding guest. He wore a loose-fitting jacket, his pants were a lightweight fabric with cargo pockets and his white linen shirt was open-collared. He wore no wedding band. She was surprised she'd looked, but even more surprised at the ring's absence because he radiated the relaxed ordinariness she'd come to associate with long-time married men, not the restless charm of players like her father. She shrugged. Maybe he wasn't a ring wearer.

"Are you in town for the wedding?" She tucked an auburn tendril behind her ear.

He considered. "Yes. That and to catch up with a friend."

She nodded. The couples on the dance floor moved to the make-out session rhythm as the song neared its end, some intent on their partner, others on the band or the bride and groom. This was the third hour of the reception, and it was grinding to a close. She wondered if Mark danced. Maybe if the band started a more up-tempo number she'd make her way on over to ask him. Shyness, thank God, had never been her problem. It wouldn't serve in politics, where straightforwardness or at least fearless lying was a part of the job.

The man – Patrick – seemed to be on the verge of saying something just as a high-pitched, "There you are!" made her turn. Kate's high-school friend and fellow bridesmaid, Becky Schaal, was scurrying towards her, arms outstretched. Kate jumped up to take advantage of the proffered hug. "They need me for a picture," Becky cried, breaking away and waving. "See you on the conga line." Kate hoped she was kidding. As she sprinted away she caught Kate's eye and pointed to Patrick behind an open hand. "Cute!" she mouthed.

Cute? Kate looked again. He *was* cute in a sort of teddy-bear kind of way. There was something about middle age that lurked sexily beneath the surface of some men. Some men, like some women, didn't earn their attractiveness stripes until much later in life. But he was way too old for Kate. What was Becky thinking?

Patrick was smiling. "A frosted watermelon blur."

"Moondance" had ended. The guitar player hunched over the mic. "When a ma-an loves a woman ..." Kate caught Mark's eye. This was number two on his list of "Top-Three Overplayed Wedding Songs". She grinned.

"Kate," Patrick began.

"Would you mind?" She put a staying hold on his sleeve. "I'm going to pop over there to say hello. Watch my stuff."

The tweedy hue in his eyes sparkled. "Will do."

The only good thing about the dress, Kate thought as she made her way across the room, was the fact the overlapping folds of satin made her B-cup breasts look twice as big as they actually were – though that sort of *trompe l'oeil* was definitely a doubled-edge sword if said breasts were called on to make a live appearance.

Mark put down his drink and straightened. "I called it."

"You did," she said. "Two in a row. Know any other party tricks?"

"Yeah, but the last time he did it," Mark's friend said, "the other ponies got jealous."

Kate giggled, and Mark gave them both a good-natured smile. He sensed the infinitesimal pause and handled it deftly. "Kate, this is my room-mate at Penn, P.J.; P.J., this is Kate Garrett. Mayor's office, right?"

Kate nodded and shook P.J.'s hand. "You going to law school, too?"

"I wish. Archaeology. All that logic stuff is beyond me. I'm more of a shovel man. If two sharp whacks with a blunt instrument doesn't take care of the problem, it's out of my league."

Kate laughed again and P.J. beamed.

Mark offered his hand. "Can I assume you'd be interested in a few moments of living *la vida loca*?"

"My Spanish sucks," P.J. said. "Do I need to deck him for you?"

"*Gracias pero no*," Kate said and added to Mark, "I would love to."

He led her by the hand to a relatively empty spot on the parquet and began to dance. While no Ricky Martin, he moved with exuberance and responded to Kate's moves with a happy ease. He even managed to lead her through an under-the-arm twirl. Kate found herself smiling even more than she'd expected.

"I'm sitting next to the guy you came with." Kate had to raise her voice as the band was bringing the song into its final lap.

"P.J.?" Mark was doing a very funny move as he avoided the violent rhythmic swinging of a beaded scarf belonging to a woman who'd apparently been waiting all her life to dance to "La Vida Loca".

"No," Kate said. "Him."

But when Mark turned in the direction she pointed, the table was empty.

"Unless this guy hid in the trunk, I can assure you, it was just P.J. and I in the car."

"He said he knew you. Older guy. Medium height, grey eyes, named, um – Oh, wait, there he is."

But when Mark turned again, the scarf nailed him. He clutched his eye, wincing. "I think I got some spangle in my eye."

Kate led him off the floor and scored some eye drops from one of the contact-wearing bridesmaids, but Mark kept closing his lid whenever he tried to apply it.

"Jesus, you're worse than my three-year-old nephew," she said.

"I -I - It's my eye, you know," he whined.

"Now you're sounding like him, too."

She ordered him on to his back on the floor and was pleased to see him submit without a complaint. Then she told him to close his eyes.

"The last time this happened," he complained, "I ended up with a bad case of crabs and someone else's shoes."

"You'll be pleased to know you are in danger of neither tonight."

"I don't know if 'pleased' is the word I'd use," he muttered slyly, and she gave him a look.

She had to hang over practically on top of him to get the right angle. He smelled like the really expensive French-milled soap she once found in the bathroom of the re-election campaign's biggest donor. She wondered if she'd ever smell as good. "Now, close," she ordered, and when he did, she let one eye drop fall into the inside corner of each eye. "Open."

"What? Now? There's stuff on them."

"Do it."

"*Arrrrrrrggghhh.*" The drops floated glossily over his eyes and down his temples.

"There. Feel any better?"

"What I feel is strong-armed," he said in a mock sulk. "Misused and strong-armed."

"Maybe write your congressman." She helped him to his feet.

"Don't think I won't." He test-blinked his bad eye. "You know there's a name for someone like you."

"Hero?"

"I'm too polite to say it."

"Why do I doubt that? Is the eye better?"

"A little." He smiled. "Thank you."

"Bouquet!" cried Bethany, a junior bridesmaid in bare feet and a borrowed sweater, racing by. "C'mon, Kate!"

"Oh, crap."

Mark stopped his eye rubbing. "Not a fan of the bouquet tradition?"

"Ranks right up there with the pencil in the eye tradition."

"I could provide an excuse." He gave her an interested look. "Cover, as it were."

"Are we back to the crabs and shoes?"

"I was thinking a stroll in the courtyard, but, hey, I'm always open to suggestions."

"Oh, that's you, a real people pleaser." She had to admit she was tempted, but she could just see Carly's face if she wasn't there. "I'm going to have to pass. The bride's my best friend. I'm afraid I owe her this one last blow to my ego."

"Ah, if I had a dollar for every time I've said that."

She laughed. "Wish me luck."

"Would that entail catching it or not?"

"I'd settle for avoiding the woman with the ninja scarf." She picked up her skirt, but he caught her hand.

"Kate?"

"Yeah?" His eyes were a clear, bright blue.

"I'd really like to see you later."

A marvellous tingle shot up her spine.

"*Kate!* C'mon!" The junior bridesmaid was back, clutching Kate's other hand and pulling.

Kate shrugged, gave Mark an encouraging smile and scurried off after Bethany.

At the gathering for the bouquet, Kate found a spot at the back, close enough to look engaged, but far enough to the side for the possibility of actually catching the accursed thing to be remote.

Carly appeared, beaming, and turned to toss the bouquet. But Carly had been a shot-putter in high school and somehow managed to put enough English into the release to send it spinning towards the speaker mount where, with a *tink*, it careened straight towards Kate.

Kate flung up her arms to ensure the arrival didn't come with the double humiliation of getting smacked in the face and, an instant later, a rousing cheer rose from the crowd.

Kate opened her eyes. Bethany clutched the bouquet giddily, aloft in the arms of Mark's room-mate.

"I figured you wouldn't mind," he said and swung Bethany to the floor.

"Kate, look!" Bethany held the bouquet just like she'd seen Kate do it in the ceremony. The bouquet was half as big as she was.

"Amazing," Kate said. "You look like a princess." She gave P.J. a smile.

Mark was in the distance, chatting with other guests. He'd made an interesting offer, one she could spread like fresh blueberry jam over the toast of the evening, savouring the crisp, sweet scent and glossy mounds of purple and blue whether she decided to partake or not.

"Are you staying for the foosball championship?" Kate asked Mark's room-mate. Carly's husband, Joe, was a foosball fanatic and had arranged a midnight tournament in the adjoining game room for those willing to stay the extra hour, and Kate could see Joe across the room, tie loosened, making the starting bracket on a sheet of paper taped to the wall.

"I agreed to collect the tuxes. I'll be here until they lock the place up."

The band started to play. Kate lifted a glass of champagne off a roving waiter's tray, considered jumping into a conversation about the new light-rail line being considered in the city but elected instead to return to her seat, kick off her shoes and spend a few minutes rolling that blueberry taste around in her mouth.

Beside her, the seat was empty. She was reminded of the incident with the man – Patrick – who hadn't come with Mark and P.J. as he'd claimed.

Weird.

She stretched her legs and let the strains of Billy Joel's "Scenes from an Italian Restaurant" roll over her.

This time she felt the emptiness beside her fill. She knew it was him, even without looking, though this time his presence seemed tinged with a different sort of emotion.

He didn't speak, which surprised her and, when she gave him a sidelong glance, he seemed intent on the bottom of his wine glass. At last she straightened. "Great band, huh?"

"Yes. Good covers. I hate to say it, but they remind me a bit of the White Stripes – the guitar playing mostly, not the song choice."

Kate smirked inwardly. Her freshman room-mate had managed to bring every musical conversation back to the White Stripes. She hadn't thought of that in years, though it struck her as odd that a middle-aged man would make a White Stripes comparison.

"I never took my eyes off your purse, by the way," he said.

"What? Oh. Thanks. I appreciate that."

Suddenly, he pushed his glass away and looked into her eyes. "Kate, I need to ask you a favour?"

"Me? Sure. What?"

"Take my hand."

Instantly, she retreated a few centimetres. "What?"

"I swear, I'm not a weirdo, but I need to tell you something and I can't do it unless I'm holding your hand."

She didn't want to. She'd had enough bad experiences with men, but he looked so harmlessly earnest, she relented. Nonetheless, she was glad there were still a number of partygoers circulating.

Even after she nodded 'yes' though, he didn't offer his hand. In fact, he appeared to be gripping the tabletop as if any movement on his part might scare her away. So Kate extended her hand. He took it gently, and she immediately felt a light charge, like the one she got touching her tongue to a nine-volt battery, only more pleasant.

"You gonna read my fortune?" she said with a nervous smile.

But however pleasant the current she was feeling, it was clear he was feeling something else. He gazed at her hand, face tight with emotion.

"Patrick?" she said after a beat.

"Sorry, it – do you feel it, too?"

"Yes."

"It's OK, though?"

"Yes."

His hand was cool and dry, and he let her do the gripping.

"Kate," he said, "I know things about you."

Kate's heart seized. He was going to try to get her to join his church or his cult or his drive to eliminate the secret magnesium vapours the government was putting in our food.

She began to pull away. "Ah, Patrick, um –"

He caught her. "You have a dog named Klondike, your sister's name is Liz and you *hate* the White Stripes."

Kate blinked, alarmed. He was right – on all counts. He saw her attempt to cover the surprise. "Anyone could have told you that," she pointed out carefully. "Besides, doesn't everyone hate the White Stripes?"

The flecks of green danced in his eyes. He liked her sense of humour, which lowered the creep-out quotient considerably. She'd let this go on a little longer. "So, you've been asking questions. This is election year. You're, like, what? Part of the opposition?"

He relaxed his grip, flashing an apologetic look. "In a sense. But this has nothing to do with politics."

"My sister and my dog. Not exactly Harry Houdini stuff, OK?"

The corner of his mouth rose, buoyed by her challenge, and his eyes narrowed in a calculating squint. "I'm walking a fine line here between trying to convince you and trying not to scare you," he said after a long pause.

"Oh, you passed that line a few minutes ago, my friend." She gazed at the bronze of his skin and the intricate pattern of hairs peeking from his sleeve. His was a fine hand to hold, she noted objectively, strong and generous, and that odd tingle of connection still burned pleasantly across the surface of her palm. That, more than anything, made her curious enough to continue.

He gestured to her clutch. "Are your keys in there?"

She nodded.

"You stuff your purses with Kleenex to make them hold their shape, you always carry some kind of lime-green-coloured lip balm, and your keychain has a Powerpuff Girl on it – Buttercup, I believe – which, for a reason I have never understood, seems to represent both empowerment and revolution to you."

He picked up her purse. "May I?"

She was too shocked to do anything but nod.

He gently shook out the contents of her bag: about a dozen crumpled tissues, Buttercup on the ring that held her keys, Bonne Bell Kiwi Lip Smacker lip balm, a twenty, a Triple A card and her cell phone. He picked up the keys with his free hand. "More?"

"You had access to my purse," she pointed out. "I left it on the table."

"Fair enough. You went to Sarah Lawrence and majored in politics," he said, "though you should've probably majored in literature, since you're a voracious reader, mostly historical fiction and mysteries, though when no one's looking you pull out one of the romances you keep hidden under your bed. There's some tiresome character named Jamie in one of them you wish all men would emulate. You drive a shiny new Subaru; you made the down payment on it with your first pay cheque, which is one of the things that first made us friends, because I drive one, too. You love to rollerblade, and you always wear a helmet, but a knee injury from ninth-grade tennis tends to make you look like a penguin on wheels, and you're about to make the biggest mistake of your life."

Kate exhaled, her mind racing in every conceivable direction. Was this a trick? These things weren't impossible to know, and yet, why would anyone bother? "I . . . I . . . don't believe you."

"About the mistake?"

"About any of it."

"Kate, your mother had a lump removed from her breast. You feel guilty because it happened while you were doing your finals senior year and you think you should have been there, and your worry for her is something that's always in the back of your head."

"What do you want?" He'd gone too far. Her shock had boiled into anger. "This is rude."

"But she's going to be OK," he said quickly. "All right? She's going to be OK. I promise."

She froze, the thin layer of defence that keeps our emotions at bay torn away, and against her will a tear striped her cheek.

"It doesn't come back, Kate. She's cancer free at five years and, at ten, the cancer is something you hardly think about any more – either of you. She's there for you, Kate. She's always there. And I know this because I lived through it with you. Not the college stuff – I didn't meet you until later – but all the rest."

Her heart ached, so badly did she yearn to believe what he said. "I haven't told this stuff to my best friend."

"But you told it to me. I'm not your best friend, but I'm close."

"I don't understand what you're saying." Her words were hot. She hated feeling exposed.

"I . . . I . . ." He stole a glance at her, evidently considering the limits to which he might go. "I come from the future and –"

"Bullshit." She nearly yanked her hand away, but the temptation to hear more was too strong.

"I understand why you'd not believe, Kate. I do. What I'm doing is something almost no one ever gets to do."

"So you're special."

"Lucky," he corrected. "I guess." He gazed at his shoes.

"Lucky" was not the emotion he was radiating.

"So what is this mistake?"

"Are you sure? I mean, do you believe me?" He worked the key ring in his palm like Queeg in *The Caine Mutiny*.

"'Believe' is a strong word. Let's say I'm willing to prolong the, well, whatever this is. Go on. You have my attention."

He chewed his lip. At last he leaned forwards. "The man you were just speaking to—"

"Mark?"

He flushed deeply. "After him."

Kate frowned, thinking. "Mark's friend? One of the ones you said you came with?"

"What I said was I came *for* them."

Then it hit her, and her heart kicked like a rabbit in her chest. "You look like him." Medium height, medium build, same grey eyes.

"There's a reason for that," Patrick said softly. "And what I said was a lie. I came for you." The keys stopped moving, and he gazed at the place her thumb met his palm.

"What's your name? Your whole name?"

"Patrick McCann. Patrick John McCann."

P.J.! He had to be P.J.'s father. There couldn't be any other explanation, or rather, there could be, but her mind simply wouldn't process it.

"I don't have kids," he said, answering the look in her eye. "I also don't have brothers or a nephew – well, except one, but he's half Filipino and lives in Singapore. I come from the future, our future, where I'm the best friend of your husband."

Kate's eyes bulged. "I marry *Mark*?!"

The key ring began to rattle. "Yes."

She sat up to put her hand on his arm, and he caught it. "You can't let go, Kate. The things I can tell you, I can only tell you with your hand in mine."

"Why?" Her head was reeling from what he'd already told her.

"Because," he said carefully, "telling you about the future is very dangerous, or so I've been told. I can tell you what I tell you for one simple reason: so long as our hands are clasped, you'll remember what I'm saying, but as soon as you let go, it will all be gone."

"Gone?" She thought of her mother.

"Gone."

She was dizzy with questions, though the sceptic in her, whose voice was fading fast, kept a low "uh uh," rumbling in her ear.

"Mark, then? Where do we live? Is he a politician? Am I a strategist? Am I successful? Are we happy?"

He gave her a weak smile. "That's a lot of questions. Let's see . . ." He lowered his gaze to her hand, as if reading her fortune in the topography of knuckles and minute lines. "You live here, in Pittsburgh, in an immense condo overlooking the river, where you host a lot of parties. Mark is a partner at a law firm, though he's a power broker in politics here and in the state."

Kate frowned. A power broker was hardly the idealist she'd visualized in that flash of imagining. Nonetheless, they were still in the thick of it. "And me?"

"You run a not-for-profit – disadvantaged kids, that sort of thing. You've made a huge impact in the city," he said with an obvious pride, "and it keeps you very busy."

This was like going to your high-school guidance counsellor to find out what job the vocation test says you're suited for and discovering it's some vaguely improbable position at the top of a corporate food chain. Admirable, maybe, but for someone else.

"Really?"

"You do a great job, Kate."

"But why not politics?"

The odd distracted reflection washed over him again. "I could speculate, but . . . but I think I should stick to what I know."

"You're supposedly one of my closest friends." The voice in her head was growing louder. "Didn't I tell you?"

"What you told me was that politics was a place for the cold-blooded."

"*I* said that?" She'd never been a cynic. Not about politics.

"Yes. And I can see you're disappointed," he added quickly, "but I can tell you, you never look back. Your work brings you immense joy. Immense."

"It sounds like you're trying to convince me."

"No," he said, agitated. "What I'm trying to do is be fair."

"*Fair?*"

"Kate, I'm about to ask you to give it all up, and I don't ever want it to be said that I didn't present the case fairly."

It was almost too much, she thought, to have pictures of her life laid out before her and then immediately snatched away. "Give it up? What are you asking me to give up? And why?"

Before he could answer, Mark appeared in her peripheral vision, and instinctually she withdrew her hand.

* * *

Patrick felt the cool air on his palm. All for naught, he thought with a philosophical chuckle, looking at that gorgeous, strong profile as she turned her gaze towards Mark. He stood at the centre of the remaining wedding guests, riveting them with a story. But it wasn't Mark to whom Patrick's eyes went when he'd finished feasting his gaze on the full, knowing lips he'd never know and the long, pale neck, fringed with dark blonde hairs that fell from her effortless French knot; his eyes went to himself, albeit a much younger version, standing to the side of the circle, eyes fixed on Kate.

Ah, my friend, if only you'd find the courage to approach her now, before that fated foosball game, he thought, and ached with the memory of how that longing felt.

But though the decades had given him the confidence he lacked then, even now, at fifty-six, after years of being there for her whenever she called, of sharing every step of her personal and business life, of being the recipient of all but her most precious secrets, he knew he'd never have the confidence – ever – to believe he could possess her. And yet, here he was, certain that what he was about to do, an act that would not only ensure he didn't possess her, but almost certainly tear her from him for ever, was the only choice he had.

He'd been given one hour. How it worked, he didn't know, but the woman in the souk with the coal eyes and the *hookah* pipe did, and in exchange for a thousand Egyptian pounds and his silence on the matter of the stolen *cartouche*, she told him the rules: You may tell the girl what you wish about her future so long as her hand is in yours, though nothing you say will be remembered. After an hour you will awake as if from the worst sort of drunken indulgence. Under no circumstances are you to make contact with your younger self.

When he asked if it was possible to change what would happen – his past, her future – the woman pulled a long drag from the pipe, grinned a horrible, black-toothed grin and said, "Changing the world is an effort of the heart, Yankee Doodle, not the mouth."

Then she'd mixed him his own *hookah* cocktail and handed him the pipe. That was the last thing he remembered.

He returned Kate's keys and other items to her purse surreptitiously. An instant after he closed it, Kate turned back to him. He gave her a polite smile. She'd forgotten everything he'd told her.

"Oh, sorry," she said with a start. "You were saying something about the . . . White Stripes?"

"The guitar player, I said. He gives it a sort of White Stripes sound." Of course, at this point, the band had finished with Billy Joel and was a few bars into "In Your Eyes", so the comparison made considerably less sense than it had before. Nonetheless, she pursed her lips again in that way she had, and he knew she was thinking of Robin, the miserable freshman room-mate he'd heard her mention over the years. He'd always been able to make her laugh with a White Stripes reference. He'd miss that.

He looked at her hand, considering.

"Kate, could I interest you in a dance?"

She felt the touch of his hand on her elbow as he led her to the floor. There was something both intriguing and protective about it. He was like the sexy uncle your girlfriend always wants to chat up at parties.

"In your eyes, the light, the heat. In your eyes, I am complete . . ."

He took her waist and held out his hand. She placed her palm on his, and a warm rush went through her, like the shower of sizzling sparks after a sky-filling firework.

She made a small mewl of surprise. "You told me things," she gasped.

"You remember." He laughed. "I didn't know."

Mark, disadvantaged kids and her mother's cancer, the ideas tumbled through her mind – narrow, concrete glimpses of a future that had until now been vast and ill-defined. "You wanted me to give something up. What?"

"All of it."

"What?"

"Kate, I don't have much time." He glanced at his watch as they moved. "To the end of this song, maybe a few minutes more, so I want you to listen. When that foosball game ends, Mark, my friend, is going to ask you out for a drink. Don't do it. Tell him you're tired; tell him you're dating someone else, whatever you want. Just don't go with him."

"You said we were getting married. You said we were happy."

His face contracted, and she felt her stomach knot.

He hadn't said they were happy, had he? "What happens?"

He lowered his eyes.

"Patrick, you're supposed to be my friend."

A long sigh. "Look, I'm not going to tell you this unless I can be completely fair. He's a good man. He shares your love of travel. You hold his hand at dinner parties. For years you guys would have won couple of the year."

"And then?"

"A woman."

"A slip."

He met her eyes.

"Does he leave me?" she asked, slightly ill.

"No," he said sadly. "Though I wish he would."

"Like my father, then?"

"Kate, I watched you fold in on yourself. I watched the Kate who set the room on fire everywhere she went just go out, like someone shot out a porch light with a twenty-two. It was like an eclipse, Kate. The spark was gone."

She refused to believe she could let that happen. She refused to believe she'd have invested so much in a man like her father. All her life had been about feeling strong and empowered. "How do we know I can't change it? How do we know?"

"I have to be honest, Kate. I don't know. I hope it *is* possible to change things. After all, that's the reason I'm here."

She looked at P.J., trading quips with Mark. "I can't believe the Mark I've met would do that, and I *really* can't believe I'd be attracted to that kind of man."

"People change, Kate. I told you."

"Did you?" She wondered what his story was.

"No."

"Did you marry?

"Yes, once. For six years. But it was mistake."

"Why?"

He turned his head. "The usual reasons."

"Why?"

"Kate."

"Why, Patrick?"

He led her into an unexpected turn. "I was in love with someone else."

Her eyes came to rest on P.J., who was looking straight at her. When their gazes met, he pivoted and took a long swallow from his beer. She wondered what else she had missed tonight.

"I'm sorry," she said honestly. "I didn't know."

Patrick shrugged good-naturedly.

"Am I nicer to you in the future than I am tonight?"

He laughed. "Yes. Much."

"I'm glad." She looked into those grey eyes. "Do I love you then?"

A flash of pain crossed his face. "Er, not that way, no."

She considered the courage and immense love it took to come so far for someone who didn't return your feelings. "So why don't you talk to him?" She indicated his younger self.

"Not allowed. Causes some kind of cosmic run-time error."

"And you're not willing to risk it?"

"I was told my time here would end instantly if I did, so, no," he said with a significant look, "I wasn't willing to risk it."

The music soared, and the singer made Peter Gabriel's lyrics her own.

"If you could," she asked, "what would you say?"

"Oh, gosh." He looked into the distance, his face breaking into the first truly unburdened smile of the evening. "Don't be such an idiot. Don't use Mark as an excuse to not at least try for what you want. Don't underestimate your own overpowering potential with women." The smile turned lopsided, and he dipped her with a flourish. "Oh, and do *not* bet against the Pirates in the '22 World Series."

She lifted a sly brow. "That last bit, good to know."

"Yeah, enjoy it for the next four minutes."

She laughed, but suddenly four minutes didn't seem like enough – not nearly enough. "What do I look like then?" She wondered if she were still battling a weight problem. It was a stupid question, but somehow she felt if she knew, some of the rest might be easier.

"You're asking the wrong person."

She looked at him quizzically.

"OK, here's what I see," he explained. "You walk in a room, fireworks go off. Your hair sends off sparks of gold like a halo. I see your smile, of course – at least when you *were* smiling. And a body that just exudes—"

"Hey!"

"Let me finish. That just exudes this sort of grace and openness to the world. And, well, let's face it, curves that just won't stop."

He squawked as she elbowed him.

"I am a man, all right?"

She let her hand drift to his lapel. He felt so solid, so constant. She'd never felt that before.

"I want that grace and openness for you always, Kate. That's why I'm here."

A thickness in her throat made it hard to speak. She didn't know this man, really. And yet he spoke in a way she'd barely allowed herself to imagine she might be spoken to someday. She must do something right to deserve a man like this in her future.

"What do you become?" she asked.

"Other than a slave to unrequited love?"

She grinned. "Yes."

"Um, an archaeologist. I think I, er, *he* might have mentioned that." He gestured toward P.J.

"Geez, am I that self-absorbed?" She chucked her forehead. "Why can't I remember what you told me?"

"Because you, my friend, have just entered the altered psychological state known as Mark Donovan. It's like cocaine, only more enthralling. P.J. McCann, on the other hand, makes up in longevity what he lacks in luminosity. Mark's like the spotlight at a movie premiere. I'm like a glow-in-the-dark rock. Four-point-five billion year half-life."

She laid her head on his shoulder, feeling the soft weave of his jacket and the softer chest below. Four-point-five billion years. She liked that.

The singer, while no Peter Gabriel, brought a heartfelt yearning to her desire to come back to the place her love was.

"I'm seeing just one problem," she said.

"Just one?" The rumble of his chuckle tickled her cheek.

"Just one. When I let go of your hand, I'm not going to remember any of this. Not one word."

"I guess," he said slowly, "I'm hoping for a miracle."

"Like the '22 Pirates?"

"Yeah, but this one, I'm not betting against. In fact, I've pretty much put all my chips on it."

"Well, at least I'll still have you. Do you think, I mean, is it possible, we'll fall in love if we change things?"

He was silent so long she lifted her head.

He looked wretched. "We won't."

"But it's possible, right? I mean, anything's possible, right?"

"Not with us."

"But if someone can – wait," she said. "I still have you, don't I?" Her head spun toward P.J. and back to him. "I still keep you, Patrick, even if I lose Mark. I mean, you're right there."

"Kate . . ."

"Tell me!"

"Think about it. I'm from Boston, which is where I – the younger I – at least at present, am planning to find an assistant professor position. I take the job at Pitt when I graduate for one reason: to be near you. And the only thing that impels me to do that is that I've fallen in love with you while you're dating Mark. No Mark tonight; no P.J. later." He shook his head sadly. "Dominoes, Kate."

"But you're standing right over there. Can't we just connect?"

But she already knew the answer. As soon as Patrick released her hand and this conversation was wiped from her head, she'd be too drunk on the thought of Mark to take the slightest notice of his pleasant but unremarkable friend.

"Don't beat yourself up," he said. "It's me, too. Look at me over there, for God's sake. I try to work up the courage to talk to you all night and never do. I have to collect the stupid tuxes, so I'm the last person here. I watch you leave with the final bunch of partygoers. I actually stand in the parking lot and watch Mark get in the car with you. How sad is that?"

She gazed across the nearly empty dance floor, out beyond the ballroom windows. It seemed so unfair. How could she be given such a gift for such a tiny period of time?

"I won't do it," she said simply. "I won't change what happens if it means I lose you."

He stopped so abruptly she nearly stumbled. "Kate, why do you think I've come here? I'm not trying to keep you from some pain. I wouldn't dare – hell, I wouldn't need to! You're one of the strongest women I know. I would have happily stood at your periphery for the rest of my life as you worked through it. I came because you're gone, Kate. Kate the woman who lit any room she walked into is gone. And I can't live with that." Tears appeared in his eyes. "When it happens, it obliterates you, Kate. It absolutely obliterates you."

She touched his arm, stunned. "So you're giving up your own happiness to save me."

"No courage required, Kate. You're already gone." He averted his face and dragged a sleeve across his cheek. "Jesus, look at me."

She thought he meant his tears until she spotted P.J., who stood at attention, beer forgotten, his eyes cutting between Kate and Patrick.

"Let's dance," Patrick said. "He's afraid you're in trouble."

She returned her head to Patrick's shoulder, navigating the apprehension of a sacrifice so selfless she wondered if she would experience it again in her lifetime. Oh, how she was dreading the end of the song.

The singer had reached the place where, alone and stripped of her pride, she'd reach out with all her heart and hope her love was returned.

"Promise me," he said huskily.

"What good is a promise," she cried. "I won't even remember."

"It's the only hope I have."

What could she say to a man who'd come from half a lifetime away? There was only one choice, and he had earned it. "I promise."

He took her in his arms as the singer began the last, lingering chorus. She clutched Patrick's shoulder, trying to absorb enough of him not only to carry her through tonight, but through a lifetime. She could feel the flutter of his breath in her hair. They had not even kissed. She laced her fingers into his.

The keyboardist played the last plaintive chord, which drifted and drifted until it was gone, and the room fell silent.

"That's it, kid."

Another moment, she wanted to scream, but she knew he deserved her strength. "Yep."

"Foosball, Kate!" Carly waved at her from the entrance to the game room. "It's our turn."

"Here's to changing the world," he said.

He released her waist. Their fingers, intertwined, relaxed. She drew hers down his palm, prolonging that last electric touch.

"To changing the world," she agreed, and he withdrew his palm.

Carly, thank God, was as wired as a dollar-store Christmas tree, for Kate felt like she'd had way too much champagne, though she could only remember drinking two glasses. Nearly every foosball shot taken and every attempt defended was the work of her teammate. The best Kate seemed to be able to do was to keep from stepping on Carly's train.

She was so muzzy-headed, in fact, she decided she must be seeing things when she spotted that nice man at her table – was his name Patrick? – going through the pockets of the coats on the coat rack. He seemed to find what he was seeking, however, for when she gave him a questioning look he held up a set of keys and smiled. Probably too drunk to find his coat. Drunk at a wedding reception? Imagine that. The next time she looked he was gone.

They won that round and two more, but they lost in the finals to Joe and Mark, who aimed every shot at Kate, sending her into uncharacteristic giggles, which she also blamed on the champagne.

"A gentleman," she said to him as they were gathering their coats, "would have let the drunk girl win."

"No one ever accused me of being a gentleman – especially with a drunk girl."

She laughed. He helped her on with her coat. He had changed into street clothes now, and he was looking great in jeans and a blazer.

"I, ah, don't suppose you'd be interested in one last glass of wine? There's a wine bar next door to my hotel that looked kind of interesting."

There it was, just like she'd been waiting for. She snapped open her purse. A glass of Cabernet on this chilly night. Knees touching at the bar. A pair of strong arms and soft lips.

"You know," she said. "I think . . . I think I'll take a pass."

He looked surprised. She felt surprised. But something in her head just kept saying no. And she'd been trying to teach herself to listen to that voice. Tonight, it was stronger than it had ever been. She'd make the right choice. No doubt. Nonetheless, when he gave her a goodnight kiss, she felt as if she was making a turn on a street she thought she'd follow the rest of her life.

She fished out her keys, and they made their way out to the parking lot. Mark lassoed a couple of others to join him for a glass. Kate waved as she headed to her car. She heard them drive off. The moon was out, which made the thin layer of snow sparkle. She tried to slip the key into the lock, but it wouldn't go in. She pulled it out and tried again. Nothing. The lock couldn't be frozen. It hadn't snowed in a day, and it was close to forty out. She tried one more time. It wouldn't budge.

She gazed around the lot. She could walk back to the hotel, she supposed, and try Triple A, but she spotted Mark's room-mate, ah, ah . . . She scoured her memory banks. P.J.! *There! I've remembered* some*thing at least.*

"P.J.!"

He had an armload of tuxes, though it looked like he'd been standing just outside the hotel exit.

"Need some help?" He trotted over, transferring the bundle to one arm.

"Yeah, apparently I'm too drunk to get my key to work."

"Wow. Who knew Subarus offered such hi-tech safety features?" She laughed.

"You must have the premium model," he said. "Mine just flashes a light that says, 'Pull him over, officer.'"

"You have a Subaru?"

"Damn right, sister. Best cars ever." He dropped the clothes on the trunk and extended his hand for the key.

But he was no more successful than she'd been. He tried the passenger door and the trunk. Nothing budged. Then he fished his keys out of his coat pocket.

"What the hell, right?"

"What the hell is right," she said. "It's either that or walk. And I live eight miles from here."

"Well, I could drive you." He slipped his key in – and it worked.

"Wow," she said. "That's weird. Though now that you mention it . . ."

"What?"

"I probably shouldn't drive."

He chuckled. "C'mon. Where do you live?"

She picked up a handful of tux and started heading towards the only other Subaru in the lot. "South Hills. Mt Lebanon."

"It's right on my way."

"Really? Where do you live?"

"The North Side."

"That's nowhere close."

"Depends how you define 'on my way'. I have to circle the city three times before I can sleep. I'm very doglike in that way."

His car was white, just like hers.

"Best colour," she said, pulling up to the passenger door. "Best colour, best car."

He leaned down to unlock her side. "What the hell?"

"What?"

"Now my key doesn't work." He dropped his armload on the trunk again.

"Well, I suppose we could use your key to drive my car to my house."

"Give me your keys."

She put them in his hand.

"Cross your fingers," he said.

She did. And the door opened. Like magic.

MacDuff's Secret

Sandy Blair

One

Edinburgh, Scotland
Present day

How bad could it be?

That was Sarah Colbert's only thought when Mr Morrow, the leader of their school's tour group, had announced he was ill and that she, alone, would be taking their unruly crew of sixth graders on their first tour of Edinburgh. Eyeing her five jostling charges in the Hotel Balmoral lobby she now prayed they'd be better behaved than they usually were in class.

Her gaze settled on the tall lanky heir to Elgin Aircraft Industries standing in the back. "Mr Elgin, where's your windbreaker?"

"Aww, come on, Miss Colbert."

"Mr Elgin, you know the rules."

While Peter grumbled and dug inside his backpack for the bright yellow windbreaker each student had to wear on every field trip so their chaperons didn't lose sight of them, Bryce Allen, the son of movie mogul Mike Allen, cuffed him on the head and started bouncing around like a prize fighter. Not to be outdone, Jeremy Babcock, an investment banker's prodigy, put his fists up and, laughing, took a swat at both of them.

"Gentlemen, knock it off."

God grant me patience. Having been an only child, she'd had little experience dealing with children prior to accepting her teaching position at the London branch of the prestigious American

International Schools, and her students, sensing it, regularly ran roughshod over her. But she took comfort where she could. Today would be a trip down memory lane, to that carefree summer when she'd been an exchange student in Edinburgh. And she'd be able to put her hard-earned degree in European history to excellent use.

Seeing Peter had his windbreaker on, she started walking. "This way, gentlemen. We're off to tour the 140 acres known as Edinburgh's New Town where at one time the greatest minds on earth could all be found living shoulder to shoulder. Our first stop will be Charlotte Square, named after King George III's wife and designed by renowned architect Robert Adam."

Three hours later, having described every nuance of Georgian architecture and the gruesome details related to Edinburgh Castle's body-laden moat being drained and turned into the lovely garden in which they now stood, Sarah, hoarse and dead on her feet, asked, "Is anyone hungry?"

"Yes!" they all shouted.

Ty Clark III queried no one in particular, "Anyone see a McDonald's around here?"

Behind him Bryce whispered, "You think the Spaniel will let us order some stout?"

Peter Elgin answered for her, muttering, "Hell, no."

Sarah sighed. "Watch the profanity, gentlemen."

A creative lot, her students had code names for all their instructors. Her boss was the Bull. Their headmaster, the Bear. They'd tagged her Spaniel the day she – running late – had shown up at school with her shoulder-length hair curling about her shoulders. She'd never made the mistake again but the moniker had stuck.

Sarah looked about. If memory served there was a nice pub that specialized in fish and chips two blocks west, near the intersection of King's Stable Road and Lothian Road. All kids like French fries, right? "OK, boys, this way."

The pub, awash in dark wood and stained glass, reeking of ale, fried fish and tobacco, hadn't changed in her ten-year absence. The hostess warily eyed Sarah's boisterous crew then led them to a private room at the back of the pub. As the boys settled around the long trestle table and tried to convince her that just *one* Guinness wouldn't kill them, Sarah opened her menu. Mmm, Arbroath

Smokie and stovie tatties. She hadn't had smoked haddock in years. Haggis? No. Forfar Bridies –

"What's Hotch-Potch?" Ty Clark III wanted to know.

She grinned. "A thick mutton stew. It's good."

He made a face.

To her left, Peter asked, "What's in 'authentic Shepherd's Pie'?"

Sarah looked over the top of her menu at their school's star soccer player. "Think about it, Peter. What do shepherds tend?"

"Oh." He went back to studying his menu.

In the end, they ordered six servings of fish and chips, five colas and one Guinness. For her. Their next stop was Edinburgh Castle. She could only pray the castle's armour displays would still be standing when they left.

"Miss Colbert, do you have a boyfriend?"

Bryce's question startled not only her but his classmates who, laughing, slapped his shoulders. She didn't have a boyfriend – never had. She'd spent the last twelve years either caring for her mother who'd had Alzheimer's or attending night school to get her degree. But that was none of their business. "Why do you ask?"

He shrugged. "You're always at school, never—"

Booooooommmm!

The violent explosion knocked them off their benches. The wall separating their private dining area from the main room collapsed around them. As they cried out, tried to make sense of what was happening, the customers in the front of the pub, buried beneath collapsed timbers, brick and glass, screamed.

Sarah, choking on smoke, her ears ringing, scrambled out from under their upended table. Reaching for her nearest charge, she shouted, "*Bryce*, are you OK?"

"Yes . . . I think." He wiped ash and tears from his eyes as he struggled to his knees. "What happened?"

"I don't know how but we've got to get out of here." Flames were consuming what little remained of the front of the building. People continued to scream. As the fractured ceiling above them groaned, she grabbed the edge of the table. "Help me lift this!"

Together they shoved the table away and found the rest of her students, choking and bleeding. Peter Elgin was the first to come to his senses. As he staggered to his feet, he took hold of Ty's arm and pulled. When his friend remained rooted where he'd fallen, Peter shouted, "Help me!"

Sarah crawled over rubble, grabbed Ty's left arm and hauled the stunned kid to his feet.

Tears streaming, Peter told her, "His parents died like this."

Sarah nodded, frantically searching for a way out. "I know . . . in Indonesia. There, behind you. There's a door. Take him out that way. I'll follow with the others."

She had her students on their feet and at the doorway before realizing the door didn't lead to a back alley as she'd hoped but into a cellar. Bitter bile rose in her throat. "Shit."

Peter called from the bottom of the stairs. "Down here, Miss Colbert! There's a way out."

At the bottom she found Peter and Ty standing hip deep in rushing water.

"Oh, God. A water main must have broken." Above them rafters screeched then collapsed, sending more dust, debris and smoke raining down the shaky staircase. Several of the boys cried out seeing the doorway they'd just passed through fill with rubble. There was no going back.

"Peter, did you see a door, a bulkhead?"

"No, but I can see daylight over there." He pointed to his right past an ancient cast-iron coal burner. "A window."

The frigid water continued to rise, now lapped at their chests. "OK. Can everyone swim?" When only Peter nodded, she screamed, "Answer me, damn it! Can everyone swim?"

She wasn't about to pull them from a fiery hell only to have them drowned in a flooding cellar. At her elbow, Jeremy said, "Ya, we all can."

"Good. OK. We can do this." *Please God.*

She knocked a floating carton out of her way. More debris took its place, the water starting to churn around their shoulders, their necks. "Everyone follow Peter. Swim towards the light." She'd take the rear. Make sure they all got out alive. And maybe she would too.

Heart thudding, she slogged past the burner and saw the window only to gasp when the stone wall behind them gave way and thousands of gallons of high-pressured water swept her off her feet. As water closed over her head, she prayed the pressure of so much water would blow out the window, for her children to survive. If only she'd learned how to swim . . .

Two

Hamish MacDuff jumped into what he'd come to think of as his magical pool, scrubbed his skin, then surfaced. Raking his wet hair back, he turned his face to the sun and sighed. 'Twould be another glorious day. "And sad that only I get to enjoy this place."

Aye, but 'twas safest.

Plush hemlock and pine surrounded his wee glen and pool, but they hadn't when he'd first arrived ten summers past. Then there were no birds or hares, no bees or hedgehogs. The only sounds to be heard then were those made by his ragged breathing and pounding feet.

Wounded, bleeding, parched and panicked, he'd somehow managed to outrun his enemies – the only one to survive out of more than 2,000 clansmen – only to stumble and fall face first in this very spot where a wee bit of cool water had soothed his slashed face. Had he the strength he would have laughed. He'd landed in a puddle no bigger than his fist, the only water he'd seen in days. He drank his fill from what he now knew to be a spring and then passed out.

He awoke to find wispy columns rising like ghosts from charred timber for as far as the eye could see. Not a soul stirred save him and a few beetles and the many-legged meggy monyfeet sifting through ash and charred branches, all that was left of the ancient forest after the Norman-set fires had done their worst. And the wee puddle had grown to the size of his head.

Deplete of strength, no longer having hearth or kin after the battle, having had his fill of grasping incompetent princes and kings, of fire and war, he remained, surviving on water and whatever hapless creatures happened to venture close to the pool.

With time his wounds became scars and his renowned strength returned. And as he mended, so did the land. Grass sprouted and scraggily saplings became bushy boughs. He cleared the dead wood from around the pool and his wee glen began to take shape. And the crystal clear pool continued to grow. 'Twas now the breadth of two oxen standing nose to tail, was bottomless at its core and loaded with fish and happy he was for them.

His middle rumbled. He climbed out of the water and wrapped his woollen *feileadh-mhor* about his waist then over his shoulder and across his chest. Securing it with his belt, he again noted its holes and sighed. A new garment would come dear and require a trip to Edinburgh, something he was loath to do. His middle rumbled again and he picked up his fishing pole. As he readied to cast his line, the normally calm water at his feet began to bubble and roll. Startled, he dropped the pole. "What's this?"

Before he could contemplate a reason for the water roiling, a thrashing lad popped to the surface gasping for air.

"St Columba's God and the fairies!"

Would wonders never cease?

He grabbed the tow-headed lad by the scruff and tossed him on to the grass like a landed fish.

Staring down at the dripping, gasping pup of a man he asked, "And who the hell might ye be?"

"What? I don't understand."

English!

Before he could ask how this could be, the water roiled again and another head and pair of thrashing arms shot out. Hamish grabbed the second lad by his bright yellow cloak and tossed him next to the first. Before he was through snatching and tossing there were five gasping lads dressed in yellow at his feet.

Hands on his hips, he glared at the youths. In the language he'd learned at his grandmother's knee but hadn't used in more than a decade, Hamish growled, "Dinna just sit there gaping like besot asses gleaming yer first teats, laddies. Answer me. Who be ye?"

The tallest lad, all joints and long bones, scrambled backwards like a crab. "Who the hell are you?"

Affronted the whelp should use such language when addressing an elder, Hamish reached out, but before he could snatch him, the black-headed lad jumped up shouting, "The *spaniel*! Where's the spaniel?"

They all rose, shouting at once in obvious panic. The fair-haired lad pointed at the pool. "*Look!* Oh crap, oh crap . . ."

Having no idea what a spaniel might be, Hamish looked. The pool was roiling again and at its centre floated yet another lad, this one the largest yet, face down and lifeless. Cursing, Hamish jumped into the pool. Careful not to step off the hidden shelf at the edge of the pool because he couldn't swim, he snagged the drowned lad's legs and hauled him into his arms.

The yellow-clad lads drew close as Hamish strode from the water and dropped to his knees, draped their hapless companion head down over his lap and pressed hard on the lifeless lad's back. On the second push water gushed from the lad's mouth. Hamish pushed down again. More water rushed out, the boy gagged then finally gasped.

Greatly relieved, Hamish rolled the hapless lad face up and placed a hand over his heart. To his shock his palm rested not on bony rib as he'd fully expected but on something round and soft. A breast. Aye, he'd not been alone so long or grown so auld that he'd forget *that* particular feel.

He scowled at the lads now kneeling around him. "'Tis a woman!"

The tall blond brushed a water-matted tress from the woman's face. "No shit, Sherlock."

The woman in his arms coughed, then sputtered, "Watch . . . your –" she coughed again "– language, Mr Elgin."

The lads issued a rousing cheer as the woman *Spaniel* stared up at him from bonnie brown eyes rimmed by thick spiked lashes. Liking the soft feel of her, the smooth contours of her oval face, the way her full lips were parted in surprise, he smiled. "Good day to ye, mistress."

"Uhmm . . . Hello." Her gaze then swung to the lads and her eyes grew larger still. She bolted upright, her arms reaching out to the lads. "Oh, God! Are you all OK?"

They clustered about her like hungry pups around their bitch, babbling excitedly in English but not in a manner Hamish had heard before.

Teeth chattering, Spaniel staggered to her feet and gave each lad a hug before looking about. Marvelling at the way her strange clothing clung to her lithe form, Hamish grinned. How could he have possibly thought her a lad? Ten summers were apparently far too long for a man to go without a woman.

He rose and she, clutching the closest lads to her sides, took several hasty steps back. "Who are you and where are we?"

He bowed. "Hamish MacDuff at ye service, and ye be in MacDuff glen."

"And where is that exactly?"

He scowled, not understanding what more she needed to ken.

One of the lads whispered, "He looks like an escapee from *Braveheart*."

Spaniel signalled the lads to silence and smiling at him asked, "How far is it to Edinburgh?"

Sarah stood atop MacDuff's watchtower and stared in utter disbelief at the small stone and wood fortress perched atop the huge stone promontory she knew as Castle Rock, upon which *should* have bristled formidable Edinburgh Castle. There was no city – old or new – no church spires, no anything but forest for miles and miles around her. Mouth dry, she stammered, "Wh . . . what year is this?"

At her side, Hamish MacDuff shrugged.

Deep breath, Sarah.

OK. If all she feared was true – that she wasn't simply trapped in a ghastly dream but they'd truly time travelled – then the powerfully built giant at her side probably didn't have a concept of time beyond the passing of seasons. "Do you know who lives there?"

"Aye. The Malcolm."

Her heart nearly stopped at the mention of the eleventh-century kings.

"After the Norman war, the ravages of which ye can still spy yon," he pointed to the blackened timber poking up through new growth, "Malcolm became ruler of this territory."

Oh God. Lonely as she'd been of late she could well imagine herself concocting a dream about a beautiful glen and a handsome Highlander, but she seriously doubted she'd have included an explosion, nearly drowning and five rambunctious, pampered students. Which made all before her that much more frightening . . . and real. "Do you know the way there?"

Logic dictated that if – and she would only concede *if* – they'd time travelled then they'd have to get back to where they'd entered the time warp in order to return to the twenty-first century.

"Aye, but I shan't advise you go." He started down the spiral steps he'd made by imbedding thick half-timbers at ninety-degree angles to the stones that made up his tower.

Grabbing what purchase she could on the ragged stones, she chased after him. "Why not?"

He stopped two steps below her and turned, his long broad sword sheathed in a simple leather scabbard strapped to his back scraping stone. Standing at eye level, he frowned as he studied her.

God, he's magnificent.

Standing well over six feet tall, heavily muscled, blue eyed and blond, he wasn't handsome in the classic sense, but definitely arresting. His chiselled features were almost gaunt. And that scar running from his left cheekbone to his jaw. The wound hadn't been stitched but had healed on its own, drawing the left corner of his lips up, giving him a permanent smirk. As if he knew a secret he wasn't about to tell.

He fingered one of the curls draped around her shoulders, startling her. "Ye are most fair and fulsome, lass. Without a clansman to guard ye, ye'll be harassed, if not claimed. Ye and yer bairns."

Had he just called her *pretty*? She couldn't be sure. Chaucer and his ilk's writings hadn't been her strong suit in college. "But we wouldn't be alone. You'll be with us."

Left to her own devices within the dense woods below, bracketed by hills and ravines, she'd lose her bearings. He had to guide them.

He started down the steps again, his broad shoulders rolling with each step. "Nay, I shan't."

As they stepped into sunshine she grabbed his thick forearm bringing him to a halt. "Why not?"

His right hand covered hers. "Look at me, mistress. 'Tis obvious I'm a warrior. Should I be caught I'll be forced to my knees and they'll demand I swear fealty to Malcolm . . . or die."

"Is he your enemy?"

"Kith but I'll slit my throat before swearing fealty to another errant hedge-born mammon."

She shook her head. "I don't understand. If he's kith, a friend—"

"Mistress, unbridled avarice has nay friends. I – and thousands more – lost all we held dear thanks to one such liege. I say never again."

Good Lord. "Do you never go to Edinburgh then?"

"I go on rare occasion. But only whilst in the guise of a leper to keep them at bay." MacDuff brought her hand to his lips. "My apologies, lass."

As her heart stuttered, he strode towards her students, who sat in only their briefs before his stone hut. She followed, asking, "We're in Scotland. How is it that you speak English?"

"My mother's people fled the south to escape the Norman invader."

"And your father?"

"A Highlander." Coming abreast of her students he asked, "Have ye had yer fill, lads?"

She should hope so. They'd decimated the huge mound of oatcakes, honeycomb and berries MacDuff had set before them. How they'd managed to eat so much was beyond her. Her stomach was still in knots, had been since the explosion. When they nodded, their host grunted and strode towards their clothing which they'd draped on branches to dry in the sun.

While Hamish MacDuff frowned and fingered Velcro closures and zippers, Mark Gibson asked, "Does he have a car? Will he take us back to Edinburgh?"

She squatted before them. "Gentlemen, I hate to tell you this but we're miles from Edinburgh and there is no car." She took a deep breath and related as best she could what she knew and what she feared.

Peter jumped to his feet. "No way! I have a soccer match this weekend. This is all bullshit."

Before she could admonish him, MacDuff was at her side and had Peter by the upper arms, holding him at eye level.

"Laddie," MacDuff snarled, one hand moving to Peter's jaw, "heed well for I shan't spake of this but once. Spaniel is a lady and ye shall treat her as such."

Fearing he'd snap Peter's neck, she grabbed MacDuff's arm. "Put him down! *Please*."

Ignoring her, MacDuff hissed, "Do ye ken me, lad?"

Peter, white faced, nodded. MacDuff *humphed*, opened his hands and Peter, gasping, fell to the ground. Sarah dropped to her knees and checked the red marks beneath Peter's jaw. "Are you all right?" When Peter nodded she snarled, "MacDuff, you could've killed him!"

MacDuff, standing with legs splayed, hands fisted on his hips, shook his unruly sun-streaked mane. "Nay. He appears a good lad for all his ratsbane of a tongue." To the others he said, "Who among ye best wields a sword?"

Mark, turning pale, raised a tentative hand. "Uhmm . . . I'm on the fencing team."

MacDuff eyed him then, apparently satisfied, asked, "Who best tends coos?" When they looked at him blankly, he pointed to the three shaggy, long-horned beasts grazing beyond the pool. "Who kens those?"

When they all raised hands, MacDuff pulled a rough-hewed bucket from a peg imbedded in his stone croft's wall and tossed it to Ty. "Dress then milk, laddie."

Apparently deciding it was wiser to obey than admit he'd never milked in his life, Ty elbowed Bryce. "Come on."

Sarah whispered to the other boys, "Gentlemen, why don't the rest of you get dressed." She had to speak to MacDuff. Alone.

They took off at a dead run as MacDuff settled on his haunches to pick up the remains of the boys' lunch. "What say you, Spaniel? Do you stay or go?"

She folded her arms across her chest and glared at him. "You can't manhandle children that way."

His eyebrows shot together as he came to his feet. "Is it not the rule of clan and church to discipline in a parent's absence? Ye told the lad three times within my hearing – and God only kens how many more times without it – to mind his tongue and he had yet to pay ye any heed."

"Yes, but—"

He leaned forwards and tapped the tip of her nose. "Nay *buts*, mistress. Ye want them to grow into good men who respect women, aye?"

She heaved a sigh. "Yes, of course. But please don't pick him up like that again."

MacDuff grinned. "Ye'll find I shan't have need. He's learned his lesson."

"And please don't call me Spaniel."

"Oh? 'Tis what the lads shouted when they could not find ye."

"My name is Sarah."

"Why then do they call ye Spaniel?"

Bone weary, she settled on the grass and tucked the huge, coarse linen tunic reeking of male musk, sawdust and smoke that he'd loaned her about her legs. "They think I look like one." When his brow furrowed, she said, "A spaniel is a spotted hunting dog."

Laughing, he sat down next to her. "Ye have bonnie brown eyes and charming spots upon yer cheeks, but without a long snout and tail I have to say nay, ye do not."

"Thank you."

He studied the boys for a moment. "Ye call them children, not bairns. Are they of royal blood then?"

She watched Peter, Jeremy and Mark romp through the field as if they hadn't a care. "In our world, yes."

"And ye?"

"I'm their teacher. Well, one of them. The children often move from place to place. Our school, with its many branches in different cities, provides continuity, some measure of stability."

"And where is yer world?"

Dare she tell him? Would he think the boys and her bewitched? "You won't believe me."

He grinned. "I believe there is more to life and this place than priests will allow."

Didn't she know it. "We live in London but in a different—"

"*Nay!*" MacDuff had jumped to his feet and was pointing at Bryce and Ty who'd been peering beneath one of the long-coated cows. "Are ye daft, lads?" he shouted. "Them's bollocks!"

Bryce straightened and looked over his shoulder. "Huh?"

MacDuff grabbed his crotch. "Bollocks!"

When the boys just looked at each other then shrugged, MacDuff raised his kilt and swung his hips. "These, lads!"

"Ohmigod, MacDuff! Stop that!"

MacDuff didn't so much as glance at her as his kilt fell back in place and he pointed to the two hairy beasts grazing to the boys' right. "Ye yank on *coos*, lads. Those with *teats*!"

Boyish hoots and laughter erupted on both sides of the field as understanding dawned and MacDuff blew through his teeth. Turning his attention to her, he said, "Two of yer princes were nearly knocked into the morrow. What have ye been teaching them that they have yet to ken the difference betwixt bullocks and teats?"

Aghast that he had the nerve to call *her* to task, Sarah shouted, "I can't believe you just exposed yourself like that! Are you out of your mind?"

MacDuff looked at her blankly for a moment then laughed, a deep and rich rumble that rolled like thunder about the glen.

When he finally collected himself he asked, "And what did my lady see?"

Heat flooded her cheeks. "Well, nothing – naught, but—"

He tapped her nose. "Then 'tis naught for ye to fash over, now is there? Men ken these things." He pointed to Ty and Bryce in earnest conversation squatting beside a cow. "The quiet one has the look of ye about the eyes. Is he yer bairn?"

The man was impossible. "No, I have no children, and his name is Ty. He's an orphan."

MacDuff's brow furrowed. "And the rest? Have they no parents as well?"

"The rest do have parents." Parents, who are doubtless going out of their minds right now, listening to news broadcasts, punching cell phones, wondering why their children aren't answering their calls, can't be reached.

He bent and plucked a blade of grass. Chewing it, he eyed her in speculative fashion, the corner of his eyes crinkling. "Are ye not spoken for, then?"

"No." Men rarely gave her a second glance. So why was he scrutinizing her so closely?

"*Humph.* Ye've slothful kin, then."

"No, no kin, slothful or otherwise. My parents married late in life, never expected to have a child, then I came along. My father died when I was three and then my mother developed Alzheimer's." Seeing his frown deepen she clarified, "A disease that destroys the mind and then the body. She passed – died – last summer." Which, although leaving Sarah bereft, had been a blessing for her mother.

"My sympathies." To her relief he turned his attention back to the boys. "Ah, they're done."

A heartbeat later, Bryce and Ty, grinning from ear to ear, placed their bucket on the ground before her.

She was amazed to find it half full. "Wow!" They'd not known the difference between a bull and cow when they started. But them drinking raw milk was out of the question. Their parents would never forgive her if they came down with tuberculosis.

To MacDuff, she said, "Before they can drink it—"

"Drink it? God's teeth, woman, why would ye have them do that?" He shuddered and grabbed the bucket. "Nay, 'tis for making crowdie. Come along, lads, we've much to do."

Skipping to keep up with MacDuff's long strides, Bryce asked, "What's crowdie?"

As she said, "Cheese," she heard MacDuff say, "Ye've not had crowdie?"

When they shook their heads MacDuff gave her another incredulous look then, leading the boys away, muttered, "'Tis a wonder any of ye live."

Hamish looked about his crowded croft, at the exhausted lads curled in sleep on their pallets, and warmth bloomed in his chest. Far too many years had passed since he'd shared a meal or heard bairns laugh. Were it not so unmanly to shed tears, he would have.

He sighed. If only the Spaniel were as relaxed as the lads in his company.

She would have taken her brood off to Edinburgh had the lads, consumed with their fishing, not begged her wait just a wee bit. Thankfully, gloaming came early to his glen.

By the time the lads were done fishing, the sun was setting and they were hungry. Then the moon rose and the wolves of the forest started to howl, which proved too much for the lady and she agreed they should spend the night.

He reached out and ruffled Ty's hair as the lad sat beside him carving a rabbit from a soft hunk of pine.

In a whisper Ty said, "We were at this pub when a bomb went off. Miss Colbert got us into the basement but it was flooded. Then we somehow ended up here."

"What means bomb?" The Spaniel had said much the same but he'd been loath to admit to her that here was yet another thing he did not understand.

"A device made from gunpowder and metal that can kill hundreds of people all at once." When Hamish continued to frown in confusion Ty crafted an imaginary ball in his hands, lobbed it, then saying *kaboooom*, fell backwards and feigned death.

Alarmed, Hamish pulled him upright. "Ye have such weapons?"

Ty, his brown eyes welling with tears, nodded. "My parents were killed by a bomb two years ago. Dad was a foreign diplomat."

Hamish brushed a tear from the lad's cheek. "My heart greets for ye, lad."

"Mine, too."

"Here ye may rest easy, lad. We have no such weapons. To kill ye must look a man in the eye as is only right."

After a long moment Ty whispered, "Did she tell you that we come from centuries ahead of this time?"

Hamish nodded. "But 'tis difficult for me to give such wild tales credence."

"You should because it's true. You saw Peter and Mark's iPods. We have loads more stuff than that. Like aeroplanes and computers. Stuff you haven't even dreamed of yet."

Hamish had no idea what he meant by *air plains* but had seen the lads' *pods*. Not that the shiny boxes adorned with strange squiggles did anything, much to the lads' consternation.

Taking up his carving and wee blade again, Ty asked, "I don't suppose you know how we came to be here?"

Hamish did – or rather suspected he did, but he wasn't about to speak of it just yet. "Tell me about the Spaniel. Is she content where she lives?"

Ty gave the question some thought. "I don't think so. She doesn't smile much and the kids take advantage of her."

"How so?"

"They horse around in class. Throw stuff. Talk too much. She doesn't send them to the headmaster like she should. I think she's afraid he'll fire her, make her leave."

"Ah." Their world was most odd. No man in his right mind would ever think to cast out so lovely a lass as Sarah Spaniel.

Ty shrugged. "I like her though. She's nice."

"Aye." And lonely, if the haunted look he'd caught in her eyes had meaning. "Ye need put yer whittling away and get to sleep. Dawn will be here 'fore long and the coos will need milking."

"They're cows, not coos."

Grinning, Hamish ruffled Ty's hair. "Ye say it yer way and I'll say it mine."

When Ty settled on his pallet Hamish stood and found Sarah in the doorway. When he smiled, she blushed, making him wonder how long she'd been standing there listening. She pointed behind her. "It's raining."

"Is it?" He eased past her, caught the heady scents of rain and woman clinging to her – that caused his blood to stir – then looked at the sky. Seeing light weave in brilliant arcs across the western sky, it was all he could do to keep from grinning like a village dolt. *Thank ye, St Bride!*

"Ach, lass, the sky does not bode well for ye leaving come morn. If the rains continue the bog betwixt here and Edinburgh will swell to a river, become impassable."

When they woke to more rain on the second day, Hamish did his best to keep them from worrying. He'd taught Sarah how to separate hull from oat kernels using a stone pastel. At her side Ty and Peter tried their hands at whittling simple animals out of small blocks of dry pine. Mark and Jeremy were stripping bark from foot long hunks of sapling pine, which they'd make into buckets. Bryce was in charge of making the cheese.

Hamish put more wood on the fire then set a crock full of milk before Bryce and lifted the lid. "Ah, 'tis ready."

Bryce wrinkled his nose. "It's spoiled."

Hamish, laughing, reached for one of the small crocks lining the shelf above Bryce's head. "Nay, 'tis just clabbered. Now 'tis ready for rennet, which will turn the milk to curds and whey."

Frowning, Bryce asked, "What's rennet?"

MacDuff opened the small crock and poured several tablespoons of dried beige powder into Bryce's palm. "Dump that into the milk and stir."

Bryce sniffed the powder then did as he was told, muttering, "Is this some kind of plant?"

"Nay." Hamish looked at him and winked. "'Tis the dried lining of a calf's stomach."

Sarah tried not to laugh as her students shouted, "Ewwwwwwwww!"

As Jeremy nudged Mark and whispered, "The Lion's joking, right?" Bryce looked at her in horror. "Miss Colbert?"

Sarah nodded, liking the boy's moniker for MacDuff. He did look like a lion. "It's true. And there's no need to *ewwww*. You've all eaten rennet custard at home and liked the cheese Mr MacDuff gave you yesterday. Rennet provides the acid needed to turn milk into cheese."

Ty, looking worried, asked Hamish, "Did you kill the calf?"

"Nay, the poor wee beast died during a late spring blizzard. Nearly broke my heart finding him that morn, but there was nay undoing it, so . . ." He shrugged.

When several continued to *eww* and shuddered, Sarah reminded them, "We eat veal and lamb at home, gentlemen. The parts not suitable for the table aren't wasted but used to make custards, gourmet cheeses, leather products like lambskin blazers – which several of you own – pet food and fertilizer. It's simply a case of waste not, want not."

Beside her, Jeremy muttered, "That's it. The minute we get home I'm going vegan."

"Miss Colbert, he's cheating again!"

Sarah, shielding her eyes against the brilliant sunlight, laughed. Hamish had Jeremy under one arm like a sack of grain as he bobbed and weaved his way down the make-shift soccer field he'd made in the hopes of easing the boys' melancholy after two days of solid rain. Their soccer ball, made from straw and leather, had flattened and was tucked neatly under his other arm, the game having degenerated into a free-for-all football.

As he scooped up Mark, she hollered, "Get him, Ty! Grab his belt and pull him down!"

When Ty lunged and missed, Sarah raced towards Peter, their goalie, who stood before two sticks set in the waterlogged ground. Emulating Peter's stance, she spread her arms and legs wide and shouted, "We got you now, Highlander!"

Hamish slowed and an evil glint took shape in his eyes. He put the boys down, then, laughing, charged straight at her. As he caught her by the waist and spun, Ty and Mark caught his belt and Hamish toppled, making a great show of being brought down, as much a boy at heart as her students.

"*Ooomph!*" While her victorious students shouted, Sarah tried to catch her breath. MacDuff held much of his weight on his arms, but had a muscular leg nestled squarely between her thighs.

Oh my God! Is he aroused?

Grinning down at her, his blue eyes dancing with mirth, he asked, "Did I score, mistress?"

Oh yes.

She'd long imagined what a man's heat and weight might feel like, but my, oh my, her imagination hadn't taken flight nearly far enough. Her heart was racing, sending warmth and need sluicing through her.

"Miss Colbert, is it dinner time yet?" Peter wanted to know.

I neither know nor care, Peter.

"What are we having?" Jeremy asked.

Hamish, his hooded gaze fixed on her lips, slowly rose to his knees and cleared his throat. "Crowdie and havers," he told them, "unless ye can garner more blackberries."

Almost in unison they groaned.

When the boys walked off, Hamish slowly rocked to his feet and held out a large calloused hand to her. "We'd best get the rest ready. Ty alone can eat his weight in oats and honey."

Dazed, she took his hand. "He's . . . He's grown very fond of you."

"And I of him."

"In ten months this is the first time I've seen him really smile. He's blossomed under your attention." And he wasn't the only one. She too had blossomed. She laughed and pondered what might have been under Hamish MacDuff's sometimes awkward, usually funny, and occasionally heated perusal.

Watching the boys, Hamish absently toyed with the broad brass cuffs decorating his wrists. "He longs for a father."

Sarah nodded, only too familiar with that particular heartache.

"And they all lust to be home. Aye?"

"Yes, they're homesick." With their game over, the boys were again quiet, walking with slouched shoulders and worried expressions. Last night in the darkened croft she hadn't been able to tell who'd wept in the wee hours of night but several had.

"And ye, mistress? Do ye lust to be home as well?"

Did she?

She no longer had any family, nor any close friends after caring for her mother for so many years. She'd applied for the overseas teaching position in the hope of finding a new beginning. Instead, her lonely life had simply changed addresses. Home was no longer the rented Chicago duplex she'd grown up in but a tiny rented flat in a grey London suburb full of strangers. Her days were still challenging and worrisome. Her nights filled with mundane television and Chinese takeout.

And then there was Hamish MacDuff. He was everything she had ever dreamed of in a man: strong, handsome, funny, not the least self-conscious. Tender and considerate. Firm when he thought it necessary. And he thought her pretty, followed her every movement with hungry eyes when he thought she wasn't looking. When she did look at him, he simply smiled as if he hadn't a concern or desire in the world.

No, she didn't lust to go home, but then it never mattered what she wanted. She just put her head down and did what was expected, what *had* to be done.

Knowing she had no choice but to do so again, she reached out and boldly took Hamish's hand, threading her fingers through his, memorizing the feel of his touch, of his calouses and strength, of what might have been.

Hamish finished his tale of how he'd come to be in his glen and wished the lads goodnight. 'Twas time to speak his heart to the Spaniel.

He found her, arms wrapped about her shapely legs, sitting at the edge of his pool. Watching her curly hair billow like a dark cloud under the light of a full moon his chest tightened. God's teeth, he longed to hold her, to claim her.

But then he was only a warrior without a liege. He had his sword and this glen but naught else to tempt her to remain. She was one of the gifted, a teacher, who could read and write, which he could not. Aye, she was well beyond his grasp, yet he wanted her. Wanted her as he'd wanted little else in his life, with a need so bone deep it hurt.

At his approach she looked over her shoulder and her full lips parted into a smile that made his heart stutter.

As he settled next to her on the lush turf surrounding his pool, she asked, "Are they asleep?"

"Aye or soon will be."

She pointed skywards. "Look at that." Her voice, soft and sweet, was filled with awe. "In a world without street lights – lit only by fire – you can see *so* many stars."

Seeing only the heavens as they always were, he cleared his throat. Before he could speak his heart, however, she asked, "Do you have many visitors?"

"Nay. Ye and yer bairns are the first." When she frowned, he shrugged. "I think it odd as well." Peddlers and armies had marched past many times over the years yet no one had ever taken notice of his glen. 'Twas almost as if he and this wondrous place did not exist. "'Tis almost as if this place were . . ."

"Shrouded in magic?" She smiled.

"Aye, so why not remain? Ty's most content here, blossoming as ye say."

She sighed. "If I had only Ty to worry over, I think I would remain. I've been content here, too. Happier, in fact, than I have been in years."

Emboldened by her words, he ran a finger along her jaw. When she looked up at him and smiled he cradled her cheek in a broad calloused palm. Looking deep into her eyes, he whispered, "I dearly lust that ye do remain, Sarah. I truly do."

Dare he kiss her? Aye, he must. How else would she ken what lurked beneath his breast, in his soul? He settled his lips on hers, marvelling at their soft texture. When a groan escaped her, he, heart soaring, deepened the kiss, his tongue sweeping into her mouth, stroking her as his hands longed to do.

Please say aye, that ye'll stay.

Too soon she pulled back and his arms, which had boldly found their way about her, reluctantly fell away.

"Oh, Hamish." She traced his lips with a delicate touch. Seeing her bonnie brown eyes grow glossy, his hopes again soared.

"I want to stay. Truly. But the other boys have parents and they're doubtless frantic with worry by now. I *have* to get them back. Somehow, some way. I don't want to leave. I *have* to." She took a deep shaking breath. "I understand why you can't take us to Edinburgh but would you be willing to lead us part of the way? So we won't get lost."

So, 'tis the end after all.

He took her right hand in his and heaved a resigned sigh. "Ye dinna have to go to Edinburgh, lass. I think – nay, I believe – all ye and the lads need do to return home is to wish whilst in this pool. 'Tis all I did to make the fish and coos come. To make ye and the lads come."

"I don't understand."

"Whilst bathing, I was pondering this place, how lovely 'twas but how lonely. I wished I had someone to share it with and—" he snapped his fingers "—there ye all were."

She shook her head. "An explosion sent us here."

"Mayhap, or mayhap my wish and your world simply aligned."
He forced a smile. "Or collided."

The next morning at dawn Hamish stood in his magic pool next to
Sarah. The lads, silent and dressed again in their yellow livery, stood by
her side. Praying his stoic countenance would remain intact – wouldn't
collapse and expose the heartache already tearing him asunder – he
reached betwixt the folds of his plaid and pulled out the five wooden
animals he'd made for each of the lads. The most complex, a long-
horned coo, he gave to Ty. "To remember me and the coos by."

Lastly he turned to Sarah. He removed one of the brass cuffs
that had belonged to his father and his father before him, a symbol
of his once proud lineage, and placed it about her upper arm for it
was too large for her wrist, and squeezed. When satisfied it would
not fall off, he took her right hand in his. "I shall miss ye most
dearly but wish ye well."

"And I you." She placed her free hand upon his chest where
his heart beat painfully. Did she ken the agony their leave taking
was causing him? Aye. Her bonnie eyes were filling with tears. She
stood on her toes and kissed him.

Too soon she pulled away. He swallowed the aching thickness in
his throat and stepped out of the pool. "Now make yer wish and fall
backwards into the water."

Three

Gasping and gagging, Sarah staggered to her feet and raked wet
hair from her face. She opened her eyes and blinked in disbelief.
"Oh my God, it worked."

She was in modern-day Edinburgh, standing in the Princess
Street Gardens' fountain. She quickly counted heads. The boys
were all with her. Across the park she could see the ruined pub, a
half-dozen satellite news trucks, a dozen emergency vehicles and
hundreds of milling people.

"Look!" Peter shouted, pointing to a man and woman huddled
together, their arms locked about each other's shoulders. "That's
Mom and Dad!" He scrambled over the edge of the fountain and
took off at a run.

"Jeremy, your parents are here, too," Bryce shouted, "and there's mine!" The boys bolted over the granite rim shouting, 'Mom! Dad!" As Mark followed suit, Sarah fell to her knees.

She'd done it. Done what she'd had to do. Gotten them home safely. Now she could cry, grieve.

"Miss Colbert?"

She looked up to find Ty standing before her and dashed the tears from her eyes. "Hey, why are you still standing here? Go, join the others."

He shook his head as she came to her feet. "There's no reason."

"But your grandmother—"

"She's in a nursing home, doesn't even remember who I am any more. Dad's lawyer oversees my schooling . . . and the money."

"Oh, Ty, I'm sorry. I didn't know."

He shrugged as he took a shuddering breath. "I want to go back. The food's terrible and there's no doctors and stuff but I was happy there." He studied the destroyed pub through unshed tears and whispered, "He made me feel safe. He cared."

Her tears spilled. "Yes, he did care. Very much."

On the other side of the park her students' happy reunions were being interrupted by a gaggle of excited reporters shoving microphones in their faces. Shaking her head in disgust, she murmured, "I want to go back, too, but I don't know that we can."

Seeing his classmates point towards the fountain, Ty put his hand in hers. "We won't know that unless we try. Please. Before they come, before it's too late."

Reporters began pointing at them, shouting orders to cameramen who lumbered forwards with large shoulder-mounted cameras.

She looked down at Ty. He was right. Why not try while they had the chance? She and Ty had so much to gain and nothing to lose should they fail. She'd fallen in love with Hamish MacDuff and him with her. Of that she had no doubt. More importantly, Ty needed a caring man in his life; a father, not an investment lawyer.

Sarah took a deep breath then squeezed Ty's hand. "All right. Let's do it. Wish as hard as you can and, for God's sake, don't let go of my hand."

Hands locked, they closed their eyes, squeezed their noses shut and together fell backwards, the fountain's cold water closing over their heads.

*   *   *

A world away in a lovely glen Hamish stood in his pool, his hands pressed to burning eyes. He'd not wept in years but did so now. His lovely Spaniel and lad were gone. He wished with all that remained of his heart that they might return then threw back his head and roared to the gods of his forebears, "*Why?* Why did ye give them to me if ye only meant to take them away?"

Receiving no answer, unable to bear the thought of life in the glen without them, he took a step on the slanting shelf upon which he stood. Only six more strides and he'd step into the abyss. Aye, 'twould be better this way than to simply exist until his bones grew too frail and his spirit too weak to hunt.

He took another step forwards then another, his warrior's heart beating a painful tattoo of protest against his ribs. As he took his next step the water before him began to churn and roil.

To his utter astonishment and joy his bonnie Spaniel popped up – then Ty – sputtering and flailing for all they were worth. Heart soaring, he nearly fell over the edge, grasping at his heart's desires.

Lost and Found

Maureen McGowan

A billy club to the hip was not the worst way Jake had ever been woken up.

"Get up, asshole," a voice boomed, and the weapon slammed down again, higher this time.

Straight to the ribs. *Damn. Another bad start to another bad day.*

"Easy. He's asleep." A velvet-soft voice drifted over him. "Give him a chance to sit."

Jake opened one eye to witness the speaker – surely an angel – but all he saw was a wall of dark-blue slacks in his face.

Angel, my ass. Two cops. Uniformed. Modern dress.

Even in the dim light, he deduced he'd woken in his own century. At least he wasn't lying on damp ground. At least New York City, the park, the bench, existed today.

He slowly pulled his face off the wooden slats and blinked his eyes fully open. The sun had barely turned the sky pink. Six twelve, he guessed, and then glanced at his wristwatch. Off by a minute. And although the watch wasn't one of those ones where the date clicked off in a bevelled box in the three's spot, he knew it was April 17. Question was, what year?

He drew in a deep breath and winced at the pain in his side.

"You hurt?" the female cop asked.

He looked up at her and stared without answering. She was tall for a chick, probably only three or four inches shy of his six foot two, and her dark hair was pulled back, mostly hidden under her cop hat, exposing pale skin that gleamed in the pink light of dawn. She might be cute – out of that uniform.

Apparently women's libbers had changed a few things. No girl cops walking the streets in his day.

Ha. His day didn't mean shit any more.

He was a man with no time, no life – just a place and one day to endure, over and over again.

"What the fuck is that on your face?" The male cop slammed his club on the bench and pointed to the flower Jake knew was drawn on his left cheek in metallic-blue eyeliner, matching the three teardrops trailing down his right. So enduring they might as well be tattoos, no amount of cold cream could wipe them off for more than twenty-four hours.

"Fucking fruitcake." The cop sneered.

"Hey." The female shot her partner a scolding look.

Cop ignored it. "Get up, pretty boy. We're taking you in."

The male cop was ugly. But not in an unhandsome kind of way. He had that whole square-jawed, clear-skinned, masculine look Jake knew women went for. No, his ugly came from the angle he held his chin, the way he kept one hand close to his gun, the other on his club, the way he stood with his knees locked, his feet spread six inches wider than was natural, projecting the repulsive look of a power-hungry asshole. He was why hippies and Black Panthers called police *pigs*.

The female cop talked in low tones to her partner, and then he grunted and stepped back. She reminded him of someone, but who?

Her blue eyes flashed a hint of kindness as she thrust a card towards Jake. "Here's a list of shelters. You can't sleep here."

Jake dismissed the offered card. "I just did."

The male cop lurched forwards ready to strike, but she blocked him.

"Let's go. He's not hurting anyone. Besides, time to go off shift."

The male cop's nostrils flared and his fingers flexed over his gun. "Yeah. Bum's not worth the paperwork." The pair turned, and the heels of their heavy black shoes clomped on the concrete path as they left. He should let them go. Couldn't.

"Hey, John Wayne," Jake yelled after the cop. "Who you calling a fruitcake? You take orders from a broad."

The cop spun and charged, club raised.

The female started after her partner, but Jake was quicker. He ducked the club and dived for the cop's legs, taking him down in a tackle on to the damp grass at the side of the pavement. The club came down on his back. More bruises, but who gave a shit. They'd be gone in the morning. Always were.

"Freeze," the female yelled.

Hearing the click of her gun's safety, he wondered whether the command had been directed at him or her partner. Didn't matter.

Jake let the male cop flip him on to his face and pin him to the grass. No point in resisting the cuffs, either. At least in jail he'd have a fighting chance of being fed.

At least jail was something to do.

Kara studied the homeless guy they'd picked up in Central Park, now sitting in the metal chair beside the desk she shared with three other street-patrol officers. Sending Tony home to breakfast and his wife had been a good move – their opposing philosophies on anti-loitering by-law enforcement was a nightly source of conflict. All bets said she'd saved her partner another excessive force charge.

The man pulled a clean-looking white handkerchief from his jacket pocket. "Mind if I wipe this artwork off my face?"

Without waiting for her answer, he traced the flower petals and swiped down the stem with freakish accuracy, and then moved on to the teardrops, hitting those with precision, too. Even without a mirror, he knew exactly where to rub. Finished, he balled up the blue-stained handkerchief and tossed it into a trash can about five feet away.

"Don't you want that?" she asked.

"Nah, it'll find me." He grinned and her heart skipped a beat.

The man was oddly familiar – she must've seen him loitering in the park before – but something didn't add up. His sandy hair, curling loosely around his sideburned face, looked clean – too clean for a man who made a habit of sleeping on park benches, and the golden stubble on his strong jaw and upper lip looked like he'd had a proper shave in the past twenty-four hours.

His clothes insinuated a thrift-store pedigree, but even there, something was off. Although his brown-and-beige plaid suit and mustard-coloured shirt were rumpled, they looked clean and, except for the retro style, new. Plus, he didn't have the obvious reek and grime of a man who lived on the streets. In fact, when she'd removed the cuffs, he'd smelled good – hints of fresh, citrus tones, under healthy sweat. But what was with that hippy stuff he'd just wiped from his face?

Time to stop wondering and start asking. "Name?"

He glanced up, his piercing eyes the colour of an angry ocean. "Jacob Reddick."

Her breath hitched. "It's you, isn't it? I know you."

"Believe me, honey." He barked out a sharp laugh. "Not a chance in hell."

He was right. It wasn't possible. Like an eyewitness, thinking she recognized a mugshot on her third viewing, Kara was falling prey to mistaken identity syndrome. After all those years of searching for her mystery man, imagining him everywhere, and recreating his face in her dreams, her memory was muddled. Faulty synapses crossing a face from her past with this man's.

Best to get this done and head home for a glass of wine – breakfast of night-shift champions. "Address?"

"Honey, you've already been to visit. South side of the lake, near the terrace, Central Park, NY, NY."

She rolled her eyes and wrote: "no fixed address". "Date of birth?"

"April 17—" He paused. "What year is this?" His mouth twitched to the side.

"Excuse me?"

"Year." He leaned back. "How many years past the birth of Christ has mankind survived on this fine morning?"

"Uh, it's 2009." Maybe she'd been too quick to rule out the psych hospital option?

He looked to the ceiling for a moment and then tapped her form. "Put down April 17, 1977." He flashed a gleaming white smile that sparked in his eyes.

Her stomach tightened and she blinked, hoping to negate the familiarity she felt. Loneliness had driven her to conjure up a connection pulsing between them. A trick of the mind. Clearly it was time to start dating, again.

"Mr Reddick, there's no point in lying."

"Sweetheart—" he leaned forwards "—last time I checked, I was thirty-two years old. So if this is 2009, it follows I was born on April 17, 1977." He was grinning again. Clearly amused.

But she wasn't amused at the effect his sexy smile was having on her insides. Kara gathered up a healthy dose of irritation to drown it.

Nineteen-seventy-seven sounded right. She'd been born a couple of years later and he looked roughly her age – further proving he wasn't who she'd thought. Where was the joke?

She realized. "Oh, happy birthday."

He leaned back. "No need to throw me a party, honey. Every day's my birthday."

His mocking grin hit her right in the belly.

She pressed back and crossed her arms over her uniformed chest. "Officer."

"What?"

"It's officer, not honey."

He rolled his eyes and then raised his palms towards her. "Look, *officer*, I'm no chauvinist pig. I think it's cool they're letting chicks carry guns these days. Just trying to be friendly."

Friendly, my ass. "Look. You're in some serious shit here. You assaulted my partner."

"Your partner's a pig."

Hard to argue with that one. She chewed the inside of her lip to keep from smiling.

"Listen, Mr Reddick. I get the feeling you're not really such a bad guy, and I'd love to help you get into a shelter, or send you home to grovel to your wife, or whoever tossed you out on your ass last night, but for some reason you seem hell-bent on making me regret helping you. Do you want to spend the next couple of months in lock-up?"

He shrugged.

She leaned on to the desk. "We're real backed up right now. It'll be ages before you see the inside of a courtroom."

He cocked up one eyebrow. "Do what you want. I know exactly where I'll be tomorrow at dawn and it won't be in your jail cell. I guaran-*damn*-tee it."

"Oh, really. You think I won't do it, don't you?" He'd read her like a book. She hated that.

Hand in his pocket, he pressed a sharp edge up and into the fabric of his slacks.

Heart racing, Kara stood, squared her stance and moved one

hand to her weapon. "Empty your pockets. Now." She was off her game not doing this sooner.

He shrugged and dug into his blazer to come up with a gold lighter and a pack of gum from one, a crumpled envelope and a small key from the other. The gum's label said "Wrigley", but must've been bought overseas, because it was unlike any pack she'd ever seen. She kept her hand over her gun as he dug into his pants pocket and then slapped a handful of bills and coins on to the desk. Three one-dollar bills, but something was off. Counterfeits? Maybe. Not recently issued bills, that's for sure.

"The other pocket."

He pulled out a necklace and let it dangle for a moment before dropping it to the metal desktop. The enamelled butterfly pendant hit with a clink, and then the chain snaked around it like sand falling in slow motion.

Goosebumps erupted on every inch of her body. "Where'd you get the necklace?"

"From a kid in the park – teenaged runaway."

The air rushed from her lungs and she squeezed her muscles to hinder the earthquake emanating from deep in her bones. She shook her head to dislodge the impossible conclusions scrambling to take hold.

His eyes widened. That they quickly snapped back to indifference didn't matter. The few seconds of intense recognition, of wonder in his eyes, had swept her from the squad room and back in time. Back to a day in 1994 she'd started to think she'd imagined.

She was imagining this.

"Get out of here." It wasn't him, and if it was, he was fucking with her.

"What? No jail?" His pissed-off tone fuelled her confusion-induced anger.

She pointed towards the entrance. "Out. Now."

As she watched him stuff his possessions into his pockets and walk away, her mind, her whole body, felt as if she'd been set in a paint mixer.

This man, his smile, his eyes, his dated clothing and hairstyle, were so much like the man who'd saved her life. But he couldn't be. Not unless fifteen years could pass without him aging a day.

★   ★   ★

Jake played with the pendant in his pocket. Hard to believe it was the same girl, but her reaction to the butterfly had been unmistakable.

From the second he'd heard her voice, something about her had been familiar, but it wasn't until he'd brought out the pendant that he'd seen the oh-so-obvious truth. Even all grown up, in that cop uniform, and without the heavy black eyeliner he'd wiped from her cheeks with that same damn handkerchief, it had to be her.

Across from the police station, he leaned against the brick wall, unable to leave – obsessed – like some chick waiting for the Beatles to emerge from a hotel. Pathetic.

And useless.

Chances were there was some back entrance the cops used. And even if she did see him waiting, she clearly wouldn't want to. She'd tossed him out.

The year they'd met in the park she'd been a teenager – lost, terrified, out of her depth – and he'd been the big brother figure who'd shared his story, hoping his life lessons might help her.

Her reaction to him that day had been text-book obvious, given her age and the circumstances, and didn't mean she'd give a damn about, or even remember, him today. She was a fully formed person now, no longer broken. Probably had a husband or boyfriend, at least friends to support her.

More to the point, even if she *were* curious, wanted to find out if they shared the same memory, what would be the point?

In spite of today – even *because* of today – the odds were freakishly long that he'd ever see her again. If there was a next time, he'd be just as likely to find her playing on the swings as a toddler, or pushing a walker as a ninety-year-old woman. Both were thousands of times more likely than seeing her on anything resembling tomorrow.

For him, there were no tomorrows.

He pushed off the wall and started down the street. A small car pulled out from the kerb and a line of yellow cabs honked. His first visit to the twenty-first century. Didn't look that different from the last.

"Mr Reddick. Jacob. Wait. Please. Jake."

He stopped, but didn't turn.

"Wait a minute," her voice pleaded, coming closer.

Talking to her was a dumb idea, yet his feet remained clamped to the sidewalk. Time – however meaningless the term had become – had taught him that interacting with others, making any kind of connection, was pointless.

Human connections only made his existence harder to endure.

Kara slid her hand on to Jake's shoulder and his head tipped back a fraction of an inch. His sandy curls hit the collar of his plaid jacket, bending like soft springs, and it was all she could do to keep her hand from traversing the few inches required to stroke those curls, confirm their softness, and run the back of her finger along the warm neck beneath.

Crazy. Insane.

She barely knew this guy. They'd spent one day talking when she'd been all of fourteen, yet he'd been the leading man in her dreams for years.

As Jake slowly turned, her hand slipped from his shoulder and stung at the loss of contact. "It is you, isn't it?" Her voice came out low and breathy.

He reached out, but dropped his arm sharply. "I don't know what you're talking about." He stepped back, but she grabbed his jacket's sleeve.

"Yes you do."

He glared and pulled his arm out of her grip. "I've never seen you before."

"Yes you have. I can prove it." Her chest squeezed and heat rose in her face. "Your mother died of cancer when you were twelve. Just like mine. Then your father died too. You regretted how you'd cut him out of your life and blamed him for things he couldn't control. You blamed him for not being your mother."

He stared at the ground, his jaw clamped so tightly she wondered if his teeth might crumble. So stubborn.

"You ran away at fourteen. Just like me. And you regretted that, too. Had to live hand-to-mouth and work nights to finish high school and land a job that paid enough to cover your rent." She sucked in a sharp breath. Had his stories all been lies designed to manipulate an impressionable young runaway?

If so, they'd worked.

She stomped her foot like a child – felt like one. "I did what I promised. I went home. I apologized to my dad. I kept away from drugs. I finished high school."

He didn't move.

"You're why I became a cop. You inspired me to help people." Her voice hitched and she hated how her throat kept strangling her words. "You saved my life."

His head snapped up, eyes soft, but his expression quickly switched back on to cold. "If that's true, I'm glad."

"So you admit it's you."

He nodded.

"Then talk to me. Where have you been? Why didn't you call me like you promised?"

"I never promised." He backed up a step.

"Tell me what's going on." She reached out to rest her hand on his forearm.

He jerked back. "There's no point."

"You can't know that."

"Believe me, Kara. I can."

Her breath hitched. He remembered her name.

That small fact melted the iciness he was casting towards her. She had to keep trying. If nothing else, she owed him. She owed him her life.

"You have three or four dollars in your pocket. That'll barely get you a coffee. At least let me buy you breakfast. Please."

His mouth cocked up in a half-smile. "What will the waitress think if I let the lady pick up the tab?"

She laughed, hoping to lighten the mood. "What year did you step out of?"

He didn't laugh back.

Jake, on round two of breakfast, swallowed a huge bite of pancake and wiped syrup off his chin with the back of his hand.

Across the table in the diner's window booth, Kara pushed congealed egg yolk around her plate with a crust of toast as she told him about her still-shaky relationship with her father.

Even though her black sweatshirt and jeans weren't exactly feminine, she was so much softer in street clothes. Unconstrained by that cop hat, little tendrils of hair had fallen around her face, and he gripped his fork to kill the temptation to lean over and brush one back. The angry young girl he'd met fifteen years earlier had turned into one hell of a beautiful woman.

"You still like butterflies," he said without thinking.

She raised one hand to her earring and a smile lit her face, the whole room. "I can't believe you kept my necklace all these years – or the ridiculous coincidence you had it with you, today."

He stuffed his mouth with pancake and bacon. He'd been trying to quash the persistent notion that the necklace was no coincidence. The last time he'd felt hope it'd almost killed him.

"Look." She reached her hand across the table. "You completely changed the course of my life that day. Seriously. And now you seem down on your luck. I'd like to return the favour, help you."

"I'm beyond help, honey – sorry – *officer*."

She pulled back. "Why are you being a jerk? I just spilled my life story, and you've barely told me a thing. Not even why you were sleeping in the park."

Her eyes were coaxing him to say more, so he studied his last slice of bacon. He was a shit for caving in on the free breakfast, a shit for acknowledging they'd met before, and an even bigger shit for revealing a second of joy when she'd told him she'd dumped her last boyfriend almost a year ago.

After today, he'd never see her again.

Frustration urged him to pound his fist through the plate glass window beside him, but he turned back and her concerned expression released some of the pressure. He rested one elbow on the table. "It's been a while since I've had a real conversation."

"These are tough times. Being homeless isn't anything to be ashamed of." She stretched out her hand and he longed to touch it so badly he ached.

He leaned away. "Homeless sounds great compared to my life."

"Tell me what's wrong." She drew a deep breath and her breasts pressed against her top. "No way have you been living on the streets for long. I swear you haven't aged."

Damn. She wasn't going to give up easily. Maybe it would help if she thought he were crazy.

He patted his full belly. "Thanks for the breakfast. I hadn't eaten since 1824."

She smiled. "Funny."

"Might be, if it weren't the truth."

Her expression hardened. Not what he'd aimed for, but angry would do. Time to toss lighter fluid on to the flames.

"You want more truth? Well, here it is." He pushed his plate to the side and leaned on to the table. "On my thirty-second birthday, a hippy in the park gave me a tab of acid. Like an idiot, I took it, and ever since then, no matter where I am or what I'm wearing, no matter what I'm doing or where I fall asleep, I wake up every morning in that same spot, on the same day, but a different year, in the same fucking clothes, with the same fucking things in my pockets."

He slapped his palm on the table. "I can't even count how many days I've endured since this started, or how many different years I've been to. Can't keep track, because the paper's never there when I fucking wake up."

He'd never used the f-word in front of a lady. His mom would've been disappointed. Dad would've slapped him. He barely cared.

Her posture had stiffened during his rant, but she softened and stretched her hand out again. "Why are you telling me this crazy story?"

"Because it's true."

"Do you hear how ridiculous you sound? Explain to me how one thing you've said is even possible."

He pounded the table. "You think I know? You think I understand how, even if I change out of this suit, even if I tear it or burn it, I wake up in it every morning as if it's brand new? You think I know why, even if I go to bed with cuts and bruises from a beating, or fall asleep in the arms of a whore, I wake up alone and in the exact same state of health as I was in 1967, the last year I lived a fucking normal day?"

Face burning, he thumped back in the booth and realized he'd shouted and a few heads had turned.

Worse, her eyes had glassed over. She was trying so hard to help him, to recapture the closeness they'd felt when they'd met before.

And he was an asshole.

He reached for her hand, still resting on the table, but she jerked it away and blinked back the tears.

One escaped and she swiped it away, clearly angry at its unwanted appearance. "How dare you yell at me? All I did was ask a question and you act like a jerk. You might look the same, but you've changed."

He wanted to apologize, but what was the point? Civilized conversations were something from his past. He focused on the table's scratched surface.

"Is being cruel fun for you?"

Shame swarmed around him. "I'm sorry."

She slid her hand on to the table again. "Please, at least tell me why you were sleeping in the park. Fifteen years ago, you told me you had a job on Wall Street. Did you lose everything in some hedge fund mess?"

He hadn't been to that job in forty-two years. What could he possibly tell her?

Transfixed by the long slender fingers of her hand, he wondered how skin-on-skin contact would feel. Her hand looked so soft and it'd been so long since he'd touched a woman, touched anyone. He craved the sensation, yet knew it would prove a mistake. "There is no way to explain my life."

"How bad can it be?" Her hand reached an inch further towards him. "Are you on the lam? A spy? A terrorist? In a witness protection programme, or something?"

"All those options sound terrific."

"I know." She grinned. "You're Osama Bin Laden."

"Who?"

"OK, OK. I give up." She raised her hands. "You'll tell me when you're ready."

The sun had come around to stream through the window and her hair, her skin, shone. Lord, she was beautiful. And was still as kind-hearted and generous and funny as she'd been as a kid. If only he could stay here, in this time. But it wasn't possible and seeing her today had made his life worse.

Even after this short time with Kara, he knew he'd forever grieve losing the opportunity to know her, grieve what might have been, grieve what could never be. Spending time with this woman was salt on his open wound of a life.

Darkness attacked from every direction, forced the sunlight from his eyes and filled every thought in his head, every cell in his body. He rested his elbows on the table and grabbed his head in his hands. "When will this end? I need to end it."

She leaned across the table and her warm palms landed over his hands. The contact was better than he'd imagined, more fabulous, more painful, and a buzz rushed through her body into his, invading his soul to push back the dark.

With a finger under his chin, she coaxed his glance back to hers. "You don't mean ending your life . . . You wouldn't . . ."

"If only I could."

Kara shifted around the booth to sit next to Jake, her heart nearly bleeding. "No. You don't mean that." She'd been the suicidal one when they'd first met – on a quick road to an OD or getting murdered. If he were serious about wanting to end his life, she'd do everything in her power to get him the help he needed. Finally, she could pay back the kindness he'd shown her.

He gave his head a sharp shake and turned towards her. "I didn't mean it like that. I'm an idiot. No social graces." He cocked one side of his mouth in a faux display of levity, but his hands gripped the table's edge like he thought the entire booth might make a run for it.

After she peeled one of them off, their fingers entwined, but she couldn't say which one of them had initiated the gesture. Her body flushed.

"Kara," he said, his voice low and deep. "You've already helped me, saved my life more than you could possibly know. Your necklace – it's the only thing I've ever held on to."

Her belly squeezed and flipped. He'd kept her childish gift, proving that day had meant something to him, too. The heat from his leg next to hers was too much to resist and when she shifted to increase the contact, he drew a husky breath and their bodies, their faces, inched closer together.

The man who'd starred in her hormone-riddled teenaged dreams, whom she'd fantasized about meeting again, was inches away. Physically, he was exactly as he'd been back then – hadn't aged a day – and even though fifteen years had hardened his outlook, she could sense the man she'd known hidden under the jerk he was cloaked in this morning.

It was crazy she hadn't recognized him the instant he'd raised his head from that bench. This man was the reason none of her relationships had lasted. He was the man she'd wanted the others to be.

With each breath, his hard biceps pressed against her breast, and her shallow breaths hitched, as if the air around them had thickened. All she'd have to do was lean forwards and their lips would join. The kiss she'd wanted for fifteen years would turn from fantasy to reality.

He pulled back.

She stifled a gasp.

"This is wrong," he said as if trying to convince himself. "We'll never see each other again. It's not possible."

Chest squeezing, she inched towards him. "Nothing's impossible."

"For me, most things are impossible."

"Why? Please. Tell me what I can do to help you."

Still leaning away from her, he chewed on his lip so hard she worried he might draw blood.

"George," he finally said. "You can help me find my friend, George."

Two hours later, Kara walked down the street, her mind in a fog. Although their bodies were a few feet apart, she felt Jake's heat, his energy, at her side, proving he was real and here – not a dream.

Everything he'd told her was true.

Or at least based on what she'd seen and heard, she could think of no better explanation. Could find no way to refute the evidence Jake's friend George, a retired judge no less, had set before her: photos of the two men together, in the late fifties and early sixties, and then in multiple years over the past four decades. In each progressive photo, George, now in his seventies, had aged, while Jake remained the same – exactly the same. It was all a little insane.

His hand brushed down her arm and she jumped.

"Are you OK?" The concern in his eyes was palpable and so much better than the anger and indifference that had filled them before.

She reached for his hand and he took it, anchoring her in reality. "It's a lot to absorb, that's all." They stopped at a kerb to wait for a light and her mind continued to swim through murky waters, struggling to find the surface.

George claimed to have seen Jake on fourteen separate April 17ths between 1967 and now, but had experienced his visits in a different order than Jake. Made an odd sort of sense. But a tab of acid didn't explain how this had started.

"What else happened in 1967?"

He ran a hand over his chin stubble. "That was forty-two years ago."

"Was it?" She stopped. "Have forty-two years passed for you? And every day of them April 17ths?" The idea made her dizzy.

His hand moved to her waist and he pulled her from a bicycle courier's path. He leaned against a store window. "I don't think so, but I don't experience time the same way any more. I'd guess I've lived through a few thousand days since this started. Many days I'm alone in the forest. Some days there are Indian villages. A few times everyone I've come across speaks Dutch. I mostly try to survive."

"It must be horrible." Her heart pinched, conscious of every twitch of the hand, still at her waist. She leaned forwards.

He shook his head, dropped his hand and pushed off the window away from her. She shivered.

"You must be busy." His voice was colder than ice. "I don't want to keep you."

She reached for his arm. "Keep me from what? I already called in sick for tonight while you were talking to George."

He looked down. "Kara, there's no point to this."

She reached up to touch his face but he pulled his head back and she winced. "You're such an asshole. Why go to the trouble to make me believe what's happening to you, if an hour later, it's buh-bye?"

"You're right." He ran a hand through his hair. "I'm an asshole. I shouldn't have taken you to see George. I shouldn't have had breakfast with you. I shouldn't have waited outside the police station. I am a total shit."

"I'll accept your weak-ass apology, if you promise not to leave me."

"Kara," he stepped forwards, "you know I can't promise that."

She took his hand and held on tight. "I'm not looking for a promise that goes past today, but if this is the only day you'll live in this year, you have to promise me we'll spend it together. Don't you get how long I looked for you the last time? How wanting to find you consumed my life?"

He looked into her eyes with such longing her insides squeezed. Desperate to feel his lips against hers, she leaned forwards.

He wanted to kiss her, she was certain. But something else mingled with the heat in his eyes. Something was holding him back.

The kiss could wait. "Come on, birthday boy. Let's party."

Kara sat cross-legged on the floor of her small apartment and sipped her red wine. Jake had eventually relaxed after she'd stopped hitting on him.

Instead, they'd talked all day and into the night, learning they were both dog people, neither liked anchovies on pizza and both preferred vanilla ice cream over chocolate. Fabulous to know they had more in common than dead mothers and dysfunctional relationships with their fathers, but her hold-off-on-the-seduction strategy was growing old. She'd wanted this man for ever and he was right here.

Across from her on the area rug, Jake leaned back and bent one arm up on the sofa at his back. The NYPD T-shirt she'd loaned him stretched across his body accentuating his deliciously solid shape. Tubs of take-out Chinese and a half-eaten chocolate cake stood between them like a shield to deter her from crawling across to explore the planes of his chest, his abdomen, with her fingers, her lips.

Given the chance, she could even learn to live with the sideburns, that suit. She'd had her fair share of men over the years, and while many had been physically handsome by any objective standard, not one had been able to stir her insides with just a look the way Jake could.

"You must be tired," he said, setting his wine glass down.

She shook her head. "Not a bit." Staying up through the day was an all-nighter for her and although bed beckoned, sleep was the last thing on her mind.

Time to blast down the shield.

Pushing the picnic remnants to the side, she crossed the few feet between them and pressed her lips against his.

His body stiffened, and her heart sank, fearing he'd push her way, but then a groan rose from deep in his throat and he wrapped an arm around her, pulling her in, tipping her back, intensifying their kiss. Drawing deep breaths, his tongue plunged into her mouth.

For years she'd dreamed of his kiss, but reality far exceeded her fantasies. The perfume of red wine and chocolate lingered as his lips devoured hers and his tongue stroked and suckled with the fervour of a starving man served his first meal.

Lost in Jake's kiss, the room spun, drifted, and she lost all concept of time, space and where she belonged in either. There existed only his lips, his tongue, his hands and the heat from their bodies mingling to form a white hot inferno.

When they came up for air, she found herself stretched across his lap, his hardness pressing into her hip through those crazy plaid pants she wanted to get off him as quickly as possible.

She moved and he groaned, capturing her lips in another ravenous kiss. Leaning on to his shoulders for support, she shifted to straddle him as his large clever hands continued to explore every inch of her body. She rubbed the seam of her jeans against him, igniting more fires as he pulled her in tighter.

"Jake." She pressed her lips into the pulsing vein at the side of his neck. "Let's move into the bedroom."

She pushed back and rose to her feet, pulling him with her.

"Kara, wait." He stopped before they reached the bedroom.

"Sorry, sailor." She slid up against him. "I'm done waiting."

"I need to give you something." He reached for his blazer, balled up on the sofa, and pulled out the envelope and key.

"Can't this wait?" Her body ached to be naked and pressed against his.

He took a step back. "It's important."

She nodded, wondering what could be more important than having him inside her.

"I picked this up at my dad's lawyer that day in 1967. The key's for a safety deposit box and the letter gives the holder of the key access. If you have problems, George will help."

"I don't understand."

"Everything my dad left me is in that box. There's a whack of gold bars, stock certificates, a few other valuables. According to George, it's worth quite a bit now."

She leaned into him, drew a deep breath and his scent made her eyes flutter shut. "What do you need me to do?" She pressed her lips into his throat.

He ran his hand up her back, and waves of electricity shot through her like welding sparks.

"The key and envelope might be gone when you wake up

tomorrow – might follow me. If it does, go see George. He can get you access to the deposit box."

"But why?"

"I want you to have it. All of it. It's no good to me. George doesn't need it or want it. It's yours."

Her throat squeezed. "No. You'll need it, for when this ends."

"Kara, this is never going to end." He kissed her and banished her will to argue.

Battling his better judgment, Jake let Kara pull him into the bedroom, let her tear off his clothes and watched with heat as she removed hers. He let her press hot kisses into his chest, into his belly, let her grasp and stroke him. How could something that felt so good be the cause of so much future pain – for them both?

Crazy with desire, he found the strength to pull away, panting, aching, heart shredding.

"What's the matter?" She reached for him. "Jake."

He forced his gaze away. "This is wrong."

She tugged on his shoulder to pull him around. "Wrong? It isn't the sixties any more, you know. I want this. I want you." Her back stiffened. "Or do you still see me as a kid?"

He cupped her face with his hand, hating that he'd caused the hurt in her eyes. "Kara, I've never wanted a woman more." He dropped his hand. "That's the problem."

"I don't get it."

"I'll be gone in the morning. It's not fair."

"You idiot." She smiled as she placed her hand on his chest. "I get to decide what's fair for me. I seduced you, remember?"

He looked into her questioning eyes, even more disappointed and angry than Kara. How could he possibly explain something he barely wanted to admit to himself?

He turned from her. "If we make love, it'll kill me."

She gasped. "What haven't you told me? Will you get sent to the Ice Age or something? What's happened the other times you've had sex?"

He turned to face her and the look in her eyes constricted his chest. "If I make love to you, my life will be unbearable." Bad enough now. He couldn't face jumping from year to year with such a huge piece of his heart ripped out and left behind, with knowing she existed on some different plane in time, inaccessible. Torture.

She crossed her arms over her luscious body, still glowing pink with arousal.

He sat on the edge of the bed, closed his eyes.

She joined him and her hand landed softly on his back. "I'm sorry. I've been so focused on the thought of having to wait at least a year to see you again. I didn't even think how it might affect you. That for you it might be longer. Or the next time you see me, it might not be 2010. I'm so selfish."

"No, I'm the one who's selfish." He dropped his lips to her hair and inhaled the sweet scent. "The next time I see you, you'll have moved on. I can't take that."

"Not a chance."

"Kara, it could be another fifteen years. It could be never. I couldn't bear to think you'd live your life hoping to see me at best once a year. If we make love—" He dropped his head.

She slid back on the bed and slipped under the covers. "You win. I get it. Just let me hold you." Her arms reached for him.

His heart nearly ripped from his chest and he joined her under the covers. They wrapped their arms around each other and she drew one leg over his thigh. He felt safe, at home.

She rubbed her cheek on his chest. "I love holding you."

"I love it, too."

He loved *her*. But knew saying it, or loving her, would make everything worse.

Her heartbeat penetrated his body as they clung together like hurricane victims. A hurricane would be a lesser threat. He'd never felt such happiness, such sadness. The duelling emotions overwhelmed his senses.

"Maybe if I hold hard enough I can keep you here." She pressed her lips against his chin.

He smiled. "That's a nice thought."

"I'm serious. You kept my necklace – and nothing else – over thousands of jumps through time. That must mean something."

He kissed her nose. He wanted to believe it, too. He really did. Holding on to the necklace couldn't have been a coincidence. It was almost as if fate had pulled him through time since their first meeting. Pulled him to a year when Kara was single and ready to meet him again as an adult, ready to save him, ready to make this all stop.

But thoughts like that only bred pain. The hope he'd felt on first finding her necklace added to his pockets' inventory had drained away over hundreds of jumps, drawing with it his will to live. This time would be worse.

She stifled a yawn. "Promise me one thing?"

"If I can."

"Promise me if we're lucky enough to find each other again . . ." Her voice was growing softer, her words slowing. "Promise me that the next time you land in another year I'm alive, you'll make love to me. Even if I'm ninety."

"I don't know." He grinned. "Ninety?"

"You had your crack at twenty-nine tonight, buddy. You blew it." She playfully pulled on his chest hair. "Now promise."

"Only if you promise to live your life as if I don't exist. You can't wait for me."

"OK." Her breath warmed his neck.

He'd make sure he didn't live to break his side of the promise.

They held each other without speaking, and soon Kara's breathing deepened, her body caving to the sleep it needed. He pressed his lips into her hair and watched the clock's blue numbers glowing in the darkness. A digital clock, she'd called it.

She was right about one thing, he'd be crazy not to hold her for every last minute he possibly could. He would not fall asleep. He'd stay awake and watch the minutes flash by with her in his arms.

Although the impending dawn would force him back into that hideous suit and dump him into the park in some other century, he was going to stay conscious, anchored to her and this time as long as possible.

He'd tried staying awake many times before. Hadn't worked. Neither had hopping a freight train to Florida.

Maybe tonight. Maybe if he stayed awake he'd remain here. Hope pierced the deep sadness filling his heart.

Two thirty-seven.

Three fifty-five.

Four fifty-six. Dawn was too close.

His eyes blinked open, heart racing.

Four fifty-eight. He'd missed a whole minute.

He held one eye open. Just over an hour left. No way would he fall asleep now.

Jake woke with bright sunlight against closed eyelids. Strange. Usually someone or something woke him before the sun got so high.

He ran his hand forwards to feel the surface. Ground or bench? Cotton sheet?

He bolted upright and spun. "Kara?" He was in her apartment, but where was she?

Oh, Lord. What had he done? What if she were now travelling across the centuries in his place?

His heart pounded, and pain flooded every pore in his body. No. No. No.

"Coffee?"

He looked up. Kara was standing in the door to the bedroom, his hideous suit jacket over her otherwise naked body.

Joy rushed over him and in one leap he had her in his arms. "Is this real?"

She held up a newspaper to show him the date: April 18, 2009.

"How? Why?" Without giving her an instant to answer, he kissed her. Nothing had ever felt so right.

Even if he'd never know the answer to how, he knew why.

Why was because he belonged here. Belonged in this place, in this time. Belonged with her.

Kara pulled her lips away, took his hand and drew him towards the bed. "Listen, mister, lots of time to ponder the secrets of the universe. Right now, I plan to cash in on that promise."

Stepping Back

Sara Mackenzie

1905
Victoria, Australia

She lifted her long skirt away from her riding boots with one hand, and stepped up on to the mounting block. Her horse waited patiently as she settled herself on the side saddle.

Helen glanced up at the sky.

It would be a fine day, one of those crisp, clear autumn days, perfect for riding. And she desperately needed to clear her head, to decide what she was going to do. What had seemed impossible only weeks ago was now dangerous reality.

She could not remain here.

But if she was to save herself then she must plan carefully, she must choose her moment, and she must not make any mistakes.

She set off at a slow trot along the lane that passed between the paddocks, soon increasing to a gallop. The chill wind whipped away any lingering doubts, crystallizing her determination.

"Tomorrow we will leave this place," she told her horse. "Tomorrow we will go."

2010

Sunrise turned the dry, brown land gold and for a moment there was beauty in the valley. Claire sipped her coffee and squinted her eyes against the light, watching as the shifting sun touched the roof of Niall McEwen's homestead. Now that the water in the reservoir was so low, the old homestead was completely exposed, although still unreachable. A deep moat kept the curious at bay.

Claire hadn't slept at all well. Once she used to fall into darkness every night, her dreams barely more than a surface ripple. Now instead there were vivid images in her head, nightmares, sending her tossing and turning, struggling upwards to wakefulness. And wondering if they really were just dreams, or memories of the past she couldn't remember.

Last night, as she forced back the smothering folds of sleep, the usual doubts crowding about her, Claire had heard the dog barking. Sharp jarring barks that had her peering from the windows. The sound was coming from the reservoir, but just as she thought she had pinpointed it, the barking moved on. And then vanished altogether.

Claire had not felt this unsettled since she woke up in hospital four years ago. That had been like being reborn, painfully. Apart from the physical injuries, there had been no identification on her and she could not remember who she was or where she had come from. One of the doctors had a daughter called Claire and so the patient had become known as Claire too, and Claire she remained.

Claire tried not to think about the past. The hospital seemed to think that some trauma had befallen her and her previous life had been stolen – severed like a falling climber's rope – so there was no point in longing for it. Either it would return when it was ready, or it wouldn't.

Besides, this was her home now, she told herself firmly. The house above the reservoir, and the newspaper where she worked, and her friend Gabe. Before didn't matter.

Now, as though to underscore the point, Claire stood up and tipped the remains of her coffee over the verandah railing on to the long-suffering roses.

The drought had been going forever and most of her garden was dead, but the roses persisted. Maybe it was their morning dose of caffeine that did it, she thought, with a smile.

She lifted her face and allowed the sun to bathe it. The air was already hot and dry, taking all the moisture. Summer was stretching into autumn and there was still no sign of a let-up. After five years of drought people were beginning to wonder if it would ever rain again. The town had been carting in water for months, and the reservoir was down to puddles. Unheard of in living memory.

Again, Claire narrowed her eyes at the view in front of her, and reminded herself she should take some photos for the *Bugle* – the local newspaper, and her employer. The homestead had not been visible like this since the valley was first flooded in 1910. Some years it had come close, but this was by far the most exposed it had ever been.

Every morning, sitting on her verandah, looking out over the reservoir, every morning watching the waters recede, as the homestead slowly revealed its secrets.

She'd begun to dread stepping out of her house. There was a curious sensation in her stomach, a tangled skein of fear and longing, that made no sense. And as the waters receded, the nightmares had definitely got worse.

Now it felt as if she were waiting. As if each passing day was another day ticked off on her way to . . . something.

But if she were waiting, she didn't understand why.

Or maybe it was simply that she couldn't remember.

The waiting seemed endless as the evening dragged on. All she wanted to do was go to bed and lie there, awaiting midnight. And then he made some excuse to come into her private parlour, eyes everywhere, threatening her by his very presence.

"You're mine," he said. "I don't care what anyone else thinks, we both know the truth."

"Go away." And then, her voice shaking, "Please."

He smiled then, knowing he had her measure. But he didn't know about her plan, and thank God for it. Because if he knew then he'd stop her. She wouldn't put any evil past him. And he'd already told her that if he couldn't have her then no one could.

Work was much the same as it always was. Today it was Claire's job to write up the sport section. It was Gabe's newspaper now, but it used to be his grandfather's, and everything was still done in the same old-fashioned way.

"Professional, as always," Gabe said, when he read her piece. "Thank you, Claire."

He allowed his gaze to rest on her a moment, blue and intent, and as usual Claire felt as if he could see much more than the tired circles under her eyes. Gabe was her saviour – he had found her bruised body and driven her to the hospital – and when she was well enough, he'd given her a job and helped her relearn the myriad details of life she'd forgotten. For a time she'd felt like a stranger in a strange land, surrounded by the terrifyingly unfamiliar.

"Will you come to dinner tonight?" she said, surprising herself.

He smiled. "I'd love to. Any special reason?"

Just to say thank you, she thought, but didn't say it. Gabe didn't want her gratitude, he'd told her often enough. What did he want then? Her love? She thought she might be in love with him but Claire knew that somewhere in her past love had been a threat to her life and she found it difficult to trust anyone. And Gabe didn't pressure her in any way. He was willing to wait.

"Just because," she said now, with a shrug, and left it at that.

During the afternoon she found time to visit the newspaper archives and look up the file on the old McEwen homestead. There was a photograph of the building as it used to be, before the valley was flooded to provide water for the town and district.

Claire stared at the tattered old photo and tried to imagine the house and land as it had been then. She closed her eyes – that was better. Now she could see long stretches of paddock, with horses running beside a wooden fence, and men gathered by pens where sheep were being rounded up by working dogs. A woman servant in an apron was carrying laundry in a basket, her dust boots peeping out from beneath her long drab skirts.

A door slammed.

A man came striding along the homestead verandah and down the steps. He was tall, with thick dark hair, and he was wearing a brown jacket and trousers, with boots up to his knees. The way he walked, with his head up and his back straight, the way he looked around him . . . Well, it was as if he owned the whole world.

It must be Niall McEwen. There was no one else it could be.

With a start Claire opened her eyes. She felt dizzy, her head woozy, light, as if she'd been asleep. She had been daydreaming, that was all, and yet the dream had been very real.

"The curse of a good imagination," she told herself with a laugh.

She let her gaze drop once more to the old picture of the homestead. It would be good background for her own photo, and whatever story she could cobble together. And yet, niggling away in her mind, was the knowledge that that wasn't the only reason she wanted to find out about Niall. There was something more. If only she could remember what it was.

"Do you remember how low the reservoir was four years ago?" Gabe waved his wine glass in the direction of the view below Claire's house.

"Not this low, surely?"

"Almost. And then there was a thunderstorm, gallons of rain. It kept raining for weeks. We thought the drought had broken but it was only a brief respite."

"I was in hospital then, Gabe."

"Of course." His gaze rested on her, calm, gentle. She felt safe with Gabe. "Has anything come back to you? Do you remember?"

Claire shook her head. "Sometimes I get a sense of . . . of dread." She laughed, to lighten the word. "But nothing concrete."

Gabe was silent a moment, and when he spoke again he'd moved on. "There was a bad drought in the 1930s. My grandfather was just a boy then, ten years old. He told me how he'd come down here to take a look at the old McEwen homestead, and then something very strange happened. He spotted a horse swimming across the reservoir. It reached dry land and shook itself and stood a moment, as if confused. He coaxed it with some sandwiches he'd brought with him and took it home. No one claimed it. He ended up keeping it."

"Where had it come from then?"

Gabe shrugged. "Another odd thing. My grandfather swears that some of the old people alive then told him they remembered that horse. It belonged to Helen McEwen. And it disappeared the same night she did."

Claire smiled. "A ghost horse then."

"A time-travelling horse," he retorted.

When it was time to go, she walked Gabe out to his car.

"I worry about you up here on your own," he said, staring down at the homestead in the reservoir below.

"Why? I'm perfectly all right, Gabe."

When he kissed her his lips brushed hers rather than her cheek, and before she knew it her arms were tight around his neck. The kiss deepened and if Gabe had let her she might have led him back into her house and her bed, but he drew away.

"I want you to be sure," he said, his palms cupping her face, his eyes intent on hers. "I wish—"

But whatever he wished remained unspoken. Claire watched him drive away, feeling emotional and confused. If only she could remember her past. No wonder Gabe was cautious. What if she had six kids and a biker husband waiting somewhere? The thought made her smile despite herself, and then yawn.

Time to get some sleep before she rose early tomorrow morning to take some photographs of the homestead in the pre-dawn.

Helen waited until it was well after midnight before she began her escape. Her bag was packed, just a few things, and Moppet was sleeping on the end of her bed. The little dog looked up at her as she dressed, head tipped to one side, aware something was out of the ordinary. Helen knew she couldn't leave Moppet behind.

"You must be very quiet," she murmured against his warm body.

Her horse was waiting and quickly she readied the saddle and tied on her bag. Moppet was at her feet and she tucked the little dog under her arm. A moment later she was riding out into the starlit night, moving towards an uncertain future.

Claire climbed out of bed in the darkness, wondering whether her job was really worth it. She slipped into jeans and a loose, long-sleeved shirt. Her camera bag was ready, and she opened the door and was outside before she knew it. The world was silent, black and empty, and as she looked down on what was now a valley of baked bare earth, Claire experienced a shiver of unease.

Quashing it, she pulled on her gumboots – there were still muddy patches and debris to negotiate – and found her flashlight. Pointing the circle of bright light before her, Claire walked more jauntily down the gentle slope than she felt. The sun wasn't up yet, but the scene was certainly creepy enough. It would make the perfect set for a horror movie.

The idea slid through her mind and away again. She let it go. No point in frightening herself any more than she had already. She slung her camera bag more securely over her shoulder and began to pick her way out towards the homestead.

The few patches of water between her and her destination were shallow, but there were obstacles like the old fence posts. She trudged towards the rise where the homestead stood. From her window each morning, the building had appeared small, a doll's house. Now, the closer she got the larger it seemed. The more real.

Several times she stopped and took some photos, but the silence and sense of isolation compelled her to keep moving. She glanced over her shoulder, towards the light left on in her home, as if to remind herself she wasn't so very far from safety. There was another flicker of light, further down the valley, where the spillway had been built. Startled, Claire stopped, staring towards it.

Someone is watching me.

Just for a moment her heart began to beat hard, and then she told herself not to be stupid. It could be anyone – a maintenance crew at the spillway, or Merv, her neighbour.

She walked on, her steps ever more reluctant, until eventually she had to stop. The puddles around the homestead were still too deep to walk through, forming that strange circular moat. As if Niall McEwen was protecting his property from trespass, even beyond death. Claire stood, surveying the glint of water, and knew she couldn't risk it, didn't want to. Give the drought another week, she decided, and the water would be gone. Then there'd be nothing between her and the homestead.

From where she stood now she could see the gaps of the windows and a doorway, no glass or door, of course. All the fittings were gone. Nothing left but a shell, and even that appeared twisted and warped. One wall was leaning far more dangerously than she had realized. Could be, she thought, as she moved slightly nearer, that the homestead would not be around much longer. Best take the photos while it was still standing.

As Claire lifted the camera to her face she could hear the faint drip, drip of water.

The body of Niall's wife Helen was never found. Was it still somewhere under the mud beneath her feet?

The nasty thought entered her head like a sly whisper and she lowered the camera. Her heart was pounding and she didn't like that; she didn't like not being able to hear. But what was there to listen to, apart from the dripping water?

Once again, Claire lifted the camera and this time took a series of shots looking down the valley towards the spillway, capturing the old verandah in part of the frame. She adjusted the lens and stepped back, preparing for the next shot. But her heel landed in a deep hole in the mud and her knee buckled. Off balance, she tried to save herself, and then realized there was nothing she could do – she was going to fall. The camera! She held it against herself protectively as her side hit the ground. Mud squished beneath her hip and shoulder, but although soft the ground still managed to jar her unpleasantly. Her breath came out in a whoosh.

She saw stars, or at least she thought she did. For a moment the sky danced around her, and then a shadow moved over her and a man's voice said, "Helen?"

And then she was up on her feet again. Rigid. Staring at the empty old house and listening to nothing at all.

Claire got her photos. The sun came up eventually, and she took several from further along the valley. But she did not go back to the homestead. The moment when she had fallen was as clear in her mind as the memories she no longer had, but she did not want to think about it. She could not think about it.

But as she trudged home, ignoring the prickling urge to glance over her shoulder, that voice reverberated in her head. Deep, hoarse and despairing.

Helen . . .

Someone was following her. She was hardly beyond the gate when she sensed she was not alone after all. Moppet struggled and began to bark and she was forced to set the dog down. It ran back the way they'd come, barking steadily.

Helen didn't know whether to go on, and while she hesitated, torn at the prospect of leaving her pet behind her, he came out of the darkness.

"Where are you going?"

There was no point in lying. He would know.

"I'm leaving."

He steadied his horse, blocking her path, body tense and ready if she tried to sidestep him. "I don't think so. That was never part of the bargain, Helen. 'Till death us do part', isn't that what the vicar said?"

"I made a mistake."

"I knew you were up to something. You're not very good at lying."

"And you're an expert."

"You're not leaving." His face was implacable.

She knew then, even as she tried to ride past him. Even as he caught her reins and grabbed her arm, hauling her from her saddle. She knew he was going to hurt her.

The following morning Gabe and Claire met as usual in the cafe to discuss upcoming stories for the *Bugle*.

As soon as she sat down Claire became aware of the weariness in her body, and at the edges of her mind. She hadn't slept well. There had been the usual nightmares, of course. The faceless stranger watching her. An endless fall into darkness.

Perhaps the nightmare was symbolic of her coma, or perhaps it really had happened, perhaps someone had hurt her deliberately and left her for dead. The police had said her head injuries could have been sustained in a fall, and there were other bruises, old and new. But they couldn't tell her for certain and she could not remember, so how could she ever really know?

As well as lack of sleep from the nightmares, Claire now found herself replaying in her head, over and over again, the moment out in the reservoir when she had slipped and fallen. It was like a clip from a bizarre movie, only this wasn't a movie. Real or fantasy? A figment of her imagination or an actual happening? No wonder she was tired.

They had gotten quiet, Gabe reading and Claire eating her breakfast. She didn't know she was going to ask the question until the words came out.

"Tell me what you know about Niall McEwen?"

Gabe seemed startled, although he took his time putting down his paper and looking up at her. "Probably as much as you."

"Oh, come on, you've lived here all your life. I've only been here for four years. You *must* know more than me."

Gabe seemed to be gathering his thoughts. "Niall's grandfather was the younger son of an aristocratic family in Scotland, and there's some debate whether he came to Australia to make his fortune or because he was being disinherited for some misdemeanour. Anyway, it hardly mattered, because he struck it rich on the goldfields and used the money to buy land. Set himself up, and formed a dynasty.

"Niall was the favoured grandson. He was a bit of a scoundrel, with plenty of money and a handsome face and probably no one in his entire life had ever said no to him. So, when he set eyes on

Helen, he wanted her, and for Niall that was it, really. He wanted her and so he had her."

"Gabe, you make him sound appalling," she laughed.

"Helen wasn't as well bred as Niall, but far more respectable. She held out for marriage, and eventually he proposed. It was a big wedding."

"You sound as if you didn't like Helen," Claire said.

Gabe looked down at his coffee cup. "Do I? My grandfather had a photograph of her in his desk drawer – I think he was half in love with her despite the fact she was long gone before he was born. She was beautiful, and she used her looks to get what she wanted. A bit like Niall used his charm. It made them well suited."

"Was it a happy marriage?"

"Niall was a womanizer but despite that he always insisted he loved his wife. Then Helen disappeared. Vanished completely."

"They searched?"

"Oh yes. Looked everywhere. The police believed she'd run off with a lover – although who that lover was was never discovered. But the people around here thought differently. A rumour started that Niall had murdered Helen and hid the body. The rumour was never substantiated but it was enough to make Niall's life unbearable. He sold up and left the district. The valley was flooded and that was that."

Claire was quiet, mulling over his words. She knew the story, of course, but somehow Gabe's blunt retelling of it made it all more real to her. "What do you think happened to Helen?"

"I don't know, Claire." He was frowning, and now he pushed his coffee cup aside. "Why this sudden interest?"

Something stirred in her mind but she couldn't grasp it. Tantalizingly it remained just out of reach. And there was that niggling feeling in her stomach again, that urge to find out what really happened. That sense that something wasn't quite right.

Claire met Gabe's intelligent eyes and for a moment she was strongly tempted to tell him what had happened last night, but almost immediately she knew she wouldn't. Gabe was a rational man and what Claire had experienced, if it wasn't an auditory hallucination, wasn't rational.

"Last night I walked across the reservoir, closer to the homestead, and took some photos," she admitted.

"By yourself?" Gabe's frown deepened. "Claire, it's dangerous out there!"

"I was alone."

He shook his head. "That's my point. You were alone and the ground is treacherous. You could have fallen ... been hurt ... anything."

"I was fine," Claire said firmly.

Gabe seemed to know it was time to back off. He rearranged his teaspoon. "Are they good?"

"The photos? I think so. I haven't developed them yet."

"Why don't you use one for the front cover on Thursday?" A peace offering.

"Thanks. I will."

Gabe nodded, and then his mouth quirked up into a smile. Claire smiled back. I do love him, she thought. That's why I don't want to burden him with any more of my problems.

"Do you still have your grandfather's photo of Helen?" she said.

Gabe hesitated. "Somewhere."

"I'd like to see it some day."

"I'll look it out," he said casually.

Helen's body was one long ache where she'd landed on the ground when he pulled her from the horse. She opened her mouth to scream but he was already on her, hand covering her face, dragging her towards the barn. She kicked and struggled, but then he raised his fist and struck her hard on the jaw, and everything went dark. When she came around she was lying on the ground just inside the barn, her head throbbing and her vision woozy.

Was he gone?

But no, even as the hopeful thought entered her head she heard his steps as he made his preparations. Helen knew she was going to die and anger and regret filled her. A single foolish mistake had brought her to this violent end.

"Niall ..." she groaned.

He laughed. "Too late to be sorry," he mocked. "Far too late for that."

Claire had an assignment with a local farm-machinery supplier, taking details for a paid promotion. Afterwards, on a whim, she drove out to the town cemetery, where the gravestones spoke of past joys and sorrows, good times and bad.

The iron gate clanged shut behind her. Heat shimmered from the ground and the smell of eucalyptus filled her nostrils and cleared her head. High among the drooping leaves a bird rustled and then flew off with a slow, lazy flapping of its wings.

The McEwen graves were in the older, pioneer section. Her gaze slid over Niall's grandparents and parents, but there was no stone for Niall. Wherever he'd died it wasn't here. There was nothing for Helen, either.

It would be impossible to bury someone whose body had never been found, but there could be a memorial with her name and a brief rehash of the circumstances of her disappearance.

No body, no memorial and no way to put Helen to rest.

The heat was getting worse, the air so still and hot Claire found it difficult to breathe. Still no hint of rain. Sometimes Claire wondered if it was ever going to rain again. Drought, with its accompanying water restrictions and daily worries and irritations, had become a way of life. Nothing stirred, nothing moved, and yet there was that sense of watching.

Hastily Claire turned back.

It was late by the time she began to transfer her photos on to her computer. They were good, especially those where the homestead sat lonely within its moat, the water reflecting the first dawn light. Claire began to set aside the ones she thought would make a good front page for the newspaper, turning her full attention to each new shot.

One of them puzzled her until she realized that the camera must have gone off when she fell over. A dark, confusing shot, with a partial view of the front of the homestead, some of the sky, and the gleam of light on the water. All shadows and angles.

She was about to move on when something else caught her eye. Reaching for the zoom button, she leaned closer to the computer screen. Her heart seemed to stop.

There was a face, barely visible within the gloom of the doorway. Had there been a door? Claire didn't remember. The face was only half a face, the gleam of an eye, the shine of cheek and lips, but it was a face. Surely she could not be mistaken?

No, she wasn't. Something or someone had been there. Watching her. She hadn't been alone out there after all! Some stranger had been waiting, observing her, hiding from her. Then the voice; the word "Helen" had been spoken by a real man and not a ghostly presence?

She felt relief fight through her fear. Claire peered more closely at the photo, but it was impossible to accurately make out the features in the dark and light smudges that mingled to make up the man's face. She could show Gabe, see if he recognized anything about the man, but Gabe was protective enough. If he thought she was in any sort of danger he'd be here, babysitting her. Better if she kept it to herself, at least until she knew what she was dealing with.

It was probably nothing to worry about.

Helen could hear Moppet barking. A warm wet tongue woke her from her half-conscious state. She murmured reassurance, but when she tried to take the little dog in her arms she found her ankles and wrists were bound with cord. The barn door was closed, too, and it was dark inside.

At least she was still alive. For now.

Moppet barked again and she tried to hush him, discovering that her mouth was also bound with some sort of cloth gag.

Helen wriggled on to her back, wincing, and sat up. He'd tied her hands in front of her and it only took a moment for her to find a pitchfork among the bales of hay. She rubbed the cord against the prongs until they frayed enough for her to break them. Even so, her skin was raw and bleeding. Hurriedly she removed the gag and then the cord about her ankles, then staggered to her feet.

Moppet ran to the back wall and Helen followed, realizing there was a gap in the boards, half hidden behind a barrel. The little dog darted through and Helen began to follow, ignoring the stabbing pain behind her eyes and the queasiness in her stomach.

Behind her the barn door opened.

Angus had once been a big man but age had bowed and shrunk him down into something less formidable. Angus ran a small museum in an old house in the main street.

Claire knew she should be working but she still had that squirmy feeling in her stomach and she needed distraction. It was more than that, though. The idea of solving the mystery of Helen and Niall had taken hold of her. It wouldn't restore her own lost self, but it would help. It would give her the self-confidence she needed to tell Gabe she was in love with him.

"Do you have any photos of Niall McEwen's homestead?"

"I do have a few photos. Why do you want to see them, Claire?"

"I thought I'd do a story on Niall. Now that the homestead is no longer under water, people are interested."

"Are they?" Angus looked sceptical. "There was always something nasty about that whole Helen thing."

Nevertheless he went and found the photos, packed in a cardboard box. When Claire asked if she could take them with her he gave her a hard stare.

"I'll be very careful," she promised.

Reluctantly he put the box in her arms and she carried it out to the car, closing the trunk just as her cell phone rang.

"Claire? Merv here, how you doing?"

Merv was her neighbour further along the reservoir towards the spillway.

"You haven't lost a dog, have you Claire?"

"A dog? I heard one barking one night in the reservoir. I thought it might be yours."

"Well, it's here but it's not mine. Not yours either then?"

"No."

"Just turned up in the middle of the night. Strange thing was it was covered in mud and all wet. Must have been in the water, I reckon."

Claire felt a prickle of unease. What about the man who had been in the homestead, the man in the photo? Was the dog his? And if so, why had he left it behind?

"Claire?"

She realized she'd fallen silent, standing by her car, the phone pressed hard to her ear. "How about I come over and take a look at it now? I'm about to drive home anyway."

"See you then."

Merv, man of few words, hung up. Claire climbed into the car, telling herself that it was probably just a stray dog, dumped on the highway further out of town. Animals could smell water for miles, couldn't they?

Merv was waiting for her, his shock of white hair even wilder than usual. Inside a dog was barking. Short, sharp yaps. It sounded like the dog she'd heard the other night. As Merv opened a door a small bundle of newly washed white fur ran past him and straight at Claire. Before she could stop it, the small dog was jumping at her, blunt claws scrabbling at her legs as it barked hysterically.

"Whoa there, boy!" Merv caught the sturdy little animal up, holding it away from her, but it continued to bark. Bright eyes peered at her through a mop of white fringe, and a pink tongue lolled as it fought to catch its breath. Merv looked at Claire. "You sure you haven't met before? He seems to think you're his."

She shook her head, laughing, and reached out to rub the dog's head. It was white and woolly. This wasn't the sort of dog that an owner dumped on a highway; this was a pet, healthy and well fed.

"I wonder where he came from?" she asked, smiling as the animal licked at her hand, little tail wagging so violently its whole body shook in Merv's arms.

"Your guess is as good as mine. He's an intelligent little fellow, and friendly."

Claire gave the woolly head another pat. "I'll put something in the paper for Thursday. Perhaps we can find his owners."

The dog seemed calmer now, and Merv put it down. It trotted over to Claire and sat, gazing up at her with adoring eyes.

"Love at first sight," Merv quipped.

"I've never had a dog," she said, stooping to tickle the animal under the chin. "Well, not that I can remember, anyway."

Merv leaned against the doorjamb. "Nothing's come back to you then?"

Claire grimaced. "Nothing. It's as if I never existed. As if I'm nobody."

"You're somebody in this town, Claire," Merv reminded her levelly.

It was nice of him to say so, and Claire smiled.

"I hear you're digging into Helen's disappearance." The humour had gone from Merv's eyes.

"Yes, I am. Do you think Niall killed Helen? Is that what everyone thinks?"

He shrugged. The little dog barked, breaking the tension.

"Do you want to take him? Might be company for you until his owner's found."

The dog was watching her, panting, and she nodded. Why not?

But as she drove away, the dog sitting proudly in the back seat, questions began to fill her head. If the dog belonged to the man in the homestead then why had it run away? Could . . . could the man have fallen? Claire's heart began to pound. Was he still out there, inside, too hurt to call out? Trapped and injured and expecting her help.

Guilt swamped her. The other night all she had wanted to do was get away from the place, and it hadn't occurred to her that the man might need her help, that she was running from an injured man and not a ghost.

"Damn it," she muttered to herself, and pressed down hard on the accelerator.

He was coming closer. She heard him throwing aside hay and tools and empty crates, anything in his way. Helen reached through the gap in the wall, fingers like claws in the earth, and pulled herself through. A moment later she was on her feet and running towards the homestead. There were people there. She could get help. Someone would help her.

The water had receded some more, leaving a line of newly formed crusts over the mud around the edge of the moat. It was still too deep for Claire to wade across despite her gumboots, but she could see the bottom now and from the feel of the sun scorching her back, it wouldn't be long before it had dried up enough.

She shaded her eyes and squinted up the slope towards the homestead. The barns and other buildings that must once have encircled the main house were long gone, either rotted into the mud or dismantled before the water covered them. In daylight the homestead had lost its poignancy and looked forlorn, with one wall leaning dangerously, the boards buckled and warped, and the window frames empty dark squares staring inwards.

"Hello!"

The word seemed to stop, as if it came up against something solid. No echo, no carry. She called again. There was still no real sense that anyone who might be in the structure would be able to hear her, or that she could hear them. Especially if they were injured and unable to answer loudly.

She should have gone back for Merv. But she admitted that she wasn't sure enough to risk making a fool of herself – the amnesiac who imagined ghostly voices. Claire would just love for that rumour to begin to circulate.

Cautiously she stepped closer, her gumboots sinking into the mud with an evil squelching sound. The heat of the sun stung her skin and perspiration dripped down her back. Everything was so still, the air wavering like steam from a kettle, but it was an uncomfortable tranquillity. And the sense of being watched was back, and with it a feeling of menace.

Ignoring her unease, Claire focused her gaze on the ground leading up to the homestead. No footprints that she could see, nothing to show that anyone had ever walked or crawled up there. Not even the little dog.

And yet they must have. She had proof in the photo.

"Hello! Are you all right?"

Again that odd sense that her voice had not carried as far as it should have.

Claire began to make her way around the edge of the moat, grimacing as her boots sank in the sucking mud. Finally she found a shallow causeway that looked crossable. Slowly, gingerly, she walked out into the warm water, feeling her gumboots begin to fill, but she plodded on. When one of her boots sank into the mud and stuck fast, she cursed, tugging at it and balancing on her other leg. All of a sudden it came free with a horrible sucking sound, and she lost her balance, staggering forwards. Before she could stop herself she fell, landing on the ground on the other side of the moat.

But where she expected to land on rock-hard earth her hands touched grass. Soft, sweet, green grass.

She thought she must have passed out.

Slowly she lifted her gaze from the grass – so green it hurt her eyes – and up the slope that was stretching in front of her. There was a long sweep of garden. An orchard to her left and borders of perennials. Lavender grew around her in big untrimmed shrubs, the spikes heavy with bees.

Horses stood in a railed yard, their tails swishing at the flies, and a couple of men were unloading a wagon, while a girl with a white apron was carrying a bucket awkwardly towards the rear of the house.

Still stunned, lying frozen upon the grass, Claire stared up at the homestead. A moment ago it had been a ruin but now curtains fluttered from the open windows and smoke rose from the chimneys and a door banged shut as someone strode across the verandah.

Claire shook her head. No. It wasn't possible. It wasn't true.

A man was striding down the front steps. He was dark haired and wearing a brown jacket, riding breeches and boots. He moved with such an air of authority that Claire knew who it was without seeing his face.

Niall McEwen.

A moment ago she had been too frozen to move, but now she dug her fingers harder into the soft green grass beneath her and pushed herself up. The scent of the lavender, the sounds of life about her, the utter impossibility of it all, made her head spin as if she were drunk. Claire swayed, trying to catch her breath, trying to keep her grip on the shifting reality about her, as she stood waist deep in lavender.

Just as Niall McEwen turned his head in her direction.

His body went rigid. His chin lifted. He quickened his step. In a moment he'd be running.

Terror ripped through her.

She stumbled backwards. Water washed over the heels of her boots and, as they sank a little into the mud of the causeway, the scene in front of her faded. Like a photo that has been overexposed. Niall was still moving towards her but there was no sound and she knew he would never reach her. She backed away another step and into the hole that had claimed her boot previously, toppling into a pool of water. Her head went under.

Helen! The voice was in her head, a cry of anguish and need. When she surfaced and pulled herself out on to the mud, she was spluttering and choking. Her wet hair hung in her eyes and she pushed it away with a trembling hand and turned back towards the house.

It stood drunkenly above her, a ruin baking in the sun. No garden, no horses and certainly no Niall McEwen. Nothing but bare ground and warped timbers and a harsh blue sky.

He was gaining on her. She tried to scream but the sound was breathless and barely louder than the other night noises. She ran to the side, towards the garden, where flower stalks rose starkly. She'd insisted on tidying them herself and now she would never finish.

He reached for her arm but at the same moment Moppet ran between his feet and tripped him. The dog yelped, the man cursed and Helen ran

*on. Before her was the lily pond. Would he follow her in? He couldn't
swim, she knew that much. It was one of the only weaknesses he'd
admitted to her. He was afraid of water.*

   Perhaps she could save herself after all?

By the time Claire had showered and changed daylight was fading.
Sunset was a glorious crimson and orange affair, and Claire sat on
her verandah and watched it, a glass of cooled wine in her hand,
the dog at her feet.

   He had forgiven her for shutting him up in her house earlier and
now seemed content to rest by her side, following her with his eyes
whenever she moved, clearly intent on attaching himself to her.

   Her own eyes continually drifted to the old homestead, as if
she expected any moment it might transform itself. She had no
explanation for what had happened. If it was a hallucination, it was
a pretty good one, but she knew it wasn't a dream. She wanted to
discuss it logically, but who would listen to her? Gabe? He might,
or he might just ring for the doctor.

   Perhaps the most disturbing part of it had been the sense of
familiarity. Her daydream had already shown her what to expect
and when she stood in the lavender it had not seemed foreign at all.
And he had not seemed a stranger.

   But still her rational mind argued, needing proof.

   Claire got up abruptly and hurried out to the door, the dog
trotting along behind her. She came back with the box from the
museum and set it down on the kitchen table, then poured herself
another glass of crisp white wine.

   A quick search found mostly junk. There was a photo album,
however, and she eased it out and opened it up, expecting great
things. She found disappointment. The first photo had been eaten
away by mildew, the faces unrecognizable. The next page was
worse. Claire turned another page and then another, but it was
all the same. The damage to the album had been extensive and
irreversible. Even a master restorer could do nothing with this
mess, there was simply nothing to restore.

   Claire had come to the end of the album. The last photo. And
it was undamaged. She stared down at it. A man in a high white
collar, his handsome face stern and still, a lock of dark hair falling
over his brow. His gaze was intense but it was also faintly amused,

as if he knew the effect he had on those around him – especially women.

Claire shivered.

It was him. The man she'd seen.

Niall McEwen was alive. He lived in a place that could be reached through a moat of water that surrounded the homestead. He existed in the past, but he also existed in the here and now, and only Claire knew it.

Only Claire could reach him.

But that was madness, impossible! Wasn't it?

There was only one way to prove it. She had to go back there and do what she'd done earlier. She had to cross the causeway and step on to the island where the homestead was. She had to go and face her fears.

The knock on her door almost gave her a heart attack.

Gabe's smile faded when he saw her face. "What's happened?"

Claire knew she could tell him. She could burden him with everything and he would help her, look after her, as he had before. Or she could solve her problems herself and come to him as an equal partner.

"I had a headache. It's gone now."

He appeared to accept her word.

"I didn't expect to see you tonight, Gabe."

By now he'd taken in the box from the museum and the photo album. She closed it before he could see Niall McEwen, some sense of self-preservation driving her.

"You were talking about Helen," he said. "I thought you might like to see the picture of her that belonged to my grandfather."

"Oh. Yes, thank you." She found a glass and poured him some of her white wine. "How did he come by Helen's photo anyway?"

It was just idle conversation but Gabe seemed to find the question awkward. "Belonged to an uncle of his, a cousin of Niall McEwen's who worked as Niall's foreman. He was fond of Helen, and when she vanished . . ." He shrugged. "He kept the photo."

They sat down in the lounge and Claire tucked her feet up under herself. She remembered how, after she had left hospital, she always sat so straight and formally, feet together on the floor, hands clasped in her lap. Gabe had teased her, gently, and gradually she had learned to relax.

She realized Gabe was talking about his grandfather again.

"He believed there were places in the world where the veil between our time and the past was thinner, more able to be breached. The valley was one of them, according to him."

Claire tried not to let him see how much his words had affected her. Thankfully the room was dimly lit with candles, her preferred form of lighting.

"Why did he think that?"

"He was told things and he saw things himself, things he shouldn't have been able to see. His belief was that the past and the present ran at different speeds. For instance, whereas a hundred years might have gone by here in the present, only a day might have gone by in the past."

Claire took a gulp of her wine, her fingers trembling.

"You haven't been down there again, have you, Claire? To the homestead?" And, when she didn't answer, he added, "It's not safe. Promise me you won't go alone."

"You worry too much about me, Gabe. You shouldn't have to worry about me. I feel as if I've become a weight around your neck."

He stood up and crossed to her, then took her wine glass from her hand and set it down. She looked up at him.

"Claire, I've been in love with you since I first saw you. I wanted to wait until you were . . . better, so that you could be sure about your future, but now I think I've waited too long."

She went into his arms. It seemed foolish to deny herself any longer. Gabe's mouth closed on hers. His body felt familiar against hers, but only because this was Gabe. And he showed her how he felt with every touch, every caress, every stroke. For the first time in her life Claire knew what it was to be with the man she loved, and who loved her.

The water was chill against her thighs as she waded deeper. Her skirts dragged about her and she was gasping for air. He stood on the bank, watching her, his face full of fury.

For a moment she thought it would be all right. She almost believed she was safe. But then he stepped down into the pond, the water rising over his boots and up his legs, and she knew.

Stumbling, trying to hurry, she moved towards the far bank. Her foot slipped and she went under. The murky water closed over her head, and

suddenly everything was quiet. Like a church. She couldn't breathe, her
lungs were bursting, but she couldn't seem to find the surface.

The next moment she rose up from the water, gasping and spluttering,
crying out. But when she opened her eyes she was somewhere else. He was
gone, the valley was gone, and when she turned back to the homestead, it
was nothing more than a derelict ruin.

Claire opened her eyes, confused. She'd fallen asleep in Gabe's
arms, content and happy. Now the sound of the dog barking was
sharp and clear in the night, and for a moment she felt as if it was
all still a dream. That she was Helen, running for her life, coming
through Gabe's grandfather's thin veil in time.

And then reality clicked in and Claire eased herself out of bed,
careful not to wake Gabe, and took her clothes into the lounge. She
dressed, then went out on to the verandah. The sky was a marvel,
full of starlight, and beneath it the empty reservoir echoed with
the intermittent sound of barking. Something small and white was
bobbing about, just outside the moat.

Somehow the dog had escaped the house while she slept and was
now running back and forth outside the ring of water.

A terrible sense of excitement, of anticipation, gripped her. As if
she had been waiting for this moment for a very long time. And at
the same time fear flooded through her body, lifting every nerve to
a new state of anxiety.

The air was like warm silk against her skin, heavy. She plodded
along in her gumboots, her gaze fixed on the homestead, the
occasional flash of lightning and rumble of thunder warning of an
approaching storm.

The dog had noticed her at last and came running towards her.
Jumping up, paws scrabbling at her legs and whimpering a greeting.
She reached down to pet him, ruffling the thick, curly coat.

"Where did you come from, boy?"

The dog looked up at her, its eyes gleaming darkly, tongue lolling.
He knew a secret and he wasn't telling.

"Be like that then," Claire murmured.

She picked the dog up and tucked his firm little body under her
arm. He felt warm and solid, and comforting. The water of the
moat sloshed against the toes of her boots, then up around her
ankles, her calves. Did she really want to do this? She knew that

some part of her did, some part of her was hungering to see the past again, to understand what it all meant. The rest of her was just plain terrified.

The water had evaporated even more since yesterday and soon there wouldn't be a moat at all. What would happen then? Would the past spill into the present like an unstoppable tide?

Claire moved out on to the causeway, the dog still clasped in her arms. The little animal seemed quite content to remain with her, quietly, trusting her, and besides, he was only a companion on this strangest of journeys.

Claire thought she might even manage to cross without getting wet feet, but the water was just deep enough to slosh over the tops of her boots and run down inside. With a grimace she found her way to the shallow water on the far side and took one step out and on to the bare desolate ground of the island.

It happened the other way around this time.

The overexposed picture began to come into focus, quickly gaining colour and definition. It was night-time here just as it was in the present, but there was a sense of life, of movement, all about her. The scent of lavender was strong in the air and she realized that once again she was standing among the thick bushes. An owl hooted and something snuffled in the flowerbeds, small feet running swiftly. The little dog whimpered in her arms and she hushed it, gently holding its muzzle so it couldn't bark.

She was back.

Claire moved forwards, along the path that wound through the fragrant garden and up towards the homestead. Above her the same storm she'd just left behind – or was it a different one? – was rattling the heavens. That sense of waiting sent shivers across her skin. The homestead was in darkness but it wasn't deserted, it wasn't empty.

It was waiting.

Waiting for her?

A candle flickered in one of the windows, as if someone was still up, but there was no sound. She stepped onwards, reaching out her hand towards the verandah post, to touch, to feel.

"It's you. You've come back."

The voice came out of the shadows before her. Claire stood, frozen, as he stepped towards her, his face a pale blur beneath his dark hair. The dog struggled, sensing that something was very wrong, but Claire held on to it.

"Where did you go?" There was something threatening in his voice. "Everyone has been searching for you, Helen. They're blaming Niall."

Because this wasn't Niall. As if a shattered window suddenly began to reform in her mind, bit by bit, she saw the truth. This handsome man was Maurice, Niall's cousin and his foreman, and she'd been stupid enough to spend one night in his bed. She'd done it in revenge for all the women Niall betrayed her with, but this man would not accept that. He'd always been jealous of Niall and one night made her his. He threatened to tell Niall, to blackmail her, he threatened to make her life a misery if she did not give him what he wanted.

So she was leaving him, and Niall.

"Helen?" he groaned. "You know if I can't have you then no one can."

"Yes. I am Helen." Her voice was a whisper.

The dog struggled again and he noticed it for the first time. "Moppet?" he said angrily. "You came back for Moppet?"

Of course, this was Moppet, her dog. "I could never leave Moppet."

Her placing her dog above him seemed to infuriate him even more. "Where have you been? Tell me the truth."

"Through time," she said, and laughed.

His features went hard, and suddenly he was no longer handsome.

Fear streaked through her, and Claire turned and ran. Back down the path, back towards the line of water that separated his world from hers. His boots thumped on the path behind her, his breathing heavy and gaining.

His hand closed on her shoulder, fingers pressing hard into her skin, imprinting themselves upon her. He pulled her around and into the hard grasp of his arms. Moppet leaped to the ground and Claire was dragged against his chest, aware of the faint scent of cigars and leather.

She'd returned to the past only to die here . . .

"Claire!"

Faint, desperate, a voice she knew like her own heart.

She began to fight Maurice. A flash of lightning showed his face and the determination to finish what he'd started all those years ago – or was it only an hour or two?

"Let her go!"

Suddenly Gabe was ripping her out of Maurice's grip, knocking him backwards so that he fell heavily into the shrubs. Claire was gasping, stumbling into his arms, and Moppet was barking wildly. The little dog had been barking all along, she realized, but she'd been too occupied to really hear its cries for help.

"Come on," Gabe said, voice rising against the growl of thunder.

And then Gabe was leading her through the water of the moat and the past was fading away behind her. A moment later they were standing on the baked surface of the reservoir, lightning and thunder creating havoc around them.

"He'll be able to come into the present," Claire said, wild-eyed, shaking uncontrollably. "The moat is drying up and soon he'll come."

Gabe reached down to pick up Moppet and put the dog into her arms. A big fat drop of rain plopped on to the ground beside them. And then another.

She turned her face upwards in amazement and joy. The drops were falling faster now, painful against her skin, but wonderful too.

"No, he won't," Gabe said confidently.

Later, as they sat on the verandah and watched the world through a curtain of rain, Gabe told her his story, which was her story, too.

"My grandfather had a photo of you. It belonged to his uncle Maurice. There was something secretive about the man, and my grandfather always had a suspicion it was to do with Helen. When Maurice died he told my grandfather that he and Helen had been lovers and that he'd tried to kill her, but she'd vanished. Just . . . vanished."

"And your grandfather began to work on his time theory."

"Exactly. Although I didn't really believe in it until I found you four years ago. I knew who you were. I recognized you from the photo, and I remembered what he'd told me. It was you, Helen, but I was the only one who knew it."

Claire rubbed her forehead. "The photo . . ." She went into the kitchen and found the old album, then carried it back to Gabe open at the photo in the back. "I thought this was Niall."

Gabe shook his head. "Maurice. They were alike. Must have made it even harder for Maurice to end up working for the man he wished he could be."

"If he couldn't have me then Niall couldn't either," she whispered.

"I found you down in the reservoir. You were dressed in old-fashioned clothing, like something from a costume drama. I got rid of the clothes, pretended I'd found you up in the hills. I didn't want them poking around the homestead with so much of it exposed, but it started to rain about then anyway. I hoped it would keep raining but it didn't, and . . ."

"And I decided to find my past," she said, reaching for his hand. "I wish I'd trusted you, Gabe."

"I wish I'd trusted you, but you see my difficulty? When you couldn't remember anything it was a blessing for me, really. But I always knew that eventually your memory would return and then we would have to deal with it. I thought I'd tell you everything then."

They sat a moment in silence, contemplating the incredible truth.

Gabe smiled. "I meant what I said before. I've been in love with you all my life. I feel like I've known you all my life."

Her own smile trembled at the edges. "But who am I, Gabe? Helen or Claire?"

"Who do you want to be?"

"Claire," she said. "I've grown up from Helen, I'm different now. I want to be Claire."

"Then Claire you shall be. And just in case someone tries to make trouble . . ." He slipped a photo from his pocket and handed it to her. Claire looked down into her own face, held stiff and unsmiling as the old-fashioned equipment recorded her image. She held one corner to the candle flame and watched it burn, turning the past and all its bad memories into ash. She raised her chin and kissed Gabe's lips.

Sexual Healing

Margo Maguire

One

The Old City. Autumn, AD 2743

The temperature was well modulated in the residential unit and the sound level comfortable as D499-DG-098 observed the chairperson addressing the group.

"The population decline has reached a critical level," said M277-CZ-398. She was the leader of GreenPiece, an ancient organization believed to have promoted the good health of the planet. It had been revived in recent years to address the concerns of the world's troubled scientists.

M277's demeanour was perfectly calm as she stated the fact they all knew. In 237 years, humanity would die out, becoming extinct, leaving only the fauna and flora to prosper without restraint. "The spiral will soon be irreversible," she added.

"It's time, then. Have we decided who will go?" one of the members asked. "D499 seems the likely candidate since he can gain access to a tempis-disc."

D499-DG-098 remained on the fringe of the room, and listened with a growing fascination. The biologists of GreenPiece had studied the problem of the Federation's population decline from many different angles, and had come to one simple conclusion. In order to save the human race, the inventor of Fusion XJ would have to be stopped before his creation came to fruition – before it could render increasing numbers of humans essentially infertile.

GreenPiece was meeting in M277's unit, ostensibly a study group, so that the authorities would not perceive any change in social conduct. The Federation strictly enforced the Natural Progression, and interfering with past events was absolutely forbidden. The world had become a balanced place, where emotions were subdued and rationality prevailed. Where war and famine did not exist, nor violence or disease. Where knowledge was king.

It was a cold, tightly regulated world, and while humans no longer had the impetus to create chaos for themselves, they'd also lost the impetus to mate. The process of Fusion XJ had cured a multitude of diseases, and the side effect of diminishing libido had not been a problem at first. It had hardly been noticed. Once the change was detected, it was viewed as a positive social development.

But it was not. In 2514, scientists had finally understood the full effect of Fusion XJ. The lauded genetic splicing that had bred out the propensity for vascular disease and tumour growth, had had an insidious side effect. The offspring of parents who had been treated had little interest in sexual coupling.

It had taken generations for the effect to become widespread, though not everyone was desensitized. A small segment of the population remained untouched by the genetic alteration. But they were in the minority, so, over time, sexuality had fallen into disfavour. It was considered a necessary evil by society at large, and very few Federees would practise any form of it without good reason: an obligatory pregnancy.

D499 was not desensitized, but there was a dearth of stimulation in the Federation's world, so his libido was rarely a problem. He had told no one that he was a Deviant, because it was no one else's concern. And, besides, he didn't want to deal with the stigma of Deviance. Even though his genes were intact, he and everyone like him needed to be circumspect in order to avoid alienating their friends and co-workers. He kept his sexual urges to himself, as did every other Deviant.

Certainly, the gradual population control that had occurred without war and epidemics had been a welcome relief from continuous growth. But in two centuries hence, human life would arrive at a critical point. The decline in numbers would wreak havoc with civilization. There would be insufficient numbers of people to maintain life as it was known. There would not be enough workers to produce necessities or consumers to use them. Humans would retreat into small, subsistence enclaves, separated by thousands of miles. There would be no world community.

Cloning had been considered a fair solution to the drop in population, but there were flaws – especially in the intellectual capacity of the subjects. And until those flaws were corrected, the Federation could not rely upon clones for the perpetuation of the human species.

The group had decided that the creator of Fusion XJ could not be allowed to invent his process. GreenPiece's scientists had calculated the likely consequences of Fusion XJ's absence. Population growth would remain steady, due to death from war and disease. There would be no artificial decline due to a genetically engineered aversion to sex.

"Correct. D499-DG-098 is the logical choice to go. He is a temporal-spatial physicist," said M277, sitting on her sleek white sofa, wearing the white uni-suit that was identical to everyone else's, "and with his interest in history, he knows States better than any of us."

"*United* States," D499 muttered. He'd studied the available information, but the documentation was fragmented, with very few info-discs that survived the terrible wars of the twenty-third century. D499 believed the year he needed to visit would be fraught with the dangers of violence and disease. The people of that long-ago era allowed their emotions – and their libido – to rule their actions. It was likely to be absolute hell.

"My mistake," M277 said. "*United* States. Now that our data is in, it is imperative that we act."

D499 knew it was his duty to go. Someone had to stop the man who would invent Fusion XJ, and change the course of the world.

Time travel was not exactly trivial, but it was not the impossibility pronounced by scientists all through the Technical Age. Certainly, it posed problems, but they were solved by the advent of the *computrons*, the thinking machines that were immeasurably superior to the computers of the Technical Age. He was a physicist in the Knowledge Age and, as every Federee knew, knowledge was power.

"I'm prepared to go," D499 said. He knew that people of the distant past used family names. There were no Identi-Checks, and people exchanged currency for goods and services.

"Do you need time to make preparations?" M277-CZ-398 asked.

D499 shook his head. Expecting to be the one chosen to go, he'd already considered what he needed to do to fit in. He'd made arrangements. "No. Just a few hours to assemble what I'll need to take with me."

"Then we'll meet in the Old Town factory at first light."

For the past two years, D499 had added an additional hour of exercise to his daily regimen of swimming and running, in the likelihood that he would be called upon for this mission. He'd wanted to be ready, both physically and mentally, for the task. An added benefit of his weight-lifting and vigorous Aten-Ra exercises was that his physical fatigue had helped him control the lust that often plagued him when he retired at night.

He left the group and took a transit to the Restoration Center for one last workout before his departure. Though he was the lead scientist on the Federation's Temporal-Spatial team, he was vaguely nervous about the undertaking. "Sliding" through time was not something to be taken lightly. Creating a wormhole was no simple feat.

And there was a possibility that they had some of the historical details wrong. Andrew Gibson-Booth might not have done his breakthrough work on Fusion XJ in the year 2015. If that was the case, D499 might arrive a year or two late, too late to do what he needed to do. To compensate for this, his colleagues agreed that he should arrive a few years early.

He'd chosen a name, one that he'd found in his own sketchy family records. He would be Sean Dugan, and once he arrived in 2010, he would be able to use the rudimentary computers of the Technology Age to locate Andrew Gibson-Booth, and make any necessary arrangements. Perhaps the old machines could be used to create the credentials he needed to become one of Andrew Gibson-Booth's colleagues. However he managed it, he would stop Gibson-Booth before he ever got started.

Two

Chicago. April 2010

"Where's your backpack, Drew?" Erica Gibson-Booth asked her son. "Hurry up, honey. Mitch's guy will be here in a minute!"

"Who is Mitch's guy?" asked five-year-old Drew as he went into his bedroom for his pack.

Erica didn't want to frighten her son with talk about stalkers and bodyguards. She just hoped her smarter-than-average little boy would accept a bare-minimum explanation. "He's just a good friend of Mitch Crandall who wants to come to work with me."

She heard a knock at the door. Looking through the peephole she saw that it was indeed the bodyguard, a man she'd never seen before, and she would have remembered this one. The guy must be six-five. He had a face that looked like it had been chiselled from granite, and those shoulders . . .

Erica felt a twinge of something that hadn't been active in her life in a very long time, in spite of the profession she'd been forced to turn to. She hadn't felt the pull of attraction since Andy's fatal car accident five years before, when they were both grad students and had a promising future ahead of them.

Back when she was pregnant with Drew.

She took a deep breath and opened the door. "You're right on time." She put out her hand. "I'm Erica Gibson-Booth. And we're almost ready."

Her bodyguard's formidable dark brows lowered over his brown eyes and he hesitated for a moment before taking her hand and looking into her eyes. "Sean Dugan," he finally said, his voice deep, his hand warm. "Is Andrew here?"

The bottom of Erica's stomach fell out at the strength of the man's gaze. His hair was thick and nearly black, and he wore it short, almost military. He seemed to be in complete command, and yet he stood quietly, as though waiting for . . .

Erica gathered her wits and put away every lascivious thought that had just flown through her brain. *She* wasn't the one with overblown hormones. It was the guys who came to drool over her when she danced. "Drew will be ready in a sec. Drew?" she called. "Come on! It's seven-thirty!"

The apartment was so tiny that when she went into the kitchen alcove, she was standing only a few feet from Mr Dugan, who seemed to take up a great deal of space. "We'll be ready in a moment," she said. "Make yourself comfortable while I make this PB and J."

But he didn't look comfortable at all. He glanced around the apartment as though he'd never been inside an 800-feet flat before. He was almost too big for it. Too big for her apartment-sized furniture anyway, and Erica had a sudden image of him lying naked in her double bed, and taking up almost all the space. *Almost.*

She cleared her throat and refocused. "I know it's not much, but Drew and I manage." She took bread out of a drawer and slapped together a peanut butter and jelly sandwich, then wrapped it in wax paper.

"Don't say anything to Drew about why you're here," she said quietly as she grabbed her coat and purse, and Drew's sweatshirt. "I don't want to scare him."

He frowned at that, and at the sandwich she'd just made. She was going to ask him if he wanted one, but Drew came out of the bedroom with his backpack just then, and they wasted no time heading out of the apartment. She couldn't feed *everyone.* "Where did you park?"

"Park?" he asked.

"You didn't drive?"

"No. I—"

"We'll take my car, then. It's probably better if I drive and you keep an eye out for the bald guy, anyway." Her stalker. A man named Bernie Sandino. She'd learned his name from the cops, and knew that he used to be a prize fighter, but there wasn't anything the police could do about him. He hadn't made any threats, and rarely came within ten yards of her.

But he gave her the creeps, and he always seemed to be around. It was pretty obvious that he was following her. Mitch had told the bouncers at the Purple Moon to keep him out of the club, but he always seemed to be lurking nearby, after hours. "It's a relief to have you along, Mr Dugan," she said quietly, hoping not to alert Drew to any danger.

It was true. Sean Dugan had an imposing presence, even though he looked at her as if he'd never seen a woman before. Maybe he's never seen a redhead?

In any case, Sandino wouldn't dare come near her with a man like Dugan standing with her. "Did Mitch show you any pictures of the creep?"

"Creep?"

"You know, Sandino – the guy who's been following me."

"Uh, no."

They walked towards Sheffield Street and when they reached the corner Erica tossed the sandwich to the homeless amputee who hung out in the same place every day. He shouted his thanks and they moved on.

"You feed the . . ."

"He's harmless and, well, look at him. He needs help."

She led them to her eight-year-old Corolla and unlocked the car. "Andrew, into the back."

"I know, Mommy."

"And you, Mr Dugan," she said, "can ride shotgun."

Three

D499 wasn't quite sure what had just happened. The colours here were more vivid than any he'd seen in his time, the sounds louder and the smells far more intense. He could not get over the height of the trees. They were tall and . . . *majestic* was the only word he could think of, even though it was an archaic usage. Federation trees were mere shrubs compared to these. And they only grew in neat clusters, or straight rows that lined the laz-tracks.

The pure sensuality of the woman – Erica – was something he couldn't possibly have anticipated. She wore a light blue sweater, which hugged feminine curves that had obviously been bred out of the women of AD 2743, and black pants, which fitted her like a second skin. He felt the punch of something hot and sultry, and so intense he could barely swallow.

She had red hair. *Red*. It was something D499 – or rather, Sean – had never seen before. It looked smooth and glassy like sheets of styron, and had streaks of gold running through it. Amazing. Her eyes were green and her lips were full and pink. Sean's gaze was drawn to them so often, she was sure to notice if he didn't get his bewilderment – and his Deviant urges – under control.

With the assumptions she'd made about him, he hadn't had to use the ruse he'd come up with to get close to Andrew. But he wasn't quite sure what she expected of him.

In consternation, he dragged one hand across his mouth and got into the vehicle, folding his long legs uncomfortably into the small space. She had the engine started before he could bring himself to turn back and look at the child whom she'd called Andrew. *Could this be the Andrew Gibson-Booth he'd come for?*

"Buckle up, Mr Dugan," said the boy.

He didn't know what the child was talking about, and in his hesitation Erica leaned over him and reached for some sort of wide belt hidden beside his shoulder, which she pulled across him and fastened into a metal holder that lay between their two seats.

He closed his eyes and inhaled deeply as she did so, taking in the pleasant scent of what could only be her warm, feminine body. Scents that had all but disappeared in his time.

What a mistake that was.

She drove out into the street and Sean turned his attention to the business at hand. "Where is the boy's father?" he asked Erica. Even her name was sensual, the sound of it resonating through his brain almost as much as her enthralling scent.

"My daddy went to heaven before I was born," Andrew said.

Sean tried to mask his shock. He knew that the father of the man who'd developed Fusion XJ had died a few months prior to his son's birth. Which meant that the child – *this child* – was the inventor.

And Sean was meant to stop him, using whatever method he deemed necessary. Many of the members of GreenPiece believed Andrew Gibson-Booth would have to be killed.

Sean swallowed hard. He was no child-killer. But what was he supposed to do? GreenPiece had sent him back to deal with the scientist who'd invented Fusion XJ. Clearly, the records they'd pieced together were wrong. Gibson-Booth must have patented the process years later, certainly *not* in 2015, as they'd concluded. Sean had come twenty or thirty years too early.

The boy resembled his mother – he had fair skin, though his hair was more yellow than red. His bright, intelligent, green eyes watched the road.

Sean could easily *slide* ahead in time in order to deal with Andrew as an adult, but he could not quite bring himself to leave the Erica Gibson-Booth of 2010, possibly to face her twenty or thirty years in the future.

She drove through traffic, and Sean's attention was violently whipped away from his quandary by the speed they were travelling in her uncontrolled vehicle. There were no laz-tracks to keep this and the rest of the speeding vehicles in place, nothing preventing them from careening into one another.

"How fast does this vehicle travel?" he asked.

Erica shot him a sidelong glance and he felt more than a small degree of alarm, wishing she would keep her eyes on the road. "You're not from Chicago, are you?"

He swallowed, hanging on tightly to the sides of his seat. "Why do you say that?"

"Your white knuckles," she responded with a laugh. "Don't worry, I've been driving in this kind of traffic for a long time."

He shuddered as Erica pulled to a stop in front of an old house and got out of the car. Andrew did the same, so Sean followed suit.

"I'll pick you up in the morning, sweetheart," Erica said to her son, "as usual."

"OK," the boy replied.

"I love you, baby," she said, crouching down to pull the boy into a tight hug.

"I'm not a baby," Andrew said as he kissed his mother's cheek. "I love you, too, Mommy."

"Behave for Carolyn."

Even at a distance, Sean could feel the strength of their bond and the power of their emotions. And he realized that it was yet another aspect of humanity that had been lost with the development of Fusion XJ. Love wasn't a highly valued item in his time. Logic and progress, intelligence and order were the qualities that mattered.

As Erica turned her son over to the smiling woman at the house, Sean tried to sort out the situation. Erica was on her way to work, and she had just dropped her son at a place where he would be under supervision overnight. Now she would go to her lab, and she obviously believed that Sean was associated with her work there. He was not going to disabuse her of that belief until he could figure out what to do. About Andrew.

"Ready?" she asked him.

It must be an idiom, because of course he was ready. She was the one who'd needed to stop. He nodded and got back into the vehicle. Reluctantly. She resumed driving, and he found himself adjusting to the speed, and becoming even more aware of her.

The vehicle's cabin was small, the seats close together. His thigh was touching hers, and the slight contact made the electrons in his skin switch charges.

At least, that's what it felt like.

Her scent intrigued him, as did the sway of her hair. She glanced at him, her gorgeous eyes appraising him, looking at him in a way that was completely unfamiliar. Sean wondered if—

No. She could not possibly be showing sexual interest. Could she?

"Where are you from?" she asked.

He swallowed. "Atlanta." It was the first ancient city that came to mind.

"You don't sound southern," she said. She licked her lips and Sean's eyes locked on to the sight of her moist, pink mouth. He wondered how they would feel against his.

He shrugged as casually as he could. He'd had a lifetime to practise suppressing his libido and he could surely continue to do so now.

"Do you have any family back there?" Her voice was soft, the timbre alluring.

"No, I'm on my own." That much was true. He had no one here, or in 2743, either. "What about you?"

"Just Drew and me," she said. "He's all I've got."

Something in her voice jarred him. If he was not mistaken, it was the sound of complete and utter devotion. She would do anything for her child.

And Sean felt the strangest yearning to feel that kind of dedication. To be the one she cared for.

He pressed his hands against his thighs and tried to focus on the problem he faced rather than the fierce attraction and confusing emotions that were flooding his body and mind, but failed miserably. He wanted to know what it would feel like to touch Erica Gibson-Booth, to link with her in the primal way of humans – body to body, soul to soul. So much for controlling his libido.

"Why did you take food to that man on the street?"

"Poor guy is homeless," she said. "It's not his fault he got his legs blown off in the war."

Sean gave a short nod and realized he had just seen, first hand, a not unusual result of the mid-world wars that had plagued the planet for decades. His era's info-discs had not demonstrated the human losses so dramatically.

Nor had they exhibited any of the kindness that had been shown by people like Erica, who cared.

Four

He was looking at her as though he wanted her for dessert, but not in the creepy way that the patrons of the Purple Moon Club ogled her. She reminded herself not to scorn those clowns at the P.M.C. too badly, because it was only because of them that Erica was able to pay her bills, and Drew's asthma meds were expensive.

Her body hummed with awareness of Sean Dugan. He might want her for dessert, but she couldn't stop thinking of him as the main course. He ran his big hands down his thighs, his discomfort at their proximity palpable.

He was attracted to her, and he hadn't even seen her dance.

Erica took a deep breath. Dugan was hot, but no matter how strong her urge to lick him all over, she wasn't going to fall for a big, dumb-ass bodyguard, just because he had a pretty face and a body that could make a virgin beg. She was only a dissertation away from finishing her doctorate in neurobiology, and as soon as the economy improved and she could get some student financing, she was going to quit her sucky job and finish the degree.

And then maybe she'd meet someone – the right kind of someone, and not just some loser who hung around strip clubs.

"Hey, I appreciate Mitch bringing you in," she said, turning away from his chiselled jaw and that mouth that was made for sin. "I've never had a stalker before – that I know of."

He nodded. Not big on small talk, she'd noticed. And he kept his eyes glued to the road ahead of them.

"Most of P.M.C.'s patrons are pretty harmless," she said. "Or at least, none of them have ever tried to follow me home."

"And this . . . stalker?"

"He's been hanging around the stage door for the past week, and then I saw him near my apartment two days ago," she said. "He scared the daylights out of me."

He looked at her as though she'd spoken in another language and she decided he must be new to the bodyguarding gig. Or maybe it was strip clubs in general. That would be something new.

"You don't look like a typical bouncer."

"Uh, it's my first time."

She looked over at him, her mind opening to a few possibilities. "I guess I'm not the only one trapped by the bad economy. What did you used to do?"

"I'm . . . was . . . a temporal-spatial physicist."

"Really," she said, fascinated. She'd known he was no typical bouncer, but a scientist? "I've never heard of your field before. Did you lose funding?"

He gave a slow nod.

"Wow. Maybe we could have coffee after the show and you could tell me all about temporal-spatial physics."

A muscle flexed in his strong jaw and she sensed that he was uncomfortable talking about his lost profession.

She exited the freeway, and started to prepare herself for the night at the club. She'd been in her current line of work for only three months, and dancing half naked for a bunch of drooling lechers hadn't gotten any easier than the first time she'd done it. One of the other dancers had told her to fix her eyes on one spot near the back of the audience as she danced, and pretend she was all alone.

That had helped, but it didn't get the sound of the catcalls and whistles out of her head. So she thought of Drew's asthma attacks and pharmacy bills that dancing enabled her to pay.

Turning from the service drive, she wound her way through the heavy Chicago traffic, then turned on to Kingsbury. She saw that the club was hopping already and swallowed hard, bracing herself for what she had to do. She felt Sean Dugan's gaze on her.

"You seem nervous," he said, sounding puzzled.

She gave a quick nod. "I . . . I'm just not used to this line of work."

He still seemed bewildered by her statement, but otherwise didn't respond. She pulled into a parking space behind the club, put the car in park, switched off the engine and turned to face him.

"I'm really glad Mitch hired you. Scientists aren't usually as buff as . . ." She couldn't believe what she almost said. "You won't let anything happen to Drew. Or to me. Will you?"

He gave a shake of his head, his gaze roving from her eyes to her mouth. Staying on her mouth. "No. I . . . What does the man – the stalker – look like?"

It was hard to catch her breath when he looked at her like that. She leaned a little closer, hoping to catch the scent of his aftershave. "He's tall, but not as tall as you," she said quietly. Sean moved a fraction closer. She could see every one of the thick black lashes that framed his eyes. "H-his head is completely bald, but he has a tattoo on the back of his neck. I think it's a bird – maybe an eagle – with its wings spread."

Dugan touched the edge of Erica's hair with one finger, then slid it down the side of her face. Her eyes closed and she felt her heart speed up as he cupped her cheek. No one's touch had ever affected her so quickly, so potently.

She felt his breath on her face, and then a soft feathering of his lips against hers. Shivers skittered up her spine.

Erica leaned in. Slipping her hand around to the back of his head, she pulled him closer, meeting his kiss, deepening it. She hardly noticed how chaste a kiss it was until she slid her tongue past his lips and felt his gasp. He pulled away and looked at her, stunned.

"I – I'm sorry," she whispered. "I never should have—"

He pulled her to him and kissed her, a hard, open-mouthed, hungry kiss, full of promise, full of . . . wonder.

Erica lost herself in it, in the pure, raw sensuality of his kiss. She'd never been touched this way before, with pure sexual heat in tandem with an unexpected sense of something entirely different. Reverence? Astonishment?

He tasted fresh and pure. His passion seemed innocent and safe, but at the same time it was sophisticated and dangerous. Confusing.

She pulled away, touching his lips with her fingers. "I-I have to go, Sean. I'm on in ten minutes."

"On?" He looked as stunned as she felt.

"Stage." She blushed for the first time in a long time. "Dancing. You know."

"But . . . The neuro lab. I thought—"

She looked at him, startled. "How do you know about that? Did Mitch tell you?"

He cleared his throat. "Yeah. Mitch."

She put her hand on his forearm. "Listen. This was the only job I could get that pays the bills. As soon as the economy turns around, I'm going to finish my PhD and get out of here."

Five

Sean was in so far over his head, he didn't know quite what to do. Erica jumped out of the vehicle and practically flew to the door of the building. Sean didn't get out right after her, but stayed where he was, looking around for the bald stalker while he tried to gather his wits.

And do something about his unfortunate state of arousal.

Nothing like this had ever happened to him before. He'd never been kissed or even thought of kissing a woman the way Erica had kissed him. Sex in Sean's time had been downgraded to one of the lower functions, done only when absolutely necessary. And certainly without the kind of zeal Erica had shown.

He jabbed his fingers through his neatly cropped hair and turned his thoughts to M277-CZ-398 in her plain white jumpsuit. The leader of GreenPiece was an even-featured woman without any of the curves Erica Gibson-Booth possessed. She did not make his pulse hammer with desire or his senses shimmer with excitement. The thought of her cooled his fever almost instantly.

He could only assume this physical intensity was a facet of sexual attraction, something he'd never experienced because nothing in his time was even faintly alluring. Combined with devotion and affection, it would be a powerful force. *Love*, he supposed, finally getting an inkling of the emotion referred to by the ancients. It was an all-encompassing kind of caring – something Sean could imagine feeling for a woman, even beyond the urge to mate.

Everything about this era seemed geared towards mating. Most of the huge signs he'd seen were at least subtly sexual in nature, and some were utterly blatant. Females and males in their prime wore seductive clothing that showed enticing curves or strong muscles. Women wore their hair long and flowing. Sensual. Lots of men let their facial hair grow to different lengths, from slightly scruffy to full beards. Primal.

People here had names, not cold, dry numbers that brought no individuality, no personality to their bearers. Sean felt a palpable energy here, and he realized that the lack of verve and liveliness in his own time was due to the loss of sexual drive. And they would never know what they were missing.

At least, not until he dealt with Andrew Gibson-Booth, preventing him from inventing Fusion XJ. The future would change significantly, but Sean had no doubt it would be a much more interesting future than what was in store for them now.

It took a few minutes before he was finally able to exit the vehicle. He glanced around once again for the man Erica was worried about, but the fellow wasn't anywhere to be seen. Neither was the neuro-science lab that Andrew Gibson-Booth's mother was supposed to have run, according to the sketchy information they had about her. She had been a scientist, that much was certain. But there was no documentation indicating that Erica had also been a dancer.

Taking one last glance around the area, Sean saw no one suspicious, so he went inside through the same door Erica had taken. The sound of hard, driving music hit him the minute he entered the building – a heavy drumbeat, shrieking chords and a hoarse, male voice carrying a discordant tune. There was very little light in the back corridor, but the air was full of something – some kind of smelly smoke, but nothing seemed to be on fire.

He went further in, noting two closed doors on either side of the hall. One of them flew open, and a man burst out of it, arguing with a half-dressed woman, who also came out.

Half naked was more like it. She wore heavy paint that accentuated her facial features, but Sean's attention was drawn to her full, swaying breasts.

Fortunately, the two were so caught up in their argument that they did not notice him gaping. He tried not to stare, but it was all too weird. Nothing had prepared him for such a sight, and in spite of her nearly complete nudity, he found the woman surprisingly unappealing. Pure, physical sexuality was not that interesting.

He pushed past them towards the front of the building where the music was loudest, and looked for Erica.

Another shock. He found himself in some sort of theatre, with a circular, elevated stage in its centre, surrounded by cheering spectators. The walls were black, and the audience sat at tables in the dark fringes of the large room. Sean couldn't see where the music emanated from, but colourful lights were focused on the stage where he saw two women, each one wearing nothing but a tiny strap of cloth between her legs. The barest essentials were covered, but nothing else.

They twisted and turned their bodies to the beat of the drums while the men in the audience cheered and tossed money to them.

The entire scene before him was far more lascivious than anything his Deviant brain could have imagined. And suddenly the music changed tempo, the two women danced away, and another one appeared.

Erica.

At least she was wearing clothes. She climbed the steps to the stage and the cheers became louder. Men started whistling, and calling, "Mona! Mona!" Sean looked at the faces of the avid spectators and suddenly realized what was about to happen. He stood frozen in place, and watched as she moved in a sultry, sexual dance to the rhythm of a heavy drumbeat.

She remained expressionless until her eyes lit on him, then she focused on him as she danced, removing one article of clothing at a time and tossing it away. She danced as though he were the only man in the room, as though she was undressing just for him. Sean felt his knees go soft, but the rest of him hardened considerably. His mouth watered and he swallowed hard, watching her undress.

Never would he have believed this if someone in his time had told him about it. Her movements were incredibly erotic, but he suddenly remembered what she'd said in the car. She wasn't accustomed to this kind of work. *She was being paid to do this.* And probably didn't like it.

She was down to one thin layer of some soft, shimmering white undergarment. All but the tips of her breasts were visible beneath the filmy white cloth, and they bounced deliciously as she moved.

Her narrow waist flared to beautifully rounded hips, and her long legs were encased by some sheer, white, amazingly enticing stocking, which rose only to the tops of her thighs. He felt an extremely powerful surge of pure, male possessiveness. And when she let one of her straps drop over her shoulder, Sean knew he couldn't let her go through with it.

He was onstage in one leap, lifting her and carrying her off, quickly taking her to that back hall where he'd come into the building. He carried her into one of the closed rooms, set her on to her feet and looked into her stunned eyes for only a second before taking her mouth in a searing, all-encompassing kiss. She belonged to no one but him.

He breathed in her scent, felt the smooth, soft give of her skin. She pulled him tightly against her, grinding her hips against him. He felt her shudder with pleasure just before she pushed him away.

"You shouldn't have done that, Sean," she whispered. "I'll lose my job!"

"Forget this job," he replied, his voice a harsh rasp.

"I can't!"

They heard footsteps, and she grabbed his sleeve. Pulling him through another doorway, she closed the door behind them and locked it. "Mitch will be after you – *us* – in another second. You've got to get out of here."

"I'm not leaving you in there. With all those . . ."

She rose up on tiptoes and kissed him lightly. "I talked to Mitch. I know you're not the bodyguard he hired."

"No, but I—"

"I don't care who you are," she said, her voice quiet and urgent. "I . . . I've never . . ." She bit her lower lip and Sean felt a quantum leap in the intensity of his arousal. She was killing him.

Sean heard a man bellowing somewhere nearby, "Erica!"

"He'll find us in a second. Go out to the car and wait for me there. I'll come out after I finish this set."

"No. I'm taking you with me."

"Sean, I need the money I can make here tonight. I can't just leave."

He cupped her jaw, his emotions in a jumble, every one of them stronger than anything he'd ever felt before. "I have more than enough. Take what I have and leave here with me."

She looked at him sceptically.

"I . . . This is all very foreign to me," he said. "I . . ." What could he tell her that would get her out of there? "I didn't understand when we first got here. I thought you were coming to your lab. To work."

"*Erica!*" Mitch was getting closer.

"Wait here." She slipped through yet another door and returned with her coat. She pulled it on over her skimpy underclothes while Sean stood quietly, trying to collect himself. He was aroused and protective and alarmed all at once.

"There's another way out," she said. "Let's go."

Six

They took a side exit out of the building, one that Mitch would never think of, and jumped into her car. She started the motor and pulled away, drove a short distance and then stopped. Geared herself up for what she needed to say.

"Something happened to me when you stepped into my apartment," she said. "The things I'm feeling . . ." She shook her head, unsure how to continue without sounding like a love-struck idiot. But that was exactly how she felt. "I haven't felt this way about anyone since Andy was killed. I've never *been* with anyone . . ."

He touched her then, on her hand that rested on her thigh, sliding his open hand under hers until their palms touched. The contact was electric.

"It's not always this way?" he asked. "Between men and women?"

It was obviously a rhetorical question. She leaned towards him as his hand closed around hers, and kissed him softly. Then she drew away and put the car in gear, burning rubber as she started for home.

They drove in silence, and Erica could not remember ever being so aware of a man before. He was tall and imposing, possessing a strong presence, a kind of poise or self-assurance that radiated off him in waves. He made her want to wrap herself up in him for the strength and security he could provide.

There'd been no one in her heart since Andrew, but she knew to the depths of her being that Sean Dugan had the potential to move in alongside her first love. Her rational mind told her that it wasn't possible, that she'd only known Sean for a few hours. She'd done extensive coursework and research in neuro physiology and biology, and knew that her endocrine system was telling her brain how to react to this man.

But her heart and soul told her it wasn't just hormones.

He rested his hand on her thigh as she drove, and she pushed her coat aside so that the skin of his palm touched her thigh above the silk of her white stocking. She wanted him to slide his hand up, to make her body sing with pleasure. The change in his breathing pattern indicated that he wanted it too, but he kept his hand where it was and caressed her gently.

It was fortunate that at least one of them was in control or they were liable to crash. Shivering with the most incredible sensations flowing through her veins, she drove the last block to her apartment with a building impatience.

She found a parking space and pulled into it, then put her hand on his where it rested on her thigh, and moved it where she wanted it. His fingers touched her silk panties and he made a strangled sound that mirrored her own hard, hot arousal. "I want you," she whispered. "Come upstairs with me."

She quickly unsnapped her seat belt as she threw open her car door and stepped out. Assuming Sean was right behind her, Erica made a dash towards her apartment building, but was startled by someone who darted out from behind a large SUV. He grabbed her, closing a filthy hand across her mouth, and started to drag her towards the vehicle.

"Come with me, Mona," he rasped, using her stage name, and she knew it was Sandino.

Her heart pounding in her throat, Erica tried to scream, but it wasn't necessary when her attacker dropped her suddenly.

Sean had grabbed the stalker by his jacket and then spun him around. Erica pushed herself up to her feet and looked for some way to help Sean, but she didn't even own a cell phone to dial 911. She felt paralysed. Part of her knew she should run up to the apartment and call the police, but her legs would not move. She could only watch helplessly, as Sandino beat Sean to a pulp.

But Sandino wasn't winning. Erica couldn't see Sean's exact moves, but his technique wasn't like anything she'd ever seen in action films. He moved like a big, wild cat – smooth, quick and deadly, and without regard to gravity. Sandino must have wondered what hit him before he slid to the ground, unconscious. Sean tossed the brute into his vehicle, then came to her, pulling her into his arms.

He bent for a kiss and Erica pulled him to her, feeling his shudder deepening their kiss. She wanted him desperately, in a way she'd never wanted anyone, and sensed his need to touch her, too.

He broke the kiss and touched his forehead to hers, pausing for a moment, breathing heavily, yet never letting go. "Are you all right?"

She was still shaking with all the adrenalin rushing through her body, but somehow managed to nod. "I don't have a cell phone. We should go up and call the police."

Sean didn't reply, but just slipped his arm around her waist and jogged to the apartment building beside her. Impatience roaring inside them, they hurried up the stairs, and, when they finally entered her apartment, she closed the door behind them and fell into his arms.

His mouth was on hers immediately, his hands sliding across her back and down to her hips, pulling her against him. Erica's lungs felt as though they would burst if she didn't get her clothes off and feel his skin against hers. She yanked at his sweater and pulled it over his head, then started on the buttons of his jeans as they fumbled their way to her bedroom.

The light from the street lamps was faint, but she could see, could admire, the thick bunching of the muscles in his arms and shoulders, the densely sculpted surface of his abs. He pushed her coat from her shoulders and it fell to the floor, just as he sat down on her bed and pulled her to him.

Seven

Sean set his tempis-disc on the floor, thinking he would explode before he even got his jeans off. Erica was absolute temptation, wearing the slip of a garment that barely covered her. She peeled the straps from her shoulders and let the thing fall to her waist.

He groaned when he saw her full breasts free of the shimmering white cloth. Touching a finger to her nipple, he pressed his lips to it, circling it with his tongue. She made a low sound and then he felt her hand at his head, bringing him closer.

"Take these off," she whispered, reaching down to his jeans. She stepped back as he stood and divested himself of the rest of his clothes.

He had mated before, in a completely clinical fashion, with women who wanted his DNA in their offspring. This was something entirely different. Each of his cells burned with awareness of her, and his olfactory and tactile senses were overloaded. His eyes could barely take in her spectacular features, from her gorgeous eyes to her soft breasts and enticing legs.

"Touch me, Sean."

He felt like a primitive beast, wanting to devour and worship her all at once. He kissed her hungrily, dragging his hands down her back, rubbing against her smooth belly.

She slid her hands up his shoulders and to the nape of his neck, making him cry out with desire. He could not imagine living without this, without *her*, in some distant, sterile future.

He came down over her, bracing himself on his hands, lowering his head to her breasts, giving attention to each one in turn. Moving lower, he swirled his tongue in her navel, then followed his instinct and slid farther down.

She sighed when he kissed her there, and whimpered as he licked her. Then he shifted position and entered her in one quick thrust.

The thought of leaving her, of leaving the bounty of sensation in this world, was impossible. From the moment her attacker had grabbed her, Sean had known he would do anything to keep her safe. Keep her happy.

He moved then, sliding with her in the rhythm that had been created at the beginning of time, and lost with the advent of Fusion XJ. He would correct that aberration, but not by doing anything to hurt Erica's son, even though he knew GreenPiece expected it.

He heard her rapid breaths and she wrapped her legs around his waist. Her orgasm drove him to his own peak and he held the backs of her thighs as he plunged deeply one last time and exploded inside her.

He couldn't move when it was over.

Somehow, he'd managed to pull them on to their sides, but he was still inside her, still contracting with the most intense sensations of pleasure he'd ever felt.

"Wow," she whispered.

He swallowed.

And he knew he couldn't go back to his own time . . . unless Erica came with him.

She looked up at him. "I . . . I've never felt like this. Meeting you, making love . . . *amazing*."

Sean could only nod. It wasn't just the sex. It was as though she had opened another dimension to him, a dimension that had been hidden away all his life. He and the rest of humanity had become so accustomed to the monofilaments of their world, and he suddenly understood the diverse filaments that were possible. There were colours and textures and smells that had been lost over the centuries. Even the sounds of their language had changed.

They no longer used names for each other, but cold, raw numbers. They did not relate as human beings, but almost as machines.

"More than amazing," he said. "I've never experienced anything like this day."

She nodded against him.

He withdrew from her body, closing his eyes and relishing the sensation. He tucked her against him.

"Have you ever been in love?" she asked.

"No. Not until now," he said bluntly, and she lifted her head to look at him.

"I wouldn't have believed it, but yeah. Me, too." She spoke with wonder in her voice, as though she were stating the impossible.

He needed to talk with her, to make his proposal and discuss what he hoped they could do. But it could wait until the morning. For now, he just wanted to hold her until she slept.

Then he would use the tempis-disc to send Sandino and his vehicle to some distant place where he could never bother Erica again.

Eight

They got up early every day for a week, making love in the morning before Drew woke up, and sipping coffee together in the intimacy of her tiny kitchen. Erica didn't know what the future would bring, but she did know that she would have to return to the Purple Moon at some point. Sean wasn't going to like it, but she couldn't let him pay her bills, and Drew's inhalers were almost empty.

Drew liked Sean, and the two of them got along amazingly well. Both of them seemed to enjoy their jaunts to the park and the occasional quiet hour watching Nova or the History Channel on television. Erica's heart contracted with cautious optimism. There hadn't been much that had worked out for her in the past few years and she was afraid to count on this.

"You always look as though you've never tasted coffee before," she said, casting off her doubts and worries as Sean savoured each sip. She finished spreading peanut butter on toast and set the plate on the table.

"I haven't," he said, slipping his arm around her waist and pulling her close. He breathed deeply, as though he could inhale her with one breath.

She laughed, enjoying the intimacy of the morning. Idiot that she was, she'd fallen in love, and it had happened overnight. Or rather, it had happened in the span of about five minutes. She'd looked out at him that first night from onstage, and wanted to dance only for him. And when he'd carried her away from the stage and out of the club, she'd been hooked.

"I know you're from Atlanta, but they've got coffee there!"

"I'm not actually from Atlanta."

"I didn't think so." She laughed, completely unconcerned that he hadn't been honest. She knew there had to be a reason for his little deception, maybe something embarrassing.

She didn't care. He was strong and utterly male, yet sweet and thoughtful. He'd savoured every kiss and every caress they'd shared, and yet everything, *everything* seemed new and different to him.

He wasn't very forthcoming with information when she asked him about himself, always turning the conversation to her or to Drew. Erica wondered if maybe he'd been in prison. Or raised in Tibet or something.

He raised his eyebrows and then shrugged, a gesture she'd come to love during the past week. "My home is so different from everything I've encountered here."

Sensing that he was ready to open up about himself, she sat down next to him at the small dinette table in the kitchen. "Where are you really from?"

He reached under his sleeve and removed a black metal disc from a strip fastened around his upper arm. Placing it on the table, he turned it so that she could see small silver markings on its surface.

"What is it?"

"We call it a tempis-disc," he replied.

"Tempis . . . temporal? It has to do with your profession?"

He nodded. "I am part of the team that works on wormholes, time shifts, spatial distortions."

"Time travel? It must be top secret." She picked up the disc and looked at it more closely. The metal was unlike any she'd ever seen before, but she was no geologist. It could be highly polished . . . anything.

"Careful," he said, and she set it back on the table.

"What does it do?"

"It brought me here. To this time and place," he said. "Which turned out to be an error."

"What do you mean?"

"I came from another time."

Erica gaped at him, incredulous. She was a scientist. She knew what was and was not possible. And time travel? Not possible.

"I know it must be difficult for you to believe."

Erica frowned. Sean wasn't a kook or a flake. She'd learned that very well during their week together. He was well grounded and possessed a tremendous sense of scientific curiosity. She knew that there were breakthroughs in science every year, but moving through time was more science fiction than science fact.

He broke into her thoughts. "Would you like a demonstration?"

She nodded and he stood. "Come here."

He picked up the black disc and Erica stood beside him. "I'm going to move your chair five minutes into the future."

Erica watched as he pressed a tiny button on the disc and a small window opened. He scanned the chair, then used his thumb to push several symbols that appeared on the screen. "Now watch."

She looked at the chair and observed as it disintegrated before her eyes. "Impossible," she whispered.

"Maybe for the science of this age. But in my time—"

"What is— *When* is your time?"

"Twenty-seven forty-three."

A giant hole opened in her stomach. "That's more than 700 years from now."

He nodded. It made a strange kind of sense to Erica. He'd seemed like such a stranger to her world, so amazed by everything he saw and smelled and tasted. "We've made progress, Erica. Energy, technology, medicine, culture . . . Things have changed radically, and now that I've been here, met you, seen your world, I know that it's not all to the good."

"I'm not sure I understand."

"Our race is dying out," he said. "And it's attributable to a form of genetic manipulation that will be discovered and implemented in your time."

"And you came to stop it?"

"Yes."

"Won't that cause a whole avalanche of repercussions in the future?" she asked, realizing that she had accepted his theorem. She actually believed he was a time traveller.

"We hope so. I was sent to interfere with the scientist who develops the process that causes our world to become physically and culturally sterile."

"How?"

"Any way necessary. Even kill him."

"Kill? As in murder?"

He nodded. "But I'm no killer, Erica. And I certainly can't kill a child."

"*What*? You're scaring me, Sean!" she said, just as the chair reappeared. She sat down on it, hard. "What child?"

His jaw clenched and he looked away. "We had the dates wrong. We thought he would develop his devastating procedure in 2015. I came to intercept him a few years early – or so I thought – just to be on the safe side."

He reached into his pocket and pulled out a handful of stones that glittered in the light.

"Are those diamonds?" Erica asked.

"Yes." He dropped what had to be a hundred diamonds on the table. "I didn't know how long I would need to stay, and we knew diamonds have value in your time. I sold one the day I arrived. That's the reason I have some money, how I was able to buy these clothes."

The diamonds were astonishing. Erica didn't know a lot about jewellery, but all of Sean's were larger than any engagement diamond she'd ever seen. "These must be worth a million dollars."

He shrugged. "When I first met Drew, I knew I'd come far too early. He probably developed Fusion XJ in 2035, not 2010."

"Wait. Drew? *Drew* is the scien—"

She stood abruptly, her heart in her throat. She'd never believed the damn thing could break. But now she knew differently. "*It's Drew that you*... Get out! Get out of my apartment, now! I can't believe I ever—"

"Erica, wait. I'm not going to hurt Drew. I couldn't hurt your son. I have a plan."

Her eyes welled with tears, but she brushed them away and marched to the front door. She felt defeated inside, as though he'd just crushed every one of her newly rejuvenated emotions.

But when he came to her and embraced her, Erica found she didn't have the power to resist. She'd been so sure they'd connected in an elemental way. She closed her eyes and tried not to feel the overpowering sense of belonging, of security, in his arms.

"Come to the future with me. You and Drew. He can grow up there and pursue his scientific career far more effectively in my century. You both can."

He eased away from her slightly, and put a couple of fingers under her chin. There was an intensity in his eyes, a look of restrained passion. "I love you, Erica. And I'll always want you."

He kissed her lightly, then released her and returned to the table. Gathering up the diamonds, he brought them back to her and poured them into her hand. "These are yours to keep. You can stay and finish your studies here in 2010 without financial worries."

She bit her lip as she gawked at the incredible wealth in her hand.

"Or you and Drew can come with me, to a world that will be new and different for all of us. Because, yes – what I'm doing now will have repercussions for the future."

She glanced over at the strange, incredibly advanced black disc that rested on her ridiculously commonplace Formica table, and then up at Sean. She knew there was no question of what she would do.

She hugged him close, then slid her hands up to his neck and pulled him down for her kiss. "I love you, too."

He held her close and returned her kiss, and Erica felt him pour everything he had into it before easing away. "Let's go and wake Drew," he said. "We've got a big day ahead of us."

The Wild Card

Sandra Newgent

One

"The game's Texas hold 'em. Are you in, little lady?"

Startled, Camille Desmond stared at the grey-haired gentleman seated behind the green felt-covered table. With swift movements, he flipped cards to the group seated. His soft brown eyes fixed on her. "Ante up?"

Cami shook her head. "I . . . ah . . . no thank you. I'm n-not playing." She'd never played poker before and didn't want to start now in Atlantic City.

She took a step backwards and bumped into her best friend Gina.

"Oh, come on Cami." Gina grabbed her shoulders. "Play poker with me. I'll teach you the ways of the world." Gina winked at her as she snagged an empty chair.

"I *know* the ways of the world. Remember? Roger cheating? Leaving me in debt up to my eyeballs? Besides, I'm saving any spare money to open a Warner school."

"But you should be celebrating your financial freedom. You just paid off Mr Mistake. Try investing a little time in yourself. Find Mr Right-Now, let loose and have some fun."

Cami's face burned hotly in the over-air-conditioned casino. "Gina, I can't ignore the past. And now I'm ready to go home. I'm not about to blow the rest of my money on a silly game of cards and a one-night stand." Cami softened her tone, not wanting to ruin Gina's fun. "You stay. I'm not ready to 'let loose'. I'll window shop or take a walk on the beach."

Gina nodded. "OK – for now – but I'm not giving up on you." She squeezed Cami's hand. "See ya later."

Cami left the card pit and wandered through the crowd surrounding the huge array of slot machines. Looking at the spectacular show of flashing lights, this was certainly the place to let loose. The casino of the legendary Caesars Hotel was pulsating with people willing to take any risk.

"Would you care for a complimentary drink?" Cami turned and ran her eyes over the blonde-haired server. The swooping neckline of her skimpy cocktail dress was only outdone by her black fishnet-clad legs and heavily made-up face.

"No thank you." Cami watched the woman walk away, her voluptuous hips swaying with feline grace. A pang of jealousy tweaked her. The woman was obviously comfortable in her own body and sensuality. Cami peered at her own wavy reflection in the shiny chrome side of a slot machine.

A gawky child of Irish parents, Cami had grown into a tall, willowy redhead. At twenty-seven, Cami knew she had curves in all the right places. Instead of teaching elementary school kids, she could have risen from her financial nightmare by working in a bar, nightclub or even a strip joint. She'd been told she was sexy. Trouble was Cami didn't *feel* sexy. Roger had taken that from her. Nope. She was going to open up a school for underprivileged children; she didn't need anything else. Certainly not a man.

Cami turned away from her reflection and fought her way to the second floor where the crowd had thinned. She wandered down the quiet, tiled hallway and peeked into several shops.

She stepped into a luxurious bath shop. The exotic aromas of expensive toiletries encircled her. She'd splurge on bubble bath, treating herself to a soak. The thought of sliding into the large roman tub in her room, enveloped by sensual, frothy foam lifted her spirits.

But then Cami came to her senses and bought a less expensive bar of soap and a scented candle that reminded her of sultry tropical breezes. She might not need a man, but tonight she'd have a tiny part of her secret fantasy.

After paying for the items, she glanced at her watch. Time to retrieve Gina. They'd have to hurry to freshen up and change clothes before dinner and the show. Cami left the store and moved quickly through the crowds surrounding the check-in desk, slot machines and the bar. She paused in front of a roulette table to search the cavernous game room.

Not seeing Gina, Cami moved away from the table, but a hand on her arm stopped her.

"Excuse me." The man's rich, baritone voice slid over her like a lingering caress.

She turned back.

Elegantly dressed in a simple white shirt and black vest, he stared at her with intense green eyes. His dark hair, long and sinfully thick, framed the hard planes of his face.

"Yes?"

For a moment he said nothing. Cami's heart did a somersault. Good Lord, the man was gorgeous. Her body warmed under his regard and her pulse flickered and leaped.

He held out his hand, offering her a single, white chip.

"I believe you dropped this."

"I don't think so." Cami pulled away, but didn't break his contact.

"Take it. Your wildest dreams will come true."

The heat from his touch seeped into her blood. Cami couldn't think of a response. She couldn't think at all with him standing so close. She felt compelled to accept the chip. It would be rude not to. Her arm reached out.

"Say it." Though the words were softly spoken, there was underlying steel to them.

Cami licked her lips. "My wildest dreams . . . will come true."

He slowly, seductively placed the chip in her open hand.

Two

Cami's palm burned as she closed her fingers around the chip. The room wavered and she fought the urge to drop the coloured plastic in her hand. Then her world went dark.

Oh great, I meet a gorgeous man and I faint at his feet. Cami reached for him, but found nothing.

His voice, a low vibration shimmering through her soul whispered, "Take a chance."

The lights grew brighter. Cami blinked. "Take a what?" The man was gone. "Hey, where are you?"

Cami stood in a darkened corner of a room she didn't recognize. The roulette table was gone, as well as everything else that had been there. In fact, the room was significantly smaller and more opulently decorated than Caesars casino, with a marble fireplace, matching sofa and loveseat, some wingback chairs, even a billiard table. It looked like the parlour from a Victorian bed and breakfast.

The few round tables scattered throughout the room were occupied by men seated in straight-backed chairs, playing card games. A man in the far corner played a piano, the upbeat tune mixing with the sounds of light conversation and laughter.

Cami blinked again. Nothing changed. What on earth was going on? She felt as if she'd been dropped on to the set of one of those stupid reality shows. Modern woman is whisked away to live the life of a caveman. She must eat woolly mammoth and pee in a cave to experience the true nature of her new world. By the looks of things, this reality show had a Victorian motif. And the "guests" were dressed for the part.

Gina had to be behind this charade. It was just the type of "fun" she'd dream up. Gina must have sent in a sob story about her friend's sorry life and *poof*, Cami was dropped into this scene without any warning. That made sense. Fine, she'd go along, for now. But, there'd better be lots of money for starting her school at the end of this or Gina would burn.

Mr Gorgeous Green Eyes at the roulette table must have helped transport her to a studio or another casino. But she didn't remember travelling anywhere. Cami looked around again. Where were all the cameras, microphones and spotlights? She'd call Gina. Cami tapped her empty pocket and remembered she'd left her purse and cell phone in her room.

Walking away from the parlour, Cami found the front desk and an attendant. Behind the man, a sign announced in bold blue lettering: WELCOME TO THE FREMONT HARBOR HOUSE. She'd never heard of this casino.

"Can I please use your phone?"

"Excuse me?"

"Your telephone. I need to call a friend."

The man looked at her quizzically. "I'm sorry, madam, but we don't have a telephone yet."

"What do you mean 'yet'?" OK, very realistic extras.

Cami put her hands on the counter. "Look, I need to find my friend, so if you'll—"

She stopped suddenly as the chip she'd been holding tumbled on to the scarred surface. Except it was no longer a chip at all.

Cami picked it up and studied the silver coin, noting the eagle on one side and the profile of Lady Liberty with the date of 1893 on the other. A five-dollar American eagle coin.

How did it get in her hand? She could have sworn the man at the roulette table had given her a gaming chip. Whew. Maybe she did need this reality diversion. She must have blacked out and now couldn't remember anything.

"Madam, may I summon your travelling companion?"

Cami closed her hand around the coin. "No thank you. I'll find Gina myself."

She turned and strode through the old, double front doors, tripping on her way down the steps and stumbling into a group of men. This time, strong hands steadied her; one man's grip the only thing keeping her upright. *What was wrong with her today?*

"I'm so sorry, sir."

He held one of her arms. His other hand rested at her waist. "Are you hurt?"

That smooth voice. Cami looked up. The man's eyes connected with hers. Mr Gorgeous Green Eyes. Every hormone in her body sizzled at his touch. His stare seemed to suck the air out of her lungs. She hadn't had sex in three years, but this was ridiculous. Cami took a slow, deep breath. He didn't fit into her plan. She needed information from him, *not* to jump his bones.

Cami broke away, trembling from the rush of hormones. "No, I'm fine. Thanks for catching me."

She noticed he'd changed into period garb, his grey pinstriped suit covering broad shoulders. The jacket was open revealing a coordinating vest and tie. Very handsome indeed. So that's where he'd gone earlier.

The two men flanking his sides looked her up and down, as if she were a tasty morsel to be devoured. Cami shifted away from them, uncomfortable to be their centre of attention.

"Excuse me, gentlemen, but I need a word with . . . him." Cami pointed to Mr G.

A lock of black hair fell across his eyes. Cami reached up to brush it away, but stopped before she touched him. *What has possessed her?*

The shorter, balding man answered. "You'd best run along, little lady. We have *business* with him."

"'Little lady'?" Cami crossed her arms. That was twice today she'd been called that particular name and she didn't like being dismissed. "I'm not going anywhere. Not until someone tells me what's going on."

The flippant man moved in front of her, blocking her from Mr G. "It's only a game of cards, darlin'. No need for you to worry your pretty self."

He winked at his partner and then reached a pudgy hand towards her. Before she realized his intent, he picked up a lock of her hair and rubbed it, his fingers grazing her neck. "I say we finish this game and see what we can show the *lady*."

The taller one snorted. "She ain't dressed like no lady."

Cami gasped, for the first time afraid.

Mr G. yanked him back by the collar. "Remove your hand, now."

He whined. "We don't mean no harm. We just wanna finish our game, get what's due."

Mr G. released the man and shoved him away from her. "I intend to make good on my bet. It will be in the form of something other than coins."

The coin. Cami realized she held Mr G.'s money. He'd only given it to her as part of the reality show. He obviously needed it back. She'd get paid later.

Cami held up the American eagle. "Will this be enough?"

Three

Seth Warner reluctantly tore his gaze from the beautiful woman who'd come to his aid and glanced at the ruffians. He saw their lust turn to greed at the prospect of more money.

"Sure it will, darlin'." Both men slapped each other on the back.

Seth gave the woman another assessing look, agreeing with them on one point: she *was* most oddly dressed. Blue trousers moulded to her very seductive curves and a white blouse, buttons scandalously open at the neck, gave him a glimpse of her lacy chemise beneath. Her long, reddish hair hung in waves past her shoulders, free from any clasp. He felt as if he'd been punched in the stomach. Who was this siren of a woman? Why did she want to help him?

Seth approached her, intent on finding out. The other men had gone inside. He took her arm, guided her to the parlour and said, "To what do I owe this favour?"

The lacy fringe of her lashes lifted, genuine surprise on her face. "It was yours. I'm returning it."

They arrived at the table and he pulled out a chair for her.

"Oh, I . . . really can't stay," she said.

Seth pressed her lightly into the chair. As he slid her towards the table, he bent in and whispered, "We'll discuss your act of kindness after the game." Her unique scent of lavender lingered as he took the chair next to her.

Seth put his hands on the table. "Gentlemen, I believe I have a benefactress for good fortune. Shall we proceed?" There were a few grumbles, but the dealer flipped cards face down to each player. Good. He may be down, but he wasn't out.

The dealer said, "The game is five-card draw." He nodded towards the woman. "In honour of our guest, queens are wild."

Seth looked at his dealt cards: the nine of clubs, four of diamonds, eight of hearts, jack of clubs, and the five of spades.

Blast. He'd need a miracle to win this hand. He had to stay in. It was his last chance to get the money.

He leaned over to the woman and said, "Throw in the coin." That was a mistake. Her scent beckoned him. He moved closer. She held out the coin to him. "I don't want to play."

"You'll bring me luck. Let me show you." He gently wrapped his hand around hers and steered her to the centre. "Now let go." The coin clinked as she dropped it into the pile of money.

Keeping his face unreadable, he said, "I'm in." Yet he was far from unresponsive to her. His body's primal reactions heated up with a vengeance.

Two of the other players also stayed in. Only the man on his right folded.

When it was his turn, Seth chose the four, the five and the eight and tossed them into the pile of other rejected cards.

He tried to ignore the woman next to him, but he was aware of her nearness, the heat of her skin. Unable to stop himself, he angled towards her again. "Draw three cards from the stacked deck."

Her face was pale and a droplet of moisture beaded her upper lip. He struggled to keep from touching her as another spike of desire caught him.

She handed him the requested cards singly: the eight of clubs, the ten of clubs and . . . the queen of hearts.

A wild card.

The fellow across from him folded. Only one other player remained and only one hand that could better his.

He allowed himself a small amount of hope. "Call."

The last man laid down his cards and snickered. "I got a full house."

"Very admirable." Seth spread his cards on the table and smiled. "But it doesn't beat a straight flush."

Seth shoved his winnings to the edge of the table and into his coat pocket. The other men stirred.

Seth stood and whispered in the woman's ear, "Let's get out of here."

He pulled her outside, then walked quickly down Pacific Avenue away from the hotel.

"Where are we going?" She tugged back. "I want to stay close to the hotel."

He tightened his grip on her upper arm and kept going. "I don't want those men following us."

"Let go of me. I can walk myself."

He eased his fingers away, but didn't let up the pace. When they were a safe distance from the hotel, he stopped and drew her aside, out of the main flow of pedestrian traffic. She looked beautiful with temper flaring in her hazel eyes, colouring her cheeks. "Thank you for your help. But why?"

She threw up her hands, clearly agitated, for what reason he couldn't fathom. "Look, no one is more perplexed about all this than me. I really don't know. Call me crazy. It just goes with the rest of my day."

Shaking his head, he chuckled. "Has it been so bad?"

"You have no idea."

"Then it shall be my mission to make the rest of your day better, Miss . . .?"

An unwilling smile tugged at her lips. She held out her hand. "Cami Desmond."

Seth took her hand, bowed low and gently kissed her knuckles. He straightened and said, "Seth Warner, at your service."

"Wow. A real gentleman."

Seth tensed, uneasy at the number of curious stares cast their way. "As much as I'm intrigued by your clothing, you should change into more . . . appropriate attire. You're drawing unwanted attention."

She looked down at her clothes. "Well, yes, I see your point, but I don't have anything else with me."

"I won't permit you back to the hotel. It's too dangerous." He looked up the street, focusing on a storefront. He took her arm again, this time with less force.

"Allow me to provide what you require."

Four

Seth led Cami into a woman's clothing boutique. Even this "shop" appeared to be part of the set. It was small, quiet and totally Victorian. Richly crafted garments hung on hooks scattered throughout the room and several mannequins were dressed with complete outfits.

"Good afternoon, sir." The woman who addressed Seth was plump, dressed to the nines in high fashion, from her lace-embellished pink shoes to the ornate hat decorated with ribbons and bird feathers perched on a mop of curls.

"What may I show your lady today?" The woman barely glanced at her, but Cami could hear sympathy oozing from her voice.

Seth turned to the proprietor and gave her money, probably as a tip. "I must see to an errand. Please outfit her with anything she needs."

He bowed to Cami. "I shall return. I believe you are in good hands." Cami watched Seth walk out the door, wondering if she'd see him again, or if another stagehand would come for her. Where was Gina?

"Shall I show you some day gowns?"

Cami turned her attention to the woman. "Yes, I suppose so. But maybe something less . . . elaborate than what you're wearing."

Cami spent the next hour trying on several outfits of varying fabrics, colours and styles. Standing before the large floor mirror, she couldn't believe her transformation, even though it had taken some convincing to lace her into the tiny corset.

She'd chosen a simple walking dress in lightweight wool. The lichen-green, flared skirt draped to the floor. Her white silk blouse was high at the neck, buttoned at the side and fronted with lace. The matching fitted jacket had puffy sleeves that tapered to her wrists, a wide collar, and was accented with gold trim and darker green velvet, the colour reminding her of Seth's eyes.

The shop owner had swept Cami's hair high on her head, revealing her gold hoop earrings. But Cami had drawn the line at wearing a huge bonnet. Instead she chose a simple, tailored straw hat with one saucy feather tucked on the side. Cami twirled, the skirt flowing around her legs. She couldn't remember the last time she'd worn a dress. She felt feminine and sexy, in a totally new way.

"I approve of your choice. You're stunning."

Cami turned. Seth leaned casually against the wall near the door. He pushed away and came towards her.

"Good, because I don't think I'll ever get out of this corset."

A wicked gleam darkened his eyes. He whispered, "I could help."

Cami felt her cheeks flush. "Confidence killed the cat, not curiosity." She turned away and regarded Seth in the mirror. He'd also changed. His clothes were more casual, but he looked dashing in solid, light-brown trousers with a matching waistcoat, a darker brown vest and a crisp white shirt. Seth also wore a straw hat, his dark hair curling at the collar.

"Would you stroll with me on the boardwalk?"

"This dress-up time has been fun, but shouldn't I get back to the hotel? They'll be looking for me."

He stood before her and touched her hair, just a light stroke. "Who will be looking for you?"

"My friend Gina."

"Then I shall deliver you safely to her. Now that you're less conspicuous, we'll take the scenic way, along the boardwalk. I promised you an enjoyable afternoon. If possible, I intend to keep it."

"Are you always this persistent?"

"When I want something."

The corner of his sensual mouth lifted in a lazy half-smile, revealing a sexy dimple in his right cheek.

"What about my clothes?"

He held up a brown paper package tied by a string. "Any more objections?"

Cami smiled. She wanted Gina to see her walk into the hotel dressed in high Victorian fashion and with Seth. She *could* have fun.

Seth offered her his arm. Cami wrapped her arm through his.

"I'll give you an hour."

Cami walked with Seth down Pacific Avenue, relieved that the other actors were similarly dressed in period costumes. They turned right on to Kentucky Avenue which brought them to a wide wooden footpath. The famous Atlantic City Boardwalk. Yet it wasn't. At least not the boardwalk she knew.

Nothing looked familiar. They walked past several hotels, some under construction, their signage identifying them as The Ambassador and Chalfonte House. Where were the larger casinos on the Boardwalk – Bally's, the Taj Mahal and the Showboat? She understood the streets close to the hotel were made to look Victorian as part of the reality-show set, but they were well away from there.

A flicker of apprehension twisted her stomach. Something wasn't right.

Cami studied the planks of the walkway. "These boards look new. I'd think they would be made to look old, like everything else."

Seth looked at her speculatively. "Why would you think everything here is old? This city is the height of fashion and innovation."

"Let's just say it's not what I expected."

"The Boardwalk *is* new. A hurricane a few years back destroyed the old one. The city only recently finished its rebuilding."

Hurricane? She hadn't heard of a hurricane destroying Atlantic City. That would have made the national news, like New Orleans. She wiped her damp palms on her dress.

Seth led Cami across the wooden footpath to walk along the ocean side of the boardwalk. She said, "You must live here. You seem to know the city well."

"No, I have small farm near New York City. I've made several excursions to the Boardwalk recently. Where do you call home?"

"Iowa, a little town near Des Moines."

"You are very far from home. Little wonder that at the hotel you looked lost."

Cami watched the waves welling up from the deep blue ocean, lapping at the ankles of sunbathers wading in the surf. The women and girls wore dresses, stockings and shoes, even in the water. The men had rolled up the legs of their trousers or wore knee-length knickers and suspenders. They couldn't be part of any reality show. It was too far from the hotel and the people playing in the water were not acting.

A thought hit her. What if she wasn't in her world any more, but in theirs?

Cami stumbled and then doubled over, a whalebone from the corset jabbing her in the ribs. Seth's grip on her arm tightened.

"Are you ill?"

"Yes. No. I'm not sure. Let me catch my breath."

"On your left." The voice called out close behind.

Seth's gut clenched. He grabbed Cami and whirled her away in time to avoid being run over by a cart on wheels racing down the boardwalk at breakneck speed.

"Hey, slow down," she yelled at their backs. "Give me your cell phone. I'm calling the police. They're going to kill someone."

Seth nestled her closer to him, enjoying her pliant body. He could feel her heart racing. "Do you always attract so much trouble?"

"Apparently."

"I don't know what you meant by cellophone, but the police are not necessary." He tipped her chin to meet his gaze. "I'll keep you safe."

"Safe maybe, but what about sane?"

She clutched his arm, her expression deadly serious. "Seth, tell me about this year. Don't ask why. I need to know." Her voice sounded strained. Did she regret walking with him?

"There's not much to tell, except it's the year of the great World's Fair in Chicago. It begins in a few days."

"Oh God. That makes it really 1893." She buried her face in his shoulder and trembled. "Gina won't be waiting for me. It can't be. I can't be here."

Seth held her tighter. "Yes, you can. Forget those men. No one will hurt you. You're with me now."

"You don't understand. The future's been decided. I shouldn't be with you."

He didn't understand her distress, but wanted his future to include her. He ached to kiss her. But a small insistent voice at the back of his mind told him this was not the right time.

She shifted restlessly, her movements a whisper of silk against wool as she pulled away. "This has been a nice diversion, but I must get back to the hotel."

He brought his hands to his chest and covered his heart. "Oh, Cami, you wound me greatly. I've only rated a 'nice' when my goal has been 'spectacular'."

She grinned, his teasing breaking the visible tension on her face. "Seth, it's not you. You've been nothing but kind."

"Is someone other than Gina waiting for you? Perhaps a husband or fiancé?"

"No. There's no one waiting for me now."

"Then I can't possibly let you go without gaining a higher rating. Permit me one last chance to win your heart."

Five

At the next street corner, Seth drew Cami into a small candy shop. "Wait here. I have a surprise."

Where would she go? It wasn't as if she could board a bus or train and ask to be taken to the twenty-first century.

A few moments later, Seth returned holding a small bag. "No one can resist famous Atlantic City saltwater taffy."

He offered her a piece. Cami took one and began walking again. She'd spent way too much time with him. She was worried.

Silence, as thick as mud, oozed between them as they chewed the taffy.

Cami kept her voice even, distant. She didn't want to become too involved with his life. "Why was that poker game so important to you?"

Seth sighed and furrowed his brows. "I wanted to do something I believed in. That game was my last chance to help my nephew, but it no longer matters. I'm done." The wistful sound in his voice caught her off guard.

"Why doesn't it matter? If you believe in something, you should fight for it. Don't give up."

"It's too late. Tomorrow is the last day I have to get the bank loan I need to open a new school in New York, a special school to help my nephew. Although I won the card game, it wasn't enough. It's over."

Cami didn't think she'd heard him right. "Who are you?"

"Seth Nathanial Warner."

"Warner . . . Warner, oh my God. You're *the* Seth Warner. I should have put it together before now. You've got it all wrong. You're the beginning of the Warners who've built several schools for needy children in *this* area, not New York."

"Whoa, slow down. I don't know who or what you're talking about, but it's not me. I only desire to open one school to help my nephew and maybe a few others."

"I know. It's how they all started."

"How what started?"

Cami stopped speaking. If she revealed what he ultimately accomplished in his life, would she have a negative influence on the present? She had to take that risk. It must be the reason she was here: to inspire Seth and prevent him from quitting.

She took his arm. "Come with me. I have something I want to show *you*."

Cami led Seth back across the boardwalk and down several quiet side streets. She wasn't sure she could find it again, but knew it was near the lighthouse. They passed many summer cottages, elaborate two- and three-storey homes, displaying beautifully coiffed lawns and wide porches.

Cami continued walking, scanning each house. Halfway down Artic, she stopped. "There it is."

"There what is?"

"Your new school."

Seth groaned. The dilapidated, three-storey house needed fresh paint, the roof was riddled with Swiss-cheese holes and the wide, wraparound porch sagged in several places.

"No. It's too small." He shook his head. "It isn't at all what I had in mind."

Cami grabbed Seth's hand and pointed to the house. "Yes. This is – could be yours. Imagine the possibilities. You can't give up on your dream now. Not when you're this close to success."

Seth pulled her to face him. "What makes you passionate?"

Cami was surprised at his question. "My work. I love to teach, same as you."

"No." He tapped her heart. "In here. All you've spoken of is what you *must* do for others. What do you dream for yourself?"

Cami was taken aback. There wasn't anything she did for fun, for herself.

"I don't know. I don't let myself dream . . . in there."

"I'd like to change that." He took her face in his hands and brought his mouth down to hers. Their lips touched, lightly at first, then more demanding as they both tumbled into the moment, their tongues entwining. He tasted like everything she'd always wanted; sweet and dangerous. Hot desire clawed at her.

Cami clamped down her emotions and pulled away. "I . . . can't do this. Not now, not ever."

"I can't believe you don't feel me in your heart." His hand skimmed the front of her jacket, sending tremors through her.

Cami ran a finger along his jaw, enjoying the slight rough texture. "I believe in you and your school. If you go to the bank tomorrow, you'll find this house is not only for sale, but will sell at a very reasonable price."

As she drew back, he captured her hand and covered his heart. A strong, rapid beat thumped against her palm. "Come with me."

Cami had no idea what the future held for her, but knew his future didn't include her. "I can't."

The last rays of sunset had faded to a deepening blue as they stopped in front of the Harbor House.

"Seth, I've had a 'spectacular' day. You'll never know how great it's been."

He stroked her cheek. "You deserve 'spectacular' every day."

Cami's mind was in turmoil, her heart in an uproar. She hadn't realized how much she missed being kissed and touched and held in a man's strong arms. "This isn't my reality."

"I can make it so. It doesn't have to end here . . . now."

Cami shivered. More suggestion, more heat. No. She wasn't a one-night-stand girl. "Yes, it does. I have to go."

Seth nodded and opened the front door for her. "I'll escort you to your room."

"I don't have a room here."

"Where are you staying, then? I'll walk you home."

Cami paused, her situation striking her hard. "I . . . I don't know. I don't have any room and I have no money."

"Then you shall be my guest."

Cami hesitated, the implication thick between them.

Seth said, "I'll purchase you a *separate* room. It's the least I can do to repay you for showing me the house."

A very practical and convincing argument. It was either accept his offer or sleep on the beach.

"OK, but promise me you'll build your school."

"I promise."

While Seth made arrangements for her room, Cami went into the parlour to look for the roulette wheel, the white poker chip, or even the guy who looked like Seth from the present. Anything to lead her back home.

There was nothing she recognized. She couldn't get home. Tears formed in her eyes. Gina must be sick with worry.

Seth was beside her. He tenderly wiped at a tear slipping down her cheek. "Don't fret, my sweet. You're not alone."

He took her hand and placed a silver coin in her palm, the same coin she'd given to him earlier. "This should be enough to provide you with safe transportation home, whenever you wish. You may need these as well."

Cami accepted the coin and her package of clothes from the dress shop. She whispered, "I wish it were that easy."

Maybe she should tell him the truth. No, it would only complicate matters for him and Cami knew he had his own destiny to fulfil. She couldn't sidetrack him with her problems. She truly was alone in this.

Seth led her upstairs and stopped before a closed door on the third floor. He unlocked it and held out the key for her. "It's yours for however long you need it."

She took the key, their hands brushing. A crackle of energy passed between them, hot and raw. Cami jerked away.

As she walked into the room, he said, "I've also made arrangements for a bath. Someone shall be up promptly with hot water and towels."

Cami turned for a last look at Seth. Their gazes locked. She wanted him with a ferocity that terrified her. She opened her mouth. "Thank you."

"My room is next door, adjoined to yours."

His eyes smouldered with unspoken desire. He said, "If you need anything, all you have to do is come through the door and ask."

Six

The invitation was very clear. All she had to do was ask. For anything. He'd be there. Cami leaned against the closed door and sighed. She didn't know how to ask for anything for herself.

Resigned to being alone, Cami explored the room. A large canopied, four-poster bed stood in the centre, as if mocking her for her fear. Cami tossed the gift bag, package of clothes, key and coin on the bed and turned away. Yet, she couldn't help having thoughts of tumbling on that romantic bed with Seth.

A beautiful, hand-painted screen stood in one of the corners of the room. Cami peeked behind the screen and gasped at the porcelain claw-footed bathtub. She stepped back and moved the screen aside. It was beautifully white and clean. Heaven on earth. She'd get her sensual soak after all.

A secretary desk and straight chair sat near a fireplace. On the desk was a small silver tray piled with cheeses and, beside the tray, a pitcher of water.

She selected one of the matching Victorian water glasses. She ran her finger over the beautiful ovals cut along the side before pouring the glass full. She nibbled on the cheese and took several sips of water.

Now what?

With Seth gone, she felt a surprising void. Trying to fill the emptiness, Cami unwrapped her old clothes from the paper covering. She'd make sure to wear them tomorrow. She grabbed the coin, intending to put it in the pocket of her jeans for safekeeping, but had an idea.

She held the coin tightly, squeezed her eyes shut and concentrated. She even prayed to return home. After several minutes, Cami opened her eyes, but she was still in the same hotel. Deflated, she stuffed the coin in her jeans and tossed them over the chair.

A knock sounded at the door. Cami's pulse sparked. *Seth.* Her heart sank when the hallway door opened and several hotel workers brought in buckets of steaming water. They poured the water into the tub, filling it about two-thirds full, laid several towels on the bed and left the room.

The looming emptiness nearly suffocated her. How could she miss Seth when they'd only just met? Cami flounced on the bed. Another stay from the corset poked her. She couldn't breathe. Her temper flaring to life, she unbuttoned the jacket and shook out of it. The remainder of the Victorian garments flew off, until she stood in only the fine cotton chemise and drawers.

She threw up her hands. Damn it, why was she here? In this time? In this room, alone? She thought once she'd convinced Seth to build his school, she'd *poof* back to her own time. There must be more to it.

She heard the echo of Seth's question. What did she want? Work? No. She wanted passion. And connection. The harder she tried to ignore the truth, the more it persisted. She wanted love.

Oh God. She'd been so wrong. No wonder Seth thought she was lost. She'd given up on herself . . . years ago. In her quest for security, she'd lost her emotional identity and suppressed her needs. She'd let her baggage from the past dictate her future.

Her eyes strayed to the connecting door. Take a chance. Her vow not to become involved shattered. She didn't want to be alone any more. He was here, ripe for her taking, and she needed him.

Cari dumped the contents of her gift bag on to the bed.

She couldn't just show up in his room. She lit the candle with matches she found near the fireplace and grabbed the bar of soap.

Cami approached the door and listened, not hearing any sounds. She wondered if he was asleep, but decided to push ahead before she lost her nerve.

She knocked lightly. "Seth, are you awake?"

There was no answer. She tried the knob and found it unlocked. The door opened with just the slightest creak. Soft light from the candle spilled through the dark opening.

"Seth?"

A movement on the other side caught her eyes. Then she saw him, outlined by the light at the window. He turned towards her.

"Cami. What's wrong?"

"Nothing. I . . . I just wanted to talk to you." It sounded lame even to her ears. She held up the soap, as if it explained everything. "I have some . . ."

He was in front of her before she realized he'd moved. His skin smelled clean, yet musky and very, very male. He was bare-chested and had changed into clean trousers. Light from the candle turned his skin a golden brown and flickered off his toned muscles.

Cami glanced beyond him and saw a wet floor surrounding the tub.

"Oh, you've already washed. I'm sorry, I shouldn't have bothered you."

Cami turned away, but his warm hand on her arm stilled her.

"I said all you had to do was ask. Walking through that door is asking."

What could she say? She was asking for more than words.

"I . . . ah . . . yes."

Seth lifted Cami in his arms and carried her into her room, elated she'd come to him. He'd been standing at the window watching the moonbeams flickering on the water, thinking of her.

Seth looked across the room and discovered her tub full of clean water. "You've not bathed."

"No."

He placed her on the bed and tested the water. It was still warm. "We shall remedy that."

He took the soap from her hands and placed the candle on the bedside table. He wanted this night to be perfect. He didn't think there'd be another.

Coming to stand before her, he drew her to her feet. He pulled the pins from her hair and spiked his fingers though the silky tangle of waves. "I've been longing to do this since the dress shop."

"Seth?"

He nipped lightly at her earlobe and she shuddered. "Umm?" He placed feather-light kisses on her neck and then drew her chemise over her head.

"I am a little . . . lost."

Seth stroked the curve of her back, down to the first hint of her buttocks. "I know, my sweet. I'll help you find your way."

"No, I mean really lost. Like as in from another time, another place."

He planted a searing kiss on her mouth, gently sucking her lower lip, and then pulled the string on her pantaloons. They fell to the floor.

"I know so little of you, my mysterious traveller. Yet I know you've changed my life."

She caressed his face, tracing his cheek with her velvet-soft fingertips. "As you've changed mine."

Seth lifted Cami in his arms and carried her to the tub. "I've only just begun."

He set her gently in the water. She closed her eyes.

He knelt beside the tub, dipped the soap into the water and rubbed, producing a thick lather. His brain faltered when her scent enveloped him. Desire twisted in his groin, making him hard.

Seth gathered her thick, silky hair and drew it over one shoulder. He placed a last wet kiss along her neck. Scooping warm water over her bare shoulders, he gently rubbed the bar in languid, swirling circles on her back.

At his first slow caresses Cami relaxed, bending forwards, bracing her forehead on her knees. At some point the hard bar disappeared, and Cami felt his soapy palms and fingers run up the muscles on either side of her spine, creating the most delicious sensations of her life. Oh God, this was her fantasy. She'd stopped dreaming of a happy-ever-after.

She gave another sigh, this one coming from deep within her throat.

"Feel good?" His voice was low and thick.

"Oh God, yes."

"Your skin is so soft."

His slippery thumbs dipped lower in the water, massaging the small of her back. Chills of pleasure caused gooseflesh to appear.

"I want to touch you here."

From behind, Seth's warm hands cupped her breasts and her breath caught in her throat. Cami felt a gush of heat.

"And here."

His hands smoothed down her abdomen. She quivered with pleasure from his strokes.

With a low, harsh groan, Seth raised her from the tub and carried her to the canopied bed.

Seven

Cami awoke in her bed alone, the sun higher than usual. She stretched, feeling her muscles flex, remembering the workout they'd received the night before. Sounds from the room next door alerted her to Seth's whereabouts. She actually heard whistling.

Cami's stomach growled. She hadn't eaten much yesterday, substituting lovemaking for dinner. What she wouldn't give to have the luxury of breakfast via room service. Cami swung her legs over the edge of the bed and stood, wrapping the sheet around her naked body while she searched for her clothes.

Cami found her blouse draped neatly over the chair and smiled when she saw the silken cord hanging above the desk labelled SERVICE BELL. Dressing quickly in her jeans and shirt, she pulled the cord, excited at the prospect of surprising Seth with breakfast in her room.

Cami reached in the pocket of her jeans for the coin, but instead drew out the white gaming chip.

Her vision wavered. Oh no, not now! What about Seth? Everything in the room spun and then went dark.

Flashing lights slowly came into focus. Cami once again stood in Caesars casino in front of the modern roulette table. A pang of disappointment shot through her elation. She was home.

The man in the white shirt and black vest stood inches from her, his gaze making her body tingle. He had Seth's gorgeous eyes, but they now seemed a lighter green. Cami also noticed his hair was shorter and his face leaner, less angular than Seth's.

"Your wildest dreams will come true." He smiled, no dimples forming. "It's written on the chip, so it must be true."

Cami scanned the casino. All seemed normal. No time appeared to have passed in this place. Cami held up the white chip. "You knew this chip wasn't mine. Why *me*?"

He shifted on his feet. "I saw you standing there, beautiful, yet lost. I wanted to meet you. I guess you could say the men in my family have a thing for redheads."

There was vulnerability in his tone that touched a place inside her.

He held out his hand. "I'm Shaun Warner."

Warner? Hope swelled her heart. Because of Seth, for the first time in a long time, she felt there were possibilities to be explored.

Cami took his hand in hers. "Cami Desmond."

When their hands touched, she had a brief flash of déjà vu, but it passed. This time was for her.

"My wildest dreams have already come true."

The Eleventh Hour

Michelle Maddox

I saw the little boy standing on the corner crying his eyes out. Lugging my heavy portfolio, I went directly to him.

"What's wrong?" I asked as I crouched down in front of him.

"My mommy's gone," he sobbed.

"I'll help you find her."

"You will?"

I nodded. "I promise."

He looked at me warily through damp, but clear, blue eyes the exact same colour of the sky today. "Who're you?"

"I'm Sophie Shaw. What's your name?"

"I'm Adam."

"It's very nice to meet you, Adam."

He sniffed and looked at my portfolio. "What's that?"

"This is where I keep my art."

"Your art?"

I unzipped the top and reached in to grab a small self-portrait I'd done on a scrap piece of paper that morning while looking in the mirror. Practice makes perfect after all. I had a hard time with eyes, getting that spark of life to come into them, but in the simple five-minute pencil sketch I felt like I'd done a decent enough job.

"See?" I said. "That's supposed to be me."

He took the sketch from me and looked at it with wide eyes and smiled. "Cool."

With a review like that, I really wished the kid was an art buyer. Since he didn't look more than seven years old, I could only hope he'd grow up to be one. A rich one.

"I'm trying to be an artist," I told him. The more I spoke, the more his mood seemed to brighten. "I have a show next week at a gallery right around the corner from here. My first one. Now, enough about me. Where do you live?"

He looked around. "I don't know."

I stood up and offered him my hand. "Let's go find your mom."

"Really?" He seemed surprised by this and hope filled his blue eyes. I nodded. "Really."

"That will be difficult since his mother is dead," a deep voice said. I turned to see a man standing next to us. If I were to draw his eyes, there wouldn't be a whole lot of friendliness there.

My stomach sank. "Oh, I . . . I'm so sorry. I didn't know. I thought he was just lost."

"He's my nephew and he lives with me now." Something that vaguely resembled a smile crept over the man's face. He reached out his hand. "Come, Adam."

But Adam didn't let go of my hand, instead he held it tighter. My heart broke for the little boy, crying on the sidewalk because his mommy was gone. And she wasn't coming back no matter how hard we would have searched for her.

Since I'd lost my mother when I was about his age, I could definitely sympathize.

"Be brave for me, Adam. Can you do that?" I touched his face, wiping a tear away with my thumb before brushing the jet-black hair back from his forehead. "You're going to be OK, I know it."

"I'll be brave." Adam inhaled, and it sounded shaky. He still clutched my sketch in his left hand. "Th-thanks, Sophie."

"I didn't do anything."

"You're nice."

I smiled at him. "Your uncle will look after you now."

He shook his head as he finally let go of my hand. "He's not really my uncle."

I frowned. "But I thought he said—"

"You should mind your own business. It'll get you in trouble one day." The man pulled Adam away from me, his large hand clamped on the boy's small shoulder.

I looked over my shoulder to see if there was someone around to help. A police officer would come in real handy right about now. "If you're not his uncle, then who—"

When I turned back, they were both gone.

Feeling confused and shaken I walked up and down the street for ten minutes but there was no sign of them.

It was as though they'd vanished into thin air.

The bus nearly killed me.

My heart rate went a million miles a minute as I stood shaking on the sidewalk. Somebody had yanked me back just in time and saved me from my monstrous stupidity. I'd been glancing down at my BlackBerry to check an email that had just come in and wandered on to the crosswalk before the light changed.

I was also still distracted about what happened last week with the little boy. I couldn't seem to stop thinking about him, seeing his sorrow-filled little face whenever I closed my eyes, and worried about where he'd gone and if he was OK. I'd lost a lot of sleep that week over Adam.

However, just because that man wasn't really his uncle by blood, it didn't mean he wasn't an official caregiver. Adam would be OK. I hoped like hell I was right about that.

Looked like I really should have been more worried about myself, though. One wrong step – one moment frozen in time – put me inches away from becoming a splattered piece of modern art on the pavement.

"You didn't even see the person who saved your life?" my best friend Anna asked that night at the gallery.

"Nope. There were a bunch of people there witnessing me wandering aimlessly about in traffic like an escaped mental patient, but my guardian angel never revealed him- or herself."

"You almost died."

"Yeah." It was still a stomach-churning thought.

"Dead on arrival. Like, you wouldn't have even had a chance."

"Thanks for rubbing it in. Really helpful. And by the way it was an email from *you* I was reading at the time, smarty-pants."

"Don't even try to pin the blame on me, Sophie." Anna grinned, obviously not taking my brush with death even remotely seriously.

It was so great to have friends who cared.

She snagged two glasses of sparkling wine off a passing tray and handed one to me. "To your first official show. May Sophie Shaw and her fabulous talent with oils become the next big thing."

I clinked glasses with her. "I'll drink to that."

"You know what's funny?"

"Please tell. I could use a laugh."

"If you'd died today, every painting here probably would have gone way up in value."

I drained my glass in one big gulp. "The sad thing is you're probably right. Only I wouldn't have been here to enjoy spending money frivolously for the first time in my life."

She grabbed me another full glass. "Then I think we should toast to a long life, to huge success, big bucks and to the guardian angel who kept you from dying before you've had the chance to really live."

I looked at her. "Is that a crack at how boring my life is?"

She gave me innocent eyes. "I have no idea what you mean. Me, making a crack about your wildly exciting and romance-filled life?"

"I'm focused on my career right now. I'll find a man when the time is right."

"Sure you will." She nodded as if to humour me. "OK, so let's drink to the life of an eccentric twenty-something artist who hasn't dated anybody in as long as I've ever known her. One who creates gorgeous paintings of romance and love and desperate, aching need even though she chooses not to partake in such unsavoury endeavours herself. Until the time is right, of course."

"'Eccentric'," I repeated. "Sounds way better than pathetic, doesn't it? I'll definitely drink to being eccentric."

"You would." Anna rolled her eyes and laughed. "Cheers, Sophie."

Anna left the gallery early, but I stayed till the bitter end. Three paintings sold, although they were some of the cheaper ones. Still, a minor victory and one that would pay the majority of my rent for the next three months.

I'd had too much wine and tottered unsteadily on my heels as I made my way to the street to hail a cab. That was when somebody grabbed me from behind.

A scream tore from my throat but was muffled by a foul-smelling cloth clamped down over my mouth. My attacker held me there prone until my head went cloudy from whatever chemical was on the cloth and I fell head first into darkness.

"Wake up."

It was a command not a request. And when I ignored it since I was only semi-conscious, I felt the stinging pain as a slap resounded across my face. My eyes shot open and I gasped for breath.

I found myself seated in a hard chair and my hands bound behind me. The room was dark but there was a light shining in my face – a flashlight, I thought.

"What's going on?" My mouth felt dry and the words rasped out.

"That's a very good question," a man said. I couldn't see him clearly apart from a shadowy outline. "And something we're trying to figure out as well."

I pulled against my restraints but the rope bit into my wrists. "Who are you?"

"We're the ones asking the questions."

Panic gripped my chest. I'd been kidnapped. It was the sort of thing that happened all the time, but I never thought it would happen to me. Which was probably why I'd felt confident leaving the gallery after midnight by myself – something I'd done dozens of times before.

"Sophie Shaw," he said. "Born December 17, 1983. Raised in Albany and moved to Manhattan to attend the New York Academy of Art. Never married, no dependants. Both parents deceased. Is that right?"

My mouth moved but no sound came out. How did they know me? What did they want?

He smacked me again and my head rang from the pain.

"Is that right?" he asked again.

"Y-yes, that's right."

"Dammit, Harris," another voice said sharply. "There's no fucking need to abuse her, is there?"

"Just let me do my job." I heard paper shifting together. "Date of death is listed as September 15, 2009."

I stopped breathing for a moment. That was today's date.

"What?" I managed. "Please, I don't know what you're looking for, I just want to go home."

"That's not possible, I'm afraid," he said. "Tell me about the bus, Sophie."

"Th–The bus?"

"The one that was supposed to end your life today."

"I . . . I don't know."

"What happened?"

"I almost got hit but I didn't. It was close."

"Yes, so I'm gathering. Not close enough, unfortunately." He sighed and it sounded annoyed. "You are causing me a great deal of paperwork, do you know that?"

I felt utterly confused and totally afraid. "What do you want from me?"

"Answers only. According to my papers you're supposed to be dead. That bus, the one you avoided by the skin of your teeth? It was supposed to kill you. You were fated to die today. So what I want to know is why you're not lying in a morgue right now."

How could he say something so horrible with such a cool, detached tone? "Fated?"

"Yes."

"I . . . I don't understand."

"No, I don't suppose you do. I'll let my associate explain the rest to you since he seems to have a problem with my bedside manner right now. He's more than welcome to take over."

Another man shifted partially into focus behind the light, but he was mostly a shadowy outline. I could see broad shoulders and the edge of a strong, stubbled jawline as he turned to look at the other man. A glint of light brushed against his cheekbones and brow.

"It's law that we explain it to you first," he said. His voice was much more pleasant than the first man – less detached and cold. Unfortunately, a nice voice didn't change my situation one little bit or lessen my fear.

"Explain what?"

"The Books of Fate. They're . . . transcribed daily by seers. The names of people who die as well as those who are born. And they are rarely wrong –"

"They're *never* wrong," the other man said.

"No, but . . . but sometimes there's a glitch and someone fated to die doesn't. This poses a threat to adversely affect the future. It's our job to ensure that doesn't happen."

I licked my dry lips. "You sound completely crazy, you know that?"

"Turn the light on, Harris," he said. "She's terrified. There's no reason for us to scare her more right now."

Harris snorted. "Terrific. Our best agent's going soft on me over a random blonde?"

"No," he said immediately. "Just do it OK?"

"Won't change anything."

"Just fucking do it."

"Whoa, OK." A chuckle. Then a switch was flicked and light flooded the room.

I squinted and looked around. I had no idea where we were: a generic room of some kind that only held the chair I sat in and the two men in front of me. Both were dressed in black. One was middle-aged, blond, with weary-looking grey eyes. The other was younger, dark-haired with light blue eyes. Both were tall, muscular and looked very dangerous.

It was all I could do to keep my teeth from chattering at the sight of them as they looked down at me tied to the chair.

It was strange, but the dark-haired one looked vaguely familiar. Where the hell had I seen him before?

"I don't have any money," I said. "So this is a waste of your time if that's what you're looking for."

He shook his head. "We don't want money."

"What we want," Harris, the blond one, said, "is to get this finished so I can get home. I have vacation time coming to me."

The dark-haired man scowled at him. "Have a little respect, would you?"

Harris held up his hands. "What is with you tonight, Adam? You're acting bizarre. This is just another job."

That's who he reminded me of. The little boy from last week. Adam was his name too. Same black hair, same blue eyes. However, this guy was a whole lot more than seven years old – by at least twenty years.

"What happened with the bus?" Harris asked. "How'd you miss getting creamed?"

"Somebody grabbed me. Pushed me out of the way."

"Really?" His eyebrows went up. "Well, that's unlikely."

I scowled at him. "Unlikely or not, that's what happened. But what difference does it make? And these Books of Fate . . . I don't understand why it makes any damn difference. I almost got hit but I didn't. So what?"

"Because you being alive right now when your name is on the list to die today is wrong. It has the potential to screw up the future."

"Says who?"

"Says us," Harris said, then he grinned. "Because that's where we're from."

I gaped at him. "Sure you are."

"I know it's hard for you to believe, Sophie, but it's true," Adam said. "We are from the future. We're part of a government organization that regulates fate, according to the Books, and controls any potential fluctuations that affect the future. It's an important job and one we must take very seriously."

Something slid behind his gaze as he said it despite his confident words. Regret? Why would he feel regret about this?

Then it dawned on me what these two crazy men were getting at.

"So because the bus didn't kill me," I began, my voice barely audible, "because I didn't die on the day your so-called Books of Fate said I would, you've been sent here to finish the job?"

"Holy shit," Harris said, amused. "And they say blondes are dumb. This one's a regular brainiac. Impressive."

I was shaking now, harder than before. "You're going to kill me?"

"That's the general idea," Harris confirmed. "I'll make it quick, though. I promise."

"But . . ." I swallowed hard. "But why would you even bother to explain this to me? Why wouldn't you just kill me outside the gallery?"

"Because it's policy to explain what's going on first," Adam said. "It's an important part of the process – for you to understand why we have to do this."

"I *still* don't understand. This is wrong and you have to know that." I shook my head and felt hot tears slide down my cheeks. I felt utterly helpless tied to the chair. These men planned to kill me and I couldn't even fight for my life.

"What I want to know is who yanked you out of that bus's path this morning." Harris pulled a gun out of a shoulder holster under his black coat. "It's a fucking mystery to me. It's as though they knew what was going to happen."

Adam looked at him. "You think it was one of us? Somebody with access to the Books of Fate? And they might have travelled back in time to save her?"

I couldn't keep my eyes off that shiny silver gun Harris now held with ease – the one he was going to end my life with. Fix the mistake. Erase the budding artist before she'd even had a chance to live just because her name was listed in a book somewhere in the future.

It didn't matter if I believed them or not. My belief in time travel or fate didn't change what was going to happen here one little bit.

"Yeah," Harris said, grinning. "But that would be a really stupid move, wouldn't it? And what would the motivation be?"

"Don't know." Adam shook his head. He'd barely taken his eyes off me since the lights came on. "Maybe somebody who's started to doubt our missions. Somebody wondering if we're sent out as an easy answer to a difficult problem. Somebody who has begun to question exactly what fate is and why we need to kill innocent people just because we're told to. Somebody who never questioned these things until he saw the name Sophie Shaw in the Books and it jarred him out of his obedient daze enough that he travelled back twenty years through time to pull her out of the way of that bus."

My eyes widened a little during his insightful speech.

Harris turned to look at Adam, his shaggy eyebrows held high. "That's one hell of a hypothesis. But whoever that agent might be, he'd be in deep shit if he was ever caught. You know the penalty for fate interference, right?"

Adam's jaw set. "Of course I do. I've seen others executed because of it."

"Besides, it doesn't make a difference anyhow. We're here to put things back the way they're supposed to be. So if you're finished gawking at our pretty little target, that's exactly what I'm going to do right now."

I clenched my teeth as he pointed the gun at my head and pulled the trigger.

But Adam kicked Harris's arm just in time and the bullet embedded itself in the wall behind my right shoulder rather than in my forehead.

Harris turned to him with a frown. "What the hell do you think you're—"

Adam swung the heavy flashlight, hitting Harris across the side of his head. The blond man crumpled to the floor unconscious before Adam's blue-eyed gaze returned to me.

"OK," he said, "so I'm thinking that's why my name was added to the book today as well. Jesus. I just signed my own death warrant."

It sounded as if he was talking more to himself than to me.

"What?" I managed.

Adam's eyes flicked back to his partner. "I honestly didn't plan to do that. I thought I might be able to talk him out of it, but I should have known better. He's stubborn." He smiled a little, but it looked shaky. "Then again, so am I."

"What is going on?"

"That is a very good question, but one I can't answer right now." Adam threw the flashlight to the ground and then began to undo my bindings. The ropes fell away from my sore wrists. "There are other agents stationed outside. When Harris and I don't report in very soon, they're going to come looking for us. We have to get out of here."

He held his hand out to me, but I didn't take it.

"Come on," he said. "There's no time."

I shook my head.

His dark brows drew together. "I know you don't trust me, but you have to. I'm not going to hurt you. I swear I'll protect you."

"Was it you?" I asked. "You're the one who pulled me away from the bus today, aren't you?"

His chest moved under his black coat to show he was breathing hard. "That was me."

"And everything you just said to Harris—"

"Was how I really feel. Yeah. Now come on, or saving your ass twice today isn't going to mean a damn thing."

I took his hand and he practically yanked me out of the chair to my feet, then roughly pulled me behind him as he kicked open the door. We hurried down a hallway leading to a staircase.

"Who are you?" I asked him.

"Name's Adam. Adam Rizer."

"And you're from the future."

He looked at me sideways. "I am."

"And you just knocked your friend unconscious in order to save my life."

"Looks like." He shook his head. "Although, Harris wasn't exactly somebody I considered a friend. When you're in my line of work, friends can be a liability."

"Being a cold-blooded assassin must be hard work."

I tried to keep up with him but he moved very fast. I didn't have much of a choice, though. He had my hand clutched in his so tightly that if I fell, he'd still be dragging me along behind him.

"We're called auditors, not assassins."

"Of course you are. Such a bland government title for something so horrible."

He eyed me. "Yeah, well, it's not exactly the same as painting pretty pictures of people having sex, but it pays the bills."

I glared at him. "Is that what you think I do? Paint dirty pictures?"

"Of course not. They're supposed to represent true love, right?" He said it sarcastically. "The fact that the people are naked just helps raise the collectible value."

Despite my gratitude for his saving my life, I didn't like his tone. It was hard enough to get respect in the art world without somebody else labelling my work pornography. Although, I suppose without that notorious reputation, I wouldn't have gotten half as much press as I'd received since getting out of school.

We headed down another floor and I tried not to twist my ankle as we quickly rounded each corner. "I don't care what you think."

"If it's any consolation, the work of Sophie Shaw will be very sought after a couple decades from now. I saw one recently for nearly a hundred grand."

A hundred grand? I remembered what Anna said to me earlier that evening. That if I was dead, my paintings would be worth way more. Looked like she was right.

"Adam, you have to—"

"Shh," he commanded. We'd reached the bottom of the stairs of whatever building we were in. He had a gun drawn and, with his back flat against the wall, he peered out of a window to the side of a set of doors.

"They're out front," he said. "This is the back exit. I think we have the chance—"

"Adam!" an angry voice bellowed from above us. "Where the hell are you?"

It was Harris. He was awake and he sounded mad as hell. The sound of hard-soled shoes thundering down the stairs echoed around us. Without waiting another second, Adam pushed the door open with his shoulder and we burst outside.

"Stop!" Harris shouted.

I heard a gunshot. Then another.

"Watch out," Adam snapped, wrapping his arm around me to pull me out of the way. Part of the door frame splintered off as the bullets made contact.

Relying on instinct only, I ran with Adam away from the building and down an alleyway. Several alleyways, in fact, until I was hopelessly lost. It was dark and cold and my feet were burning from running in my heels. I was exhausted and scared and shaking like a leaf.

"Please, stop," I begged. "I can't go any further."

"No, you're right." Adam looked around, before putting his gun away. "This is a good place."

"A good place for what? I need to go home. I need . . . I need to go to the police."

He shook his head. "They can't help you."

"What do you mean they can't help me?"

"They're in on this. They *know*. Maybe not all of them. But the right people know about auditors from the future. It's fully condoned. They understand why the future must be kept pure. If you go to them, they'll hand you right over to Harris and the others with no questions asked. They get the list of any problem cases just like we do."

"The present and the future working together for a common goal."

"Pretty much. The only thing separating us is twenty years."

"What about the past – all the horrible things that happened then? Why didn't you kill a few bad-asses – dictators, serial killers – who hurt a lot of people?"

"Because it wasn't in the Books, of course," Adam replied simply, his jaw tight. "We only take care of the glitches. Otherwise, the past and the present stand as they are. As they *were*."

"So you'd kill me but you wouldn't go back and kill Hitler because that wasn't your assignment."

"We have to operate within a two decade time frame, but even if we could go back further, you're right. We wouldn't have killed him without a direct order like yours. But I *didn't* kill you, did I?"

My head ached even attempting to wrap my brain around everything, but I tried to think. "I need to go home. Grab a few things. Then I can go into hiding for a while. Maybe I'll go to Mexico or Brazil or—"

"No, that doesn't work. They'll find you."

"But I have to talk to Anna. I have friends who'll wonder where I am."

Adam's expression was tense. "It's over, Sophie. Your life. The life you knew. You can't ever go back to it. Not if you want to live another day."

I just stared at him. "But I have to."

"No, you don't. The life you knew ended the moment that bus was supposed to hit you." He rubbed his forehead. "Fuck. Maybe I shouldn't have done anything. Maybe I should have let fate run its course. Dammit, I had to do something, but I wasn't thinking straight. I didn't think through all the repercussions." His gaze was intense. He closed the distance between us and grabbed me by my shoulders. "But I just couldn't let you die. Not like that."

"Why not?" I struggled to breathe as the warmth of his touch sank into me. Despite my fear and this bizarre and dangerous situation, I found myself oddly attracted to this strange man who'd now saved my life twice. Being pressed up close against him didn't help. "Maybe you should have. You don't know me. Why would you screw your own life up to save somebody you don't even know?"

"But I do know you." Adam looked away and raked a hand through his black hair, his strained expression lit only by the moonlight.

"How?"

Adam reached into the inner chest pocket of his long black coat and pulled out a piece of yellowing folded paper. He handed it to me.

I took it with trembling hands and unfolded it. It was the sketch – the self portrait I'd done last week. The one the little boy had looked at and never returned to me before he'd disappeared. Only now it looked old and faded. The pencil marks were practically too light to see.

"Sorry for the shabby shape it's in," he said, a sardonic curl to his lips. "That's what twenty years'll do. And I must admit, some of them have been a bit cruel. But I still have it. I've kept it as safe as I could."

I looked up at him. "How . . . How is this possible?"

"What part? How I've stared at that drawing of you for twenty years, imagining who you were, what you were like, what you wanted? How I've dreamed about you countless times?" He laughed, but it was humourless. "Funny how the mind can play tricks on you. One blonde lady who was nice to me all those years ago and I've never been able to forget her beautiful face. Funny how when nobody's ever been nice to you, you remember the one who was – even if it was only for a minute. And a little boy's gratitude can change to something else as he gets older. Something that makes him willing to fuck up his own life when hers is in danger."

The realization hit me like a tidal wave.

It was him.

This handsome, dangerous man with the haunted blue eyes who stood before me in a dark alleyway – the one I couldn't help but be attracted to even in the midst of running for my very life – he was the little boy from last week on the corner who was missing his dead mother.

"You . . ." But I couldn't figure out what to say. I was utterly stunned.

Adam paced to the other side of the alley and then back. "I looked you up ten years ago, thinking stupidly that I'd find you and you'd fall madly in love with an eighteen-year-old kid like me," he said, with a wry twist of his lips. "But . . . that's how I found out you were already gone. That you'd died the week after I met you and there wasn't a damn thing I could do about it because there were no details about the death of Sophie Shaw, the famous erotic artist. But when I found your name in the Books, I knew . . . I just *knew* I had to do something about that. And here we are."

I chewed my bottom lip. "My paintings aren't erotic."

"Doesn't bother you that you were dead, just that I'm labelling your art erotic." He stared at me for a moment before he laughed. "This is not something you want to argue with me about. I know your work. I've studied every piece for hours. It's incredibly erotic."

My face warmed and I looked down at the sketch again. "I can't believe this."

"Believe it." He drew closer to me until I could feel the warmth from his body shielding me from the cold night.

"So you did all this, you put your own life at risk, because—"

Adam blinked. "Because I'm in love with you."

My mouth dropped open.

He grimaced and looked away. "I shouldn't have said that. This is complicated enough without –"

I pulled him closer to me and kissed him, stroking my fingers through his black hair. He resisted for a moment before kissing me back, hard and deep and filled with need. He pulled me closer to him so my breasts flattened against his chest and I felt his arousal press against me. My hands slid down the sides of his face as his tongue slid between my lips to taste me deeper.

A sudden and uncontrollable wave of desire crashed over me. I'd never wanted anyone so much in my entire life. Or so fast. I'd only just met him.

Even though he'd known me for twenty years.

I'd waited so long, painted so many pictures of love and passion, but it had only been a pale representation, a *guess* of what love truly was. I'd never actually felt anything that powerful for anyone before. Not until now.

Adam was the man I'd been waiting my whole life to find – I *knew* he was.

Little did I know how I'd end up finding him.

"We need to go," he whispered against my lips. "It's not safe here."

"Go where?"

He pulled the sleeve of his coat up so I could see he wore a strange watch with a large face on his left wrist. He fiddled with it for a moment, carefully turning a gear on the side of it.

"I'm sorry," he said. "It shouldn't be like this. You shouldn't have to leave your life behind, but there's no other way to keep you safe."

I thought of the friends I wouldn't see again. They'd be worried and confused about what happened to me. But Adam was right. I couldn't go back. My life here was over.

"You didn't answer my question," I said softly. "Where are we going?"

He brought his arm around my waist. "To the future. Twenty years from now. My time. I know a safe house there for those who want to escape from the Books of Fate. You won't be the first who's taken refuge there."

The future.

I nodded. My heart ached at the thought of never seeing Anna or my other friends again, but I knew he was right. "OK."

He seemed surprised I was so agreeable. "You trust me?"

"I do."

He nodded. "Good."

I folded the sketch and tucked it back in his pocket.

"It's worth money, you know," he said with a grin. "If anyone knew I had a Sophie Shaw original they'd be very jealous."

"Feel free to sell it."

"That's not going to happen." He looked at his watch, fiddling a little more with it.

"No?" Despite everything, a smile tugged at my lips. "Can't bear to part with it?"

"That, of course." Adam shook his head and met my gaze. "But also because I found my name in the Books this morning as well as yours."

My smile fell away. "But, wait a minute. What does that mean?"

Adam touched my face, stroking his warm fingers over my cheek and bottom lip. "It means I'm going to die very soon – killed by a bullet to my heart, apparently. And there's nothing I can do about it."

I heard a sound, a whirring noise, and it filled my ears as white light filled my eyes. Before I could say anything else, demand more answers from him, the world I'd known all my life disappeared forever.

"This is Gloria," Adam said when a door creaked open on the fifteenth floor of a condo on the Lower East Side.

We'd arrived in the future – as crazy as that sounded – an hour ago. Adam kept checking his watch for some sort of indication that his friends had also come forward with us. He seemed nervous about that, but not because he feared his own impending death. He was so focused on my safety it was driving me seriously crazy.

He also wouldn't discuss it any more. I asked him questions about how the auditors found people and if there was any way to talk to them rationally, but he just changed the subject. It was very frustrating.

"As I live and breathe." Gloria's gaze scanned the length of him. She had dark hair and dark skin and ruby red lips that curled with amusement. "Adam Rizer. Never thought I'd see you here."

"Didn't you know I was aware of your secret little operation?"

"Of course, and I knew you wouldn't tell anyone. But I thought you were a company man. Never go against your uncle for anything." Her eyes flicked to me. "Ah, I think it's becoming clearer to me why you'd risk so much tonight."

"This is Sophie Shaw," Adam said, averting his gaze from mine.

"The artist," Gloria replied.

"That's the one. She's going to stay here for a while. I'm hoping you can help her get adjusted to everything."

"It would be my honour. Please, come in." Gloria opened the door wider for us to enter.

"Thanks," I said. I had Adam's hand clutched in mine and I wasn't nearly ready to let him go yet. After everything I'd been through tonight, the feel of his skin against mine was the only thing keeping me remotely sane.

The apartment was much larger than I'd expected. In fact, it seemed to be the entire floor plus, according to the staircase in front of me, at least the floor above us as well. A safe house in the sky.

"So, breaking all the rules now, are you, Adam?" Gloria asked with a smile.

"Seem to be."

"I told you she'd be a keeper."

That caught my interest. "You told him that?"

"I did. When he was younger Adam showed me the sketch of you he always keeps in his pocket. I told him one day you would be together romantically. That you'd know he was the one for you the moment you saw him."

Adam studied the floor. "It wasn't like that, Gloria."

"No," I agreed. "The moment I first saw him, his buddy, Harris, was slapping me around."

Her eyebrows went up. "Oh my."

"It took me another twenty minutes before I knew Adam was the one for me," I finished, then smiled at her.

Gloria laughed. "See? Like I always say, fate's a pain in the butt but sometimes it's not so bad."

"How did you know?" I asked her. "About me and Adam?"

"Because I'm a seer," she said. "Or, at least I used to be. But the auditors . . . they twist what we tell them. They change things to make it pure and perfect. Life isn't perfect – it changes and undulates as we grow and move and breathe. There is not only one destiny for us all to hold true to. Fate can shift depending on our decisions. Believing differently will result in the necessity for places like this –" she waved a hand at her surroundings "– where those who have been rejected from their time, whose lives are in danger from those who wish to control our destinies, can come and know they still have the chance at a real future."

"Thank you for letting me stay here."

"My pleasure."

"I must leave," Adam said suddenly. "I've done all I can. I hope you can forgive me, Sophie. I never meant to ruin your life."

He turned and walked to the door. I ran after him and grabbed the sleeve of his coat, forcing him to look at me.

"You didn't," I said, fighting against the lump in my throat. "You *saved* my life."

"You didn't have to say that before. About knowing I was the one for you."

"I don't say things I don't mean."

"It's too fast for you. I mean, for me it's been twenty years, but for you –"

"For me it's been twenty-*five* years." I placed my palms flat against the firm planes of his chest. "Because I know you're the man I've waited my entire life to find."

"I'm an assassin."

"Still?"

"No, but—"

"What you've done in the past is finished. We can have a future together now. This can be a clean slate for both of us."

He shook his head. "I wish that was true."

"Why are you leaving?" My throat felt thick.

"Because a bullet will find me tonight according to the Books. It's fate. And if I stay here, it puts you in danger as well. It puts this safe house in danger and now I finally see how important it is."

I didn't know what to say to him. My heart ached at the thought that I was going to lose him when I'd only just found him. "What happened to your mother?"

Adam's eyebrows went up. "My mother?"

"Yes. When I first saw you, you were sad. She'd died."

He crossed his arms. "That was a long time ago."

"Maybe for you."

He gave me a sad smile. "She died of cancer."

"And the man who took you away?"

"That was my uncle."

"You said he wasn't."

"I . . ." He frowned, as if trying to remember. "I call him my uncle, but we're not related by blood. He was a scientist – still is. He's the head of the time travel division I work for. He raised me, then recruited me, thought I'd be good at being an auditor. He was right. I am damn good at it. But it always felt wrong to me. Now I know it *is* wrong."

"But you're still going out there tonight and put yourself in danger for something you think is wrong?"

"Just because I think it's wrong doesn't mean it isn't true. Fate exists. And it can be foreseen. Gloria worked with my uncle for years before she got out only a short time ago."

"Why can't you do the same?"

"Because just as there was a bus destined to kill you, there is a bullet destined to kill me. And I can't be here when it finds me." He stroked my face as if trying to memorize me. "Be safe, Sophie."

"Adam . . ."

"And just for the record, I never thought your paintings were dirty. I thought they were beautiful. Absolutely beautiful. Just like you."

He kissed me. But before I could draw him closer he pulled away, pushed the door open and left the safe house.

Fate.

It was fate that I'd spoken to that little boy. Fate that I'd given him my drawing. Fate that that bus was supposed to kill me. Fate that Adam would save me.

Was it fate that I'd fall in love with him?

It had to be. What I felt was as real as anything I'd ever experienced.

I wiped away the tear sliding down my cheek and turned to Gloria who stood by the floor-to-ceiling window looking down at the city below.

"So," I said shakily. "Did you see that coming too?"

"I did," she replied gravely, and then turned to look at me. "It was fate that Adam would leave here in search of his own death tonight."

I was surprised. "It was?"

She nodded. "Yes. Just as it's fate that you will go after him and save him from his own pig-headed stupidity."

I just stood there and gaped at her.

She put a hand on her hip and raised an eyebrow. "Are you going to stare at me or are you going to go after him? Like I said, fate changes. Just because he knows how he will die, doesn't mean it can't still change. But it won't unless you get your ass in gear and move."

Gloria was right. Of course she was. Adam hadn't accepted that I'd die from getting hit by the bus. He'd changed my fate. And I could change fate for him as well.

I turned away from her and something caught my eye. A painting on her wall. A painting I'd done of two lovers only a couple of weeks ago after a vivid dream I'd had.

I'd called it *Destiny Awaits*.

"You're an excellent artist," Gloria said. "I paid seventy-five grand for that little piece. It's filled with the fire and passion I want to see from you right now."

"Thanks, Gloria."

"You're welcome. Now move it. There's no time to waste."

The seer gave damn good advice.

Without another word spoken I ran from the apartment, headed down the elevator and emerged on to the sidewalk out front. I couldn't see Adam anywhere.

Fate.

If I was meant to stop this, I'd know what direction to go in. I'd pick one and it would lead me to him. Hesitating only a moment longer, I turned left and hurried along the sidewalk. After a minute, I took off my heels, threw them to the side and ran along in my bare feet until I finally heard something.

"Stupid," a voice said. "You are so fucking stupid, Adam. For a woman? You'd ruin your entire life for some meaningless woman?"

"Just shoot me and get it over with, Harris," Adam replied. "I know you want to."

"Your uncle would be disappointed in you. Always so perfect in his eyes."

"What the hell do you care?"

"What do I care? That nepotism earned you the perks I should be getting. It's not fair."

I flattened my back against the side of the building and sneaked a peek into the alleyway.

"Tell me where she is," Harris said.

"Where who is?"

"Your little artist bitch from the past. Despite our quarrel right now, this can still be fixed. I just need to put a bullet between her eyes and everything's the way it should be."

"And if I don't tell you a damn thing?"

"Then that's going to be a problem."

"Did you look in the Books beyond Sophie's listing today?" Adam asked. "Did you look at the Book for here? Right now, twenty years later to the day from when she was supposed to die?"

"Why would I bother with that?" Harris asked.

"Because," I said, stepping out from the shadows, "it has your name listed."

He shifted the gun to point it in my direction.

Adam turned to stare at me with shock. Did he really think I was going to stay out of this just because he'd planted me in that safe house in the sky like Rapunzel?

"You shouldn't be here," he said.

"And yet here I am. The walking dead."

"I like that you've finally accepted your fate," Harris said. "Now come closer so we can finish this."

"No." Adam pulled out his own gun and pointed it at Harris. "Let's not."

"So I shoot her and you shoot me?" Harris asked. "Is that how this is going to play out?"

"Not exactly what I'd had in mind," Adam said. "So I warn you not to even think about pulling that trigger."

Harris didn't flinch. "The thing is, I don't believe her. My name wasn't in the Book. Not a chance."

"But it was," Adam said evenly. "It was right under mine."

That surprised Harris. His eyes widened and he swung the gun back around towards Adam as if feeling threatened for the first time that night. On bare feet, and by instinct alone, I ran. A split second after Adam had fired his gun, I threw all my weight at him to push him out of the line of fire.

Adam's bullet hit Harris in the chest.

Harris's bullet ripped into Adam's shoulder.

Harris dropped his gun, touched his chest in shock, and fell forwards. His eyes open and unblinking.

I fell to the ground next to Adam. He wrapped his good arm around my chest and pulled me back behind some trash cans.

He swore, grimacing in pain. "Sophie, what have you done?"

I checked him for more serious injury, but there was none. "A bullet in the shoulder can't be pleasant," I said, "and you're bleeding like crazy, but it didn't hit your heart."

"What the hell did you think you were doing coming here and putting yourself at risk like that?"

"Saving your life," I replied. "Giving fate the finger. Losing my really expensive – and now apparently *vintage* – shoes. Not necessarily in that order."

"So that's all it takes to change fate?"

"I don't know, I'm kind of new at this sort of thing. Was Harris's name in the Book? Because I was totally bluffing."

"No, it wasn't," he said. "I was bluffing too."

"Great minds think alike. But he's dead?"

"Pretty sure. I'm a really good shot."

"Bragger." I almost smiled but I wasn't nearly ready to feel relieved yet. "But the fact that somebody not fated to die tonight ended up dead – that's probably a good indication that we changed things, right?"

He pointed at his shoulder wound. "I got shot. Just not in the heart."

"Serves you right for taking off on me like that."

He looked at me incredulously. "Why would you follow me and put yourself at risk after you were safe with Gloria?"

I looked at him sternly. "Do you know how hard it is to find a decent boyfriend in New York City? It was hard enough in 2009, let alone 2029. A girl's got to fight for what she wants, you know."

He smiled but it was edged in pain. "And what you want is me?"

I stroked the dark hair off his forehead. "I'm thinking I just might."

Adam looked worried. "They'll be after me now. Just like they'll be after you. My uncle won't make an exception for me. I broke the rules in a big way."

"Then it's a good thing we'll be watching out for each other. We'll both stay at Gloria's for a while until we figure out what to do next."

Adam kissed me, but he looked very serious afterwards. He held my face gently between his hands.

"We may have changed the future by both of us staying alive tonight. Forever."

I smiled at him, then brushed my lips against his. "I'm kind of counting on it," I said.

Pilot's Forge

Patrice Sarath

The Hatch-registered freighter *Godolphin* drifted in space, about 200,000 kilometres from Merritt's skiff, the *Crane*. The *Crane*'s sensors reported the details. The *Godolphin*'s hull had been breached and the ship had lost propulsion, engines, most life support. The distress call was on auto and getting weaker. No one could be alive – Merritt flipped the readouts to visual and zoomed in to see for himself and, sure enough, the freighter was dark.

Raiders had likely cleaned her out and taken the crew as captives for ransom.

"So why didn't they tow the boat in for salvage?" he said out loud. He was the only one on board the *Crane*, but it didn't stop him from talking. He thought better that way and, right now, he had a puzzle. The ship had been left to drift when arguably she was the biggest prize of all. He flipped back to the datastream, sat back in his chair and considered. He could tow the freighter into Crowe's World, one of their notorious chop shops, or play it the other way, tow her into Hatch station for the reward or stake a salvage claim. All without firing a shot. He let himself dream for a bit. If the ship were still sound, he could set himself up as a skipper, hire a crew, and get ahead of sector police. "You know, go straight," he told the datastream, running in heads-up display in front of him. "Settle down somewhere." Make the family proud.

It was a nice dream. He indulged it for a few seconds more, then turned down the datastream. More likely, if he towed that ship in, he'd find sector cops just waiting to bust him one more time and he would never see space again.

The *Godolphin* would have to continue her solitary journey through the galaxy's spiral arm, and Merritt would be the last one to see her. That didn't mean he shouldn't at least board her and confirm she was derelict. It was the charitable thing to do. And if he happened to pick up anything of value that might have been left over, well, even a good Samaritan deserved something for his trouble. He went to suit up.

He was surprised to see that the *Godolphin* still had atmosphere when the airlock whooshed and opened up for him, but with a hull breach the ship could vent at any time, so Merritt left his faceplate closed. His breathing was loud in the confined space of his helmet, and for a moment his readouts showed that he had elevated pulse and respiration. The ship's interior was dark and his headlamp flashed through the smoky darkness. He needed to get some lights working on the old girl. That was confirmed when he tripped over the first body. She had been killed with a pulse weapon. The woman's uniform had the Beauchamps logo on it. Beauchamps – one of the smaller merchant clans. Merritt's own clan was Crane, though he was only a distant relative of the great family and he didn't doubt they had as little care for him as he did for them. A Crane ship would not have been attacked. Raiders were smart enough to go for easier meat.

He counted three more bodies, scanning slowly. There had been a running gunfight, and there was plenty of scarring along the bulkhead.

Merritt tamped down his sudden desire to get the hell out of there. His suit sensors kept up a data feed, along with a ship schematic, which it displayed on the inside of his helmet. The hatch to the bridge was down the corridor, and Merritt headed that way, sidestepping the dead. There's not gonna be any salvage, he told himself, but he kept going anyway, knowing it was sheer stubbornness that drove him on. His helmet readout flashed a single dot, signifying his position along the schematic, and then, faintly, another dot flashed out of the corner of his eye.

There was someone else alive on the *Godolphin*.

Merritt stopped. With great care he thumbed the button on his suit to replay. The dot flashed again, flickered, came back. With his other hand he unholstered his pistol. Whoever it was might be dying, might not be human, might be trying to shield from his suit.

He got a lock on the other dot and saw that it was on the bridge. There was a hatch about twenty metres ahead. He found it, and climbed up, his boots clicking on the rungs. He was sweating by the time he got into the control room, and he found the body, suited up with the helmet latched. He muscled between overturned chairs and broken panels and knelt stiffly next to it. The man opened his eyes and muttered something that Merritt couldn't catch. Under his faceplate, blood crusted around the man's mouth and nose.

"What happened?" Merritt said, hardly expecting an answer. "Raiders?"

The Beauchamps captain moved his head slightly inside the helmet. *Yes.*

Merritt's suit beeped, letting him know he was running low on air. "I need to get you to my ship," he said. "I can't carry you. Is there a float?"

The captain shook his head again. He tried to say something, spoke hoarsely. "Get off my ship."

Merritt kept from rolling his eyes. *Man's dying and he's* still *pushy.* "Sorry, captain. Looks like this is a rescue."

"Damn fool," the Beauchamps captain said, and that came through clearly. "You. Are. In. Danger." He grabbed Merritt's arm, his bloody fingers leaving prints. "Jumped by raiders, and disabled. But they hit the D-space navigator." He stopped, gulped a lot of air. "We've been cycling in and out of space-time, each time it's getting worse. We're due for another cycle any second, and if you don't get out of here, you're dead too."

Merritt's status sensors told him what he already suspected – respiration, heart rate, adrenal glands: all pouring forth accelerated data. He holstered his gun again and knelt, trying to lift the Beauchamps captain. He grunted under the effort; his suit didn't make things easy. "Then I guess we better be going."

Beauchamps cried out in agony. "No time. I'm cycling too."

Merritt looked down and almost dropped him. Beauchamps was *fading.* D-space was happening all around them. Great for getting from place to place without having to take, say, 100 years to make the next star; not so great when a wormhole opened up inside you. Beauchamps got a lot heavier and Merritt saw that he was dead. He set the man down and backed away, then ran for the ladder. He slid rather than climbed down.

The ship shook all around him, coming in and out of reality. The central corridor seemed longer this time, even though he was sprinting. His heads-up display flared and shook, transmitting streams of unintelligible data. Merritt kept running, hit the controls for the airlock, and froze. The door had *changed*. It was now made of wood and iron and had an old-fashioned doorknob. Tentative, he touched the knob and the door whooshed open, an airlock once again. He stepped in and reflexively slapped at the side of the door to close it.

His glove hit wood and something fell to the floor. An old-fashioned key – an iron skeleton key – lay at his feet. It's not really there, he told himself. It was a ghost of the D-space nav malfunction. His brain was making sense of what it couldn't understand, creating familiar images out of multispace. The ship was coming apart at the subatomic level, and so would he. He saw the great gathering darkness rushing towards him, pulling him into the wormhole that gathered at the bow of the ship. Breathing hard, Merritt pulled the door closed.

"Come on, come on," he muttered, sweat slicking down his back. Would the airlock work, or would he be trapped inside the wormhole for ever? With agonizing slowness the rising whine indicated that the airlock had began to pressurize. Merritt heard a noise and looked out of the tiny window in the wooden door.

A face filled it, a face contorted in hatred and fear.

"Shit!" Merritt flung himself backwards, fumbling to pull up his weapon. The man was snarling, his teeth showing like spikes through his beard. That's not the captain, he thought crazily. What the hell was going on?

The power whine stopped and the airlock stopped pressurizing. The man continued to snarl like an animal, and he was trying to pull the door open. *Shit shit shit.* Merritt knelt and scrabbled for the key, fumbling in his panic and haste. He held the door closed, desperation giving him strength, and pushed the key in the lock, then turned it. The door locked with a click. Again the slow rising whine, again the long wait as the airlock pressurized. The face dropped away and Merritt allowed himself a slow breath.

Then with a shuddering crash the man threw himself against the door, teeth bared, eyes bulging. The small compartment was rocked again and again as the creature threw itself at him. Merritt drew his gun, faced the door, and waited for the moment when the creature burst through. If the explosive decompression didn't get him, he might survive.

A polite chime sounded, signalling the atmosphere had stabilized. The airlock opened behind him.

Billy's was crowded that night, the little roadhouse bar spilling music and laughter out into the parking lot. Edith parked her battered old work truck, with 'Crane Farrier and Blacksmithing' stencilled on the side, at the end of the parking lot, got out and stretched. It had been a long day. She had shoed five horses that day. Her business was picking up, but it meant that she had spent a lot of time bent over double, and some horses were lazy about supporting their own weight.

"Edith Crane!" shouted Melissa Andrews from over by the front deck with a bunch of friends. "'Bout time you got here!"

Edith made her way over to the group and slid into an empty space on the bench. Melissa poured her a beer from the pitcher and Edith sipped and relaxed.

"Oh my, that's good." Edith looked around at all of her friends. There was Melissa and her boyfriend Brian, and a half-dozen people her age, all young, all making their way in the little Tennessee town of Pilot's Forge.

Melissa leaned across the table towards Edith and spoke low. "Listen, Edith, have you heard from Sam Grenady?"

Edith felt a shiver of unease. She and Sam had dated briefly when she came to town. She was drawn by his rough good looks and a kindred liking for physical labour. He was a carpenter and jack-of-all-trades, and had an easy smile that, she realized after about a month, he could put on and take off as easy as a jacket. The smile and the charm hid a sizeable chip on his shoulder that came out when he drank, and he drank a lot. He had lots of plans for her, he told her. Big plans that she had no say in. After three dates she made sure they were at Billy's when she told him she wasn't the girl for him. The expression he gave her was cold and empty. And then he smiled, gave her a kiss on the cheek, paid for their beer, and walked away. She hadn't talked to him since.

"Why, what's up?" She asked it carefully.

Melissa said, "He's been heard making noise about you. Says you lamed Cindy Dupre's warmblood with lousy shoeing."

Edith's heart sank. Pilot's Forge was a small town and Sam was an old-timer. He could sink her business in no time. "That son of a bitch."

Melissa snorted. "Don't I know it. He sweet-talks plenty, but the minute he doesn't get his way, he goes ballistic. He was always like that, even when we were in high school."

Edith was reminded again that she was the newcomer. It didn't matter that her grandparents farmed here eighty years ago. If Sam Grenady wanted her out of Pilot's Forge, all he had to do was spread a few rumours. Well, she wasn't going to go without a fight. She'd call Cindy Dupre and all of her clients and let them know that Sam was full of it.

She looked straight at Melissa. "If you hear anything else, you let me know."

"You know it, California girl. I've been telling everyone that this town has always needed someone to put it on the map, and that's going to have to be you."

Edith laughed. "Melissa, I shoe horses. That's not glamorous."

"Oh, honey, in small towns you have to make your own fun."

It was late when Edith drove up the mountain road to her old farmhouse, her pickup growling in low gear as it rounded the turns towards home. Trees massed around her, and now and again her headlights reflected on the eyes of animals in the dark. A whitetail bounded on stick-thin legs across the road in front of her, its twin fawns leaping behind it. She was glad to be heading home but Sam's lies made her uneasy. She remembered his expression when she broke up with him. Should have known it wouldn't be that easy, she thought. She would have to look out for him.

Her porch light was a welcoming sight as she pulled in to her driveway. She got out, locked her truck, and the cool summer air swept over her. Overhead the stars glittered between the trees. She hadn't even seen the Milky Way before she moved out here from smog-filled Los Angeles. The swath of stars filled her with peace and awe.

Edith yawned. Straight to bed for me, she thought, but she needed to check on her horses. She let herself in, turned on lights, and went through her kitchen, with its jumble of mismatched crockery, Formica table and chairs, and old stove that came with the house when it was remodelled in the 1950s. Out back was the barn, well over 100 years old and still sound.

The only light came from the dusty night light by the door. Katahdin, her big seventeen-hand retired show horse nickered, but Cowboy and Blackjack both slept – Cowboy curled up like a foal. Edith made sure he wasn't cast in his stall; a cast horse could break a leg trying to get to his feet. But Cowboy had plenty of room. Edith was about to leave when she heard the noise.

She turned towards her tack-room door. It sounded like there was a machine in there. She could feel the thrumming of an engine deep in her bones. Edith backed away, fumbling for the iron crowbar she left in the corner of the barn. Behind her Blackjack snorted and whinnied, and Cowboy lunged to his feet.

Katahdin kicked at the back of his stall, shaking the wall of the barn. Edith jumped. The tack-room door jerked open and someone stumbled out.

She had little time to register before whoever it was, in a streamlined G-suit, collapsed in front of her.

Oh my God. There's a dead astronaut in my barn.

Merritt opened his eyes and wondered if he was still cycling in D-space. A woman with dark curly hair, dark eyes – and a long metal bar poised to strike – stood over him. She was good-looking too, he noted; trim figure in a simple shirt and trousers. And scared and determined enough to smash him with the crowbar. She didn't look like Beauchamps crew – where the hell was he? And where was the man from the freighter?

He stayed as still as he could. Sometimes the best thing to do was play dead and hope for the best. With her free hand the woman fumbled for something in her pocket.

"Don't move," she said, her voice coming through his helmet's comm. "I'm calling the police."

Crap. That was all he needed. He started to get up.

"I said, don't move!" Her voice rose.

He didn't have time for this. He might only have a few minutes before whoever was chasing him on the *Godolphin* came through the airlock after him. He pulled his gun and trained it on her. Her eyes got big and she backed away.

"Lady, the way I see it, you just brought the wrong weapon to a gunfight." He nodded at the crowbar. "Drop it." She hesitated and set it down. "Now the comm."

She frowned in confusion, but he held out his hand for the strange little comm, and she handed it over. He tucked it into his suit pouch.

"What do you want?" she said, swallowing to get her voice going.

"Same thing you do. To get out of your hair." He gestured with the gun. "Move."

She didn't. She stood her ground. "Who are you? Did Sam Grenady put you up to this? What did you put in my tack room?"

What? He followed her gaze, turning his head. There was the door and, behind it, the *Godolphin.* The woman started towards the door, which had fallen ajar. For an instant he was back inside the scuttled freighter, the wormhole chasing him down and drawing him in, towards the crazy screaming man.

"NO!" Merritt shouted, as she pushed it open.

She flicked on the light.

Without thought Merritt plastered himself up against the opposite wall, aiming at the door, his heart hammering, as he registered what he was looking at. There was no D-space, no wormhole, no freighter, no madman: just a tidy room lined with gear, harness and metal grain bins. Stand down, he told himself, just as something big snorted just behind his ear. Merritt whirled around and almost screamed. An enormous quadruped stood there, long-necked and big-headed. It eyed him and snorted again.

"What the hell is that thing?"

"Don't shoot him!" the woman said, and she threw herself at Merritt, grappling for the gun.

They wrestled. The suit gave him extra weight and boosted his strength and he soon had her pinned to the floor.

"I swear to God, if Sam Grenady is behind this I will kill you both!" she shouted, still trying to squirm free.

"Stop," he said. "*Stop.* You keep fighting, the suit will keep compensating, and I can sit on you all day, and you'll never get up." She listened to him, sullenly, fury still in her eyes. Merritt was suddenly enjoying himself. Finally, something was going his way. And even through the suit, he could get a sense of her beneath him.

"Now, I'm going to get up and I'm going to let you up. You're not going to try that again, right?"

He waited. She didn't want to, but she nodded. He got up, and held out his hand to help her up. She ignored it and got to her feet.

"Like I said, I just want out of here. I need to know where the nearest port is. What world is this?"

She looked as if she were trying to come up with the right thing to say, and one of her choices was not going to be complimentary. Finally, she settled on, "Get the hell out of my barn."

"My pleasure. After you." He gestured with the gun and she went in front of him. He followed. One of the quadrupeds stuck its long neck out and eyed him with interest. Merritt scraped along the opposite wall, but she reached out and stroked the animal's neck. A pet? A thing that size was a *pet*?

Outside the barn the skies above the trees were filled with unfamiliar stars. Merritt stopped, enjoying the rush of wind against his face, and wishing he had the *Crane*'s nav service to tell him where he was. There was a swath of galaxy above him, but he couldn't tell which spiral arm he was marooned on from here.

She led the way through an ornate gate that swung silently on oiled hinges, past a small stone house and pointed down the mountain. In the pale starlight a road shimmered faintly before him. "That road leads to town. I don't know who you are, or what you are doing here, but I would appreciate it if you didn't come back."

"You and me both," Merritt said. The sooner he got off this rock and back to civilized space – well, the sooner he would be back to dodging the police and trying to hustle a living. He remembered the key and opened his glove. With a sudden surety that took him by surprise, he said, "I think this is yours."

She stared at it in the faint light from the stars. It lay in his glove, flat and heavy, and he waited patiently. She took it finally, and through the extra sensitive material of the glove he felt the gentleness and warmth of her fingers. He turned and began to walk down the road.

In the warm light of the kitchen, her heart still pounding, Edith began to dial 9-1-1, then hung up before the call connected. What the hell was Sam up to? If he had put this guy up to it, what could he want? To make her sound crazy when she called the cops and said there was an astronaut in her barn? She got up and paced.

What if Sam wasn't behind it? What was crazier, that there was a guy *pretending* to be a spaceman in her barn –

– or that there *was* a spaceman in her barn?

Her gaze fell on the key. It was an old-fashioned skeleton key. A shiver ran down her spine. The farmhouse had been modernized more than fifty years ago, but before that, it had a key very much like this one. And that key had been lost for generations, she knew that for a fact.

She should have called the cops on him. She could still call the cops. She looked over at her phone, but she didn't call.

Crazy guy hides out in my barn wearing a spacesuit, pretends he's an ET who doesn't know what a horse is. Yeah, she should have called the police.

Except. She remembered the sound coming from the tack room. That hadn't sounded like anything she had ever heard. And he was terrified when she pushed the door open.

And then there was the feel of his gloves when she reached out and took the key. Thick gloves, yet so sensitive that she could feel his hand beneath them. Her hair rose at the memory, even as she scoffed.

So, you are out here in the back end of nowhere, making a living at a centuries-old craft. What do you know about new technology?

Edith got up. She went around her house, closing windows and turning locks. She went upstairs to bed, and looked out of the window at her barn. The building was dark and peaceful, the small glow from the night light a comforting sight. For the first time she was unsettled by the loneliness of the mountain.

It took her a long time to fall asleep.

One-gee normal, his suit told him, and Merritt could feel every bit of it as he trudged down the mountain road, helmet in his hand. The cool mountain air felt good against his face. As the road curved down the mountain he could glimpse the lights of a small settlement in the valley below and, further away, a much larger city. There was no sign of an air-transport grid though, and surely he'd be able to see port gantries from here. He craned his neck to look up at the stars again. Through the trees he could see a tiny, fast-moving point of light. Too small to be a space station though. Most planets were orbited by the wheel-and-spoke standard stations that could be seen even in daylight.

Wouldn't that be his luck, to come out of D-space on one of the lost worlds?

Merritt stopped. He wiped sweat from his eyes. Night noises rose up around him. A faint wind rustled through the leaves, and in the distance he could hear hooting, a rippling cry, and a rhythmic call. Animals, he told himself nervously. Just basic animals. He didn't get dirtside on too many worlds, but most terraformed planets were rife with flora and fauna. This one looked like it was pretty well along in the process. Merritt checked his sidearm. It was fully charged.

The sound of an engine caught his attention. Merritt looked down the road. Someone was coming up in a groundcar, and whoever it was wasn't running their lights.

Had the woman called for reinforcements after she sent him on his way? Merritt melted back into the woods, and touched his suit controls. The suit obligingly made itself match the shadows in the woods. The smell of low-tech fuel made him gag. Internal combustion? What the hell?

When the car was swallowed up into the night he played back the recording made by the suit.

A cargo vehicle much like the one he saw at the woman's house. The man driving it was shaggy, bearded. Angry. Obviously racing up the mountain to help out a friend who was in trouble. *I better get the hell out of here before he comes looking for me on the way back.*

Still, Merritt hesitated. He stopped the video, zoomed in on the truck. There was lettering – his suit chittered as it ran itself through standard transliteration modes and finally settled on one he recognized.

Grenady Construction.

Did Sam Grenady send you?

Merritt cursed under his breath. The last time he tried to help someone, he had gotten kicked through D-space to a lost world and would likely never see his ship again. Forget it. She could handle herself. He actually took two steps down the mountain, when he stopped, swore again, and charged back up the road.

* * *

The sound of breaking glass jolted Edith out of her uneasy sleep. She sat upright. There was another crash of glass, and Edith threw aside the covers. She grabbed for her phone and remembered. The guy in the tack room had taken it. Edith ran down the stairs in her T-shirt and shorts, getting into her boots along the way. She hit the light switch and flooded her front yard with light. Sam stopped only for seconds and looked towards the house, then took another swing at her truck, battering the hood.

"I'm calling the police!" she screamed. "I see you, Sam Grenady! You will go to hell for this!"

"Screw you, bitch! I'm just giving you what you deserve!"

He swung the sledgehammer once again into her windshield. Edith ran for her kitchen phone. Nothing. No dial tone. Son of a bitch, she thought. He cut the wires. She would have to stop him herself.

Sam was sledgehammering at the back of her camper shell and had gotten the door open. He pulled out her tools and supply of keg shoes and then began to dump gasoline all over them. Dear God, nothing would stop a fire that caught up here. Her house, her barn. Her horses. She burst from the house with a wild scream, brandishing the fire extinguisher.

"Get away from my house!"

He looked up just as she sprayed him full in the face. He staggered back, scraping foam from his eyes. Then he roared, and swung the gasoline at her. It spattered over her, and she stumbled backwards, the smell of gas overwhelming. She kept spraying at him until the fire extinguisher was out and she threw the empty canister at him, screaming a wordless war cry to meet his howls of rage.

"Hold it!" came a voice from outside the pool of light. They looked up into the darkness, Sam with blood and foam cascading down him, Edith wild-eyed, reeking of gasoline. A glowing red light began to gather to a point. It was her spaceman, and he had his raygun.

"Don't move!" he ordered and came into the light.

With a curse Sam grabbed Edith and threw her at the man, and bolted for his truck. The man pushed Edith away and ran after him, but Sam was lost to the darkness. An instant later they heard the engine roar and he peeled out down the mountain. Edith looked at the destruction of her truck. Her yard was full of glass and tools, and her truck listed to the side.

The spaceman came back. "He's gone," he said, his voice grim. "I couldn't get off a clear shot."

Edith turned to him. She ached and stung all over. Adrenalin was fading, leaving her with anger. She looked at him and shook her head and then slapped him as hard as she could. He staggered back, shock turning to anger, but she didn't care.

"You stupid –" she said, her throat so thick she could hardly get the words out. "You took my phone."

The police came, their blue and red flashing lights washing over her yard and the damaged truck. They jotted down her account and took pictures, and promised they would look for Sam, though at least two of the cops were related to him. Yeah right, thought Edith, bitter and cynical now. One of the cops looked at the spaceman. He was no longer in his suit. He had hidden it and his gun inside the house, upstairs in her bedroom. Now he just looked like a normal guy, though his shorts and T-shirt were made out of an odd material that she almost wanted to touch, just to see if it felt as strange as it looked.

She hadn't wanted to cover for him, but if the police thought he was a crazy spaceman, they might be distracted from going after Sam. Better not to confuse things.

"How are you involved?" the cop said.

"He's a friend," Edith put in. "He's here visiting." The man nodded, his expression showing no surprise at her explanation, like he was used to lying about who he was and what he was doing. She hoped like hell they didn't ask her for his name.

"He can talk for himself, can't he?" the cop said. "You have a name?"

The man raised his head. "Merritt Crane." His voice was cautious.

Edith tried to keep surprise off her face. What was he playing at? The cop caught it too.

"So let me get this straight – you a friend or a relative?" he asked, suspicious now.

"Friend," she hastened. "Just a coincidence."

Now the man looked at her, his expression guarded. Secrets, she thought. There are too many secrets for one front yard to handle.

The cop went on. "So you were here for the attack?"

Merritt nodded, a helpful easy attitude. "I just went for a walk down the road a bit, to stretch my legs. I saw him drive up in his ground vehicle, and thought that looked suspicious. Especially after – my friend – here said she was worried he'd try something."

Ground vehicle. My friend. The cops looked from one to the other. "Right," one said. "All right, that's it then. We'll keep up patrols for the rest of the night. We'll find him. He won't go far."

Edith sat back in the kitchen chair and looked at the stranger. She was exhausted. She smelled of gas and she was covered with bruises. Tears bubbled up just under the surface and with the last of her effort she kept from breaking down into sobs.

"Won't this night end?" she said. "I don't think I can take any more." She looked at him, the crazy stranger who wasn't so crazy any more. He watched her with concern. She got a good look at him, finally, in the light. Handsome, with a lean face and dark eyes, short dark hair. He looked like he was around her age, early thirties. Her voice shook a little as she asked: "Who are you? Is your last name really Crane? What are you doing here?"

He hesitated and then said, "Yeah. I'm really a Crane. As for what I'm doing here – I don't know."

"Why did you come back?" she said.

A muscle twitched in his cheek. "Something didn't feel right."

If he hadn't come ... if Sam hadn't been outnumbered ... The tears came at last and she covered her face and sobbed, her shoulders heaving. He reached out and put his hand over hers, and squeezed.

"Hey," he said. "Glad I could help. You did good by yourself."

"My livelihood – my truck. I don't know how I can repay you."

"You don't have to repay me," he said, but it sounded as if he had to force the words out. "You just need to tell me. What world is this?"

She was silent for a long time, the ticking of the clock the only sound in the kitchen. If she answered his question, it meant she took him seriously. Edith shook her head. She was too tired to second-guess any more.

"It's Earth," she said. "You're on Earth."

She watched as comprehension dawned – comprehension and something else. Wonder. Disbelief. Fear. She expected him to say something but he only said, gently, "Go clean up. I'll keep watch."

"Aren't you tired too?" she said.

He smiled, and it lightened his expression. "The suit's been keeping me awake. I can push it for a few more hours."

She couldn't even protest, just got up and pushed herself away from the table. Then she stopped, remembering something. "Merritt. I'm really sorry I hit you."

He gave a rueful grin and rubbed his cheek. "I'm sorry I sat on you."

She laughed despite herself. "Even then."

"Even."

Earth. He was on Earth. The Earth Merritt knew was a wasted planet, with seas of glass and dead cities, its oceans boiled away, the losing side in a war with an unstable sun that had gone from even-tempered to angry giant in the cosmic blink of an eye. The arks had left Earth for other star systems aeons before. There were about twenty planets that called themselves Earth, but he didn't think she meant one of those. She meant *Earth*.

First things first, he told himself. Secure the house. Merritt started on the top floor, making his way up the narrow wooden stairs. There were two rooms. He opened the door to the first one. It was a sleeping room, neat and tidy, sparsely furnished, its ceiling slanting down over the window. Edith had thrown his suit and helmet up here. Merritt got himself his gun and checked the charge. Still full. He looked into the second room. This was where she slept. The bed was untidy, the covers thrown back. Clothes were piled on a round-armed chair under the window, and there was a closet full of more clothes, its door ajar. The room smelled of her, warm and clean.

He went down the stairs, hearing the water running as she washed up in the bathroom. He imagined himself in there with her, grinned and shook his head. Need to keep my mind on what I'm doing, he thought. The downstairs held two rooms in front and the kitchen in the back of the house. He figured out the controls for the lights and he flipped the switch. Light came on to show another tidy room, not used very much. A word came to him, dredged up from distant memory. This was a "parlour", for guests.

He heard the water shut off. There was one more door, at the end of the hall. He opened it and stumbled back. It opened on to a black hole, a void, and for an instant he thought that he had come upon another wormhole. He realized that he had stopped breathing, and forced himself to take a breath. He fumbled at the wall, but there was no light switch. So he turned on his torch and pointed it downwards. Now he could see stairs going down.

"What are you looking at?" she said from behind him. He turned, absurdly relieved that she was there. She still smelled faintly of gasoline, but she was in a clean sleeveless shirt and drawstring trousers, and towelled at her hair. His heart stuttered again but not from fear. He tried not to stare at the way she filled out her plain white shirt.

"What's down there?"

"The old cellar. The foundation of this house dates to the 1800s, and they gutted it and modernized it, oh, about sixty years ago. That's the root cellar." She wrinkled her nose self-deprecatingly. "It creeps me out. I don't go down there much."

Funny how he knew exactly what she meant without knowing the words. He nodded and closed the door and they both breathed a sigh of relief.

"All right. It looks all clear. Sleep sound. I'll take the downstairs."

"Thanks." She hesitated, and a bit of colour touched her cheeks. "I mean. I don't know how to thank you."

"It's all right. I'm glad to help."

He watched her go, and shook his head. Merritt, don't even think it, he told himself. But it was too late. He was already thinking it.

Sam Grenady holed up in a swale off the road. He was covered with dried foam and blood, and smelled of the gas he had used to douse her truck. Crazy bitch, he thought. He shivered in the night air, and tried to cover himself with leaves. She had found herself another guy in record time, and he had some kind of taser thing. It had glared in Sam's eyes, and he couldn't see, couldn't think. Well, if she thought she could get away with dumping him and taking up with someone else, bitch had another think coming. It was time to finish the job he started.

He'd have to do it quick though. He heard the police cars screaming up the road after he drove off into the underbrush near her place. Come daylight, they would be able to find his tyre tracks easy.

"Don't underestimate Sam Grenady," he muttered. This was his town, his mountain. He'd been hunting on Crane land ever since he was a boy, and he knew its secrets. Sam kicked his feet at the end of the hollow. They banged against wood, and he kicked again and again until he smashed it in.

There were tunnels and caves all over this mountain, some natural, some man-made from the days when the locals ran moonshine. Sam slid inside one of these as cold wet air rushed at him from under the earth and wormed his way through the low tunnel into the pitch-black underground. He'd teach Edith Crane a thing or two about her family history.

Birdsong and sunlight woke her. Edith got up and dressed quickly in jeans and a tank top, then threw on a plaid work shirt to ward off the morning chill. It was already eight o'clock. She never slept in this late. She paused before going downstairs, looking out of the window. She loved this view. Beyond the barn and her forge, the green mountain rose up over the homestead, culminating in the bare granite mountaintop. From here she could see her meadow, blanketed in low morning mist, and dotting her land were the sculptures that she had made of iron and steel. Some she meant to sell, and she was starting to get clients from the big cities, even a few museums interested in her work. Others were just for this place, and had meaning only for her.

Her gaze fell on the skeleton key and she picked it up. Someone had hammered it out of pig iron. Not a method she would have used – she would have gone with an alloy and moulded the molten metal into the right shape. It was made out of old iron, heavy and anachronistic. A mystery, she thought, part of a bigger one downstairs.

She padded down the steps as quietly as she could. Her spaceman dozed in the chair by the window, the gun lying in his lap. He didn't wake, and she just took him in for a minute. Tall and lean, with dark hair, stubble on his face. Not classically handsome – someone had broken his nose at one point and it had set a little crooked, and she bet he had been teased about his ears when he was a kid – but oh, nice just the same. She took another step down the stairs, hitting the plank that always creaked. He jerked awake, handgun up, then relaxed as he remembered his surroundings. He looked at her.

"Damn it," he said. "The stim wore off. I didn't mean to sleep."

"It's OK. We both needed it." She bit her lip. "Look, if you want to wash up, the bathroom's through there. I'll make breakfast, but I have to tend to the animals first."

He went off to the bathroom and she waited, wondering if he was going to need help with her old-fashioned bathroom. Hmmm, that might be kind of fun, she thought, then scolded herself. Bad girl, Edith, but she was grinning as she went out to feed her horses. Katahdin had his nose out the door of his stall, neighing furiously at her, kicking the walls of his box for good measure, irked at his late breakfast.

"Get over it," she told him, as she shook out flakes of hay and freshened their water. She left their stall doors open. When the horses were finished eating they knew enough to take themselves out into the meadow.

She stood at the split-rail fence, breathing in the clean mountain summer air. It stayed cool up here even in summer, and the birds sang their hearts out in the crisp sunshine. It was so peaceful, she could pretend that nothing had happened last night. Only the faint smell of gas told her otherwise.

Instead of tears, anger welled up. She was through crying. The police had better find Sam first, because if she did, she was going to make him pay.

Her kitchen door opened and Merritt came out. He looked freshly washed, his hair wet. Her mood rose.

"Figured it out?" she said.

He nodded. "I haven't washed with water for a long time. Felt good."

She couldn't help it; she laughed. "Merritt, are you bullshitting me?"

He laughed too, but a little uncertainly. "I don't—"

It didn't matter. She was suddenly happy. Sam had done his best but he hadn't broken her spirit. She put a hand on Merritt's arm, and nodded at the barn. "Watch."

He followed her gaze. Led by Katahdin, the horses filed out of the barn, their heads nodding peacefully as they walked out to meadow. When they reached their pasture, they began to trot and then to canter and buck. Merritt tensed. "Watch," she whispered. Katahdin moved in a floating trot, the big bay horse lifting each hoof as if he were in a dressage test, his neck arched. The horses circled the pasture, disappearing down the hill and then they could hear the thudding hooves as they galloped back up.

When they settled to graze, Edith finally stirred.

"Gets me every time," she said.

For a second a flash of sadness shadowed his eyes. "That was . . . That was incredible."

She still had her hand on his arm and blushed. She turned the caress into a comradely slap on the shoulder. "Come on, I'll make you breakfast. We have a full day ahead of us."

She made him scrambled eggs, grits, toast and strong coffee, and they sat at her kitchen table. Earth food tasted pretty damn good, Merritt decided after the first few cautious bites. He hadn't had a home-cooked meal in pretty much for ever. He was so deep into his breakfast, he was almost surprised when she spoke.

"That key you gave me last night. How did you get it?"

"I doubt you'll believe me," he said. "I hardly believe it myself."

"Try me."

She listened as he gave her the whole story, and when he was finished, she was silent for a long time, swirling her spoon in her grits. "You're right," she said at last. "I don't believe you. But that key you gave me last night? In the Great Depression, when my family left Tennessee for California, they brought that key with them. It was a symbol of this place. That key went missing in my grandparents' day."

He thought of how the key landed at his feet, with the wormhole behind him and closing fast, drawing him towards the attacking madman. At first he thought it was a figment of his brain, trying to make sense of the collapse of space-time. Had he conjured that key out of the past – their past? But his past was her future, and maybe in more ways than one.

"I told you I was Crane, right?" he said. "Well, I'm part of the Crane clan, though I doubt we share much of the same DNA."

"Distant cousins," she said, her voice dry.

He laughed. "Really distant. Yeah. In my time, the Cranes became one of the greatest clans in the galaxy. Three hundred years ago,

the Cranes built the arks to take humanity off Earth, and we settled
the known worlds, terraforming and transforming as we went."

She looked puzzled. "What? Why would we leave?"

"Because Earth died. The sun became an unstable red giant, way
sooner than anyone expected."

Watching her absorb the news was like watching someone
get kicked in the stomach in slow motion. She looked out of the
window and he knew what she was thinking. This beautiful country
with its horses – her home, her land – consumed by an angry sun.

"All of it?" she said. "I mean, it's all gone?" She turned to him.
"How do you stand it, knowing that Earth is gone?"

He surprised himself with his own answer, because until she
asked him he never knew that it was something he had to stand.

"We spend our lives looking for her," he said. "No matter where
we live, no matter what station or what planet, no one ever stops
looking."

She looked stricken. "I wish you hadn't told me. I wish I never
knew. I'll never be able to stand it, never."

Merritt got up and went to her. He meant only to comfort, and
he put his arms around her, but she lifted her face to his and they
kissed. Her lips were soft and he pulled her close, letting his hands
fall to her waist, smoothing over her hips. She put her arms around
his neck, and their kiss deepened.

Somehow they made it upstairs to her bedroom, scattering
clothes along the way, and in the cool breeze from the open window
they made love on her rumpled bed.

It was afternoon before Edith woke from her doze. The room had
gotten chilly. Merritt had both his arms around her as if he didn't
intend to let her go, but he dozed too, and when she stirred, he
muttered a protest.

She kissed him. "Not going anywhere." She didn't want to. It felt
good, lying in his arms, their legs entwined. The iron key lay on the
bedside table where she had put it the night before. She sat up to
pick it up. It was cool and heavy in her hand.

Merritt sat up behind her, wrapping his legs around her, nibbling
along her neck. "What is it?" he said, between kisses, keeping his
hands around her waist. She shivered, losing her concentration for
a moment.

"I think this key is the crux," she said. "Somehow this key got lost so it could bring you here. But a key is nothing without a lock." Edith pulled away and started to get into her clothes. She tossed Merritt's to him. "If this is my grandparents' key – where does it fit?"

They both hesitated at the top of the stairs to the cellar, shining their flashlights into the dark. The stairs weren't steep but they were in darkness by the bottom. Merritt got the impression of an earthen room, supported by timbers. Old ceramic jugs and rusty washtubs, and a tangle of copper tubing in one corner.

"What's all that stuff?" Merritt asked.

Edith laughed. "It's our sordid past. The Cranes were bootleggers back in the day. You'd never believe it by my grandmother, but the Cranes ran on the wrong side of the law now and again."

Merritt gave a short laugh. Some things never changed.

They picked their way through the room, brushing away cobwebs. At the far end of the cellar was a wooden door, its threshold dull with dust. Edith put the key in the lock. It fitted but resisted her attempts to turn it.

"Damn," she said. "Here, hold this." She handed him the key while she rummaged through the junk piled up by the stairs, her flashlight shining wildly. She held up a can. "I knew I saw some down here. WD-40. This and duct tape – keeps the universe together." While Merritt kept the light steady, she sprayed the lock and tried again. Sluggishly it turned. They both pulled on the door and it shrieked on stiff hinges as it came open.

With a scream of fury, Sam Grenady burst out of the open doorway.

For a second Merritt was back on the *Godolphin*, watching the wormhole close in, the figure of the man rushing towards him. It was *him*, he thought dazedly. The cycling of the *Godolphin* had brought him here, through time and space, to this moment, and sent him the key to save himself.

He realized all this even as Sam threw himself at Edith. Merritt jumped on Sam's back and pulled him off, then grabbed him under the arms and held on. The flashlights rolled away, illuminating useless corners of the cellar, so the only light came from the stairs. Sam screamed and fought, and Merritt wished he had brought his gun.

Light began to grow from behind them, and Merritt heard a
familiar noise, the gathering sound and energy of a ship's mechanics.
He could see the dawning wonder on Edith's face and he knew
what was happening behind him. The airlock had returned, and
behind it was the *Godolphin* corridor. He probably even had time
to get to his ship and cast off from the freighter, bolting before
the *Godolphin*'s final destruction. He could pull Sam through too,
and the man would remain in the stasis, forever on the edge of the
wormhole exactly as Merritt found him.

Merritt dragged Sam towards the airlock. The whining noise
rose and the soft chime of the warning system told him he was
running out of time. He backed into the open door, the white light
of the *Godolphin* airlock all around him. Sam struggled and fought,
screaming and cursing, and Merritt tightened his hold even as the
man threw himself backwards, trying to break Merritt's nose with
the back of his head. Over Sam's head Merritt could see Edith
struggle to her feet.

The airlock whooshed shut. As he waited for the atmosphere
to balance, he could see Edith through the tiny airlock window,
impossibly far away.

Edith worked steadily at the forge on her land, coaxing the iron into
shape with fire and hammer. It was a facsimile of the airlock that
had appeared in her cellar weeks before, made out of iron, to match
the key and the lock. Crazy, she thought to herself, more than once,
but the concentric rings were beautiful. Looking through, you had
the impression you could see an infinite distance.

Edith took off her goggles and wiped back her hair with gloved
hands that smelled of metal. As far as the police knew, Sam had
left town. They found his truck off the side of the mountain, but he
had disappeared. They promised Edith they would make sure they
caught him if he tried to sneak back into town. They never asked
about Merritt. It was as if he had never been there. She had tried
the key a couple of times, but the broken door always opened on
the dark tunnel leading up the mountain, and never into the airlock.
So she decided to build a new one, forged of iron and hope.

It took her all day to haul the pieces of the new door down into
her cellar, and almost all night to set it up, under a rig of lights that
illuminated the dirt cellar and the remains of an old life. The lights

shed plenty of heat and Edith was drenched with sweat. The close cellar smelled of it, along with metal and warm dirt.

Finished, she stepped back and looked at her handiwork. The iron door with its concentric rings fitted in the opening, almost filling the cellar. Merritt said he spent his lifetime looking for Earth. It didn't seem fair that he should find her, just to lose her again less than a day later. The key brought him here once before. It would just have to do it again. Plus, if she were going to found the clan that built the arks, she couldn't do it alone.

She took a breath and fitted the key in the new lock. It turned without resistance. There was a pause, and then she heard a rising whine of power gathering behind the door. A chime signalled that the atmosphere stabilized, and the door swung inwards.

Saint James' Way

Jean Johnson

The merchant was grumbling again. Phinneas grunted and hoisted his bulky girth on to the low stone wall lining one side of the rutted road. Anne nibbled on her lips to hide her smile, watching him check the leather of his left sandal and mutter about wanting a horse to finish the trip home. The monk, Thomas, tutted and reminded his fellow pilgrim that the point of making the journey on foot was to show their Creator how pious and penitent each of them were.

The two nuns, Muriel and Lisette, were plodding along in their brown and cream robes at the same slow but steady pace as always. They passed the merchant and the monk with courteous nods, but otherwise said nothing. Their pilgrimage wasn't for penance, merely for piety, but they had taken a vow of silence for the trip, allowing themselves to speak only five times each day, save for prayers.

Three of the others were up ahead, two farmers and one of their wives, and two more followed the monk and the merchant, being a miller and a shoemaker. At the head of their little parade of piety strode Sir James Fitz William, hired guard and guide. At the rear strolled Anne, quiet, soft spoken and watchful of everything.

"Can't you do something about this?" Phinneas demanded as the shoemaker drew close, peeling back the separating layers of his sandal. That wasn't what he actually said, but the transceiver behind Anne's ear translated it as such. "I cannae, m'laird, 'til be nightfall. Ye knoun it since mornin," the shoemaker shot back.

Do not forget to remind Simon to load Middle Scottish next time, she repeated silently. Even with the transceiver's help, his accent was thick. *Low Middle Scottish,* she added as the shoemaker said something else – something not so easily translatable, but which she thought might possibly be crude in nature, mainly because one of the farmers overheard it, understood it, and laughed. Guffawed was more like it.

"Hurry up, everyone!" the horseless knight called out from his position at the forefront. "The well of San Vicente Marantes is just up ahead, and we're late in reaching it. We need to be over the river before nightfall."

"If my shoes weren't falling apart, I would hasten in a more seemly manner," Phinneas countered out loud.

"We were only in Compostela for a week. They will not have fixed the flooded bridge by then, and the raftsman does not ply his trade at night. The choice is either camping out in the woods on this side of the river, or in comfort at the hostel on the other side," James explained patiently. "I suggest you make what haste you can."

The merchant hauled himself off the wall and muttered under his breath, "Whatever you say, *Saint* James . . ."

Sir James just waved him off and kept walking. The younger man was as straight-backed and strong as he had been this morning, despite the weight of his chainmail hauberk, his plate shoulder and knee guards, and the sword and dagger slung around his waist. That didn't include the roll of his cloak and provision bag slung over his back, similar to everyone else. He was the only one armed with anything longer than a dagger, save for the two farmers, who carried the yew bows and capped quivers stuffed with arrows that marked them as Englishmen. Everyone else had a walking stick, some worn with years of use and some new, selected just for this trip.

The flapping of Phinneas' loose sandal kept distracting Anne, as did the older pilgrim's constant muttering about his discomforts. Anne reminded herself firmly of her mantra as a temporal anthropologist. *I am here to make accurate observations about pilgrims in the early fourteenth century. Not to perpetuate stereotypes.*

Even if I am looking at a fat, greedy, lazy merchant. Thank goodness tonight is my last night among these people.

The one she would actually miss was James. The knight wasn't particularly wealthy; as the third son of some English nobleman up in the Middle Countries, he hadn't many prospects, particularly in the lull between French and English territory wars when there was no chance of grabbing a plot of land or bringing home loot or a foreign noble for ransoming. She didn't even know if he had a horse, but then he wouldn't be using one while escorting pilgrims down to the Iberian peninsula and back; that wouldn't be suitably pious.

What he did have was a keen mind, a good wit, and a distinct flair for observing people. A natural social scientist at heart, though he called himself a philosopher-knight. When evening fell and they gathered around the fire, whether it was in a hostel or in a camp, he would regale them with stories of other pilgrimages he had led. The cost of hiring a boat to sail from the southern coast of England to the northern shores of Castile and the Compostela region, depending upon the journey, was considered a reasonable price to pay, given the continuing squabbling between England and France as to who owned what chunk of land.

So far, the troubles, which would eventually lead to the conflicts collectively known as the Hundred Years' War, were staying up in the French territories. There were other dangers to watch out for, though. Banditry was always a potential problem even on well-travelled roads such as this one. Feral livestock was another. One of James's previous trips had involved a wild bull. He had been quick to praise the Englishmen on that trip, who had dispatched the beast while he himself had done his best to dodge the bull's horns. Anne couldn't help but think of the curly-haired knight as a matador whenever she thought of that tale, though it was hard to picture him in a matador's "suit of lights" instead of his dusty, tabard-draped armour.

They reached the well, which stood between the road and the little cluster of stone and plaster huts that passed for a village – or maybe a hamlet at best, since there were no more than five houses. Children headed their way, ready to gawk at the return of the foreign pilgrims. Their parents, used to such travellers, kept their attention on their chores.

By the time Anne reached James, everyone else had already drunk from the bucket, emptying it. He lowered it and winched it up again, giving her time to pull her drinking cup from her makeshift pack. He filled her cup, then fetched out his own. Both were simple wooden vessels, the sort which wouldn't break if dropped on the ground, and which wouldn't cost much to replace if lost. He satisfied his own thirst, then eyed her with his green eyes and smiled.

"And how fare you, Mistress Anne? Was Compostela everything you imagined?"

"I fare well enough," she murmured. Field anthropologists weren't supposed to interact much with their subjects, but James insisted on being friendly. Particularly with her. She was supposedly portraying the part of a freeholder's widow, undertaking this pilgrimage to commemorate the anniversary of her husband's death.

"And?" he prompted her.

"And it was all I imagined. And more," honesty prompted her to add. Her previous assignment had been in Germany, and had involved a similar pilgrimage, but the land and the people of the Black Forest were very different from this corner of Europe. That trip also hadn't had a Sir James in it.

He leaned in a little closer and murmured, "*I* think you'll be utterly bored when you return home. Presuming you want to return home. You take to this life on the road with great ease. You're no milksop maiden. Nor, I think, would you enjoy being under your brother-in-law's thumb."

"What makes you think that?" Anne asked, bemused by his claim.

"You told Sister Muriel you couldn't donate any land to the Church in your late husband's name, since his brother inherited everything but for a bit of coin and your personal things. And that it was a relief to be away from his family for so long, despite the hardships and dangers of taking a pilgrimage," he said.

"Your ears are sharp, to have picked up so much," she countered without directly agreeing with him.

"Anything involving an angel would hold my attention. Doubly so, when that angel is you," he murmured, leaning in close enough that she could feel his breath against her cheek and ear. Unlike some of the others, he took care daily to freshen his breath, usually with a bit of some herb plucked along the road. Today, it was mint. Yesterday, it had been parsley.

He had also picked up the habit of bathing relatively frequently. Clad in his armour, he did smell of metal, rust, oil, dirt and sweat, but she had seen him carefully washing himself on more than one occasion. He had also brought a second set of clothes, fresh hosen and thigh-length cote-hardie as clean as could be kept while travelling, and a fine, embroidered tabard. James had donned them just before reaching the cathedral, and had taken care to wipe down his armour with an oiled rag before their arrival so that it would gleam. Her own gown, a simple linen cote-hardie which barely touched the ground, suitable for her station, was rather dusty by comparison.

"I am no angel, Sir Knight, nor a creature to be venerated and adored," she demurred. Protocol demanded she turn down any such offers. Inside, however, she felt very flattered by his attentions. She kept her gaze on the nuns, who along with the others were taking the opportunity to disappear into the bushes across the road from the well, attending to the needs of nature. "You should not say such things on a pilgrimage."

"We travel on pilgrimage to know and honour the miracles of the Creator. It is well known that God made man in His image, and then made woman to be the companion of man," James reminded her.

Anne started to roll her eyes. She had been exposed to too much equality between the genders after becoming a temporal anthropologist to put up with such chauvinism. At least not in her personal life.

"And, as any artisan will tell you," the curly-haired knight continued smoothly, "the first attempt in crafting something is always the worst, while the second is always the better. If I am a good man – and I think I am – why then you as a woman must surely be better. Every evidence of my eyes, ears and mind support this idea . . . so why should I not venerate and adore you? To do otherwise would be a sin of denial against the sheer craftsmanship of God."

She blushed. The weeks spent in his company had proven him a reasonably pious man; she knew he believed what he was saying. She also knew it was the courtship style of the day, the courtly manners and florid flirting which had tamed and tempered the brutal force of the warrior caste in medieval Europe. "If you seek to place me upon a pedestal, you must know I am not a lady of noble birth."

"You are a lady in all the ways that matter: courteous, kind and competent. You have an innate nobility that no measure of birth-rank can match." Shifting so that he could look into her eyes, James touched her hand. "I chose this life because I wanted to study all manner of ranks and births, of educations and crafts. I have seen men and women of the highest birth behave with the poorest of concern for their fellow beings, and the lowliest of ranks sharing what little they have with the compassion of the saints they venerate.

"I have trod this road with women of all ages and persuasions, and no one I have found has felt so much like a . . . like a kindred spirit as you. You understand people. Like I do," he finished, cupping her fingers beneath his. His skin was calloused from his many daily practices with his blade at dawn and dusk whenever they camped, but his touch was gentle. "I care not that you come with no lands and no name of note – I am a third-born son, myself; my portion is small at best – but I care about *you*.

"When you return to your home, Mistress Anne . . . or what is left of it . . . I would ask leave to court you. I doubt I am liable to find another woman quite like you."

Involuntarily, the corner of her mouth quirked up. James smiled back.

"I amuse you? Good. A man *should* be amusing and genial," he asserted smugly.

She laughed. "You are not likely to find another woman quite like me, no." Beyond his green eyes and blond curls, she saw the merchant, Phinneas, grunting and groaning his way into the bushes. Her smile faded. "Ugh. He's making those noises again, the ones he makes whenever he's about to spend far too much time in the bushes."

"What, the merchant? Yes, I can hear it, too. I fear between his crumbling sandal and his rumbling gut, he'll keep us from reaching the raftsman before sunset." Lifting his gaze from her face, he looked off to the west. "Fill your stomach and your waterskin while you can. Hot weather makes for thirsty pilgrimages, but rain and mud are far more miserable to endure. At least the weather looks like it'll hold. For now."

Nodding, aware he had been escorting pilgrimages for at least five years, Anne let him haul up another bucketful while she drained the dregs of her waterskin into her wooden cup. She didn't say it, but she did think the thoughts uppermost in both her heart and her mind. *I'd love to accept, Sir James. You're remarkably enlightened for your day and age, and I think I'd enjoy being courted by you, wherever it might or might not lead ... but I come from the distant future, one which does not involve you.*

A pity, but for the sake of temporal continuity ... I have to leave you.

Don't look back ... don't look back ...

"Anne?"

She almost jumped out of her skin. Whirling, she faced the shadowed silhouette of her confronter. The campfire the others had built was just visible through the trees behind him. "Oh! James ... uh ..."

He moved with remarkable quietness. It wasn't until he was close enough to touch that she realized he wasn't wearing his armour. He must have taken it off while she had been gathering wood for the fire.

"Where are you going?"

"To ... to the river, of course. It's not that far," she managed as casually as she could, half turning towards it.

"Why?" James asked, moving to intercept her. "And why take your bedroll?"

"Well ... it's a warm night, so I thought I'd wash it. And myself. Away from prying eyes. I don't like the way Phinneas looks at me sometimes," she improvised. "Like I'm a widow with a fortune for him to marry."

"Somehow, I don't believe you. My instincts, which I have honed by watching people time and again ... say that you're running away from us," James stated. He cupped her shoulders, his thumbs gently rubbing her through the linen of her summer-weight dress. "Did I scare you off with my stated intentions? You shouldn't be frightened by me. I meant no harm. I just ... thought we would well suit each other. I care for you. And I really don't think it is wise for a woman to try travelling on her own. There are all manner of feral beasts out there. Some of them run on two legs instead of four, you know."

Anne could have protested that she would be fine. No anthropologist was allowed into the field without completing several courses in basic and advanced self-defence, including courses in the targeted time frame's weapon styles. *But he wouldn't believe me, and I don't have the time to convince him. Not without raising awkward questions.*

I'm supposed to leave the group by oh-one-hundred hours tonight, and it's just half-past twenty-one. How do I distract him so I can get far enough away that I can be picked up and returned to the future without anyone noticing?

He solved her dilemma for her. Sort of. "All right, so it's been a hot and dusty day. A dip in the river does sound good. I'll walk you down there. The others should be safe enough, since they have their numbers, the fire and our good yeomen-farmers to keep watch through the first and second quarters of the night. But I'll not risk you to a wild beast, or a bandit, or even a slip and a fall which might injure your head, or a cramp which might cause you to drown."

"James, it really wouldn't be appropriate –"

One of his hands lifted from her shoulder, his finger finding and sealing her lips. "Shh. I insist. Surely the night is far too dark for me to see anything . . . inappropriate."

That wasn't entirely true; the moon was waxing towards full. Though its light did shine down in faint silver patches here and there, the forest canopy hid most of its light. Down by the river, which at this part ran north–south, it would shine fully upon the water, and on anything nearby.

"Come." Sliding his other hand down her arm, he laced his calloused fingers with hers and gently tugged her through the trees. The ground sloped gradually down as they made their way eastwards, until the thickness of the underbrush forced them to detour to the south. A small break in the bushes a modest distance upriver provided access to the water. It was also far enough away that the light and the noise of the pilgrims' campfire could no longer be discerned.

This is my last night with him, Anne thought, catching sight of his face in the pale silver moonlight. *And my last and only chance to be alone with him. I'm not being picked up until oh-one-hundred hours. We have time . . . and maybe I can exhaust him into sleeping deeply.*

It wasn't exactly in the rulebook, but neither was it expressly forbidden on this trip. Anne had heard other field anthropologists being given lectures against such things for specific missions, but she hadn't been lectured. Shrugging out of the rope holding her bedroll together, she untied it with the practice gained from weeks of travel and spread it out over the ground.

James moved closer. "Aren't you going to wash that?"

"I've changed my mind. Besides," she murmured back, strolling close enough to touch him, to brush her body against his own, "shouldn't I get it dirty first, before I scrub?"

She could see his frown, thanks to a small shaft of moonlight. James stepped back. "I find I do not quite trust this reversal, Anne. Why were you so coy before, yet so forward now?"

All the instincts of a natural anthropologist, or maybe a psychologist or sociologist ... Sighing, she gave him as much of the truth as he could handle. "I'm leaving the group. A friend will be meeting me shortly, and we'll be on our way elsewhere. I was told that once I reached the river after our visit to the Cathedral, I should diverge and head upriver – and I will be *fine*," she added as his frown of distrust deepened into a worried look. "This isn't the first time I have travelled, nor the first time I have struck out on my own, even for such a short distance as this trip will be.

"*You* need to stay with the others," she reminded him. "They'll need your protection, since it's still a long way back."

"And you're offering yourself to me? What has prompted it?" James asked her.

Anne shrugged. "I decided I'd rather not leave with any regrets. I like you, I enjoy your company, and I desire you. If we weren't destined to part company tonight, I would honestly consider your offer of courtship far more seriously than circumstances allow."

He closed the distance between them, slipping his arm around her waist. "Well. If we do enjoy each other's company, and this ... dalliance ... proves fruitful?"

She smiled wryly. "After so many years of barren marriage, I doubt it will."

Particularly given the birth-control methods all field agents use... There were rumours of certain agents being sent into the past to "acquire" genetic material, but not having been approached herself, Anne wasn't sure if those whispers were true, or just lascivious gossip.

"I am not your late husband." Pulling her close, he nudged her with his loins. In specific, with the lump of his manhood. "You may find me to be the better man."

His line almost made her laugh, except she sensed he meant it in several ways, not just the most obvious one. Softening her reaction into a smile, Anne lifted her hands to his hair. Fulfilling the longing she had suppressed throughout the trip, she buried her fingers in his springy blond curls, enjoying their slightly coarse texture.

He complied with her guiding touch, tilting his mouth into the perfect angle for meeting hers. Then pulled back, apparently startled by the touch of her tongue on his lips. Anne pursued his mouth, rising up on her toes and bringing his head back down to hers. He tasted more like the roasted turnips and rabbit they had eaten than like the mint of earlier, but mostly he tasted like a man. Delicious.

It took only a few moments before he returned her caresses. His own tongue grew more bold, as did the hands on her back, one skimming up to cradle the back of her head, the other sliding down to cup the curves of her bottom. Anne caressed his shoulders, then shifted her hands to the front of his cote-hardie. He had changed back into his travelling clothes this morning, to save his good outfit for the visits to the Cathedral, but even his second-best tunic was made of a finer weave of linen than her own. Unfastening the buttons as they kissed, she reached his belt and fumbled with the knotted leather.

Stepping back, breaking their kiss, James unfastened his belt himself, along with the rest of his cote-hardie. Anne took the opportunity to remove her own girdle and work on her buttons. Their garments fell to the ground, which was sparsely covered in tufts of grass and the felted wool of her bedroll. Moonlight obscured some of the details of his body and highlighted others. She could see scars from old wounds, and the ripple of muscles bunching and flexing when he stooped to remove his shoes.

She bent over in turn, unlacing her sandals and peeling down her hosen, only to blush when she heard him speak.

"God bless widows who know what they want," he murmured. "God and all the saints. I've never been interested in a shy, retiring maiden who knows nothing of the ways of men and women."

"I thought my behaviour had been rather circumspect and demure," Anne quipped as she straightened. She pulled the pins and ribbons out of her hair, releasing it so that he could play with it if he wanted.

"Circumspect, maybe, but your experience of the world shows through in all the little things you do." Moving back to her, he wrapped his arms around her, bringing their bodies close together. "I like it."

Anne kissed him again. The evening had cooled enough that neither was damp from sweat, allowing their bodies to rub gently together. She enjoyed the crisp-textured hair of his chest brushing against her breasts, the soft press and nibble of his lips. The jut of his arousal rubbing against her belly. Her fingers skimmed through those chest curls, lightly tugging and teasing until he captured her hands and pressed them flat. She could feel the rhythm of his heart and knew it matched her own, faster than it should be, and stronger.

She couldn't remember the last time she had made love with anyone. At least a year ago. Long enough for each touch, each caress to feel new. Long enough to make her wish for a softer bed than a scratchy wool blanket laid on a somewhat lumpy stretch of ground. The shift of his lips from her mouth down to her breasts distracted her, though. He laved and worshipped them, wringing gasps and whimpers from her as he played with their sensitive tips.

One of his hands caressed her clenching belly, then slipped down between her thighs. Anne gasped and tossed her head back, thumping it against the ground, but the pain was brief and mild; the pleasure of his seeking fingers was too good to resist. Covering his hand with her own, she showed him exactly where she liked to be touched and how firmly he should rub.

James proved a willing student. Between her breasts and her loins, he sculpted her into a squirming, gasping, shuddering thing of bliss with his mouth and his hand. Drifting down from her climax, Anne sighed. "Oh, James . . . I wish I could take you with me . . ."

"If I had my way," he murmured, kissing a path back up to her lips, "you'd never leave me."

Lifting her knees, she made room for him. Welcomed him with her lips and her palms and her thighs. He pressed himself home with a sigh of her name and a slow flex of his hips. It felt better than she remembered, much better. Each inward stroke had a near-perfect angle to stimulate everything she liked best about this part of lovemaking. It didn't take him long to have her gasping and shuddering again, whispering his name until he, too, climaxed and slumped, breathing heavily himself.

He finally rolled off her, but not to abandon her. Instead, James pulled her close, cuddling with her. Sweat made their skin stick awkwardly in places, though the cool air wafting up from the river did its part to help dry them again. But the sweat and the breeze and the lumpy ground under the blanket couldn't distract her from the warmth of his embrace.

Tired from a long day of walking and a delicious round of lovemaking, Anne dozed for a little bit. She was sure James did, too. When she finally decided to move, inhaling slowly and deeply to wake up a little more, she felt his arm tighten around her shoulders.

"Ready for more?" he murmured, proving he wasn't asleep.

Her internal transceiver warned her it was getting close to midnight. *But I still have time. And this feels too good to skip a second chance.* Smiling, she pressed a kiss to his collarbone. "Nothing would please me more. Since you're a scholar at heart, the same as myself . . . let me show you some of the things I've learned."

His murmured consent was the last coherent thing he said. It didn't take much to reduce him to gasps and half-bitten oaths, just the application of her tongue, teeth, and lips from his throat to his groin. The lattermost goal made him choke on her name and bow his back, fingers tangling in her hair. From the surprise in his voice, she guessed he had never experienced this before, and applied herself with more enthusiasm and care, wanting to make it as enjoyable for him as possible.

Her attentions invigorated him so much, she found herself flipped on to her back, her head pointed down the modest slope of the bank and her legs hoisted high. Hands clenching in the blanket and the sparse tufts of grass, Anne accepted his enthusiasm for the compliment it was, and for the delights of the inventive position. He growled as he climaxed, trembling and sweating all over again. Shifting a hand to touch her folds, he rubbed as she had shown him, and chuckled when she, too, trembled in bliss. Breathing heavily, James lowered her hips back to the ground, then her legs, before slumping once more at her side.

"I think . . . I know . . . how your husband died," he muttered between breaths.

"Oh?" she managed, wary of his sudden choice in topic.

"Very, *very* happily."

Anne laughed. Not because it was the truth – far from it – but because his compliment tickled her. She wanted to tell him the truth about her so-called marriage, but between her orders and this latest bout of passion, she kept her mouth shut. Content, she snuggled against him, reminding herself not to doze for long. She still had to leave by oh-one-hundred hours so that she could be returned to the future. Her weeks of observations needed to be recorded and analysed. Including this interlude, however much she wanted to keep these moments by the moonlit river to herself.

Just a little bit of a nap ... then I really will leave him ... I will ...

The crack of a twig woke both of them. James scrambled for his belt, grabbing and drawing his sword even as he stood. Anne rolled away from him and rose in a defensive crouch of her own, eyes straining to see through the night-shadowed trees.

"Who goes there?" James demanded.

"A friend. I mean you no harm."

Anne relaxed slightly, recognizing Simon's voice. Then blushed hotly, mindful of two things: her naked state, and the hour. A mental check of her sub-dermal transceiver showed the hour was half past one. She was late. That was a potential sin in the temporal handbook, a black mark on her record. But her superior didn't sound upset.

"I do not recognize you," her lover stated, blade still bared and held between them and the source of that shadowed voice. "Name yourself!"

"James ... it's all right. It's my friend. The one I told you I was going to meet?" Touching his elbow, she gently urged him to lower his weapon. Once he did, she made the introductions. "Sir James, this is Simon, a freeholder and long-time friend of my family. Simon, Sir James, the escort hired by my fellow pilgrims.

"As you can see, I'll be fine from here on. You can rejoin the others with a clear conscience as to my safety," Anne told James.

"Did I mean nothing to you?" he hissed.

"You meant a lot. But I must go my way for now, and you must go yours. Return to the others. If I can, I'll come find you in England later."

"Actually ... he cannot return to the others," Simon stated.

The blade came back up, silver-blue moonlight glinting off the beaten metal. "Why not?"

"Simon?" Anne strained to see her superior's face. He moved closer, ignoring the threat implied in James's blade. She caught a glimpse of his expression, the pinch of worry between his dark brows. "Am I in trouble for being late, and not alone?"

"No more so than Rachael was," Simon murmured.

Comprehension dawned, relieving Anne of much of her worry. She hadn't black-marked herself in the rulebook by making love with the man at her side.

"You both speak in riddles. Make yourselves clear," James demanded.

"Peace, brother . . . and put your hosen on. Both of you. We have time for you to dress before we must go."

"Anne?"

"I trust Simon with my life, James. You can, too. More than you yet know." Stooping, Anne rummaged through the clothing scattered on the ground, separating out which garment belonged to whom by touch, since James's clothes were of a higher quality than her own.

He hesitated only a moment before accepting his hosen, undershirt and cote-hardie. Setting down his sword, he dressed as quickly as she did, shaking out his boots and strapping on his belt. After sheathing the blade at his hip, he waited while she fastened the last of the buttons on her over-gown, then faced the shadowed silhouette of their visitor.

"We are dressed, as requested. Now, tell me what you mean. Why should I not return to the others?"

"If you had been with them, instead of having followed Anne here, you would have suffered the same fate they just did. A short while ago, a group of Castilian bandits came upon the pilgrims' camp, ambushed the farmer on watch, and slaughtered the rest in their sleep. Even as we speak, their bodies and belongings are being looted."

Anne heard James half-draw his sword and quickly put her hand on his wrist. "We are not what you think. Neither of us is in league with the robbers."

"How do I know that?" James hissed. "You urged me to go back there, then lured me into staying here! How do I know you didn't decide they would be more vulnerable and thus easier to kill without my protection?"

"Because I didn't tell her what the fate of the pilgrims would be. Nor could I interfere to save their lives, even indirectly, without it causing irreparable harm to the future. Which, if you continued to live in this time frame, your own presence would also do."

James struggled to draw his sword. Anne forced it back into its sheath by pinching one of the nerves in his wrist; from his startled hiss, she guessed he wasn't expecting so much strength from her, nor the sudden pain shooting up his arm. "James, Simon and I are scholars of the past. Literally, we come from the far-distant future. We, and others like us, travel through time by a special means. We immerse ourselves in a time period, in a culture, in a situation, and observe.

"Just like you do," she stressed. "You chose to travel as a pilgrimage escort so that you could be a student of humanity, to observe people from all stations of life. We do that, too. But because we do it in the past, which cannot be changed overtly . . . sometimes we cannot stop what happens, because it is vital that it should happen."

"From the future . . . you're not actually from northern England, are you?" James accused. "Just how much of what you have told me has been a lie?"

"My place of origin, my inheritance, my brother-in-law . . ."

"Your late husband?" he demanded. "Was even that a lie?"

"Only in part," Anne confessed. "I was married, and my husband did die. It was in May, in the city of Abbeville in France, not at home in northern England as I claimed. And it was in the Year of Our Lord 1940, in an era when what you know of as the many states of the German kingdom was at war with France. I was an anthropology student – someone who studies societies and cultures and the ways how people live. My husband was also a scholar; he was giving a lecture on mathematics at a school in northern France when there was an unexpected, rapid advance of the German army. He died in the attack. I saw him cut down, and ran. I probably would have perished, too, if I hadn't seen an exchange student sneaking for the basement of the university building, and followed her instead.

"I wanted to warn her to get out of there, to follow me in making a run for safety. But instead of being trapped and killed as was happening to the others elsewhere . . . she told me she was going to rescue me. She did it by transporting me even further into the future, offering me sanctuary and a new way of life." Anne hesitated, then continued. "I honestly did not know what fate would befall the others tonight. All I knew was that I had to leave the rest by the middle of the night, so that I could be picked up and returned to the future, where my observations could be reported for posterity. I swear, I did not know."

"Most field agents aren't told," Simon confirmed. "Compassion is wonderful, but if it interferes with the path of history, it can cause complications."

"I don't understand," James murmured. "I think I can believe Anne when she says she didn't know, but . . . how could not saving their lives be the right thing to do?"

"If your grandfather was the sort to beat his serfs and tax them into starvation, if his actions had blackened your family name from long before you were born, would you want to go back in time to kill him when he was young, to stop him from harming so many people over all those years?" Simon countered. "I know I would . . . but if you went back in time and killed him before he had sired your father . . . you would no longer exist, because your father would not have existed."

"For another example," Anne offered, "if he was a good man, one who had intended to marry one woman, who died by, oh, falling off a cliff, and instead married another after her death, a woman who became your grandmother . . . if you went back in time to save the first maiden's life . . . wouldn't your grandfather marry *her* instead? Wouldn't they have different children? Perhaps a daughter instead of a son that year . . . meaning yet again that *you* would not have been born?"

"Time is tricky. We are sent back to observe and learn, not to interfere," Simon stated. "Anne has saved your life, and it is not our policy to kill those whose lives are accidentally saved . . . but your life now comes at a cost. You cannot return to your family without irrevocably altering the future . . . or risking circumstances arranging themselves so that you are slaughtered in some other way, and soon. You can, of course, leave us and take your chances . . . but the future is changeable only in tiny degrees, while death versus life is a major change. I do not know the exact pathway to your death, but it is out there waiting for you, and it will come very soon. The pressure of history will ensure it."

"So ... what am I to do? I will *not* end my life willingly; such things are a sin," James said. "But even I know that the world has changed greatly over the last thousand years. If I am to go a thousand years into the future, how much more will it have changed? How would I live? Unless you have need for a guard on yet more pilgrimages ..."

Anne smiled and tucked her hands around his elbow. "I think I know why Simon is so willing to take you with us ... and why Rachael was so willing to save me from the Germans, despite what fate might have otherwise decreed. You are as much an anthropologist at heart as I am, James. A true student of humanity. The rest is just catching up on a thousand years of history and all the many advances people have made in the ways that they live."

"You might not ever come back to this moment in time, of course, but some of our best field agents have come from centuries past," Simon added. "You know far better than we how to behave and blend in ... though as you have seen, some of our anthropologists are more adept at blending than others, even outside their natural time frame."

James considered their offer. Anne could sense him thinking, in the tensing and relaxing of his muscles, in the quiet, deep way he breathed. After a long, quiet moment, he turned to her.

"*If* I come with you ... were your words from earlier true? Would you still be interested in my ... in my courting you?"

"As you yourself said, we have much in common ... and I do care for you, James," Anne admitted. "I would be honoured to know you better."

"I *will* go to the future," he decided. "I am indeed a scholar at heart, and I find that the part of me that longed to explore distant lands is now equally curious about distant times."

"Good. We should be going – you won't need the bedroll, or anything else," Simon added as James started to bend down. "In the morning, travellers will stumble across the campsite, and your disappearances blamed on the bandits, along with the others' deaths. But by then, we'll be 1,317 years into the future ... and, once there, I think I can safely predict your lives will be reasonably long and relatively happy."

"Good. You'll answer to me if things turn out otherwise," James warned him.

Simon chuckled, and Anne blushed. Holding on to her lover, she braced both of them for the trip to the future.

The Troll Bridge

Patti O'Shea

Lia glanced around the control room. It looked so ordinary, so boring – industrial grey carpeting, neutral walls, even the windows on the far side of the room were normal. She expected something more at a cutting-edge facility like the particle accelerator. The only things that separated this place from a regular office were the curved desks with two tiers of flat-screen computer monitors lined up side by side.

Even the scientists seemed mundane, dressed in slacks with Oxford or polo shirts. Couldn't there at least be one guy running around in a white lab coat with his hair going twenty different directions like Albert Einstein?

Everyone around her was busy doing something, but she had no idea what. She'd grown accustomed to interviewing engineers as part of her job in corporate communications for Park International, but this was her first time dealing with physicists. She hoped it was her last.

The man she was supposed to talk to had listened to about three questions and answered none before he'd dumped her off on an intern. The kid knew a lot about the particle accelerator and was nervously rambling, which might have been good for her article in the monthly employee magazine except that she needed to quote someone with credentials.

It was too bad. This boy, Derrick, was going to be an asset someday. Earlier, he'd seen her blank look and had immediately started speaking in layman's terms. That was worth its weight in gold.

Today's experiment was supposed to rev the particles up to their highest rate of speed so far and she'd been sent to cover it. This was a Big Deal and the order had come from the top of the food chain, but Doctor I'm-Too-Important-To-Talk-To-You didn't care who had issued the assignment.

To her surprise, she'd found what little she'd understood about particle physics interesting, and since the kid wouldn't ridicule her, she decided to ask a question that had intrigued her since she'd researched the atom smasher.

"Derrick," Lia interjected when he paused, "I read something about the particle accelerator maybe creating black holes. Is this any kind of real hazard?"

"No, ma'am." He shrugged self-consciously. "The possibility is so minute, it's nearly inconceivable. If any do happen to actualize, they'll wink out in a fraction of a second. They're too small and unstable to maintain their existence long."

That was a relief. Although she'd guessed the odds of making a black hole that could swallow the Earth were small, it was still nice to hear it from someone who knew physics – even if he was still in college.

Derrick didn't stop, though. "It's also unlikely that we'll create any wormholes either, and, if we did, they'd be so small that only subatomic particles would be transported."

Lia hadn't read anything on that. "Wormholes?"

"Wormholes are tubes that traverse space, time, or both and if we find one and could travel through—"

"I've seen *Star Trek*, I know what wormholes are, but I didn't realize we could *make* them," she told him ruefully. OK, so it was slightly embarrassing to use a television show as reference material, but the reading she'd done on particle physics had turned her brain to gelatin.

He pushed his glasses back on the bridge of his nose. "We can't. That's what I was explaining. The idea that we might produce a wormhole is every bit as remote as the black hole theory, although it is mathematically possible."

"That's kind of disappointing," she murmured.

Derrick smiled for the first time. "Tell me about it, but it was proven that the Einstein-Rosen Bridge would shut as soon as it formed, closing—"

He stopped short when the physicist who'd ditched her called his name. The experiment was about to begin and Derrick's help was needed, leaving Lia to her own devices. She glanced over a few shoulders, but no one paid attention to her, and since they all looked so intent, she didn't ask questions. Instead, she leaned against a wall at the back of the control room and hoped something interesting would happen that she could write about.

It didn't. Had she made a note on how long this was supposed to last? Flipping through her steno pad, she checked, but before she found the information, the tension in the room shot high. She couldn't understand what they were saying in their geek-speak, but anything that ended the boredom had to be a good thing.

"It broke containment," one of the scientists called.

Or maybe it wasn't a good thing.

A man she didn't recognize approached her. "Out," he ordered and pointed to the exit.

"But—"

"Out or I'll escort you out."

When she hesitated, he took her by the arm and put her in the hall. Lia eyed the closed door to the control room and rubbed her biceps where he'd gripped her. She briefly considered going back in, just on general principle, but Godzilla had bruised her and she wasn't some hotshot investigative reporter. She wrote feel-good pieces for the company magazine and that was it. Not worth it.

Lia frowned at the treatment, but realized this had nothing to do with her, at least not specifically. Standing in the hall, though, reminded her of all the other times she'd been on the outside looking in. Her thoughts, her opinions, her way of viewing life didn't seem to match anyone else's and it made her feel alone. She didn't understand the prejudices, the arguments that antagonized people, and she'd learned not to ask questions to try to make it clearer. Others took it as a challenge and tended to get defensive.

Things hadn't been quite so bad while her parents were alive, but even they hadn't understood her. Their lives had been dull and they hadn't seen anything wrong with routine. Her daydreaming had puzzled them. How could she simply sit and stare into space? Why didn't she clean her room or take out the trash? But there had to be more than working at a nine-to-five job every weekday, doing yard work on Saturdays and golfing on Sunday.

Life was supposed to be about pursuing dreams, wasn't it? About having adventures? Lia grimaced. Yeah, she was one to talk. She'd taken the safe road of corporate communications rather than risk failure.

She didn't want to think about this, not now. Closing her notebook, she slid it in the side of her purse and shoved her pen in the metal spiral. Maybe they had a vending machine around here and she could get some crackers or something. The physicists had apparently been too excited to eat, but she was hungry.

The halls were deserted and there was no one to ask where to find a break room. She kept walking, turning down random corridors. How lost could she get before she ran into someone who could point her in the right direction?

After about ten minutes, she had to concede that she wasn't going to get a badge in orienteering or find help. Lia stopped and tried to mentally retrace her route, but she didn't remember much beyond the last couple of turns.

Before she could decide whether to go back or continue forwards, she felt a change in the air behind her. At last, someone who could give her directions. With a smile, she pivoted, but sobered immediately.

There was a giant shimmery circle closing ground on her. *What the hell was that?* She backed up.

The vortex followed and she ran. She dropped her purse, but couldn't take time to worry about it now, not when she could sense the thing gaining on her.

Lia didn't get far before it engulfed her. She felt as if she were tumbling, careening madly in mid-air, but hitting nothing. Clutching her arms around her waist, she closed her eyes, trying to stave off the growing nausea.

Her stop was abrupt and pain exploded as her skull connected with a hard surface beneath her. She took a deep, shuddery breath and, rubbing the back of her head, tried to clear her vision. It took a few minutes before Lia realized she wasn't staring at the ceiling, but at the sky. That shook her enough that she forced herself to sit up. She was outdoors and, judging from what she saw, it was early evening. This wasn't right. Slowly, she pushed herself to her feet and swayed before she caught her balance.

Unless she was mistaken – entirely possible – she was standing on top of an enormous step pyramid in the middle of a city that looked like nothing on Earth. At least nothing she'd ever seen on Earth . . . in her time.

Wormhole. Lia shivered before she scoffed at herself. Yeah, right, Derrick the intern had said the odds against it were astronomical and that even if a wormhole opened, it would be too small for anything larger than an atom to pass through. Besides she'd need, like, a spaceship or something, otherwise she'd be dead, right?

Something had happened, that was obvious. The most likely scenario was that she was unconscious and hallucinating – she had hit her head. Yeah, that was it. There was a slab of marble behind her that bore a resemblance to an altar, and Lia went over to it and sat down. She'd just wait right here until the doctors revived her.

Troll Maglaya stood at attention with his Special Operations team in the Colonel's office and waited for the man to finish giving orders to his aide. This was Troll's third tour of duty on Jarved Nine in the past seven years, but he couldn't quell the spurt of anxiety that he felt whenever he had to face 'The Big Chill': Colonel Sullivan was a badass from the word go and no one wanted to be on his shit list.

The door closed with a snick that had Troll stiffening. "At ease," the Colonel said as he took a seat behind his desk.

For a long moment the room was absolutely silent. "We've suspected for a few weeks that the coalition has an agent on J. Nine," Sullivan said finally, voice low. "Last night the MPs found her atop the pyramid in the centre of the Old City."

That surprised Troll, but he remained expressionless. The coalition had been trying for years to acquire lamordite to facilitate their space travel beyond Earth's solar system, but he hadn't realized they'd succeeded.

"Captain Montgomery, you and your team will search outside the city for the spaceship and for any other coalition agents who might be present."

"Yes, sir," Marsh Montgomery said.

"I'm pulling Sergeant Maglaya for another mission – that means you'll be short-handed – but you have permission to tap any MPs you want to join your search."

Troll went rigid, and since he stood shoulder to shoulder with Marsh and the team's executive officer, Flare Cantore, he felt them both tense as well. Why was the Big Chill singling him out?

Sullivan kept talking. "Major Brody is waiting in the briefing room – he'll fill you in. Dismissed. Sergeant Maglaya, you'll stay here."

The colonel waited until the other men had left the room and the door was shut behind them before he continued. "Sergeant, I have a special task for you. As I said, we found a woman who doesn't belong here and she's not telling us anything – at least nothing that makes sense."

Sullivan frowned fiercely and Troll watched him take a few deep breaths before he said, "Your job is to guard her."

"Sir, why not lock her up?"

"Because we don't know what the coalition is after and we need that information. If she's loose, chances are she'll try to complete her mission. That's where you come in. You're going to be glued to her side. I don't want her using the bathroom without you standing guard at the door. Understood?"

"Yes, sir." Troll hesitated, then decided to risk it. "Permission to speak freely, Colonel?"

"Go ahead."

"Why me, sir? Why not assign this job to one of the MPs and let me work with my team?"

Sullivan sighed. "Your reputation with women is well known, Sergeant, and it's been decided that you should put that skill to use. If necessary, you're to romance her to get the information we need about why she's here and what the coalition wants."

It was Troll's turn to scowl and he didn't give a rip what the Colonel thought about the display. He wasn't the randy kid who'd used his appearance to bag and bed every willing woman he could find – not any more – and he resented like hell that Sullivan was asking him to whore himself.

Before he could find a way to verbally share his displeasure without pissing off the Big Chill, the man shook his head. "I know, Maglaya, I don't like it either, but your orders came from above me and my opinion was overruled."

The Colonel had fought against this? "Thank you, sir."

Sullivan ran a hand over his chin. "She claims her name is Ophelia Stanton and that she either time travelled or has a head injury."

"Time travel, Colonel? The head injury is more likely."

That earned him a *no-shit* stare. "We transported her to the infirmary and the docs checked her thoroughly, but found nothing wrong. This is obviously some kind of ploy. She might try to pull a con on you, too."

"It won't happen, sir." Troll might not be a player any longer, but he'd spent a lot of years in the arena before he'd watched his teammates find love. Marsh had gone first, falling for Kendall during the team's initial tour on J. Nine, and one by one all his buddies had gotten married. As he'd observed them, Troll had realized he wanted what they had. He'd grown tired of the emptiness that seemed to deepen with each superficial relationship and he wasn't going back there. Not even to protect the interests of the Western Alliance.

The Colonel's briefing was short – he didn't have a lot of information – then Troll was dismissed and sent to take over guard duty. Stanton remained at the infirmary and, as he neared, he could see the MPs through the windows. They stood, but between them was a woman who was seated. Had to be her.

Troll was nearly to the door when he stopped short and drew a sharp breath. No way. He stared. No way in hell.

She had medium-brown, shoulder-length hair, an oval face, high cheekbones and full lips. He couldn't see the shade of her eyes, but he had a bad feeling they were hazel. Almost reluctantly, he reached for his wallet.

Fourteen years ago, right before he'd left for basic training, his grandmother had given him a drawing she'd done in coloured pencil. The page had already been yellowed and was more than three decades old back then, but she'd insisted he take it and made him promise to keep it with him at all times.

He pulled it out, put the wallet back in his pocket, and carefully unfolded the paper. It had been years since he'd glanced at it – he had to be remembering it wrong. Had to be. But as he looked between the prisoner and the picture, Troll discovered his memory was good. The woman Gram had drawn in 2002 was sitting in front of him, and she didn't look much older than she did in the drawing – in a sketch forty-eight years ago.

Lia eyed the closed door of the exam room and, with a grimace, lay back. She wasn't going anywhere, not with two military policemen in the hall to make sure she stayed where they'd put her. Lacing her fingers behind her head, she brought her knees up to rest her feet flat on the padded table and stared at the textured panels of the ceiling. As far as prisons went, the infirmary probably wasn't that bad, but it was impossible to get comfortable on such a short surface.

Maybe it was deliberate. Wasn't sleep deprivation an interrogation tactic? She wouldn't put it past the colonel from hell. He'd badgered her unmercifully, accused her of being a spy, and had derided her when she'd tried to offer explanations for her presence. Then there was his reaction when she asked to be taken to the wormhole that would return her to Earth 2010. She'd thought the man was going to freeze her with his death stare and *that* gaze had been friendly compared to the way he'd looked at her when she'd asked about a particle accelerator.

She tried to ignore the sick feeling that blossomed in the pit of her stomach. Somewhere during her browbeating, Lia had accepted the illogical. The unbelievable. She didn't have a head injury – she'd time travelled for real, and judging by the colonel''s response to her questions, she was going to be stuck here. For ever. Her gulp was audible.

The sureness that she was in the future hadn't come to her in some cataclysmic epiphany, but had crept in slowly. There were too many anomalies for it to be some fantasy of hers. Lia didn't know anything about the military beyond what she'd seen on television or in the movies, but what she'd observed here was a chain of command that seemed accurate and army-speak that was foreign to her.

That had held true at the clinic, too. She didn't know much about medicine and yet she'd listened to jargon-filled conversations between the doctors and nurses and watched them use some equipment that she'd never seen before.

Everywhere she looked, everywhere they'd taken her, things were familiar yet strange, but she could see an evolution of sorts. She'd always had a wild imagination, but it wasn't this good. If this were really an illusion, there'd be things that didn't make sense, but that wasn't the case. Everything fitted. Everything.

Besides, normally, when she dreamed, she only had two senses engaged – sight and sound – but since she'd arrived here, all of them had been in play. She could smell the antiseptic of the clinic, she'd tasted the awful scrambled eggs they'd given her to eat this morning, and she could feel the stiff fabric of the olive-green pants they'd supplied her with after her shower. It was distinct, solid, and Lia had no choice except to believe she was in 2050, as they'd told her.

A coma would be much more comforting.

She swallowed the urge to whimper, afraid her guards would hear it. Being confined wasn't a totally bad thing; it had given her time to think. To calm down.

If she didn't end up in prison as a spy, maybe this era wouldn't be so bad. They'd probably solved the problems plaguing her time like global warming and clean water. Maybe no one went hungry any more and everyone had health insurance. This time might be great. Although what was this coalition the colonel had accused her of belonging to? That didn't sound too good.

Lia bit her lower lip. She was worrying about nothing. Society had had forty years to advance – it *had* to be better now. She'd be fine once she got out of this treatment room, explored her new world, and saw how wonderful it was.

As if in answer to her thought, the door opened. Slowly she sat up and looked into the stony faces of the two MPs. "You, come with us," the older of them ordered.

Her mouth dry, Lia asked, "Why? Where are you taking me?"

"Ma'am," the other one said, "please come with us."

Despite the politeness, his tone was clear – it wasn't a suggestion. If she didn't go along voluntarily, they'd haul her out of here. Lia slid off the table on to her feet and started towards them.

"Take your bag, ma'am."

She detoured to grab it off the chair and clutched it tightly. Were they putting her in a real jail? Is that why they wanted her to bring the bag that contained her clothes?

Each man grasped an arm as she reached them and escorted her down the hall. Damn, she hoped they weren't returning her to that colonel. He was terrifying, and she wasn't ready to deal with him again. Not yet.

Lia tried to ignore the way the doctors and nurses stared as she went by. To her surprise, she felt shame. It was stupid, she hadn't done anything wrong, but realizing that didn't lessen the emotion.

They reached the front of the clinic and her guards put her in the waiting room near the entrance. "Have a seat," the polite one told her and Lia took the first chair she reached.

The MPs flanked her on either side, positioning themselves so that they could watch her, the door to the infirmary and the clinic itself. There was only one other person present, a young man who sat behind a half-wall with a counter on top of it. The check-in area, Lia guessed. He gaped at her for a moment before looking away.

Her nerves pulled taut as the silence lengthened. It was obvious they were waiting, but she had no idea why and bit her tongue to keep from asking. They wouldn't tell her anything.

With the exit in view, the idea of making a run for it was almost too tempting to resist. Almost. Luckily, she was smart enough to know she wouldn't get far. Lia couldn't outrun her guards – she was only five and a half feet tall and they were much bigger. And they had guns. That colonel had probably told them to shoot her if she tried to escape. Even if she somehow did get free, she had nowhere to go and nobody to help her.

Clasping her small canvas duffle bag, she wished there were a pair of ruby slippers inside that would take her home again. That would make everything much easier.

Her stomach was churning when the door to the infirmary opened. Almost afraid to look, Lia glanced over and did a double take. She'd never before, not in her entire life, seen a man this beautiful – not even in the movies. Her tension left her like an ebbing wave. "Wow," she mouthed silently.

He was dressed in camouflage fatigue pants, boots and an olive-green T-shirt that stretched across his broad shoulders and muscular chest. Imprinted on the left side of the shirt was the insignia for a sergeant – she'd watched enough TV to identify that – and although she didn't see a holster or any other sign of a weapon, she'd bet he was armed.

One of the MPs went to talk to him, but Lia couldn't stop staring at Sgt Gorgeous long enough to pay attention to what was being said. He wore his dark hair short – no surprise given his military affiliation – had a strong chin with the slightest hint of a cleft, and when he smiled at something the MP said, she saw that his teeth were perfect.

His golden skin suggested a mixed heritage, but she couldn't guess what it was and she didn't care. Vivid blue eyes met hers for an instant and a shiver of awareness went through her. He looked away and she was left feeling bereft.

As stunning as he was, Lia wouldn't use the word "pretty" – he was too rugged, too sharp-edged for that – and damned if that didn't make him even more appealing. Who was this guy?

When the men finished their conversation, the two MPs left and the newcomer walked over to her. Sgt Gorgeous smiled and held out his hand. A small shock went through her at the contact, but she savoured the warmth of his fingers. As they shook hands, he said, "Ophelia—"

That knocked her out of her stupor and she interrupted him. "Lia. No one uses Ophelia more than once, got it?"

His grin widened and she forgot to breathe. "Understood." He released her hand. "I'm Troll Maglaya. I'm assuming escort duty from Dunn and Gomez."

It took a moment for the words to sink in because she was lost in his deep voice and the way it seemed to swirl over her body and caress it. This man was potent. "Troll? Seriously? That's what your mom calls you?"

He shook his head. "No, she calls me Chris. To everyone here I'm Troll, understood?"

Lia nodded. "Got it . . . Troll." She looked at him from beneath her lashes and smiled. "Should I be insulted that I've been downgraded to a single guard?"

"You could take it as a compliment. You've gone from two MPs to a Special Ops soldier, and one of us is like a team of twenty regular troops."

His wink had her heart picking up speed. Oh, my God, she'd flirted with him and he'd flirted back. It was probably instinctual for a guy who looked like him and not a big deal, but the instant man–woman attraction she felt had Lia alarmed. "What happens to me now?" she asked and managed to sound normal.

"I thought we'd get you settled and then have some lunch. You must be hungry."

"Settled?" Her fingers tightened around the canvas. "In a jail cell?"

"Nah," Troll said easily, "not unless you insist on it."

She felt a flutter in her belly and had to remind herself not to fall for this. Maybe some people underestimated him because of his appearance, but she wouldn't be one of them. She didn't know a lot about the military, but Lia was aware of how hard it was to become a Green Beret or whatever they were called. Troll might be showing her his nice-guy facade, but below the surface he was formidable and she needed to remember that even if she was wondering how his lips would feel against hers.

"Are you ready to go?" he asked.

With a nod, Lia stood. She expected him to grab her arm the way the MPs had, but instead Troll put his hand at the small of her back. Heat unfurled, running through her body like a jolt from an electrical wire. Definitely potent, and he had manners – he held the door for her.

Lia stopped and gawked as soon as she stepped outside. Last night it had been dark before the MPs had gotten her to the bottom of the pyramid and she'd hardly seen anything of the city. She looked now, fascinated by her surroundings. There were wide, graceful walkways and plenty of grass, plants and flowers. Most of the buildings were marble and stunningly beautiful. Not quite in the same league with Sgt Gorgeous, but still worth a second glance. "Wow."

"Yeah," Troll said, "it's something, isn't it? It's too bad the aliens that built the city were long gone before we got here. It would have been interesting to meet them."

"Aliens?"

"Yep." Instead of explaining, his hand pressed lightly against her back, urging her forwards. "The mess hall closes in less than half an hour, so we need to move."

Lia walked. "This planet is outside Earth's solar system?"

"It is. I could give you coordinates, but no one from your era would get it unless they were an astronomer." He shrugged. "Most of the people in this time don't get it either and it's taught in school."

Two things occurred to her simultaneously. First, the colonel from hell, or one of his minions of darkness, must have filled Troll in on what she'd said. Second, Sgt Gorgeous was talking as if he thought she had time travelled – or at least he was going along with it. Lia pulled him to a halt and, looking into his eyes, she asked, "You believe me?"

"Yes." He didn't need to ask what she was talking about.

There was nothing flirty in his gaze now and nothing shifty either. That didn't mean he wasn't lying, of course, but she needed someone to believe her and she wanted it to be him. "I want to go home. Will you help me?"

"I don't know how I can help you."

"I need a wormhole or an atom smasher." Lia rapidly filled him in on what she thought had happened last night and he listened to her. Really listened.

"We don't have either thing here, but even if we did, have you considered that it might take you somewhere else besides your own time?"

No, she hadn't, but . . . "The odds against the first one opening were astronomical, and the chances of a second one appearing that went somewhere else must be next to impossible." That was logical, wasn't it? "To be honest, I was kind of hoping that in this time you'd mastered how to summon and use wormholes, but since you haven't, I guess I'm stuck here."

She thought she'd done a good job of concealing her emotions, but Troll's response told her she was wrong.

"I know you're scared – who wouldn't be? – and I know it's tough to leave your family behind, but I've never heard anything about wormholes being created or used."

"I don't have any family left," Lia told him and ignored the stab around her heart. The loss still hurt years later, but she'd become used to the hollow feeling.

"I'm sorry," he said quietly. After a pause, he added, "You know, if you give it a chance, you might like 2050 and I'll do what I can to help you adjust." He winked at her again, and, inclining his head, said, "Come on. I'm starving and don't want to miss mess."

Lia didn't move. "Why do you believe me when your colonel doesn't?"

Troll shrugged. "Maybe I'm more open-minded than the Big Chill, or maybe I have more imagination. Or maybe I have some sixth sense that he doesn't."

"Sixth sense?" Something about the way he'd said that caught her attention. "Do you mean you're psychic?"

His lips curved slightly. "If that were the case, don't you think my nickname would be the Prophet? That isn't something my team would let slide." Troll took her hand and, lacing their fingers, began to walk.

"If they were aware of it," she murmured, but when he simply raised his brows and smirked, Lia had to laugh at herself. She was grasping at shadows, probably because her leap forwards was fresh in her thoughts.

She pushed the idea aside and relished the warmth of his calloused palm against hers. He was a stranger, but he treated her in a way that was almost casually intimate. That wasn't what made her uneasy. The part that unnerved her was how natural it felt, as if it would be wrong if he wasn't touching her. She needed to get her mind off this before she started dreaming up really stupid ideas. Lia tugged free, trying to dispel the weird sense of rightness, and said, "This place is like a ghost town. Where is everybody?"

"Around somewhere. There're only about five hundred people inside a city that once held up to fifty thousand. It always looks like this. You'll get used to it."

Lia didn't want to get used to it. She wanted to glance up and see aeroplanes leaving contrails; she wanted to go into Starbucks and grab a cup of coffee; she wanted to deal with crowds and traffic. But she didn't say anything. It wasn't like she could change anything, and Troll couldn't either. He took her hand again and this time she hung on, needing the connection as they continued through a nearly empty alien city.

They turned a corner into a square. Smack dab in the middle was an unsightly corrugated metal building with a flagpole in front of it. Now she saw a few other people and she expected Troll to release her. He didn't. "Let me guess," Lia said, "we brought that monstrosity from Earth."

"You know it."

Something else caught her eye. "That isn't the US flag."

He gazed at her for a moment before he said, "It belongs to the Western Alliance. There are a lot of Americans here, but this is an Alliance outpost."

"Western Alliance?"

"You had the European Union in your time, right?" When she nodded, he said, "It's like that – mostly – except with more countries involved. The history is convoluted and it evolved throughout the years and with each of the wars."

"Wars?" Maybe this time wasn't more advanced than hers.

"Sorry, my explanations are only raising more questions for you. I'll stop and let you read up on what's happened the last forty years. Links will take you from topic to topic and you'll get more complete answers than I can give you." Troll's expression turned sheepish. "History wasn't my favourite class. I passed it, but I didn't pay much attention."

History. Things that hadn't occurred for her yet were events from his past. Some of it had likely even happened before . . . "When were you born?" she demanded.

"June 3, 2018."

Her eyes went wide and she did some maths. "My God, I'm thirty-six years older than you are!"

He shook his head. "If you'd lived through all that time, yeah, but you didn't. From what the Colonel told me, you're four years younger than me."

"Your colonel talks a lot," Lia grumbled.

"A briefing is different than gossip, and when it comes to a mission, there's no such thing as too much intel."

She was a mission? Blood roared in her ears for a moment. She was on her own in a time and place where she wasn't sure of the rules, but she'd ridiculously latched on to Troll as her guide. "I'm only an assignment?" Lia asked, unable to stop herself.

"You know better than that. Believe me, I don't handle my missions like this. If I did, I'd have been booted out of Spec Ops a long time ago."

And that easily, the weight on her chest eased enough to let her take in air. "What else do you know about me?"

"What else did you tell Sullivan?" Troll countered, his thumb rubbing circles on her palm, arousing as well as relaxing her. "He might have sent a request to Earth to get more information, but it's too early to have anything back yet."

Time lag in communications. She hadn't thought about that, but she should have. Lia was still mulling it over when she recognized where they were – in front of the security building. The MPs had dragged her here last night after they'd escorted her to the bottom of the pyramid. Her heart kicked into high gear again and betrayal made a lump block her throat. She dug in her heels, refusing to move forwards. "You said we were going to lunch, but you're taking me back to that colonel, aren't you?"

"No. I'm bringing you to my quarters to drop off your stuff and the quickest route happens to take us past security headquarters."

She wanted to believe him. Troll was the only one who seemed to be on her side and she needed that. She needed *him*. Because of it, Lia stared hard, trying to see the truth.

"The MPs could have brought you to security HQ without involving me." He squeezed her hand, his thumb continuing to caress her skin. "And we both know I didn't have to lie to get you here. You're not exactly operating from a position of power."

Reluctantly, she nodded. Troll was right, it wasn't as if she could refuse to go anywhere, but this ... connection ... she felt to him made her idiotic. "Your quarters?" she asked.

"Yeah, I –" He stopped abruptly, straightened, and though his left hand continued to hold hers, his right went to his forehead to salute a man drawing near.

Half afraid she'd see the colonel, Lia turned to get a better look. It wasn't Sullivan, but some other officer and her muscles unclenched. She watched the man drop his gaze to their joined hands, then look back up at them. He returned the salute, shook his head, and kept going. Only then did Troll relax.

"He's sure good-looking," she said. "Who was that?"

Troll scowled. "Major Brody. He's married with three boys and devoted to his wife so you're out of luck."

Did he sound jealous? Lia scoffed at herself for having the thought. Not only did they meet maybe ten minutes ago, but Troll had to know that very few males could measure up to him in the gorgeous department. "It was just a comment and some curiosity, not a plan to hunt the man." And before she could stop herself, she added, "But I can see how a guy like you would be insecure about his appeal. I'm guessing you were nicknamed Troll because of how ugly you are?"

One side of his mouth quirked up. "Something like that."

He tugged gently and she fell into step with him. It wasn't until after the metal building was out of sight that she asked, "Why did you keep hold of me when you saluted? Your colonel made it clear that he thought I was a spy, aren't you worried about getting into trouble for associating with me? And why did that major shake his head, but not say anything?"

This time it was Troll who stopped walking. "We're never going to make it to the mess hall for lunch," he muttered. He glanced around and led her to a bench against the front of a dove-grey building. "Have a seat."

Lia quelled the urge to ask why and did as he suggested.

Troll sat beside her, his thigh nearly brushing hers, and stared straight ahead. For a moment, he didn't speak and she had a sense he was trying to decide what to share. Finally, he said, "Major Brody shook his head because I have a reputation with women."

"Undeserved?"

Troll sighed, but confessed, "No, I earned it, but I reformed about two years ago. Not that anyone except my teammates believes it, but it's the truth."

Lia considered that and decided it was better to leave it alone. "What about you being so cosy with a suspected spy?"

That got her a frown and another admission. "The Colonel suggested I romance you if necessary to get information about your mission. If someone reports we're holding hands, it'll get chalked up to my following orders."

She tried to jump to her feet, wounded by his words, but Troll snagged her wrist and held on.

"Listen to me," he said, turning towards her to meet her gaze. "I wouldn't have told you this if I planned to do it. I informed Sullivan I wouldn't prostitute myself for the Alliance. You can ask him the next time you see him. What's between us . . . it feels right. You sense it, too, Lia."

Yes, she did, but . . . "We just met. We don't know each other."

"I'm aware of that, but it doesn't seem to matter."

It didn't. "I don't want this," she said, but Lia couldn't stop staring into his eyes, couldn't stop thinking about pressing her lips to his, as long as his mouth was this near anyway.

"Me either, but some things are too powerful to fight."

"I wouldn't have guessed you were a fatalist." She couldn't kiss him out here on the street. Could she?

Troll shook his head. "I'm not. We have free will, but I do believe in destiny and you're mine."

Heat built low in her belly. One quick peck, just to find out what it was like. "It's too soon." But he was right, it didn't seem to matter. Damn, she wanted to taste him.

"I'll back off."

He stood and she did as well. The hell with it, she decided. Lia dropped her bag and put her free hand on his nape to keep him close. "This is a mistake," she murmured.

And, leaning into him, she brushed her lips over his.

Desire slammed into her with breath-stealing strength and she needed more of him. Wrapping both arms around his neck, she went back for a second, longer kiss. Still not enough. She ran her tongue over his lips and Troll opened for her as his hands went to her waist, pulling her tightly against his body. Good. He felt so damn good.

So damn perfect.

Destiny. That thought frightened her enough to break the kiss and quickly put distance between them. One glance at his darkened eyes, the desire on his face, almost had her tossing aside common sense and going back for more, but Troll banked his heat before she gave in to the urge.

"Come on," he said thickly. "We might still make lunch."

She retrieved her bag and fell into step beside him. This time he didn't hold her hand and Lia had to curl her fingers to keep from reaching for him. It *was* too soon and she didn't fit in here. Did she? Of course not. Just because she felt in sync with this one man, it didn't mean she belonged.

If it wasn't for that damn vortex, she wouldn't have to deal with any of this crap. Maybe the Einstein-Rosen Bridge closed instantly, but her wormhole was the Troll Bridge, and it seemed it had been open for business.

"Here we are," he said, pointing towards a house.

It was small – well, small compared to some of the buildings here, but certainly not tiny by normal standards – and made of cream-coloured stone. There were two wide slate steps leading up to a welcoming front porch, but before she could appreciate much more than that, they were at the entry.

"Just drop your bag inside." He opened the door for her. "We don't have time to go in."

Lia did what he said. Troll closed the door again, took her hand, and hurried them off. "You really are hungry," she said.

"I missed breakfast helping the Z Man put together a trike for his kid. Who knew it would be that hard and take that many hours?"

"The Z Man?" She was slightly out of breath from trying to keep up with his long strides, but she didn't ask him to slow.

"One of my buddies." They reached another metal building and Troll pulled the door open. "Made it." His smile gave way to a soft groan. "A long line this late isn't a good sign," he explained when she looked at him.

They stood in it anyway. He asked the group in front of them if they knew what was going on, but they didn't. A few minutes later, Troll spotted someone. "Sasha," he called. A pretty blonde woman came over holding a tray and Lia felt her heart jam in her throat when Troll leaned over to kiss her cheek.

"The team's back?" Sasha asked and she sounded hopeful.

Troll shook his head. "No, I was pulled for another assignment. Sorry. What's going on with the line?"

"All the ovens, stoves, and anything else that could heat food crashed. Another of the infamous J. Nine tech glitches. It's a chicken sandwich or nothing." She nodded towards her plate and then looked at Lia. "Hi, I'm Sasha Cantore and you're . . .?"

"Lia Stanton," she said, but her voice was choked.

"Troll, you get Lia's lunch," Sasha told him. "She can wait at a table with me while you stand in line."

"I'll stay here," Lia said.

"Go ahead. Sash will take good care of you and it'll give you a chance to meet the team wives. Y'all are together, right?"

Sasha shook her head and said dryly, "No, I had a session that ran over schedule. Since we don't travel in packs like the team husbands do, I can only guess that the other team wives have already eaten and are either working or with the team children."

"Smart ass," he said amiably. "Sasha is married to Flare, the team's warrant officer. She's also a shrink, so be careful what you say."

Relief washed through her, but Lia refused to consider why it made her feel better to know this woman was tied to Troll's friend and not someone he'd had a romantic relationship with. His warning registered a moment later – she's a psychologist, so don't mention time travel. "Got it," she assured him. Sasha started to walk away, but Lia hesitated. "You trust me not to run off?"

"I trust you, period, Lia." He gently tugged the ends of her hair. "And there's no point in both of us waiting when you don't have to decide what you want for lunch, right?"

"I suppose," she said reluctantly and went over to where Sasha stood. As soon as Lia got there, the blonde turned and headed deeper into the mess hall.

"So you're Troll's woman," she said as she wound her way through the tables.

"I wouldn't say that."

"I would," Sasha disagreed. "Troll letting you come with me is almost as good as him bringing you home to meet his family and about as close as he can get to that on Jarved Nine."

Lia shook her head. "We just met."

"It happens that way sometimes. I knew the first instant I saw Flare that he was going to be important to me. We hit a few obstacles along the way, but we're together twenty years later." Before Lia could comment, Sasha said, "There's an open table."

The doctor waited until they were seated to begin quizzing her, but it was done with such good-natured interest that Lia found herself sharing more than she intended. The colonel-from-hell could learn a thing or two from this woman, she decided, but she liked her. Some of Lia's answers were odd, she knew it from the confusion she'd see cross Sasha's face from time to time, but the psychologist didn't look at her like she was off-centre and she liked the easy acceptance.

What was taking Troll so long? Lia swivelled in her seat and studied the line until she spotted him. He'd nearly made it to the food. She turned back in time to see Sasha's smile. "It doesn't mean anything," Lia blurted.

"No? I don't think you realize how many times you've glanced over to check where Troll is, or how your tension level has risen the longer you've been separated from him. Like it or not, you've developed a bond with him."

Lia opened her mouth to explain again that she'd just met the man, but it had gotten her nowhere with Sasha earlier and Lia doubted repeating it would make any difference. The doctor had her mind made up. With a silent sigh, Lia let it go. What did it matter anyway?

She didn't believe in love at first sight, and no matter what this woman thought, Lia hadn't fallen for a blue-eyed stranger with a sexy smile. Destiny be damned.

*   *   *

Troll held Lia's hand again as they meandered slowly through the city. Dusk was settling, but it wasn't dark enough yet for the lights to come on. He felt a pang of guilt over having fun today while his team was searching for a spaceship that didn't exist, but it wasn't like he could tell the Colonel anything, not without getting into explanations he'd rather not make about things Sullivan would never believe.

The drawing of Lia was tucked safely inside his wallet, but he couldn't stop thinking about it. From the moment Gram had given it to him, Troll had known this day would come. No psychic was ever accurate all the time – free will caused things to change frequently – but it hadn't mattered. He'd simply known.

Maybe that was why he'd played so free and loose with women when he'd been younger. No point getting attached to one when Lia would arrive someday.

Despite this, he'd still needed a good ten minutes after seeing her this afternoon to corral the fear. He'd walked away from the infirmary and paced until his hands had stopped shaking and his breathing had slowed to normal.

Free will. He had it, too. Just because Gram had said the woman in the drawing was The One, it didn't mean he had to go along with that. If he wanted, he could do his job and walk away at the end of it without a problem. Troll had long ago mastered the art of remaining disengaged on any meaningful level.

And then he'd touched Lia's hand.

As easily as that, the apprehension had evaporated as if it had never existed and he'd seen the future. One *possible* future. He and Lia had been playing together, laughing, and he'd felt the depth of the emotion between them. It had decided things for him and brought up a new concern – could he convince her to give it a chance and see where things went between them?

"You're awfully quiet," Lia said.

"Sorry. I was thinking about how much I've enjoyed spending the day with you. My teammates are going to give me shit for pulling this duty while they're roughing it outside the city walls."

"Why would they do that? It wasn't your decision."

Troll grinned. "Because I plan to rub their noses in it. If they didn't give it right back to me, I'd be worried."

Her laugh travelled through his body and left his cells buzzing. He hardly knew her, not really, and even if she was The One like Gram said, like his own vision seconded, it didn't mean they were meant to be together in this life. The idea made him want to learn everything he could about her just in case this was all he had.

"If you could do anything you wanted, what would it be?" Troll asked, picking one of the dozen questions jumping in his mind. "I mean, in whatever time you're in or whatever world you're on."

"You want to know my big dream, huh?"

"I want to know *all* your dreams."

Silence. He could sense her reluctance and decided it would help if he went first. "You know what I've always wanted to do? Buy a sailboat and travel around the world, go from place to place and stay as long as I like. Maybe dock her and head inland when the urge struck. It'll never happen, though."

Lia looked at him. "Why not?"

"The war for one. Even after it ends, it won't be safe. There are mines, old hatreds," he explained when she appeared confused. "Bunch of other issues. Money is another factor. Boats aren't cheap, not ocean-going vessels – and supporting myself while I sailed?" Troll shook his head. "The logistics aren't workable, not for a man earning army pay."

"But if you really wanted to . . ." She trailed off.

"Maybe that's it. I don't want it badly enough." He shrugged. "Definitely not badly enough to leave Spec Ops."

They walked without speaking for a few minutes before Lia asked, "Have you considered that Special Ops is your dream?"

That stopped him in his tracks and Troll thought about it. After a few moments, he nodded slowly. "You could be right. It's never been something I sat and thought a lot about, though, not like the boat."

"The boat's your fantasy, a way to leave behind the stress of life for a little while. Fantasies and dreams are different."

She said that with such authority that Troll smiled. "So your fantasies about climbing on top of me and having your wicked way are different than your dreams?"

Even in the fading light, he could see the blush stain her cheeks. "You can't know – I never said –" When his grin grew bigger, her eyes narrowed and she groaned. "Damn, you were fishing . . ."

Troll released her hand and put his arm around her shoulders instead. "Yep. So now that you probably can't get much more embarrassed, why don't you share your dream?"

"You're more diabolical than I thought."

"I prefer to think of it as ingenious." He kissed the top of her head, steered her towards a nearby park, and sprawled beside her on a bench. They had a view of the city from here, including the pyramid, but the thing was so flipping huge that it was hard to avoid it. She still didn't say anything, but Lia snuggled into his side and Troll enjoyed the warm weight of her against him as he waited for her to talk.

Lights were illuminating the buildings when she finally spoke. "You're patient, aren't you?" Lia didn't pause for an answer before continuing, "I want to be a writer, OK? Not for company newsletters or employee magazines, I mean stories. Fiction."

She tensed slightly as if bracing herself for his reaction and it made him wonder if in the past others had scoffed when she'd found the courage to share her dream with them. "Yeah? Cool. I'll read for you if you want."

"What?"

The disbelief in her voice stung, but Troll pushed it aside. He couldn't blame her since she hardly knew him. "I know, you're thinking a guy like me won't be much help, but while school wasn't my thing, I've always loved to read."

"I wasn't—" Lia sat up and stared at him. "People discount you because you're so good-looking, don't they? That's what you thought I was doing."

Troll shrugged.

"Idiot." She scowled. "I've been with you all day and you snagged me on the sexual fantasy thing. I'd have to be stupid to miss how sharp you are."

His lips twitched. She'd just called him an idiot and then turned right around and said she knew he was smart. "Why'd you question my offer then?"

"Because usually when I mention I want to write novels, I get laughed at, or humoured, or stared at in disbelief, or my favourite response – 'You weren't good enough to get a real job in journalism, but you think you can write a whole story?' Oh, wait, then there are the practical people who tell me nobody reads any more and maybe I should try writing a movie or video game script, but that isn't what I want to do. No one has ever offered their help before."

The hurt lifted and Troll could breathe again. "Well, you got it if you want it. You ever think of writing science fiction? 'Cos I gotta tell you, falling through a wormhole and winding up in the future would make a great story."

With a smile, Lia settled against him again. "It'll never sell," she told him. "And how could I write a book where the heroine returns home again while I'm trapped?"

Troll felt his gut clench, but he kept his muscles loose. They'd been playing, but her comment reminded him that he hadn't won her yet. He tried to come up with more positives about this time. "Sasha likes you."

"You can't know that," Lia argued.

"Yes, I can. She gave me a thumbs-up sign when she walked behind you."

"She didn't."

She sounded both hopeful and horrified and Troll found himself smiling again. Lia made him happy. It was scary when he thought about it too long, but, hey, he'd been anxious before and taken action. "She did. You're already making friends."

Stiffening again, she moved far enough away to break his hold. "Why do you keep trying to sell me on how great it is to be stuck here?"

No guts, no glory, Troll thought and plunged in. "New Orleans, 2002."

She stared at him blankly.

"You saw Madam Genevieve in a shop not too far from Jackson Square and had a reading done."

A furrow formed between her brows and Troll watched Lia search her memory. He was aware of the instant it came back to her. "How the hell do you know that?"

"She's my grandmother."

"Why would she talk about me so many years after I saw her? It's not like I ever went back and I can't imagine she told you about all the tourists she did readings for."

"She didn't. Only you." Troll reached for his wallet, took out the drawing, and unfolded it. For a moment he hesitated, worried about how she'd react, but he passed it to Lia anyway. "She gave me this when I was eighteen and said you were my destiny. Gram told me you asked her about your soulmate. Do you remember what she said to you?"

Her confusion was brief. "That I'd meet him . . . in the future." Lia looked stunned. "But she couldn't know – could she?"

Troll shrugged. "Maybe. Gram is eerie with what she can see, but she didn't specifically mention time travel to me when we talked."

She glanced briefly at the drawing and then back at him. "This scares me. Why are you taking it so calmly?"

"I'm not. I'm probably as edgy about this as you are, but I'm not willing to let that stand in my way, not when I've spent years wondering how we'd find each other. Let's throw the dice and discover what we could have."

Staring into his eyes, she studied him for a moment. Troll remained quiet, giving her time to consider things. "Here," she said at last and handed him the sketch.

He waited for her to say more, but she didn't and he put the drawing away. Growing up with his grandmother, Troll was used to the psychic stuff, but most people weren't and it left them uneasy or sceptical, or both. But he'd thought Lia would be different – she felt the pull between them every bit as strongly as he did, he knew it.

Fear. He sighed. She didn't have his training and experience, so he'd give her time and let her grow accustomed to the idea of the two of them. It wasn't as if she was going anywhere.

Lia pursed her lips and Troll found his attention drifting. Damn, he wanted his mouth on hers again when he didn't have to consider where they were or who might stumble on them. Maybe they should head back to his quarters. They'd have privacy there and he wouldn't have to worry how far things escalated. He had a feeling they'd both lose control fast.

Her gasp yanked him back to the here and now.

For a split second, he thought she'd read his mind about taking her to bed, then Troll realized she was staring into the city. He turned to see what had her alarmed. No one was coming towards them. "What?" he demanded.

"The wormhole." She pointed to the top of the pyramid. "It's back. It's back!"

And before he could react, Lia took off running.

★   ★   ★

Lia wasn't surprised when Troll caught up with her, but she ignored him. He didn't say a word. He didn't need to. What he'd said in the park echoed through her mind. *Let's discover what we could have.* It was tempting, but she hadn't opened the vortex and this might be her only opportunity to go home. How could she throw it away on a possibility? On a hope?

She didn't know where she was going, but she zigzagged through the streets, keeping her gaze locked on the pyramid. Maybe it wasn't the most direct route, but the wormhole was still glowing when she reached the base.

Troll took her hand, stopping her as she began to climb. Before she could pull free, he said, "There's a faster way."

Without giving her time to argue, he brought her around the corner to a tall door that led inside the structure. They travelled down hallways and he pressed crystals that made rock walls slide open. "Secret passages," Lia said, amazed.

"Yeah." Troll didn't sound happy. "Kendall, my captain's wife, will kill me for showing them to you. She's protective of this place."

He took her down a few more long corridors and Lia felt impatience bubble inside. What if the wormhole was gone before they made it to the top? The worry that they'd be too late wouldn't leave her, and it didn't matter that Troll was moving at a good clip or that it would have taken her hours to climb the exterior stairs to the altar. "Can we go faster?"

"We're at the midpoint."

Lia looked around a large open area. There was sunlight streaming in, but it was night outside and she saw no visible source that could be producing an artificial glow. Everywhere she gazed there was solid stone and carefully manicured plants. Troll led her to one of eight platforms that were arranged in an arc and stood on top of it. She followed although she wasn't sure why they were standing here.

She didn't get the chance to ask. A stone balustrade rose from the sides of the dais, not stopping until it reached about waist height. As soon as it was in place, the entire platform began to rise like an elevator. She grabbed on to Troll.

They reached the top and he silently brought her to a second elevator. When they got off that one, he took her through a door that led outside to the flat top of the pyramid. The wormhole was there, glowing and throbbing in some rhythm that only it understood. Home, she thought, taking a step forwards, but Troll put an arm around her and stopped her.

"If you're going to leave, at least think about it first, don't walk mindlessly into that thing."

"I wasn't," she protested, but he was right. She'd been mesmerized by it.

"You can't even be sure this is going to take you back to 2010. For all you know, you'll end up in Alpha Centauri seven thousand years in the past."

Lia shook her head. "It'll take me home. I feel it." She shrugged, uncertain how she knew this, only that she did. "Maybe it's trying to correct its mistake. After all, I'm not supposed to be here."

"Bullshit. That's a force of nature, not a sentient being who's trying to balance the universe. And I think you *are* supposed to be here; that's why it appeared to begin with."

"Sometimes it's not destiny, just an accident. I don't belong in this time."

"Lia, give us a chance. If you leave, what do you think the odds are that you'll be able to come back here? I'd say zilch. That particle accelerator was probably locked down immediately once they realized they had a wormhole big enough for travel. Do you think they'll let you near it again?"

"No," she admitted in a small voice.

"Just a chance." He moved, standing in front of her, and clasped her shoulders with his hands. "You told me you don't have any family left, so what's back there for you? Nothing much that I can see. Here you could have something important – *we* could have something important – but if you leave we'll never know. Isn't it worth some time to find out?"

She looked past him at the vortex. Was it pulsing a little faster now? Lia took a step forwards, but Troll tightened his hold just enough to grab her attention.

"You're frightened, I get that, but you know what scares me more? The idea of spending the rest of my life wondering what we might have had if you'd stayed. Wondering if Gram was right and you were my destiny. Can you walk away and live with those questions?"

"But this might be the only opportunity I have. What if I pass on it, things don't develop between us, and I can't get home? What then?"

Troll framed her face between his hands. "I promise you, if you want to go back to 2010 later, I'll get you there somehow." He shook his head. "Hell, if the wormhole is tied to the pyramid in some way, Kendall can probably control it. If not, I'll break us through security for an accelerator in 2050 if that's what it takes."

The vortex flickered and Lia sucked in a sharp breath, afraid for an instant that she'd lost her only chance. Troll made staying sound easy, but it wasn't. "Your colonel thinks I'm a spy. He'll lock me up or torture me or something if I remain here."

"Sullivan is a problem, but we can figure out what to do with him. We can enlist the rest of my team and their wives if we have to. Someone will have an answer."

Again, Lia looked over his shoulder at the vortex, then returned her gaze to Troll. His blue eyes were intense and she could see he meant every word he said. "But what if—"

"There are no guarantees in life, but sometimes you have to take the risk anyway. Stay with me, take this chance. We could have everything."

"Or nothing."

"That's a possibility," he admitted. "But we've got this on our side."

Troll's kiss made her toes curl and Lia clutched at him, hanging on as if *he* were the one who might leave *her*. She wanted him to distract her, to keep her occupied until the wormhole was gone and she didn't have to make a decision, but long before she was ready, he broke free.

"It has to be your choice," he said. And then he stepped aside, leaving her path to the vortex clear.

His actions paralysed her and Lia stared at the lights, watching them spin faster. She wanted to stay, but how could she? Troll was gorgeous, funny, smart, interesting, sexy – everything she wanted in a man – but even if he didn't feel like one, he was a stranger. How could she turn her back on her home when this time was foreign to her? When she was under suspicion? When either she or Troll could decide that they weren't meant to be?

The wormhole began to contract and she stepped forwards.

In that moment, Lia realized she was more like her parents than she'd known. They'd been afraid to risk anything, afraid to go for broke, and she was about to leave the only man who'd ever made her feel alive because of the fear. Maybe it wouldn't work – he was right, there were no guarantees in life – but if she left, it was over right here, right now.

Lia stared at Troll, then at the gateway home.

Her job, her car, her apartment, a life that was familiar and safe. Or a man with whom things might not work out, a possible charge of espionage held over her head, a horrible colonel who thought she was guilty, and a world that was mostly strange to her. Just the thought of staying made her nauseous.

The vortex shrank farther, and with a gasp, Lia rushed towards it.

But before she crossed, she stopped short. Life wasn't supposed to be mundane and routine. It was about change, about experiences, about dreams. About love. What if Troll *was* her destiny? What if she spent the rest of her life comparing other men to him and none of them measured up? What if she regretted her cowardice every day until she died? What then?

No promises, but a chance.

She couldn't live with the *what ifs*; she had to know whether or not Troll was the love of her life. With her heart lodged in her throat, Lia let the wormhole close.

Tremors shook her body when it disappeared, and she breathed deeply until the urge to vomit passed. It took another couple of minutes until she felt steady enough to walk over to Troll. She stared up at him, letting his steady gaze calm her. "I'm scared that I just made a big mistake, but I'm rolling the dice, Chris."

Wincing, he wrapped his arms around her and gathered her close. "You won't regret it, I'll make sure of that." He kissed her, but before she was ready for it to end, he stepped away, took her hand, and led her back inside the pyramid.

"Chris!" she protested.

He shook his head. "Why don't we make a pact? You can call me Chris when we're home – alone – but otherwise it's Troll. Deal, Ophelia?"

Now she winced. "Deal. You give as good as you get, don't you?"

His smile was wicked. "Always. You'll appreciate that when I have you in bed."

Heat settled low in her belly and Lia forgot her terror and uncertainty. Life really was an adventure and hers was about to begin.

Iron and Hemlock

Autumn Dawn

Jordon flinched and shielded her eyes. The glow of lightning lit the darkness behind her lids, persisted in dots of colour as she slowly lowered her hand. She blinked, disoriented. Death was a lonely country road?

It was no wonder she was confused. Only moments ago, she'd been crossing the street on her way to meet the bus. When the speeding Porsche had lurched around the corner, then gunned for her with an angry growl, she'd known she was dead. Only the lightning had struck *before* the car did. Had it somehow knocked her out of the way?

She drew a shaky breath and looked around. No. It was dark here, and stormy. The sun had been directly overhead in Spokane. The city had disappeared completely, leaving nothing but whispering trees and a crawling sense of unease.

A cold wind worked its way through her jeans, stealing her warmth. She hitched her light leather jacket closer and thanked God for the vanity that made her wear her cashmere and silk sweater, though it had been a little warm for it this morning. Unfortunately, the suede boots didn't fare as well, quickly becoming waterlogged in the rain.

A flash of lightning illuminated the outline of a tremendous stone wall lining the dirt road. A quick glance showed nothing behind her – no lights, at least, which would have indicated people. A hundred yards ahead, the wall was pierced by a wrought-iron gate. As she drew closer, she could see that the panels were unlatched, swaying slightly in the wind, almost in invitation. When she was close enough to touch it, the torches above the gate flared to life, illuminating the gravel path. She glanced up and started slightly at the fierce gargoyles flanking the wall on either side.

As she watched, one of them blinked.

Jordon froze. But she was not the kind of girl who screamed and ran at every shadow, even in such dire circumstances. She watched the gargoyle instead. It did not take long to convince herself that she'd imagined it. The statue was obviously stone.

Still, she felt watched. She looked behind her, but there was nothing out there. Blackness, night. And yet she had the feeling that something was watching her; something other than the gargoyles.

Shrugging her shoulders against the sensation, she slipped through the gates. Uneasy, she glanced back, just in time to observe the wind pushing the gates closed. They shut with a loud clang and remained fixed, as if they had latched. Was she locked in?

She did not have time for further speculation. The sound of hoof beats heading her way made her stiffen. When she saw what was bearing down on her, she ran. She did not need the lightning to see the flames shooting from the head of the midnight-coloured stallion charging her way. His eyes and nostrils blazed, as if he were a living furnace. Sparks flew where his feet struck the earth, and the ground shook.

She doubted he was checking to see if she'd brought oats.

She did not get far before she was snatched from the ground by unseen hands and flung on the back of the nightmare horse. "Hide her, Sam!" a fierce voice shouted as she was dropped astride. She grasped frantically for the mane, scrambled not to fall off. It seemed safer to ride the creature than to fall under its hooves.

Unfortunately, Jordon was no rider. The glance she spared to see who'd dropped her unbalanced her completely and sent her tumbling from the back of the galloping horse. She landed on the wet lawn with stunning force, too dazed to move. Winded, she lay there as chaos reigned around her.

A scream jerked her attention to the right. Jordon peered through the curtain of rain, scanning the darkness. As lightning flashed, she gasped. There was a woman out there. Battling a . . . griffin?

Jordon had no time to fight with her automatic rationalizations that griffins didn't exist; the woman was losing. Seizing a fallen tree branch, she struggled to her feet. There was a flowerbed in her way. Without a thought for the daisies, Jordon tramped through the plants and dashed across the wet lawn.

It wasn't until she'd nearly crashed into the combatants that she realized her mistake. Up close, she could see that the "woman" was nothing more that a wasted wraith, a monster with bones peeking out where pieces of her had rotted away. Jordon could see the creature's ribs through the rags it wore. It hovered over the ground, using a rusted sword to hack at the griffin. If the griffin hadn't been such a tremendous jumper, gifted with wings, it would have been dead.

When it spotted Jordon, the wraith's red eyes lit. It opened its mouth and screamed, a piercing shriek that paralysed her and sent her to her knees. She dropped the branch and pressed her palms to her ears, but nothing stopped the pain. Her ears had to be bleeding. She gritted her teeth, but couldn't hold back a moan of agony. That sound would kill her.

The banshee had forgotten the griffin. He sprang at her while she was distracted, shredding the monster's decayed flesh with his razor-sharp talons. The monster fell to the ground, writhing. With one final snap of his powerful beak, the griffin severed her head from her shoulders.

Jordon panted as the pain ceased, cautiously lowering her hands. Shuddering, she watched the griffin rip the corpse apart. Her hand felt through the grass, closed around the branch. Hoping the griffin would stay occupied, she began to back away, eyes lowered, as if she were backing away from a mad dog.

She had not gone three feet when she bumped into something. *It moved.*

With a war cry, Jordon whirled and swung her stick with all her might. She thought she had struck the head that belonged to the eyes that now hovered above her, but she didn't linger longer than it took the beast to grunt in pain. She ran towards the house she could see at the end of the gravel path with a speed that would have surprised her old gym teacher, propelled by sheer terror.

The griffin leaped in front of her, landing in a flurry of wings. Jordon cried out, tried to brake, and skidded on the wet grass. She landed on her butt with a wet squish. Terrified, she waited for it to attack.

The griffin eyed her, then sat back on its haunches. It cocked its great head, and began to clean its talons calmly.

Jordon drew a deep breath. Slowly, she got to her feet. A furtive glance to the side showed more dark shapes in a loose circle around her. The night was black, but she could hear them breathing. It was hard to contain her fear, but she put forth a mighty effort. Panic didn't seem like a good idea.

"It was brave of you to attack the banshee," the griffin said, giving her a start.

"Foolish," someone grumbled.

Jordon shifted. The heavy stick in her hand was hardly reassuring. "I wasn't attacking her." There was a short silence. "I didn't realize what she was until I got closer." She was babbling. To counter it, she bit down. It helped to still the chattering of her teeth, too. The rain may have abated, but the wind was frigid.

"You're cold," the griffin observed. "You should go in."

"Great idea," she said quickly. "If you'll excuse me?" She waited for someone to move, but no one seemed in a hurry to do so.

Another flash of lightning lit the circle around her, giving a glimpse of big, winged bodies to her right and left. It was enough to see that there were gaps in the ring, easy enough for her to slip through. Shaking, she took a quick breath and darted between the bodies.

She couldn't help a glance back, but none of them had moved. Eyes front, she speed-walked towards the house in the distance. She didn't look again to see if anyone followed. She hoped not.

The driveway must have been a quarter-mile long. Though she could only snatch lightning-lit glimpses, the mansion at the end looked old, gothic. Were there people inside? Only the darkened windows kept her from breaking into a sprint to reach the place. If it was deserted, would she find a door or window unlocked? The griffin had said she should go in. Did he know the people inside?

The storm was fast becoming one of the worst she'd ever seen. Whips of lightning split the sky with almost supernatural frequency. Suddenly one speared an ancient oak tree not fifty yards from her, splitting it in two. The thunder came so quick it deafened her, drowning her shrieks.

Jordon decided she didn't care if the mansion housed a battalion of zombies; she ran for it. Stumbling up the stone steps, she skidded to a halt at the door and pounded for all she was worth. "Hello?

Help! Please let me in." She looked quickly over her shoulder, expecting to be pounced on at any moment.

It took a determined round of banging on the old iron knocker but finally there came a deep echoing sound as the door grudgingly swung open. An old woman with black eyes, and the biggest nose in Christendom, scowled down at her. "We're not open to travellers."

Jordon stood up straight, her composure somewhat restored by the long wait. "Ma'am, I know we've never met, but I would be grateful if you'd allow me in. I—" She was interrupted by the crashing voice of thunder. There was a howling note to the wind, like a live thing denied its prey.

The old lady looked at her with more interest now. "Well now! Got the banshee after you, have you? Heh. Perhaps I ought to let you in after all." She swung the door open, smiling a rather white and sharp smile at the wind's protest. She grabbed Jordon as the wind suddenly tried to suck her away from the thick, iron-bound door, and pulled her firmly inside. The sudden quiet as the door slammed was almost eerie.

The woman sniffed. "Nothing like hemlock and iron to keep out unwanted guests." She picked up her old-fashioned oil lamp from a side table and glanced at Jordon. "Come. You're dripping on the floors."

Jordon glanced around as she followed her hostess, taking in the dusty elegance of the house. "I didn't get a chance to introduce myself. I'm Jordon Hearst."

The old lady raised a brow that was nearly as thick as her nose. "You may call me Mrs Yuimen. I am the keeper of the kitchens here." As she spoke, she led the way through a great hall with a polished table and murky floors. "The housekeeper has left us some time past and has yet to be replaced. You can see it needs attending to." She spoke as if this were somehow Jordon's responsibility.

Jordon blinked. "I see." She was unwilling to offend Mrs Yuimen, lest she be given the boot. "I really appreciate –"

"Yes, yes," Mrs Yuimen interrupted. "Now, be seated and I'll pour you some tea." She entered the kitchens as she spoke and gestured to the rocker and stool before the old brick hearth. A one-eyed cat looked up from the rug there and growled a warning as Jordon shuffled over, choosing the stool. She didn't want to take what must surely be the cook's customary seat.

She cast a wary eye at the glaring, reddish-coloured cat and the odd green flames of the fire. "I've never seen a fire burn green before."

"Driftwood," Mrs Yuimen said as she moved efficiently about the kitchen, setting up a tea cart.

"Oh," Jordon said, disoriented. "Are we by the sea?"

Mrs Y. cast her an odd look but otherwise didn't comment.

The kitchen was so spotless as to seem a world apart from the rest of the house. Mrs Y. had enormous worktables that, while nicked and battered enough to be fifty years old, were polished to a high sheen. Stacks of wooden bowls and crockery lined the shelves, and ropes of garlic, onions and herbs hung from the beams. The stone floors were neatly swept, and the tiled, wood-burning cooking stove was free of soot and food residue. Even the copper tea kettle was brightly reflective.

When she'd assembled the cream and sugar and such, Mrs Y. rolled the cart over to Jordon and poured the tea.

"Thank you," Jordon said gratefully as she accepted a piece of apple, and some cold ham and cheese from the birch platter. Cold drops of rain water still ran down her neck, chilling her. Carefully, she wrung her hair out over the basin and tried to squeeze some water out of her sweater.

Mrs Y. made an impatient sound and found her a kitchen towel. "Here, use that. You're making a mess. And take off your clothes – I'll fetch a blanket."

"Th-thank you." Mrs Y. was quick, and Jordon was soon wrapped in a quilt, her feet in borrowed bed-slippers. She watched Mrs Y. wring out all her clothes and hang them over chairs near the fire. They quickly began to steam from the heat, but Jordon knew it would be hours before they were dry. "I was wondering if you had a phone here? I'd like to call for a cab." She bit her lip, silently questioning just what help a cab would be. She wasn't exactly in the city here. Looking around, she began to wonder if she were even in the same century. Though that was absurd, right? Where else could she be?

The old woman looked at her with gleaming black eyes. Too large and black, really. Combined with her odd grey hair – like wet soot, with a subtle life of its own – she didn't look either modern or normal. "I have a suspicion you're not asking about a hansom, which you'll not find here in any case. And unless a 'phone' is an odd term for a footman, I think you'll find yourself unsatisfied."

Jordon opened her mouth to speak and was interrupted by another angry peal of thunder. She glanced warily towards the window and had to stifle a sudden cry. A man stood there in the shadows, just behind the workbench. His chest was bare, the rest of him hidden by the bowls on the countertop. "Who are you?" Jordon demanded, trying not to take a peek at the rest of him.

Mrs Y. didn't seem disturbed. "Oh, Lord Griffin! This is Jordon Hearst. She was caught in the rain tonight. Join us for tea?"

Griffin came closer and smiled into Jordon's wide eyes. "We've met."

Jordon looked hard at him. Surely he didn't mean . . . but his hair was tawny and crested, more like feathers than hair. His nose was hooked, the jaw strong, but with a rather pointed chin. The eyes were dark, with glints of gold. Her heart accelerated as she recognized the voice. "Griffin?"

He cocked his head, like a hawk considering prey. She took it as affirmation – and fainted dead away.

She didn't think she'd been unconscious long. Griffin's feathery hair was still dripping when she came to. In fact, it was probably the drops falling on her nose that woke her.

She sat up carefully, but there didn't seem to be any new aches. It was then that she noticed he was naked. Since he was crouched beside her, she wasn't particularly stressed about that – it wasn't as if he were totally on display. Oh, he was well muscled otherwise, of course. Fighting monsters must be great exercise.

She shook her head, feeling dizzy. "I think I could use some whiskey," she muttered. With a little help from him, she climbed carefully back on the stool.

He smiled as he helped to steady her. "I'll bring you some brandy. It'll take the chill out better than tea."

She watched him as he walked over to a cupboard. She numbly accepted a jam tart from Mrs Y., trying in vain not to stare at Griffin's better parts while he poured her drink. It was difficult; there was a lot to look at. She averted her eyes when he caught her at it.

"My apologies. I've run with my brothers too long," he murmured, then reached into a lower cupboard to fetch out a tablecloth. He wrapped it deftly around his waist. "Better?"

Jordon lowered her head and muttered something non-committal. In other circumstances, she'd feel obliged to correct him.

He returned to the fire and handed her the brandy snifter. "See if that helps."

It did, actually. It even helped her to maintain her calm as he pulled up a chair and sat across from her with his own cup of tea.

He smiled at Mrs Y., then commented to Jordon, "You're doing very well. I imagine most damsels would be in hysterics by now."

"Yes, well, American girls are tough," she said. "We aren't bothered by drinking liquor with half-naked, shape-changing griffins. Though if we were back home, I'd probably be having an Irish coffee . . . with a little extra Irish thrown in."

"Ah." There was silence for a moment. Maybe he was organizing his questions. "You came through our gates earlier, trailing banshees and storm gremlins. I wonder what they wanted with you?"

She released a shaky breath. If she'd had lingering doubts about his identity, his words erased them. "It really was you outside."

"Mm. My brothers were there, too." He took a careful sip of tea, then slanted a questioning glance her way, as if judging the state of her nerves.

He was right to be concerned. Hysterics threatened again, but she stared at the ceiling until they passed. "I have a question. Where am I?" It came out pleading. She felt obliged to explain. "I'm supposed to be in America."

He was silent for a long moment. Finally, he set aside his tea cup. "You're in England, darling. I *am* curious to know how you missed the transition. I'm told it's a three-month journey by ship."

She frowned very hard to suppress her distress, though she wasn't terribly amazed. Both he and Mrs Y. spoke with British accents. "I was struck by lightning. It . . . did things to my memory. Tell me, what year is it?"

He looked even more curious. "It's the twelfth day of July, 1837. We have a new queen on the throne." He frowned. "I say, you're looking rather pale. Can I get you something?"

Her lip quivered. "Starbucks," she whispered. "The internet. Real books." While she enjoyed *Pride and Prejudice*, it had nothing on modern werewolf romance. And what would she do without Stephenie Meyer? She wanted to cry.

To disguise her distress, she stared at the green fire. If she'd had somewhere to go, she'd have left that instant.

Griffin exchanged glances with Mrs Y. "Our guest is tired. Why don't you prepare a room for her? I'll keep her company until you return."

Mrs Y. left without a word. Griffin looked at Jordon thoughtfully. "I'm wondering what happened to you before you entered our estate tonight. The lads at the gate tell me you appeared, 'between one lightning flash and another'. Normally they would have smelled you coming."

Jordon drew a deep breath. The brandy was already affecting her judgment. Why not tell him? Maybe he could actually help. "The lightning brought me." When he remained quietly interested, she added, "I was crossing the road. A car almost hit me – I swear, it was *trying* to hit me – and suddenly I was here. Well, in the road, at least. I don't know how." Despair threatened her self-control. "I'd just like to go home."

"Hmm." He stared into the fire for a long moment. At length he said, "Well, I'm no Traveller myself; I don't know how it's done. Unfortunately, those who do know are not the sort you can trust to see you home. They're more the type to take you to their lair and keep you." He smiled as if he understood the urge. "I suppose we'll just have to keep you ourselves."

Jordon's hackles rose. "I'm not a lost puppy!"

"So I see," he almost purred. "However, you need a dry place to sleep tonight. I can offer that."

Her eyes narrowed in warning. "Can you guarantee I'll sleep alone?"

His eyes swept slowly over her, reminded her that she wore only a blanket and a borrowed pair of slippers. He smiled. "You will be safe here; if you wish to be."

His words made her stomach tighten under the scrutiny of this unwanted interest. The man was gorgeous, but too confident for his own good. She wasn't going to encourage him. "Not interested," she said firmly, and set aside her cup. She didn't need more brandy when he was in the room.

"Very well." He rose and offered her a hand up, then tucked it neatly through his arm. The gesture was so courtly she found it hard to object, though the feel of his heated skin against her hand was subtly delicious. She tugged free, saying, "I need both hands on the blanket."

His smile was wolfish. "Of course. We wouldn't want it to slip."

Jordon was not used to blushing, so she tried to hide her face and ignored him. As she did, movement caught her eye. She glanced out of one of the dusty windows and stiffened as lightning flashed, illuminating the large shapes that prowled the yard.

Griffin followed her gaze. "Yes. They are awake. And busy, I suspect. You've brought quite a storm with you. It's a good thing that you came to us. You seem to have stirred up some serious trouble. I don't think any of the neighbours would have dealt easily with it."

Jordon swallowed. "Are they like you? Griffins and such, I mean." For all she knew, she'd landed in an entirely different world. Tonight, anything seemed possible.

He grinned. "I'm afraid not. They're rather ordinary, for the most part. Careful on the stair; those slippers are rather big for you." His hand hovered protectively at her back as she took the marble stairs in the floppy slippers.

She wished it wasn't so protective. She was in more danger of stumbling from the heat of his hand than from the oversized foot gear. She held herself stiffly, ready to object if he got fresh, but the hand hovered, just shy of her back. It was worse than if he'd touched her outright.

Then she found herself silently following him through the draughty, dusty old house. The only source of light was Griffin's candle and the occasional flare of lightning. Stern oils frowned down at her from the walls as they passed. Sculptures of plaster and older, worm-eaten wood ones gazed at her with solemn, chiding eyes. All around her, the house breathed, expectant. She had the uncomfortable feeling that something was required of her.

To distract herself, she said, "You have a lot of art here. I expect to come upon the statue of David at any moment."

He smiled down at her. "You'll find no stone statues here. Gargoyles are touchy about that sort of thing. The idea of being trapped forever as stone . . ."

Jordon frowned. "Gargoyles?"

They had come to a lighted doorway. He paused outside and looked in. "Mrs Y. has been busy."

Jordon peered in. Mrs Y. saw them and grunted in satisfaction. "We've not had guests in years. I had to pull the Holland covers off and fetch fresh bedding." She'd lit a fire in the hearth, Jordon saw. It burned with a reassuringly yellow and orange flame.

Mrs Y. moved to the wardrobe and removed a neatly folded square of white. She shook it out, revealing a long-sleeved, cotton nightgown with a row of tiny buttons down the front. Pretty and old-fashioned, the bodice and hem had tiny blue flowers embroidered with twining silver vines. She laid it across the bed. "There you are, and I brought warm water for washing." She pulled a large jug from under a tea trolley and poured the steaming contents into the old-fashioned washstand. "And that should be that until morning."

Jordon paused, acutely aware of the man at her side. It felt too intimate with him here. "The room looks very comfortable, thank you."

Mrs Y. looked satisfied. "I'll see you in the morning, then. We rise early." She let herself out.

Jordon glanced at Griffin. He hadn't moved. "Well. Goodnight, then."

He smiled, slow and warm. "It has been. I've enjoyed your company."

Her blood felt thick, her heartbeat a little too strong. She wished now that she'd had nothing to drink. She didn't handle liquor well. She licked her lips, searching for a reply . . . and he kissed her.

She instantly forgot what she'd been going to say. His lips were soft, scorching hot. Or maybe she was the one on fire. Her insides certainly seemed to be in meltdown.

His hands were gentle, yet firm as he slid one into her hair, used the other to span her waist. He kissed her as if they were already old lovers, as if he had the right.

It was long moments before she was able to lower her head, breaking the kiss. "I don't know you."

He gently stroked the hair away from her face. "You know this." When she turned her head away, he said, "You're a widow, aren't you?"

She looked at him, startled. "How did you know?" It came to her then, just what age she was in. He would have certain ideas about "good women". It was ironic, considering her origins, that he was actually right.

"You're not afraid of me," he said with certainty.

"That's not exactly true," she hedged, backing away a step. "I don't understand what you are."

He looked at her keenly. "One advantage to being more than a man is that I can smell exactly how you feel right now. It is difficult to resist."

She swallowed. "Make an effort. If for no other reason, you don't want to father a child tonight." She had not been on birth control since her husband had passed away nearly two years ago. She had not been ready to risk her heart again.

To her surprise, his eyes flared with interest. "Don't be so certain! If I thought such a thing were possible . . ." He took a careful step back. "Children require a more careful level of courtship. I will have to consider this." He made her a slight bow. "Goodnight." Before Jordon could ask him what he meant, he was gone.

As a man of dual nature, Lord Griffin had often had to battle the animal side of himself. Tonight, he was inclined to agree with the animal. He wanted her, and when she'd mentioned children . . .

He shook his head. Well, it had been coming on him for some time now. He had fought the urge to take a mate, partially because he enjoyed his freedom, partially because he'd never found a woman who seemed right. Of course, he'd never met a woman like Jordon.

She was a puzzle. He wasn't particularly bothered by her origins, but he was interested to know why the banshee had come after her. As far as he knew, the banshee were never far from their native bogs and moors. He'd never met one in person until tonight. Had she somehow angered them?

He reviewed what she'd told him. Someone from her time tried to kill her – a man? She was brought here, apparently by lightning, and it had saved her life. The banshee attacked her. Had they been sent? A powerful fae could arrange that. Fae could also time travel.

An interesting puzzle, and griffins loved puzzles. He would have to consider this. And since the lovely Jordon was part of the puzzle, he would have to think very earnestly of her as well. Smiling to himself, he made his way to his room.

⋆   ⋆   ⋆

Jordon dreamed of her killer. She could not see his face, could not seem to remember it, either. Yet she knew it was him.

He was a shadow in her dreams. Warm, seductive. "Ah, Jordon, my love! We got off to a bad start. And here I've come to make amends." He held a white rose in his hand, a sign of peace. "Do you forgive me?"

Jordon was in the same room she'd fallen asleep in, but instead of soft quilts and a cotton gown, now her only covering was a thin silk sheet. In the dream she was aroused, deeply so. It made her angry. "Go away!"

His voice was teasing, though he pretended to be wounded. "Ah, but I've promised to make peace with my sister. She was very upset that I put you in harm's way." He moved closer as he spoke, trailed the rose over Jordon's calf. "I've been very naughty."

She gulped and kicked at the rose from under the sheet. "Get out!"

He ignored her, sat on the bed. Jordon hunched into a ball at the headboard. "You're making me angry," she bit out. Even the force of her arousal was not enough to combat that.

He scanned her slowly. "It will come to a choice, you know. There could be peace if you choose me. Griffin . . . he is an animal, you know." He shook his head chidingly.

"Jordon."

She didn't know who spoke her name, but the shadow seemed annoyed. "He would come," it said.

"Jordon!" It was Griffin's voice, and he sounded concerned.

"Interfering animal," the shadow said, and stood up. "Very well. There will be other nights."

"JORDON!" Griffin roared, and this time her eyes flew open. She sat there staring at him . . . and then she looked down at her foot. A single white petal lay on the quilts. With a cry of alarm, she kicked it off as if it were a spider. It flew into the air and vanished.

"Did you see it?" she asked Griffin, panicked. "The rose? He brought a rose!"

"I believe you," Griffin said soothingly, stroking her back. "I heard you through the wall."

"W-what wall?" she gasped. She was hardly coherent. The dream had scared her so badly.

"Mine is the next room," he said, still soothing. "I'm glad you woke me."

But Jordon was in no mood to be soothed, not like this anyway. Fear was not the only lingering effect from the dream, and Griffin was a handy outlet for her seemingly insatiable desires. She threw herself at him, ground her mouth into his . . . and suddenly it was not the dream alone that drove her.

He tasted delicious. She'd never had a kiss so luscious. His hair was like silk.

Griffin was not the least put off by her demands. After one startled murmur, he enthusiastically took over, curling a hand around her hip to draw her closer. Moments later, her gown flew over her head, apparently by magic. He was not interested in going slowly, and neither was she.

He loved her breasts with tongue and gently nipping teeth. She urged him on, gasping when he reached down and squeezed her. Her legs fell open on reflex, and he laughed as his mouth trailed down.

His lips were oh so soft, but not as hot as his gentle tongue. Jordon screamed, writhing to escape his wicked torment. It pleased him so greatly that he prolonged it, lashing her again and again.

He did not warn her when he was ready, just rose over her and thrust deep. She screamed in instant climax, then moaned as he rode her, watching her face, milking every sensation from her until she was soaked and begging. Once there, his face changed, broke into a snarl. He sank his teeth gently into her neck and drove hard, shaking the entire bed.

She fell asleep on top of him, still intimately joined, and woke again in the night. The words they exchanged during their new round of loving could not be termed conversation. "More" and "yes" were more than enough.

Jordon woke to an empty bed. Hazily, she raised her head and surveyed the tangled sheets. The quilt was sideways, and her feet stuck out. A glance at the window showed it was almost dawn.

She groaned and stuck her head under her pillow. She could still feel him inside her, was still tingling from the last time he'd seduced her. She could not have managed the fourth round without his promise that he'd do all the work. Not that he had in the end. She just couldn't help herself.

She muttered to herself and threw the pillow off. Lurching to the washstand, she surveyed herself in the mirror there, and winced. No hiding that hickey! The man did like to leave his mark. A glance at her breasts showed faint evidence of his attentions, too.

She hung her head and sighed. Stupid girl. Nice going. One bad dream and she threw herself at the first available man. Lovely.

She looked around for her clothes and remembered that she'd come up here wrapped in nothing but a blanket. Growling to herself, she cleaned up at the washstand and then wrapped herself in last night's quilt.

She kept her head high as she marched down the stairs, just in case she ran into a servant. Fortunately, there didn't seem to be any lurking about. She'd just made it down the stairs and was marching for the kitchen when she was suddenly scooped up like a doll and carried into an empty parlour.

"Griffin!" she shouted, not appreciating his enthusiastic greeting.

He ignored her and sat in an armchair, arranging her on his lap. He kissed her with great energy, as if he hadn't spent all night enjoying her. "Good morning."

She pushed him away, gasping a protest. "Griffin! Do you mind –" She broke off in a yelp as he tugged down her blanket and kissed her breasts in greeting.

"Good morning! Hell-o," he murmured appreciatively. "I've missed you."

She growled at him, but there was no heat in it. It was hard to be stern when he caressed her that way. She slowly relaxed under his soothing hands, loving the rumble of his voice as he praised her.

"Am I interrupting?" a languid voice intruded.

Jordon gasped and covered her chest. There was a man in the doorway, studiously looking at the portrait on the wall above their heads. Dressed all in white and cream, he looked like a gentleman. He held a folded newspaper in his hand, and he seemed rather disapproving of the goings-on.

Jordon struggled to get up. Griffin tightened his arms around her and stood, gently setting her on her feet. "Hello, Sage. This is Jordon Hearst. I'm afraid I waylaid her on her way to the kitchen."

"Indeed." Sage glanced over what he could see of Jordon's neck and swollen lips. "Perhaps I should escort her the rest of the way. You seem to be a somewhat negative influence."

Jordon flushed, but walked straight towards him and through the door, saying over her shoulder, "I can escort myself, thank you. I was leaving this morning anyway." Oh, she couldn't wait to get away! How embarrassing.

Griffin was at her side in an instant. "Actually, I'm fairly certain you don't want to pass through the dining room right now. That's what I was going to tell you before I got distracted."

She stopped outside the door and looked at him with suspicion, "Why? Is someone in there?"

"My youngest brother is likely having breakfast."

Jordon paled. She definitely didn't want any of his brothers seeing her like this. She shot a glance at Sage, wondering if one already had. She started to run a hand through her hair, then had to grab for the blanket again. "OK," she said shakily. "I need my clothes. Coffee, too. I think you can manage that much." She glared at Griffin as if this were all his fault. "Once I'm dressed, I'm leaving." She looked around, seeking a refuge. "I'll wait in the parlour. The front door is closer from there."

Griffin raised his brows, but seemed to agree. He inclined his head and headed for the dining room. Sage went with him.

Jordon retreated to the parlour and sat stiffly on a chair. She couldn't wait to get out of there!

Griffin met the interested face at the dining table with a cool stare. He knew his brother Samhain had heard every word. He also knew it wouldn't be repeated. Sam was no more a tale bearer than Sage. It didn't stop him from asking questions, though.

"Ms Hearst sounded upset," he said calmly. But his ears gave him away. He couldn't flatten them as a man, and the slightly pointed tips twitched. He peered through his mane of black hair as if waiting for a chance to trample his older brother.

Griffin grimaced. "She's embarrassed. Sage arrived at an inopportune moment." He fixed a plate for Jordon and poured a cup of coffee. No doubt she'd be hungry. He'd been starved this morning. It had taken two heaped plates to satisfy him.

"Is that for you?" Sam wanted to know.

"No." Griffin set the plate aside, intending to get it once he'd collected Jordon's clothes from the kitchen. He was thinking furiously of delaying tactics. He'd decided sometime in the night that he was keeping Jordon. Now he just had to convince her of the wisdom in staying.

Mrs Y. sent him a knowing look as he entered the room. Well, she'd known what she was doing when she gave Jordon the room next to his. She'd been trying to get him to wed for years.

He ignored her and headed to the fireplace. Jordon's things were dry, and most of her clothes had been folded and placed on a chair.

"I washed her socks and underthings," Mrs Y. said casually. "I'm afraid she'll have some difficulty, though. Her sweater seems to have disliked the rain."

He shot her a curious look, then lifted the soft blue sweater from the pile to have a closer look. After a moment, he smiled. Somehow he doubted Jordon would be in a hurry to leave in this.

Jordon was dismayed to see her favourite sweater shrunken to the size of a handkerchief. But she rallied quickly. She was not going to allow it to slow her down. "I'll need to borrow one of your shirts."

Griffin made a face. "Darling, it would swamp you! If you'll be patient, I'll send for the village seamstress. She's really very good."

Jordon looked at him coldly. "I am not sitting around in a blanket all day. Nor am I going to wear *that*." She glared at the maid's uniform that he'd brought along as an alternative.

He looked over her head and drew a breath as if to control his temper. He did not seem interested in helping her leave. The storm was over. She needed to go home if she could.

She worried about that as she put on the shirt he brought her, ignoring the way it hung to her knees. She grudgingly thanked him for the jacket.

"It's chilly this morning," he said off hand. "Shall we?"

She wished he wasn't the one walking her down the long driveway. Walking gave her too much time to think. She began to feel apologetic. "I'm sorry about last night."

He raised his brows in enquiry. He was still being cool and aristocratic.

She hated it. "It was my fault. If there are . . . complications . . ."

He stopped. "I suggest you stop right there. We can discuss this after you've had a look at the road. Once you've ascertained for yourself that you can't go home, we'll discuss it further."

She looked at him grimly. "I think I should say it before I disappear. There may not be another chance."

"I doubt that." He began walking again, rapidly this time. "Magic doesn't work that way."

"What do you mean?" She had to stretch her legs to keep up with him.

He saw it and slowed to an easier pace. "You were brought here for a purpose. You'd do better to spend your time discovering what that is than . . ." He trailed off. "No, forgive me. I suppose you're being reasonable enough, from your point of view."

She looked at him, surprised at his capitulation. "Really."

He smiled charmingly. "I'm merely upset that you're so eager to run away from me."

She coloured and looked forwards. "About that. I'm not in the habit of leaping on men. It's just that it's been a while." She saw that he was listening attentively. "My husband's been gone two years now. He was killed in battle."

"I'm sorry," Griffin said respectfully. "You loved him, of course."

Her throat tightened. "Yeah." They were approaching the gates now. It seemed important to make him understand. "I think it's become a habit, you know? The grief. I've been searching for a way to . . . heal, I guess. Last night, I think I used you." She swallowed.

He stopped her. When she wouldn't meet his eyes, he took her hands. "Jordon Hearst, I do not feel used. Have you considered that finding a new love is one of the best ways to heal?"

She jerked her hands back with a gasp. She wanted to berate him. How dare he? And yet . . . "I don't love you. I barely know you."

"Today, that's true. You don't know what tomorrow will bring."

She didn't want to discuss this. She strode through the gate, still hoping he'd leave her alone. She searched the ground carefully, glad for the excuse to hide her eyes. She didn't love him. There was no such thing as love at first sight.

Of course, there were no such things as griffins, either. Or time travel, for that matter. She ignored that errant little thought, concentrating on her task. She didn't have time for nonsense.

She didn't know what she expected to find on the road. In the daylight, it was an ordinary country lane. She walked over to the place where she estimated she'd arrived, looking for a feeling of *otherness*, for any sign of what had transported her last night. There was nothing. The only significance about the area was its proximity to the mansion gates. She glanced at them and sighed. She had a feeling she knew what Griffin would say about that. Annoyed, she ruthlessly began to search the trees at the side of the road for anything that might trigger a portal home.

Griffin seemed to be searching, too, though she got the feeling he was more interested in possible danger than in portals. His head was up, and his nostrils flared as if scenting the wind. After last night's fight with the banshee, she couldn't blame him. She even found she was glad of it.

It was as she searched the ditch that she felt the growing sensation that something was wrong. She glanced at the woods, as if she could peer through the trees to see what might be coming. "Griffin?" she said uncertainly.

He saw the direction she was looking. She thought she could *see* his hackles rise. He grasped her arm and began walking her towards the gate. "Quickly now."

She didn't resent his taking command. She knew something wasn't right, too. A zing ran down her spine, and her breath came faster. The feeling didn't make sense, but she hadn't forgotten the banshee. Never mind that she'd never been bothered by so much as a stray premonition before, Jordon headed for the gates at a rapid clip. She would have run if Griffin hadn't kept her at a walk. *Something was coming!*

He appeared before the house when they were halfway up the drive. Dark, urbane and unapologetically *other*. Beautiful danger, seductive killer. He stood there dressed in an old-fashioned, midnight-blue frock coat, white ruffles spilling from the sleeves and cravat. Long hair, a burnished black, spilled from under a beaver top hat. Both hands rested on a polished ebony cane with a silver knob. He studied her with blue, blue eyes.

"I know you," she whispered, appalled. "You're the man who tried to kill me with the car."

Griffin looked at her sharply. He seemed coiled, tensed to fight, but he stayed quiet and listened.

The stranger smiled slightly. "A miscalculation. I've come to pay my . . . respects."

"Your respects!" Anger flashed through her veins, tightening her muscles. She was ready to lash out at him when another thought occurred. "You know how to take me back!"

His mouth quirked. "There would be no point, you know. The house would only draw you back here."

She glanced suspiciously at the house behind him. "It's not alive."

His smile grew razor sharp. "You haven't been here long enough to appreciate it. Meanwhile, I hope to further our acquaintance. I am called Naturu. The pleasure is mine, Jordon Hearst." His scintillating smile hinted at the kind of pleasure he meant.

Griffin smiled with white, sharp teeth. "Don't be so confident, fae. She's spoken for."

"Am I?" Jordon asked sharply. She turned her attention back to Naturu. "I'm afraid you'll have to leave. I'm not usually thrilled to meet a would-be assassin." She expected him to protest, or attempt to charm her, but he only inclined his head.

"As I said, I regret the circumstances of our first meeting. As a token of apology, I came to offer a friendly warning." His tone was silky, caressing. "Do not leave this place alone, Ms Hearst. There are more than shadows waiting outside these gates."

Griffin's lip curled.

A chill kissed her spine. She remembered the fear that had made her run back to the house, knew without a doubt Naturu was right. It didn't make her like him any better, though. Acidly, she said, "You're too kind."

He smiled seductively. "I can see I've overstayed my welcome. Accept my parting gift, then, and think of me with better favour." He bowed, then disappeared in a swirl of black smoke. She glanced around, but he was nowhere in sight.

Griffin met her gaze with hooded eyes. "He's gone. For now." His eyes swept over her, his expression carefully neutral.

She followed his gaze, blinking in surprise as she caught sight of her clothes. She was now wearing a blue cashmere dress over a pale blue, silk under-dress. The sleeves and neckline were liberally adorned with pearls. There were even matching silk slippers upon her feet. It was beautiful, but ... "Stupid man! Those were my favourite jeans." She was not inclined to look with favour on Naturu's gift. He'd tried to kill her!

Sage spoke dryly from the front door. From his words, he must have witnessed most of the conversation. "Be grateful he didn't turn *you* into a lowly moth. That one could have done far worse."

He frowned at the dress. "It suits you better than Griff's shirt, at any rate."

Both she and Griffin glowered. Neither one of them liked Naturu messing with her clothes.

Griff gently took her arm. "We'll have the seamstress in today. You deserve a choice of clothing."

She hesitated, glanced back at the gates. Had she really searched as well as she could have?

Griffin leaned down to whisper in her ear. "It's not worth the danger. You can search again another time."

She considered, then reluctantly allowed him to escort her inside. He was probably right . . . for now.

Griffin waited until Jordon was settled in the parlour with a tea tray before making his offer. He worked up to it, of course, and made a very fine effort.

Jordon was not impressed. "Marriage." She grimaced and set down her tea. "There's no reason for that, Griff."

He looked at her steadily. "There is the possibility of a child."

She sighed and looked around the dusty parlour. "I think you need a maid more than you need a wife. What happened to this place?"

"We were away. Our help deserted us. Unfortunately, it is not easy to find servants who can adapt to our household. Fae work well, but they were threatened in our absence. I don't blame them for leaving. About my offer—"

"I'll entertain it, but I need some answers first. Who is Naturu? You didn't seem surprised by him."

He clearly disliked the subject change, but he humoured her. "He is the brother of our matriarch. The house, you know."

"No, I don't know. What about it?" she asked, slightly irritated. "There seems to be an unspoken assumption around here that I know things. Maybe you'd better back up and give me some of the history of this place."

He thought for a moment. "Very well. It might help simplify things.

"Many years ago, there was a fae named Hyani. As a child, she played with the young of a clan of shape-shifters. Eventually, she came to love a young shifter named Traic.

"Her family did not approve. They forbade her to be with him. Instead of obeying them, she ran away to be with her love. By the time their hiding place was discovered, they had already produced three children. Her parents, while angered, did not want to discipline their beloved daughter. Not all fae felt the same way.

"There was war. Traic was killed in battle, but his friends the gargoyles helped Hyani and the children escape. They fled to the mortal world, but Hyani could not overcome her grief. In her despair, she transformed herself into a form that could shelter her children, but would be unable to suffer the pain of loss. She became this house."

Jordon blinked. "She became a *house*? How is that possible?" She looked around, trying to see a living being in the walls around her. It looked ordinary enough to her, if richly appointed and rather dusty.

Griffin shook his head. "After all you've seen, how can you doubt? Have faith that the house is what remains of our ancestor.

"It is said that the ladies of the house sometimes hear her guidance. I wouldn't doubt she had a hand in bringing you here. It's been a long time since there was a woman she could talk to."

"Mrs Y. is here," Jordon pointed out.

He smiled. "Mrs Y. is extraordinary, but she is not family." Before she could comment on that, he went on, "Hyani's children were of mixed blood and inherited long life, something that infuriated the fae, who were jealous of the gifts. They did not want to see mortals rival them in any way. There has been strife between the two races ever since, though the fae are careful never to attack Hyani in any way that would raise the ire of her family, for fae children are rare, and she is still much loved by her parents.

"Her brother is not as reserved. Although he seems to care for his sister and is thought to commune with her still, he considers her children to be freaks. We've suspected that he works with her enemies. The attempt on your life seems to confirm it. I think he knew you were someone of interest to Hyani, a possible successor. She has been known to matchmake before, very successfully. He would not like to see another mated pair." He smiled. "He was right to be afraid."

Jordon tried not to squirm. "You don't know that's what's going on."

"It seems logical. Which brings me back to the point. Will you marry me, Jordon?"

Jordon tapped her back teeth together. "I've not given up on going home, you know. If the house could bring me here, she could send me back. All I have to do is convince her."

"Luck with that," he said, not in the least upset. "She's not known to change her mind. I'm interested to know how you would plan to raise a griffin child alone, by the way. They tend to be headstrong. She would need guidance."

"What makes you think it would be a she?"

He smiled. "Most first children tend to be, in honour of their grandmother. I would be pleased with a boy or a girl. I would enjoy being a father."

She didn't appreciate him being so nice about this. It made him harder to deal with. "You don't know that I'm pregnant. In light of that and the fact that we hardly know each other, I think marriage is fairly premature. You don't even know that we're well suited."

"Hm." He stared thoughtfully at the mantel. "A valid point. I propose a courtship period, then. What say you to a month? Surely that would be long enough to give you an idea of my character."

Jordon didn't recall specifically agreeing to his request. He somehow managed to make it seem as if she had. He even went so far as to formally introduce her as his fiancée to his brothers at lunch. When she called him on it later, he said, "I'm the confident sort."

She took it to mean that he was arrogant beyond measure.

Servants began to appear at the house over the next few hours. Jordon couldn't pinpoint exactly what was odd about them, though Griffin informed her they were the fae who had formerly served in the house. Noses were too big on some, fingers too long on others, as if they couldn't quite master the nuances of the human form. Seeing them cleaning industriously made her wonder, though. "How long were you gone, Griffin? A couple of months?"

He shrugged. "Oh, fifty years or so. They get touchy if you're gone for a while, and we've been home only a matter of days. Now that we're here, Mrs Y. has set about coaxing them home."

She stared at his face. Considering he didn't look older than thirty, that seemed amazing. It was not something she felt comfortable asking about just then, however. There was something more pressing she wanted to know. "Tell me about the gargoyles."

He looked thoughtful. "I could show you instead. You seem brave enough to handle it." He smiled, but it slowly faded. He looked at her seriously. "There are other things you should know, too."

She was wary. "Like what?"

He glanced at the windows, perhaps tracking the path of the sun. "Samhain, Sage and I are shape-shifters. It's part of who we are. We need to spend part of each day in our natural forms, or we suffer."

"Suffer how?" She pictured agonies of the damned, men screaming in pain.

"It's melancholy at first. We become moody and withdrawn, go off our feed. If left for a very long while, some shifters become suicidal. You could give us the best things in life, and we still could not cope with the grief. We need to be ourselves."

"Oh. I see." His explanation made sense.

He watched her carefully. "Good. You'll understand then when I tell you that we chose the night to be our animal forms. We are nocturnal by nature, and it keeps our neighbours from noticing. Since it's also the time when the gargoyles awaken, it is most convenient. It's also why we eat dinner just after sunset. Gargoyles wake hungry."

Jordon thought about that for a moment, then cleared her throat. "OK. You're telling me that you'll all be at the dining room table as your true selves."

He smiled at her. "This shape is also a 'true self'. I'll just look a little different."

"Right." She nodded, then kept nodding as she processed his revelation. How did a girl brace for all that?

Griffin suggested she meet the gargoyle clan first, hoping it would be easiest on her. "You might also want to ask Rook how his nose is doing. He was the one you hit with the stick. He'll be the black one, with white hair."

She winced. "Sorry about that. I was a little shook up last night."

"Hm. Well, I won't let him eat you. You should know he tends to be moody, though."

As a result of his warning, she was feeling a little nervous as they approached a gate set in the high shrubbery. The gate itself was hidden from the house by an oak tree and a group of flowering bushes. Griffin had to unlock it.

"The gate is warded to drive away any guests we might receive. We don't want visitors to wonder why the statues change positions from day to day." He held the door open for her.

Jordon stepped inside, looked curiously at the group of five statues within the large garden. Each one rested on a wide stone pedestal, and no two seemed to be the same. There were several that she recognized as gargoyles, though none of them were the squat, ugly monsters she'd been expecting. They were alien, yes, with hard, sharp angles, like the one with spikes on his elbows and wingtips. He had claws, and his face was set in a snarl, but she saw the beauty in his features, too. There were others like him, though each was unique in his own way.

Jordon hadn't known how the sight of them caught in stone would affect her. The thought of seeing them wake should have daunted her more than it did. Stronger was the urge to see them free.

She gently touched the foot of the gargoyle closest to her, felt the stone flex under her hand. She gasped and pulled her hand back. The stone subsided.

Griffin grinned. "It's all right. They're close to waking. No doubt you startled him."

She gave Griff a wide-eyed glance, then went back to watching the silent gargoyles. As the sun dipped below the horizon, the stone flexed slowly, moved like a living thing. All around her, chests expanded, drew in air. Colour bloomed over the stone, turned it to onyx, jade, carnelian, quartz . . .

Jordon paced backwards, the better to view the change. As stone slowly became flesh, a powerful joy seized her and, with it, a sense of helpless fear. She didn't know these beings. She had no cause for joy. *What was happening to her?*

She still felt awkward at dinner. By then she suspected that part of what she was feeling came from the house itself. All day it had seemed as if it were whispering to her, subtle thoughts that just brushed her mind. That was odd enough, but the reality of sitting across from seven mythical beings was almost overwhelming.

Griffin sat on her left in his griffin form, the size of a horse. A handsome, gleaming brown with golden beak and claws, he was rather intimidating. It was difficult to convince herself that he was also the man she'd spent the day with, and much of last night.

The gargoyles were able to sit, though Jordon thought they would have been more comfortable on stools than in high-backed chairs, for their wings draped uncomfortably behind them, and none of them seemed to rest their spines against the upholstery. She speculated that the pressure on their wings was uncomfortable.

Sage and Samhain stood at the table, though the stallion's food and water was actually on the floor. Jordon wasn't terribly shocked when Sage was brought a couple of whole, raw chickens. He was a giant white owl, after all, easily the height of a man. It did cause her some consternation when a bowl of freshly butchered rabbit was placed before Samhain's stallion form, along with a bucket of strong black coffee. She didn't comment, of course, but she did pour herself a little more wine.   Unfortunately, her own excellent meal was going mostly untouched. She was too tense to really enjoy it. Though they were on their best behaviour, she was just not used to such extraordinary company. She sipped at her glass of wine.

She studied them carefully, trying to be subtle. In return they eyed her boldly back as they shoved food into their maws. There was very little talking. Eating was serious business.

After a few minutes, Jordon left off picking at her soup. When she saw Griffin eyeing it, she shoved it his way. "It's good, but I'm not very hungry."

He drank it carefully, making the bowl look dainty as a tea cup. "Very nice." It was odd to hear his voice coming from a griffin's beak.

She cleared her throat. "Do you often eat human food when you're a griffin, or is meat better for your body?" Someone had poured more wine into her cup. She took a sip.

"I prefer meat, though cheese makes a nice snack. Bread is pretty tasty, too."

"But no vegetables," she said, smiling a little.

"Definitely not."

She accepted the next course from a freckle-faced boy. She doubted he was as human as he appeared. Jordon couldn't imagine too many Victorian citizens would take the sight of her present company in their stride. It wasn't too many years past the time when a supposed witch would have been burned at the stake. She assumed the same would happen to gargoyles and such, should they be caught.

She lowered her eyes to her salmon and buttery fried parsnips. She noticed the gargoyles were served the same, and plenty of it. Unlike her, they didn't seem to be as careful of fish bones. She drank the last of her wine and poured some more. "Mrs Y. is a good cook," she said, trying to make small talk. "You're lucky to have her."

Rook coughed, amused. "The local farmers are lucky we have her! Happy for them, not all of us enjoy raw meat." Like the others, he didn't bother with tableware, deeming his fingers utensil enough.

"And the farmers frown on missing sheep," a sharp-edged gargoyle called Vicious said between bites. He had black hair, blue skin and wings. Chuckles followed his statement.

"They wouldn't really steal," Sage explained to her calmly. "The estate provides for all of us. As night guardians, they hardly have to beg for food."

Jordon looked to Griffin. "If you're all awake at night, who guards the place when you're asleep?"

"Unlike the gargoyles, we can be awake in the daylight. We need little sleep," Griffin explained.

The blue gargoyle grinned a sharp white grin. "It gives him more time to cat around. The ladies like his company."

Griffin growled in warning, and Vic lost his smile. "What?"

The wolf-like creature next to him, Howl, snickered. He had roast beef stuck in his teeth. "Don't mind him. He's not too smart."

"Vic's barely thirty," the thin purple one across the table from him spoke up, cutting across the brewing fight. Jordon thought his name was Lance. "He probably hasn't noticed what's happening between you two."

Jordon stiffened, set down her fork. "I wasn't aware there was anything happening," she said with strained calm. She didn't like to think of the relationship between her and Griff as public, not when she barely knew what to make of it herself. She nervously took a sip of wine.

Lance stared at her. Cornered, he shot a glance at Griffin, and quickly changed the subject. "I'm the best flier. Howl tracks like a wolf."

"Better," Howl shot back. He crammed a whole boiled potato in his mouth.

Jordon let them change the subject, but her appetite was completely gone. What was she doing, sitting here like this? She should be trying to convince the house to take her home. She didn't belong here. "Excuse me. I don't feel well," she said. Avoiding Griffin's eyes, she quickly stood and left the table, praying he wouldn't follow her. She was quite sure she would start wigging out if she had to sit still one more minute and pretend that everything was normal.

Everything was not normal! She was trapped in a living house, out of her time, and slightly drunk. She stumbled on her skirt as she was climbing the stairs and upgraded that to "definitely drunk".

Since it was either leave the table or climb the walls, screaming, she thought she'd made the right choice.

She didn't even try to reach her room. Tonight she rather wanted to be lost. She didn't want Griffin to find her too soon, not when she felt so confused. She needed time to think.

That was how she found the balcony. Stumbling through dark rooms until she found one lit by moonlight, she followed the white path to a double French door. It swung silently open to reveal a cosy balcony overlooking the front lawns. A brisk wind blew at her, perfect for clearing her head.

Jordon closed the doors and leaned on the rail. As long as no one went for a flight, she'd have her privacy. She smiled a bitter smile and closed her eyes. Ah! How did things get so complicated? This had all come on her much too fast. Was there a way to prepare for something like this?

"Take me back," she told the house, putting her heart into it. "We are not a good match. You know it, too. I'm no good for him."

"*Is he good for you?*"

Jordon blinked. The quiet thought hung there, as if waiting for a response.

She didn't have one. Griffin good for her? Jordon broke it down, simplified it. Was Griffin good? Of course. Though she hadn't known him long, she felt sure of that. Was he good for her? She bit her lip and stared over the shadowed lawns. Though she wrestled with the question for a good long time, she couldn't find an answer.

The chill finally forced her inside. Somehow she was not surprised to find him waiting there, and in his human form. At least he was dressed.

He bowed, very formal. "This place can be confusing. I thought you might have gotten turned around. May I lead you back?"

She sighed. "I wish someone would."

They were silent as he escorted her back to her room. When they reached the door, he looked down at her solemnly. "Am I invited tonight?"

Part of her was tempted. She would have loved to be held. Instead she shook her head. "It's no good, Griff. I'm not good company tonight."

He nodded soberly, reached for her chin. He hesitated just before touching her. When he spoke, there was unhappiness in his voice. "May I kiss you goodnight?"

His pain made her heart ache. She nodded softly.

She recognized that kiss for the mistake it was an hour later, when she'd had time to think. Griffin was a ruthless seducer. Only now, draped naked over his drowsing form, did she have time to acknowledge it.

He'd worn her out. She closed her eyes, promising she'd deal better with him tomorrow.

At first she didn't realize she dreamed. She was twined with Griffin, but there was another presence in the room: the shadow man.

He studied the pair of them critically. "Well, that was quick! I see my sister has gotten her way again."

"Naturu," she whispered, barely able to speak, to move. She felt as if the air had become a pressure, holding her down. "G'way."

"I'm afraid not." He examined his cane, his tone off-hand. "You realize I don't approve. We'd whittled the numbers down to seven, my friends and I. I've no interest in seeing a population explosion." He looked at her with regret. "I'm afraid I'm going to have to kill you." He took a brisk step forwards, raising his cane that now sported a barbed tip. His eyes were locked on Griffin's chest.

"No!" she shouted as the paralysis abruptly lifted. She sat up, threw a pillow to deflect his aim. "I won't let you kill him!"

He took aim again . . . To her surprise, Griffin was shaking her, telling her sharply to wake. Her eyes flew open, and she looked around wildly. "He tried to kill you!"

Griffin's jaw tensed. He put a calming hand on her shoulder, then looked to the spot where she'd last seen Naturu. "Come out. I can smell you."

Naturu's voice came out of the air, bored, as if he hadn't just tried his hand at murder. "What would be the point in that? I find it's much easier to kill you this way."

Griffin smiled grimly. "Brave fae! Noble foe to come at your prey in the dark. I had heard that you'd become craven over the years, O hero."

"One does not require chivalry to slay an animal." Naturu's voice had a distinct edge.

Griffin smiled as he baited him. "And in your sister's house no less. She'll certainly forgive that."

"What is it you want? Shall I give you a sporting chance?" Naturu spat. "Very well. Tomorrow, at dawn. I will meet you before the house. Winner gets the girl . . . and any monsters she might be breeding." The voice held sinister promise.

They waited in tense silence. Finally Griffin said, "He's gone."

"Was he really here?" she whispered, still shaken. "He was in my dreams . . ."

He tucked the blanket around her shoulders and held her close. "He's fae. They do that." He nuzzled her temple. "This one won't bother you again, however. I'll take care of it tomorrow."

She jerked her head up, nearly clipping his chin. "What? You're going to fight him? That's what he meant, didn't he? No! I don't want—"

He shushed her, first with his voice, then with gently persuasive kisses. "I'll be careful. I promise. All will be well."

She tried to argue, but his lips stilled every argument, until she finally just pushed him back. "Look. There has to be a better way."

He took her hand in his, kissed it. Then he slowly coaxed her to lie against his chest. "Very well. I'll talk to him tomorrow. We'll sort this out."

Her breathing slowly began to calm. "You will? You think he'll listen?"

"I can be very persuasive," he said reasonably, stroking her hair. "I'll have my brothers with me, too."

That calmed her. It wasn't as if he'd be all alone. She didn't know what she could do against Naturu, but she would be there too, of course. She'd talk to the house if she had to, get her to intervene.

As her pulse slowed, her eyes got heavy. Promising herself she'd sleep lightly, Jordon drifted off.

A bone-jarring thud woke her the next morning. She opened her eyes, stared out the window with bleary eyes. An angry groan came from somewhere far below her window.

She glanced at the lightening sky and gasped. Dawn! Grabbing her dress, she dashed for the window. She was just in time to see her Griffin climb to his feet and launch himself at the giant black griffin snarling on the lawn.

Jordon bolted for the door, struggling into her dress as she went. The hall seemed endless, the stairs a dangerous slope as she flew down them barefoot. The front door was ajar, and she threw it open, skidding to a stop on the landing. The griffins were locked in unequal battle, Griff biting and feinting viciously at the monster twice his size.

"He allowed Griffin to choose the form," Sage said calmly as she stared, appalled. He didn't seem surprised to see her barefoot, with the back of her gown hanging open. He did hold out an arm to block her as she tried to run past. "He doesn't need your help."

"He needs someone's!" she cried, trying to get past. "Why are you just standing here? Help him!"

Sam moved to block her way as well, shifting sideways with his back to her. He barely spared her a glance. "What? You want the fae to continue pestering you? Griff told us he was haunting your dreams."

Jordon opened her mouth to answer, then stiffened as Sage moved behind her and began to efficiently fasten the back of her gown. She watched the battle, wincing from time to time. Naturu was fast for such a big monster. It was fortunate Griff was faster.

"You need a ladies' maid," Sage murmured, fastening the last hook.

"I need an Uzi," Jordon shot back, twitching with the urge to help Griff. She needed a weapon!

The sound of a meaty smack made her look back at the battle. Griffin flew through the air and smashed into an oak trunk. There was a cracking sound, and he was still.

When he didn't move, Naturu relaxed. He stood on the lawn in a watchful, but not aggressive, stance.

Jordon feared the worse when the men stood back and let her through. She ran to Griffin, checked as gently as she could for a pulse. She couldn't tell if he was breathing. "Griff, please wake up! Can you hear me? Please." There was blood, but she wasn't sure how much of it was his. For all she knew his worst injuries were internal.

Panic threatened, but she fought it down. The grief was harder. How could she care so much in such a short time? "Griffin? Please. I don't want you to go." Did he stir? Hoping her words were reaching him, she pleaded, "Please live – for me? I'll stay here for you. It's not so bad, really, even if it is stuffed full of griffins and gargoyles. I don't mind if you're feathery once in a while."

He actually laughed, though it was weak. "You hated dinner. You're afraid."

She drew a shaky breath. "I'm afraid of losing you. There! Are you happy now? I admitted it."

His body heaved as if he were trying to get to his feet. "I need to finish him." He groaned and flopped back down.

"You need a doctor, or a vet," she said severely, trying to push him back down. Remembering Naturu, she turned around, but the griffin hadn't moved. There seemed to be some kind of force field surrounding her and Griffin. "What is this?"

Abruptly, Naturu was his fae self once again. He smiled bitterly. "My sister has decided to take a hand in things, it seems. She has no sense of fair play." He considered Jordon broodingly. "I've half a mind to claim my prize anyway. I've clearly won."

Abruptly Griffin was on his feet, looking far too hale for a creature near death. "Not today, foul one. Why don't you take yourself off?"

Naturu's eyes sparked, but then he looked at the house. "Ah, sister! Very well. I'll humour you for now. There are other ways we can settle this matter." With an enigmatic glance at Jordon, he disappeared in a swirl of black smoke.

Jordon stared at the place where he'd been, then she turned to glower at Griffin. "You were playing possum."

He took a step towards her and winced. "Mostly."

She bit her lip, unsure if he were truly hurt. "It might help if you turned back into a human. I can't see your injuries through your feathers."

Abruptly, he was a naked man, covered in gore. He smiled ruefully as she started. "You'll have to get used to it, darling. After all, you did promise to stay here with me."

She pursed her lips. She *had* said that. She was starting to realize that she'd meant it, too. She really did want to be with him. "I didn't say how long I'd stay."

He smiled and pulled her close, ignoring the way she squirmed away from the blood. "Finicky, tricky woman. Just try and leave." He kissed her temple, smiling to himself. "You'll have to wait until the dressmaker finishes your clothes, at least. This one is ruined."

Though she suspected he'd ruined her dress on purpose, Jordon did stay until she had new clothes. She remained through the summer, in fact, and on into the fall. By then the babe she carried was obvious to all.

Griffin had let her go two days before presenting her with a ring. "We're married," he said flatly. "We'll have a ceremony here and do things the human way so that there's no doubt. You're staying with me, though."

She frowned at the ring, then squinted up at the ceiling, which was now blessedly free of cobwebs. The new maids had been busy. "I don't know. There are a lot of things about my time that I might miss. Good coffee—"

"Mrs Yuimen makes excellent coffee," he said sternly.

"Books—"

"I'll give you the library. We'll kick Sage out," he promised.

She looked at him and smiled softly. "You. If I went back, I would definitely miss you." His expression made her heart go soft.

There were many things about her new home that were strange to Jordon, and none stranger than her new husband. She loved him though, this knight who had saved her from a bad end. If she must live in a faerie tale, at least she would get a happily ever after. That was something even a modern girl could appreciate.

Last Thorsday Night

Holly Lisle

The Thorsday Night Writers were getting down to business when a cold autumn wind swirled through the room, leaving a tall, rugged blond in its wake. He stood in the doorway, looking a little lost and a lot out of place – a man who did not belong.

It's hard to look out of place in a writers' group – especially one like ours, which specializes in science fiction and fantasy.

Jason MFA-Working-on-PhD had the mandatory professorial waist-length ponytail, goatee and tweed jacket; William I-Write-Bleeding-Edge-Crossover dressed only in black turtlenecks and black jeans; Carol My-Tiny-Heroines-Can-Kick-Your-Big-Ol'-Heroes'-Asses dyed her hair carrot orange in homage to Robert Heinlein's heroines, wore elf-green contact lenses, and favoured spandex – which admittedly looked fantastic on her; Apocalypse-and-Dystopia Tophe (short for Christopher) had run out of places to tattoo, and had moved on to making sure he'd never pass through a metal detector alive; and Shora I-Only-Write-in-the-Nude (who thankfully wasn't writing at the moment), favoured low-cut skintight angora sweaters, miniskirts, and six-inch heels when she did deign to dress. An ex-stripper, she was smart and tough, hated her job as an office manager, and wrote unfinished fantasy novels about women who conquered the universe by lying on their backs.

In contrast, the stranger's summer-blond hair was short and neat, and he wore a plain dark-brown T-shirt with a pocket – no clever sayings – and faded blue jeans a little on the tight side (bless you, handsome newcomer). He did have well-defined muscles; what he did not have was a Look. "Sorry I'm late," he said to Jason, and my heart hit the floor at the rumble of his voice. Oh, that voice. "I had a little trouble finding the place. Thank you for inviting me."

He glanced at everyone in the room, studied me for a longer moment, and gave me the sort of smile a five-year-old gives an ice-cream cone. He strode through the circle of folding chairs and took the empty seat to the right of mine.

Which simply doesn't happen.

Because ... me, I'm the woman men notice when there aren't any busty twenty-something ex-lap dancers or sylphlike Heinlein heroines around. We were full-up on both, and they had empty seats next to them, too.

The new guy swung his enormous backpack to the floor beside him, where it made a substantial thud, pulled a legal pad and pen out of it, then leaned over to me and whispered, "What have I missed?"

All the oxygen leaving the room, I thought. When did that happen?

I managed to find my voice though, and I said, "Pizza. When Jason hosts, he always has pizza for us before the meeting."

"No writing yet?"

"No. Official start time is in ten minutes. You're not actually late," I told him. "We're waiting for two other writers to arrive – Narnie, who has a long drive to get here, and Tyler." I'd been half-heartedly and sporadically dating Tyler for about four months, a fact I suddenly wished wasn't true.

Tyler arrived like the king for his coronation, spotted the stranger sitting beside me, and glared at him. He came over and took the empty seat on my other side, leaned over and whispered in my ear, "Who's he?"

"New guy," I whispered back. "Jason invited him. We haven't done introductions yet. We're still waiting on Narnie."

Narnie Hampstead was our resident pro. She had fifteen published novels, plus a bunch of shorts in various magazines. Jason had an MFA and taught creative writing, but Narnie actually wrote for a living. She was the one whose crits we all saved and double-checked as we were writing and revising.

The rest of us were wannabes. I was the Wannabe-Least-Likely-to-Ever-Publish-*Anything*.

It wasn't that I didn't write. Seven completed novels gathered dust and mouse droppings in the trunk at the foot of my bed, and I could not muster the courage to send out any of them.

After a year in the group, I'd finally brought myself to read *Wall of Rivers*, the best of my trunk novels, to everyone. Narnie told me I should send it out, that it was really good.

But I hadn't. I couldn't.

Next to me, the stranger was introducing himself. I realized Narnie had come in and taken her seat while my head was in the clouds.

"Thanks, Jason," the stranger said. "I'm Per Tordönsson. I'm just getting started writing. I didn't bring anything to read tonight. I want to see how this works first."

Both Carol and Shora oozed "Hi, Per," in melting tones. Beside me, Tyler snorted.

"I'm Nila," I told Per. "I write, but I haven't sold anything yet."

Per looked into my eyes and smiled again. All he said was, "Wonderful to meet you," but he said it like he meant it. *Really* meant it. Like meeting me was the most important thing he'd done all year.

There may be a moment in every woman's life when she sees someone she doesn't know and, for just that moment, wants what she cannot have because every cell in her body is screaming at her that this . . . *this* is the person she's supposed to be with. Or maybe that's just me. But right then, right there, feeling the bass vibrations of Per's voice resonating in my chest, staring back into his eyes, with his left knee bumping my right one . . . that was *my* moment.

I wanted.

I could feel Tyler stiffen in the seat on my other side. He put his arm around me and said, "I'm Tyler Boothe Mayall, the defence attorney. I intend to be the John Grisham of fantasy." He was a Thorsday Night charter member, and he'd been using that as his introduction since *I* joined.

Per called him on it. "Terry Brooks beat you to that thirty years ago, big guy." This caused Tophe and Carol, who couldn't stand Tyler, to burst out laughing. Giggles echoed around the rest of the room. I stifled my own laugh, but not fast enough.

Tyler's arm around me tightened.

The tension between the two men grew palpable.

After Tophe finished reading his latest reworking of his third chapter, which should have been called "Why My Hero Should Drink Arsenic Right Now and Make the World a Better Place", Per gave Tyler a sidelong glance that would have killed small animals at a hundred yards.

Tyler glared at Per and groped me, and I shook him off. The two of us were not *there* – never had been.

They were two big dogs, circling. I had no idea what was going on.

But whatever it was, it made the hair on the back of my neck stand up.

Halfway through the meeting, Tyler leaned over and murmured in my ear, "Why don't we get out of here and go to your place? I have court tomorrow morning, and I don't think I can stand any more of Shora reading."

While I agreed with him on Shora – her heroine that night had already slept with a werewolf, a were-tiger, two dark elves (one male, one female, both at the same time), and was at that moment being chased by a vampire through the reptile display at the zoo, where I winced to think what was going to desire her next – I was sitting beside the handsome enigma, and the burning question on my mind was, if I hung around, would he smile at me again? Besides, Thorsday Nights only happened every other week, and I loved them. "I still haven't read yet," I told him. "I brought chapter one of my new story, and I want to get some feedback."

Tyler said, "Read it another night. I don't want you going home alone. I don't trust your neighbourhood," but he wasn't looking at me when he said it. He was looking at Per Tordönsson.

Per Tordönsson. Who rested a hand lightly on my shoulder and said, "Nila, please stay and read your chapter. I'd love to hear it." He looked past me to Tyler. "I'll see her home, or one of the other men here will."

"She doesn't know you, and neither do I," Tyler said.

Tyler had a point. Per's interest in me, in my writing . . . it was completely out of place. It unnerved me. But I didn't want to leave the meeting. I was having fun.

And Tyler was being possessive way past anything our half-dozen dates entitled him to. We weren't a couple. We hadn't slept together.

He'd driven me home one night and had stayed over because it was so late, but he'd spent the night on the couch. And brought me breakfast in bed the next morning, which he'd gone out to get, and which had creeped me out, though I couldn't figure out why.

"I haven't invited you over," I told Tyler. "And I'm having fun. My neighbourhood's good, and I'll be fine."

He looked completely unbothered that I'd blown him off. "I'll drop by first thing in the morning, sweetheart," he said, loud enough that Shora stopped reading, which was a blessing, and that everyone else looked at the two of us with surprise, which was awkward.

Tyler was one of those men who didn't *get it*. We weren't working out, but he seemed to think we were. I decided in that instant that our last date had been just that. The last.

"I'll bring you breakfast in bed again, baby," he added.

He might as well have peed on my leg. He was telling Per, "Don't be there," without actually coming out and saying it. As if Per and I . . . well, as if there were any possibility for there being a "Per and I".

"Don't," I said.

I was glad to see Tyler leave.

The rest of the evening was fun. Long, but fun. I read, and people made useful comments. Per sat silent after I finished reading, blinking like he was trying not to cry, which was crazy, because my first chapter wasn't sad at all. He reached over and touched my hand once, just brushed it, and said, "Thank you."

I didn't know what to make of that.

Narnie read. Jason read. The Thorsday Nighters talked. We laughed.

At 3 a.m., we were all packing up and telling tired, silly jokes just prior to heading out the door, when Per stepped in front of me and took a deep breath and said, "Before you go, can I show you something?"

I looked at the earnest expression on his face, and said, "Sure."

He turned so his back was to everyone in the room but me, and pulled a book out of his backpack. He put a finger to his lips, then handed it over.

I took it, turned it over, and saw the title. *Wall of Rivers.*

My title.

My heart started to race, and when I glanced at the author's name, I had to sit down.

Nila Sturgess.

It was a new copy, printed beautifully by a publisher I'd never heard of. I opened it to the middle and out of habit sniffed the pages. There is no smell like book.

I turned to the copyright page.

And closed my eyes.

Wall of Rivers was in its thirty-seventh printing, with a copyright renewal in the name of the Estate of Tyler Boothe Mayall. And a print date more than fifty years in the future.

I turned to the back of the book, to the author photo on the inside flap of the dust jacket. The picture was mine – one Tyler had talked me into having taken only a few weeks earlier. "Because you're so pretty," he said, "and when you're famous, you're going to want a nice picture of you when you were young to go inside your books."

It was the stupidest reason I'd ever heard for someone wanting a photo. I figured he'd just wanted it for himself.

But . . . there it was. I turned to the first page. The words were my words.

I handed the book back to Per, and saw how badly my hand was shaking.

Per took it, and touched my fingers lightly in the process. What he said next was the biggest understatement I'd ever heard.

"We need to talk."

We went to an all-night diner – one of those chains where you can have breakfast or dinner twenty-four hours a day. It had the advantage of being public while still being anonymous. *Wall of Rivers* was the manuscript Tyler had asked to read the night he stayed over because he said he was having trouble getting to sleep. I would have been insulted, but Tyler did not exactly have a way with tact. I'd put it down to him being him, and hadn't thought about it again.

But now I needed an explanation. How and where had my novel come to be published, what did the date and number of printings on the copyright page mean, why did Tyler's estate own the copyright? How had Per gotten his hands on it?

I ordered a diet drink. I didn't think I was going to like what he would say, and diet cola was all I could trust my stomach to keep down.

Per, on the other hand, ordered half of everything on the menu.

He started by saying, "I'm not supposed to be here, and I'm screwing things up by doing this. But I love your books. You've been my favourite author for years."

I shivered. He was heading into the territory I'd feared.

"You want a sweater?" he asked. "I have one in my bag."

"I'm . . . fine," I lied, which was clearly the stupidest thing anyone has ever said. I was a long damn way from fine. He shook his head, his half-smile telling me I wasn't fooling either of us.

"No, you're not. How could you be?"

"I started out being fine," I amended. And that was true enough. He'd sat beside me at Thorsday Night, he'd smiled at me, and he'd made my heart beat faster. But now everything had gotten scary, and I had to ask. "You're not from . . . here . . . are you?"

"Swedish Institute of Historical Research, Time Validation Division," he said. "In Helsingborg."

"That's where. How about *when*?" I'd written time travel. I was proud of myself for making the leap so sensibly, for not falling apart over the situation that was presenting itself to me. I was, I thought, at least as cool as my characters right then. I was a bit freaked out. But I'd seen one of my future books. So at least I knew I was going to eventually get up the nerve to send out my work. And that when I did, at least one of them would sell.

The idea that I might also end up marrying Tyler, though, wasn't doing too much for the residual pizza churning in my stomach.

Per nodded. "I'm from about sixty years ahead. But you and I don't have much time. We mustn't talk about me. You have to know the truth about you before you go home *tonight*."

Something about the way he said "tonight" made my skin crawl.

"Why tonight . . . specifically?"

He reached into his bag and pulled out a ring binder. It was gunmetal grey, and made of a material as cool and hard as metal, but as pliant as plastic, impressively space-age-y.

He handed it to me, and said, "Skim. You'll get the gist of this quickly."

The binder held copies of newspaper articles far more exotic than the originals had ever been: the paper was creamy with a semi-gloss finish, and the words on the first page scrolled down as I read them. I didn't have to touch anything. The paper seemed to be tracking my eye movement and helpfully putting the next words I needed to read where I needed them to be.

Any doubts I had about the legitimacy of my printed book were laid to rest by the binder with its tech-we-don't-have-yet paper. Per Tordönsson *was* from the future.

And the date on the first article was tomorrow . . . no. We weren't in the middle of Thorsday Night any more. We'd slipped into plain old Friday morning. The paper's date was today. The headline read WOMAN SLAIN BY INTRUDER IN HOME INVASION. The photo Tyler had badgered me into getting identified me as "woman slain".

I closed my eyes and wrapped my arms around myself. "I should have let Tyler take me home," I said.

"No," Per said. "You did the right thing. Just keep skimming."

There was an article where Tyler said my murder was a huge tragedy, that I'd just sold my first novel, that we were engaged, that I had no one else in the world. That we'd been so happy together. The bit about me having no one else in the world was true enough. But everything else was a lie.

Through newspaper articles, videos (also on the amazing paper, with sound included) and copies of legal documents dated well into the future, I discovered that Tyler had somehow had himself designated the executor of my estate. He'd managed my first novel sale into a bestseller by playing heavily on my emerging talent cut short by the tragedy of my brutal murder. I tried hard not to think too much about the "brutal" part.

It didn't hurt that the books had been good. But the promotion had been . . . well . . . inspired.

I looked up at Per.

"I've loved you . . . your work . . . since I found the first book by you," he said. He put his hand on mine and said, "You are a brilliant writer. And I lo—" He shook his head.

I couldn't catch my breath. "I . . . you . . ."

He touched a finger to my lips and said, "You have to understand the situation – quickly – because there are some choices you must make. I need to know what you want. Your work has become classic in my time. Millions of people have read you, have had their lives changed and made better by your stories. You're famous, you're beloved." He took a deep breath, and continued, "But all the probabilities suggest that your work only found its audience because you died so horribly – and because Tyler Boothe Mayall jumped in to market your just-sold book on your death. The odds are that if you had lived, all seven of your novels would have stayed in the trunk in your bedroom, along with any others that you might have written, and neither I nor anyone else would have ever heard of you."

So.

If I died later this morning, I could be famous. Big-time famous. My words would live on long past my final breath. I would achieve the sort of literary immortality most writers dream of – and almost none get.

If I lived, odds were good that when I was dead no one would know I'd been here.

He was watching my eyes, looking for answers there. I doubted he could find any.

I buried my face in my hands.

I loved writing. And I loved the stories I told, the characters I created, the themes I explored and pursued and eventually pinned down and answered. I *wanted* people to read what I'd done, to love it as much as I did. And I wanted to leave something of me behind when I was gone.

But I loved breathing, too. I loved waking up in the morning to the sunlight falling across my face. I loved walking the block to work, where I was a copywriter for a small ad agency. I loved the taste of cherries in summer and apples in autumn, the way my muscles burned when I stretched, and the way my heart pounded in rhythm with my feet when I ran.

I could be immortal if I died today.

I could be nobody at all if I lived tomorrow.

But the odds were I couldn't have both my life and my fame.

"Writers dream about reaching millions," I said. "But we also dream about being around to enjoy it."

He nodded. "I know. And I can't know how long you will live if you don't die today, or how much more you will write. There are no odds for that, no way to predict, no way to track what didn't happen. But I can tell you . . . having heard the first chapter of your new book, I would give *anything* to read the rest of it."

I frowned. "Only . . . whether I live or die, you never will. Because either I won't live to write it . . . or I won't manage to publish it."

"Those aren't exactly the options. Don't worry about what comes next. Or about me. Tell me what you want now. Do you want to become as famous as . . . well, not Shakespeare, but as famous as Tolkien? If you have to die today to do it? I know some writers would give anything for that guarantee." He took a deep breath, and said, "Or would you want to live, knowing that if you do, odds are no one will ever know who you were?"

I drank the last of my diet soda and put my hand over his. "How long do I have to make up my mind?"

"Your murder happens at 7.24 a.m."

I looked at my watch. It was 4.10 a.m.

I put my hand on his and said, "I have to go home. I want you to come with me."

"I . . ." He looked away and blinked and swallowed, and I saw one tear slide down the side of his nose.

Without another word, he went to the counter and paid the bill, and we walked out together.

He was staring at his shoes as he walked me to my car. "So you have decided? You want to die and be famous in the world you leave behind?"

"No, Per. I just want to know there's something worth living for.

I had to go back to my place. My gut demanded it, but my mind wouldn't say why.

I couldn't run away. Well, I could – running away had been what I'd been best at my whole life, frankly. Foster homes, jobs, relationships . . .

But holding the book I'd written in my hands and knowing I hadn't lived to see it published, that someone I didn't like much had taken my work and my passion and made it successful after I was dead because I hadn't had the guts to even *try* while I was alive . . .

Yeah. I had to go back to my place. I didn't know what was going to happen there, but I wanted to have a say in what did.

Per didn't talk much on the drive over.

He sat in the passenger seat, staring straight ahead. When I glanced over at him I could see the muscles in his jaw working. I realized he was angry. I wasn't sure why.

Finally he said, "You know why I came back?"

I should have asked that. "No."

"I've been reading and rereading your books since I was fifteen. They changed me. They gave me a way of looking at the world that I don't think I could have found on my own. I'm a better man because I read you than I ever would have been without you. And there are a lot of people like me out there, which is why your books are still selling. You said something that mattered.

"But," he continued, "the whole story of how you died never felt right to me. Your lawyer fiancé—"

"Tyler has never been my fiancé. He's someone I've gone out with about maybe six or seven times in the last four months. He belongs to the same writers' group I do. That's it."

Per bit his lip and took a deep breath, and I realized my relationship with Tyler was beside the point at the moment.

"The man *everyone in my time thinks* was your lawyer fiancé told a good story. He had all the paperwork to prove you'd made him your designated heir and the executor of your estate. The signature on your publishing contract perfectly matched the signatures on everything else he had on his desk—"

"I never signed a contract," I said.

"I know that now," he said, and the muscles in his jaw jumped harder. I told myself to shut up and let the man finish. He said, "In my time, I went through everything available on your life, because there was this air of wrongness about your lawyer."

I forced my mouth shut, but I thought, He's not my lawyer, as loudly as I could.

"When I read the interviews that didn't get wide coverage, I realized your Thorsday Night Writers were too surprised that the two of you were engaged, and absolutely flat-footed that you'd sold a novel and hadn't even mentioned it at the last meeting you attended." He glanced over at me, his expression unreadable. "So I became a field historian – a time-travelling researcher – because I needed the truth. Always in the back of my mind I held this tiny hope that one day I might be able to travel back to see you while you were alive. Maybe even talk to you. Nothing consequential, nothing that would change anything. But just . . . I held that hope." His voice broke, and his body tensed.

I sat silent for a moment. "And now you're doing something that is almost certain to change the future," I said. "Why?"

"One week ago in my time, I made a registered trip back to this morning. A few hours from now. To your apartment. I'd spent the last two years building a case against Tyler Boothe Mayall being your legitimate heir, and I presented my case to the Head of Literature Research. Because you're an important historical figure, my request to validate Tyler Mayall's story about his association with you went through. I was allowed to come back here, set up recorders in your room and in Tyler's home and office to document the specific details of your death and his actions following it. Once the recorders were in place, I had to leave. I couldn't be in the room because just my presence could break the rules of historical engagement.

"I did the standard three-month forward-time transfer to a point when I knew both apartments and the office would be empty, and I dropped myself in, extracted the recorders, and went back to my own time."

"One week ago – in my time – I saw the man who killed you break into your room, almost the way Tyler said it had happened. Except that prior to his breaking in, Tyler used his key to let himself into your apartment while you were still at the meeting, and unlocked your bedroom window. I saw him do it. And I saw the intruder . . ."

Per's voice broke again. He took a deep breath as I pulled into the parking lot in front of my apartment. The apartment in which an unlocked window would be used by a murderer intent on killing me.

I'd never given Tyler a key to my place. But he had spent a night over. Had brought me breakfast the next morning. Had left the house to do it.

Per said, "The intruder slapped duct tape over your mouth while you were sleeping, and then . . ." He shook his head. "He brought both a knife and a gun. You didn't die quickly. It was the . . . horrific details of your murder that made your death famous enough to guarantee immediate public recognition when your publisher overnighted your book to the stands. Several million copies of your first novel sold. The quality of your work – and Tyler flogging the tragedy of your death every time he and your publisher brought another one of your trunk novels to print – kept you a household name. But . . ."

He turned and stared into my eyes. "You weren't yet dead and your killer was still busy with you when Tyler got there."

"And tried to save me?"

We sat there in the parking lot, in the dark, and Per took my hand, and held it tightly between both of his. It was as if our hands had been created just to fit into each other like that.

He said, "No. Tyler told the killer to hurry up, because he had other things to do."

I had no words.

I fell into the darkness inside my head for a long time, until pain pulled me back to the world. I realized the stick shift was digging into my right hip, and that Per had his arms around me, and that I was sobbing into his shirt.

"Oh, God," I whispered. "And you came back to . . . to what? If you change history and I don't die, won't you have never read my books? Won't there be a paradox that will make it impossible for you to come back at all? The fact that you're here means that I have to die, doesn't it? You just came to be with me, to . . . give me something to put me to sleep or something so my death wouldn't be so awful, and then you're going back . . ."

"No," he said. "You *don't* have to die. I'm not here officially. It took me a week – my time – to arrange my absence and bribe the people who could get me here. If you wanted to guarantee that your work would live on after you do, I did bring something you could take so that you wouldn't wake up during your murder." His arms tightened around me, and his voice went hoarse. "*If that was what you wanted.*

"But that's not why I came back. That's not why I became a historical researcher. That's not why I specialized in literary research. Nila, I fell in love with *you* through your books when I was fifteen. You were in them, in every one of them, and I wanted to meet you. And in person, at the meeting tonight, you *were* the woman who wrote those books. I was afraid I'd be disappointed, that you wouldn't be anything like what came through in your work – but it was *you*. The you I'd known existed. The you I've loved for half of my life."

"If I don't die, you'll never read me. You'll never become a historical researcher."

"I'm here, Nila. And I've already read every book you wrote, and I loved every word, but more than the books, I love the woman who wrote them. And I'd rather have you alive and unknown than dead for the betterment of millions of strangers. That's selfish. But just knowing that you didn't die today would get me through a whole lot of years."

"If I live, you'll lose your job, won't you?"

He managed a laugh. "It's more complicated than that. But yes. At the very least, I'll lose my job." I felt his hands against my back clench into fists. "Screw the job."

I pulled out of his embrace. "How much time do we have before . . . you have to go back?"

"The killer comes through the window at 7.24 a.m. We have two hours and forty-eight minutes."

"Come on," I told him. "We have to hurry."

I nearly dragged him through the door and locked it behind us.

"You love me?" I whispered when we were inside.

"I love you," he said.

"I've never been in love," I told him. "And I've never had anyone who loved me. I've wanted, and dreamed, and hoped, and looked, but there was never anyone. There may never be anyone again." I reached up and touched his face. "But right now, just this once, I want to know what it feels like to be loved. To love. In the little time we have, can we . . . Can we do that?"

He pulled me into his arms and kissed me.

I don't know about perfect kisses. I know only that I will never forget that one. In Per's touch, in his taste, in his hunger lay the promise of a lifetime of wonder.

We held each other, undressed each other, moved over and against and into each other, and I knew that our one brief moment wasn't going to be enough.

It wasn't the sex. I'd had good sex.

This was *everything*. It was knowing that he knew me, and knowing that I needed to know him just as well. It was wanting to hear all his stories, wanting to wake up every morning to roll over in bed and find him there. It was needing to walk down the street holding his hand, and wanting to sit on the couch beside him, not doing anything in particular, because being with him, just breathing the same air, had a magic to it that I had never had before.

And was never going to have again.

There wasn't ever going to be another moment for us. And there wasn't ever going to be another him.

We lay in my bed afterwards, and I realized he was looking at me with a worried expression. "I'm . . . sorry?" he said.

I realized I was crying.

"It's not . . . It wasn't you. You were – you *are* amazing. Wonderful. I just . . ." I closed my eyes, and took a deep breath and said, "I've been waiting all my life to meet the man I wanted to be with. I knew when I found him, I'd know. And now I know. And I can't have you."

"You would want me?"

"I *do* want you."

He looked away, and I saw his jaw working again. Under his breath, he muttered something that sounded a lot like " . . . no guarantees . . ." And then he said, "Your computer . . . is it on? Is your internet connection working?"

"I shut down the computer, but I have broadband. The internet will work as soon as the computer comes on."

He nodded, pulled on underwear and his jeans, grabbed his backpack. He said, "We're almost out of time. I'll be right back. *Stay here.*"

I nodded, and he jogged out of the bedroom. I wondered what he wanted with my computer. I wondered even more what he wanted with the internet. I heard the computer's boot-up sound, and him walking around in the living room, and then a couple of quick taps on the keyboard. And then nothing. A whole lot of nothing. I waited. That "stay here" had sounded important.

Then I heard footsteps on the little patio outside my bedroom window, and I looked at the clock.

7.23 a.m.

7.23 a.m.

I stopped thinking at all.

I stared at the window, shuddering, willing my body to move. I heard the aluminum frame start sliding open. The blinds were drawn, so I was in near blackness. There were no sounds from the living room any more. Which meant . . .?

That Per had realized he was out of time, and had used the internet to connect to his time travel device?

That he'd been . . . beamed home?

Or that time had grabbed him and ripped him away from me while he was trying to stop it?

It didn't matter. He was gone.

And there was a killer outside my window.

I keep a baseball bat under my bed. I couldn't in the orphanage, when I had plenty of reason to want one, but as soon as I got into foster care, I found a way to acquire one. Mostly I didn't need it. Once, with a dreadful foster family, I did.

The aluminum bat lay under my bed.

I grabbed it and moved fast, because there wasn't much time. I ran to the window.

The digital display on my alarm clock changed to 7.24 a.m. There were no more sounds outside my window. But Per had been very clear: 7.24. He'd seen the recording of my murder.

7.24 became 7.25 a.m, and someone politely tapped on the glass. Tapped?

Baseball bat at the ready, I gave the roll-up blind a quick tug. It shot upwards and rattled around its spindle for a second before falling silent.

On the other side of the window stood a complete stranger. He had duct tape over his mouth and around his wrists. Behind him stood Per, shirtless and rumpled.

The bat dropped to the floor with a clang, and I stared. It was 7.25 a.m., and Per had not vanished into the future. He was still here.

And looking a little uncomfortable. "Let us in before someone sees us."

"Oh. Right." I opened the window, and my would-be killer came through head first, propelled by a vicious shove from behind by Per. Per followed, with a speed and grace that made my heart thud in my throat.

"You're here."

"We'll deal with that later," he said. Up close, I could see that he was going to have a bad bruise under his right eye, and that his lip was split and bleeding. "We still don't have a lot of time."

He handed me a gun. "This is his," he said, kicking the hit man in the thigh. "Shoot him with it if he so much as twitches."

I shrugged my shoulders just enough that Per caught the gesture.

"Never shot a gun?"

I shook my head.

He stepped behind me, reached around me with both arms, and thumbed the safety off. (I looked at the red dot staring back at me – "red is dead", I remembered someone telling me once.) He put me in a shooting stance with the gun aimed at the killer's chest. "He makes one move, you pull the trigger. Can you do that?"

"Yes," I said. "I can do that."

He ran into the living room and came back with a manila envelope. He thumbed through it and pulled out one of those amazing sheets of paper of his. Then he crouched in front of the killer.

"Look at this, asshole," he said.

I could not see what they were looking at, but I did see all the color drain from the killer's face.

"How did you—"

I could not see the page in front of them, but I could hear it. Moaning and whimpering, and a man laughing, and then the front door opened. "Len, you here?"

Tyler's voice.

And the voice of the other man saying, "Finishing up. You said make it messy."

"Yeah. Messy." A pause, then, "Look. I have a list of things to do after this, and I need her to still be warm when I make the 911 call. So wrap it up."

One wet noise. And the sound of footsteps.

The killer's eyes were bugging out as he tried to say something around the duct tape.

Per touched the surface of the paper and the sound stopped. He said, "I'll take the tape off your mouth, but if you make any loud noises, she's going to kill you. You understand that?"

The killer nodded.

Per ripped the tape off the man's mouth, and he cringed and bit back a whimper.

"I never did that, man. It isn't me."

Per touched the paper again. "That's what you came here to do."

"No. Just rob the place. Seriously. That isn't me, man."

"See how I can make the picture bigger?"

The man nodded.

Per dragged a finger along the front of the page I could not see. "See how I can turn the image to get your full face? I can zoom in close enough to reveal your individual fingerprints. Want me to show you?"

Len shook his head. "What *is* that?"

"New police surveillance technology."

"But I didn't do . . . that."

"You haven't yet. And what happened next hasn't happened yet, either."

From the page in Per's hand, I heard Tyler's voice. "Holy shit, what a mess."

"You said . . ."

"Yeah." I heard Tyler gagging. Then vomiting. "The smell . . . How can you stand it?"

"You guaranteed I walk on the Burgess murders is how. No death penalty, no life in prison. I get a dismissal. And this – we all have our needs, man."

"You'll get your dismissal," Tyler snarled. "Get out of here. Let me do what *I* have to do now."

I heard boots hitting the floor, and more walking.

And then a gunshot.

The heavy thud of a body falling.

"There's your dismissal, you freak," Tyler's voice said.

Len was staring wide-eyed at the paper. "He *killed* me?"

Per told him, "His story was that you tried to escape, fleeing the scene of your crime, and he shot you before discovering what you'd done. Everybody believed him, too. Except me."

My would-be murderer stared from me to Per, and back to me. "But you're not dead. And I'm not dead."

At which point Tyler walked into the room.

"Which makes this tougher for me. But not impossible."

Tyler blocked the door, and I remembered again what a big guy he was. He wasn't lean and hard like Per, but he was wide and meaty. And the gun he pointed straight at me made him a lot bigger.

The gun in my own hands had gotten pretty heavy by that time. I could feel the muscles in my forearms quivering. The muscles keeping my knees from buckling joined them.

I had been scared of the man who had come to kill me, but I was more scared of Tyler. He was urbane. Genteel. Respected and respectable. He had people – a lot of them. Law partners, parents, siblings, guys he went yachting with, guys he went big-game hunting with.

All of them would no doubt say he was the best guy ever born. Salt of the earth.

And me . . . who did I have? I had the Thorsday Night Writers, whose odd-lot appearance and diverse lifestyles would make their testimony a hard sell.

And for the moment, I had Per. He hadn't yet disappeared, but was probably going to any second.

Small picture, there were three of us, and only one Tyler.

Big picture, Tyler knew how to use his gun. And had every other advantage, too.

And then Len, would-be hit man, pond scum, violent criminal, said, "You shot me in the back, you son of a bitch." With his wrists still duct-taped in front of him, he lunged to his feet, yanked the gun out of my hands and charged Tyler with a speed and a fury that made me realize Len could have been on me and I would have been dead before my reflexes even had a chance.

I scooped up the baseball bat at my feet as Len's animal leap launched him across my bed towards Tyler. Tyler swung his gun away from me to protect himself.

Len's gun jammed, and Tyler shot him. He dropped like a bag of hammers and lay bleeding on my bedspread.

Per lunged at Tyler. I charged at the same time, baseball bat swinging in short, sharp arcs. I swung and kept swinging, and kept connecting, until Per dragged himself across the bed and pulled me away from what was left of the would-be John Grisham of fantasy.

Per introduced himself to the cops as Per Tordönsson, of Tordönsson Detective Agency, and told them I'd hired him to check out the man I was dating. He presented them with his card and a folder from his backpack that included copies of documents on which Tyler had forged my signature, giving him control of my estate, naming him as my next of kin for all my personal effects. He handed them what he said was a phone tap of Len getting the date and time of my murder from Tyler. He said it was clean, that the affidavit was in the folder.

The cops sent someone to the ER to talk to Len, who admitted that Tyler had hired him to murder me. He also said that he hadn't intended to do it.

No one believed him.

It was the end of a long, exhausting Friday. Per sat across the table from me in the hotel room we'd rented, his leg stitched and bandaged, working his way through room service steak and eggs, salad, roll and a dessert of questionable origin.

"What happens now?" I asked him.

"What do you want to happen?"

"I want to be with you forever. I just keep waiting for this beam of light to surround you and whisk you out of my life, and I want to know how much longer we have."

And there it was. That smile again. The one that melted me on the inside and made me know from the first instant I saw it that this was a man I had to know.

"I'm staying," he said.

"But your time. The research historians. Won't someone be along to drag you back?"

"I can't go back," he said. "Ever. The instant I loaded my life spider onto the internet through your computer and went after Len so he couldn't come through your window to kill you, I broke my connection to home. I created a new branch in time, a new past relative to my own time. In this past, you live. In the past I come from, you always will have died – but there's no way to this past from there. And no way there from here."

"But your family? Your friends?"

"I had them. I'll miss them. But I had a dangerous job, and they knew it, and so did I. Research historians get swallowed into alternate pasts from time to time. It's why we travel with life spiders."

"Which do what?"

"In your time, they create validation in public databases for all the information that lets me prove who I am. Every research historian working in the age of the internet carries a life spider with him that creates a name, social security number, driver's licence . . . all of it. Complete with past. In my case, even a nice bank account."

"You came planning to stay?"

"I came *hoping* to stay. Big difference. If you had not been you; if you had wanted to die so your books would live on; if you had not wanted me – then I would have disappeared. No light. No magic. I just would have blinked back to where I was supposed to be."

"But you've given up everything to be here. And you decided knowing that I had just met you. You couldn't know whether I would change my mind . . . and now you can't ever go back."

"Life doesn't come with guarantees, Nila. What it does come with is chances. You're the chance I wanted to take."

I slid my hand into his. I might never be famous. I might never change someone's life. I swear I'll try . . . but when I'm gone, maybe no one will remember my name.

That's all right.

I know what it is to be loved. I know what it means to love. And the chance I've won is better than any guarantee.

The Gloaming Hour

Cindy Miles

Savannah, Georgia
Present day

Are you awake yet?

Kylie's eyes fluttered open. The hazy light of an approaching dusk filtered through the canopy of moss-covered oaks and looming pecan trees. She glanced around then inhaled. The sweet scent of magnolia blooms blended with the sharp tang of salt marsh, and a slight breeze, barely even there, stirred the reeds and sawgrass. A pine cone thudded to the ground. It'd only been the wind. It felt strange being back on the Vernon River. As childhood recollections crashed over her, she inhaled, and the scent of Granny's fresh-fried beignets and peach cobbler drifted on a faraway memory. So vivid and real, she could taste the sugar on her tongue. If only other memories could be as sweet.

But, they couldn't. Some reminiscences would haunt her forever.

She heaved a sigh and gave the porch swing a push with her bare foot. The gentle swaying coaxed her lids to fall, the creaking of the rusty chain lulling her back to sleep.

I need your help, lass. Wake up. Besides, you'll miss the gloaming hour ...

Kylie shot up out of the swing and glanced around. Her heart pounded, her breath hitched. "Who's there?" The words squeaked from her throat.

Good God, woman. You're sae bonny.

She whirled around and stared in the direction of the deep, accented voice. Nothing. The white verandah, in desperate need of a few coats of fresh paint and bare of the gauzy Boston ferns which used to hang from the rafters, sat empty. No one was there. But God, the voice sounded as though it'd been right in her ear.

She pinched the bridge of her nose. Not only had she imagined a voice, she'd imagined it with a sexy Scottish burr. "You've lost your mind, girl." Maybe it'd been her subconscious self calling to her, pulling her out of sleep. She loved the gloaming hour – that small window of time between day and night, when a haunting darkness stretched across the land, and burnt colours from the faded evening rippled the sky and canopy above. Stars peered out, and night birds called to one another across the marsh. Seventeen-year cicadas made their presence known, and crickets sang their sweet, eerie lullabies, and the sound floated over the salty air. A slight breeze rustled the sawgrass, sounding almost like a hushed whisper . . .

Aye, that's better, girl. I knew you'd come round.

Kylie jumped and whirled around. Fear gripped her insides. "Who's there? I mean it – cut it out!" She looked around, then grabbed an old fly-swatter hanging on the post. "I'm . . . armed."

Deep laughter rumbled out of nowhere. *Aye, an' so you are, wee one.* Another laugh. *But put doon your weapon for now. I need you.*

Kylie dropped her plastic armour and ran. Skidding around the corner of the porch, she flung open the door and jumped inside, then turned and bolted the lock. Her breath came out in harsh puffs, her chest heaving as adrenalin pumped through her veins. She squeezed her eyes shut. "Oh, God, what's happening to me? Why am I hearing voices?"

A heavy sigh broke the silence. *My apologies,* mo ghraidh. *'Twas no' my intention tae frighten you.*

Her pulse quickened and she cupped her hands over her ears and squeezed her eyes shut. "Stop! Please, whoever you are, just go away." She tried to swallow. "Leave me alone."

As you wish.

Silence. Only the whir of a ceiling fan and her laboured breathing. Minutes stretched, her back aching as it pressed against the cool, hard oak. Silence. She took several deep breaths and cracked open one eye, then the other.

An empty room filled her vision. A haze filtered through the flimsy curtains, casting an uncanny glow on the long-ago abandoned home. Dust-covered canvas draped the old pieces of furniture left behind after Granny's passing. A thready cobweb stretched across one corner of the kitchen breezeway. No man, no voice – and certainly not one with a Scottish brogue. "You're going nuts, Kylie." Finally, she eased from the door and inhaled several calming breaths. What had just happened? Was it too soon to have come back here?

With a determined shrug, Kylie pushed the strange incident behind her and walked through the old, familiar house – one she knew so very well. The light filtered through aged screened windows, and tiny particles of dust caught on narrow beams of light as they shot across the wood-planked floor and tongue-and-groove walls. Slowly, Kylie closed her eyes, and in place of the canvas-covered furnishings stood the living room she remembered, with her grandpa's recliner, her granny's rocker, and the old TV that sat on four legs at the far end of the room. She easily pictured the glass coffee table near the old green sofa, where her granny had displayed several china figurines. Birds. Cardinals to be exact. Her granny always loved cardinals.

An archway led into the kitchen and, for a moment, there was her granny, standing at the kitchen sink, staring out the window as she cooked. An old black rotary telephone hung on the wall.

How she wished she could go back to those days . . .

After a full day's worth of work, the house was actually livable again. The canvas had been removed, cobwebs swept away, and the wood floors sparkled once again. She'd unpacked what few belongings she had, pulled Granny's china down and washed it, and swatted out the old braid rugs thrown here and there throughout the house. And all without the first whisper of an unseen Scotsman.

At first, Kylie felt relieved at the absence of the voice. She'd been scared out of her wits yesterday. It'd sounded so . . . real. Where had it come from? And hadn't he asked for her help?

Then, emptiness washed over her, and she found herself wondering more and more about it. It'd almost sounded *familiar*. Had she become so pathetic that the best she could do was *imagine* a man had spoken?

She glanced down at the long scars on both arms, thought about the matching one on the left side of her face. She ran her fingertips across the puckered line of skin and sighed. "Get a grip, girl."

After a quick inspection of the house, she pulled on her Keds and headed out the door. She crossed the yard to the narrow, wooden dock and started down its path over the water. The outgoing tide left the marsh with the sharp, pungent tang of salt and sea life, the bubbling of oysters in the shoal, and fiddler crabs crackled far beneath her. Crickets serenaded one another through the trees, and a breath of air shifted across the water and teased the leaves of the pecans, oaks and sawgrass. Magnolia drifted by like a whispering caress. God, she'd forgotten how much she loved this place. No, she hadn't forgotten. It'd been forced to the back of her memory, replaced by a terror she'd give anything to forget.

At the end of the pier sat the small, screened-in dock house her grandpa had built years back. She'd spent hours in there, wrapped up in one of Granny's crocheted throws, playing with her Barbies or watching a summer storm creep across the marsh. Life had seemed simple then. Home-made ice cream. Blueberry picking. Simple.

She walked down to the dock, kicked off her shoes and sat down. Warm, brackish water circled her feet and legs. A thumbnail moon hung in the fading sky, and gulls cried out over the marsh. How calm the Vernon was compared to the bustling city of Atlanta.

Lass?

Kylie held her breath, then slowly released it. "No, not again. Not that sexy Scottish voice again. No, no no." She shook her head. "No."

A deep chuckle echoed across the water. *So, you find my voice pleasing, aye?*

She yanked her feet out of the water and jumped up. Nothing. There went that fear again, bubbling in her throat, threatening to steal her breath.

Do no' bolt from me, Kylie. I willna hurt you. I need your help, if you'll give it.

"How do you know my name? Who are you?" She swallowed hard. "Where are you?"

Forgive me, lass. Major Rory MacMillan. Now please, I beg you. Dunna bolt.

A blurry haze shifted near one of the dock posts – like the sun's wiggly reflection off hot tarmac. Her heart leaped into her throat.

She tried to run, tried to scream, but a paralysing grip held her tongue, kept her feet firmly in place. From the strange haze emerged a pair of long, boot-covered legs, braced wide apart. Narrow hips. A torso. Arms folded over a thick chest. Broad shoulders. *Ridiculously* broad shoulders. A head, with dark auburn hair pulled back. White teeth split his face in two as he smiled and gave her a low bow.

Kylie placed a hand to her forehead to keep her head from spinning. She lost her breath and hiccupped, felt herself falling, and, just before her eyes rolled back, she wondered why it seemed as though they'd met once before . . .

Rory grabbed the girl before she hit the dock. Soft and limp in his arms, he held her up and thanked the saints for the gloaming hour. 'Twas the only time o' day when he could touch, taste, smell, feel . . .

He squatted down, keeping her firmly in his arms. The feel of her body against his all but knocked him over. He studied her closely. How Kylie had grown since last he'd seen her. Honey-coloured hair, pulled back like a horse's tail, fell across his arm, and brows the same colour arched over closed eyes. Specks of cinnamon dotted her tanned nose and cheeks. He lifted a forefinger and traced the raised skin of the scar on her face. What had happened? Each arm sported the remnants of a wound. An accident of sorts, mayhap? He shook his head. Poor lass.

"Wake up, *mo ghraidh*." He gave her a gentle shake, and her eyes fluttered open. Round and questioning at first, they quickly narrowed as she scrambled to get away. He allowed her to get up, then stood to face her.

Her blue eyes flashed as she regarded him. "Who are you? What kind of joke is this, huh? This is private property, you know." She glanced around, then backed towards the wood-framed house at the end of the dock.

Damn, he hated that she feared him. He didn't move. His poor knees wavered as he stared into her blue depths. "I need your help, lass. No harm will come tae you. I give you my word."

Kylie could do little but stare – and try to look as though she wasn't scared out of her mind. Yet at the same time, he fascinated her. It was the same thick Scottish brogue she'd heard earlier. "Why are you here? And why are you dressed like that?" High black boots, cream-coloured leather pants hugged heavily muscled thighs. And a blue coat with tails . . . he looked as though he'd been in the midst of a battle re-enactment at Fort Pulaski.

But good Lord Almighty, what a stunning man.

Instinctively, her hand moved to hide the scar on her face. His gaze followed her movement, and she felt her cheeks grow hot.

He lifted his stare to the darkening sky and sighed. "Your granny felt my presence, but could ne'er see me. I always hoped you'd be different."

Fear gripped her. "You knew my grandmother? How can that be? I don't remember you at all."

He smiled and shrugged. "Nay, you wouldna. 'Tis only now you can see me, and 'tis a miracle at best." He smiled, but his eyes pleaded. "I need you verra badly."

A memory flashed before her, from the summer she turned eight. She'd been on the dock, at the very place she now stood. *A voice . . .* "Why do you think I can help you?"

Sombre grey eyes stared back at her. "Because you haven't run away yet."

As if she could. He towered over her, blocking her path to the house. Their gazes locked, and her insides screeched to a dizzying halt. She couldn't take her eyes off his.

He moved towards her. "Please, lass." He reached out his hand. "I'm desperate."

Kylie stepped back, confused. His plea sounded heartfelt, and so very real. *Kylie, he appeared out of nowhere . . .* Another step back, and then the sound of wood splintering cracked the air before she could stop herself. She screamed as the dock gave way beneath her. Just as both legs plunged through the rotted wood, Rory dived and grabbed her hands.

"Please, don't let me go."

"Nay, girl. I willna." As if they'd known each other for ever, he pulled her up and into his arms. His firm chest against her cheek, his roughened hands splayed across her back, moving in a slow rhythm.

Then, just as fast as it had occurred, his warmth seeped away, a cool trace of mist remained in its wake. The solidity of his body shifted, and Kylie leaned in to capture it back. She opened her eyes and looked up – and gasped. Rory's image was growing hazier, thinner.

"Do you remember me, Kylie? You were but eight summers old."

Kylie scrubbed her eyes, trying to clear her vision. Slowly, he began to fade. She reached for him. "Wait! What's going on?"

'Tis all right, girl. I can still speak tae you. But I'll no' be able tae show myself again until tomorrow's gloaming hour.

"Oh, God . . ." Staring at the haze until it fully disappeared, she drew a deep breath and swallowed. "You're a . . ." It sounded crazy, stupid. But what other explanation, besides her pending madness, could it be? She could barely make herself say the word. It sounded absurd. But what else could it be? "Ghost?"

Nay, lass, no' a ghostie. I dunna think I could solidify, were I dead. His light chuckle drifted over the marsh. *I wish I could explain it, but that's why I need you, Kylie. But you should head back tae the house, girl. Should you fall again, I willna be able tae catch you.*

She shivered as a childhood memory assaulted her. The dock house, especially during the gloaming. A presence, perhaps – she couldn't be sure. "I always felt something, but didn't know what it was."

He laughed quietly. *Aye, your little nose would crinkle up whenever I'd come aboot.*

She exhaled and closed her eyes. "I remember."

Rory.

She opened her eyes. "What?"

My name's Rory. An' I'm desperate tae hear you say it.

A breeze rustled the reeds and cat tails, caressing her cheek as her heart pounded like a feral thing. Yeah, leave it to Kylie Robinson to be turned on by a dead guy. Or whatever he was.

"Rory." She hadn't meant for it to come out as a whisper, but it had. She wondered if he'd even heard it. Silence stretched between them as she walked across the yard and into the house. Dummy her, she'd forgotten to leave a lamp on. Easing into the darkness, she stopped after a few feet to gain her bearings.

Say it again.

Kylie jumped. His thick accent brushed her ear, surrounded and moved through her. Every nerve ending in her body hummed with awareness. What was he doing to her? She cleared her throat. "I, uh, thought you needed my help?"

Again that laugh. Sensual and strong, it filled the room and she'd never wished so hard that something could be real in all her life.

Aye, I do need your help, Kylie. Forgive me. You're most distracting.

Breathe, Kylie Jane, she told herself. She moved until her fingertips brushed the lampshade. She pulled the chain and a dim light settled over the breezeway. A quick glance confirmed that indeed, she was talking to thin air. If he wasn't a ghost, yet he was invisible, what was he? He'd certainly been very much alive on the dock – his warm, tight embrace still wrapped around her body. Yep. She'd gone and truly lost her mind.

Moving into the kitchen, she made herself a cup of tea and sat down at the table. She peered around the empty room. Again, she cleared her throat. "Rory?"

I'm right here, Kylie Jane.

Yeah, and seemingly right against her neck. Another deep breath. "I'm only called that when I'm in trouble."

Rory laughed, this time a bit further away. *I know. I heard your granny call you that more times than no'. Truce it is, lass. For now. I'll no' be able tae measure my behaviour in the future.*

She gulped. A flirty apparition? She could understand that. "OK, so tell me how you think I can help you."

Verra well. He let out a heavy sigh. *I'm sae weary, girl. For as long as I can remember, I've been searching the river for someone to help me. No one's been able tae hear or see me – save your granny – until you. I . . . canna seem tae remember things. One minute, my men and I were together, and then next, I was verra much alone.*

"You're a soldier?"

Aye. His voice moved closer. *I left Nairn in the year of our Lord, seventeen hundred an' sixty-five, where I joined the Revolution. I havena been back tae Scotland since.*

"What happened?"

I remember leading my men through a wood, no' too far from here. An ambush overtook us, killing several of the lads. We fought like mad, but were outnumbered. What few of us remained was herded into the Berkshire.

Kylie gasped. "The prison ship *Berkshire*?"

Aye, the verra one. How is it you know o' her?

"I'm a professor of Georgia History at the University."

Och, so you can help me then.

Kylie stretched and crossed her legs. "What is it, exactly, you need help with?"

I canna be sure, but all at once, I was leading my men into the ship's belly. I was shoved from behind, and went sprawling into the pit of the Berkshire's *prison. Then, I was afloat, invisible. I could see my men, and the other prisoners of the* Berkshire, *and then … they simply disappeared. The verra next thing I knew, I was here.*

Her insides chilled. "As crazy as it sounds, I think you must have stumbled into a time slip, or rift, or … something." How unbelievable, to think this man had once lived, fought for a young country not his own, and then just vanished to another time. His family, loved ones, all dead for centuries now. She ached for him.

I've waited sae long for you. I always hoped one day you'd have the gift tae see me.

"I remember playing in the dock house. I always felt as though someone stood beside me, calling my name."

Aye, I tried for many years. Then, you left.

She had left, and sorely regretted it. She'd missed a lot of things in her life by leaving home, and had encountered nothing else but pain. Now, nothing remained of her old life except the old river house. And, her memories. Rinsing out her tea cup, she turned. "Can you see me, Rory?"

A soft chuckle. *Aye.*

"So, you can see, hear and speak, just not touch and smell?"

Nor taste. At least, no' until the gloaming. And for that I have no explanation.

She shivered as the suggestion sounded in her ear. Mercy, what a sexy man, even for one so inaccessible, invisible. Maybe that's why she hadn't broken out in a cold sweat, or run away. He seemed just tangible enough to be real … yet not real enough to be a threat.

Flipping off the kitchen light, she headed for the bedroom. At the door, she paused. "You'll be here in the morning, won't you?"

You have only tae call for me, mo ghraidh.

Her heart slammed against her ribs. "What's that mean – *mo ghraidh*?"

Och – just an old Scottish endearment, lass.

She steadied herself with a deep breath as the words washed over her. Probably just her silly own wishful reaction. There was a reason she neared thirty and still lived alone. She slipped into her bedroom. "Goodnight, Rory."

An' tae you, Kylie.

Saints! What are all those?

Kylie set the crate on the dining room table with a grunt. "Reference volumes from the university library. I'm hoping to find what you're looking for in one of them. But I'll warn you, it may take a while. These are quite old, and I had to sneak them past—"

Thank you.

That sexy brogue wrapped around her, enveloped her, and she grabbed the back of the chair to steady herself. Just the way he spoke to her set her insides afire.

You feel it, too. Dunna you, Kylie?

A breeze drifted in through the screen door, like warm breath against her skin. She closed her eyes and inhaled, exhaled. She didn't want to feel it. But she did.

She opened her eyes and started unpacking the volumes. "I'd better get started on these, Rory. It's a lot of material to read through."

Several hours later, she'd managed to get through the first book. With a heavy sigh, Kylie pushed her glasses on to her head and closed the volume. "This is insane. It could take a year to go through all this information, and I'm not even sure what I'm looking for." The bones in her knees popped as she stood and stretched. The blades of the ceiling fan sent a feathery breeze across her skin, and the scent of jasmine drifted in through the porch screen.

Come outside with me. The gloaming draws near, and I want every second o' it wi' you.

Kylie sucked in a breath. "I thought you wanted my help."

It's you I want.

She gulped. It was one thing to be with a ghost you couldn't see. Quite a different story, though, when said ghost solidified, regaining all mortal senses.

Lifting the heavy volume, she moved to the cool shade of the verandah. The sturdy rocking chair creaked as she sat down. Stretching her legs out, she propped them on the railing and crossed them at the ankles. The soft, gauzy sundress slipped above her knees as she rocked, but she barely noticed. Memories of her childhood flooded back, and she welcomed the deluge.

What are you thinking aboot, girl?

He sat beside her, close. She sighed. "God, I spent hours shelling peas with Grandma and Grandpa on this very porch. It seems so ... long ago. Another lifetime even." Every scent, every sound encompassed a cherished memory. When had she allowed them to fade? When had she forgotten the scent of lilac her granny used to wear? Or how her grandpa's hands were gnarled and calloused from a hard-working life at the railroad, and prior to that, having survived Omaha Beach? Now, flashes of her as a child sitting on her grandpa's lap, holding one of his large hands in two of hers, battered her. God, how she missed them.

Cicadas tweaked and chirped, and songbirds settled in for the night. The ever-present bubbling of the outgoing tide filled the air. And a barrage of high-pitched croaks emerged from the canopy of Georgia pines and magnolias.

Just as she moved to open the volume in her lap, a heavy hand rested on her bare shoulder. Her skin heated under it.

"Walk wi' me."

She lifted her gaze and met his light grey stare. He looked so real, from the sun lines at the corners of his eyes to the muscle ticking at his jaw, to the dark auburn hair pulled into a queue. Butterflies beat madly within her, setting her nerves on edge. To think a Scotsman from the Revolutionary War, who had centuries before slipped through a crack in time, made her react in such a silly way. Oh, how Granny would roar with laughter.

She stood and he took her hand, placing it in the crook of his arm. They walked and talked, he of his life and she of hers.

It was a comfortable walk with Rory; a familiar ease that Kylie admired in wonderment. To think he'd been at Granny's on the Vernon River all these years, and she'd been ... elsewhere. So much had happened in those years she'd been gone. God, how she regretted them all.

Rory's gloved hand reached out, and a long finger traced the scar down her left arm. Reflexively, Kylie flinched.

"What happened?" Rory asked, his voice so quiet Kylie barely heard the question above the song of the cicadas.

Kylie's stomach tightened at the jarring, unwanted memory, and without her permission, her breathing became rapid. She swallowed several times. "I . . . don't like to talk about it," she said quietly. "It's something I've put behind me."

Rory stopped, pulling her to a halt. Gently, he turned her to face him. Kylie refused to look at him.

"I dunna think you've put it behind you, lass." He lifted her chin with his knuckle, traced the scar on her face. "Look at me."

Kylie forced herself to meet his pewter gaze. Her insides shook. "You can trust me."

Kylie fought back tears, not wanting to relive the events that nearly ended her life. But when she looked into the kind, trusting eyes of Rory MacMillan, her fears began to fade. Then, a feeling of certainty washed over her, and suddenly it felt right to trust him.

She'd never trusted anyone else before now.

With a deep sigh, she again met Rory's intense gaze and began. "I've tried so hard to forget," she said, and shook her head. "I'd been in Atlanta, in my first real apartment, for almost two years. I knew my neighbours. It was in Roswell, a safe suburb of Atlanta, and . . . I guess I became complacent." She focused on some point across the marsh. "I'd gone out jogging – something I'd done daily for more than a year." Tears filled her eyes, and her voice dropped to a whisper on its own. "We run for fun these days, and to keep our bodies fit. I loved it. And I didn't even hear his footsteps behind me."

Rory's body visibly tensed, and his voice, when he spoke, sounded barely controlled. "A man did this to you?" His accent was thicker, his tone deep and lethally steady.

"Yes," she said. "He'd apparently watched me daily, watched the path I took, and then, he attacked." She again shook her head. "No rape, no robbery – just brutality. He taunted me with a knife—" she closed her eyes, opened them again "—then cut me. I fought back, and that seemed to anger him further." She lifted her gaze to Rory's once more. "He would have killed me – he was so much stronger than me. But a passer-by happened upon us. A fellow jogger." She concentrated on simply breathing. "They fought, and he tried to hold my attacker, but the guy got away. The police never found him. I lived in so much fear – fear that he'd come after me again. Finally, I decided to come home."

"Christ, lass," Rory finally said, and anger tinged his voice. Then, he simply pulled her close. His lips brushed her temple. "I would have found him. And I would have killed him."

Kylie leaned into Rory. He smelled of leather and the salt marsh and strangely enough, gunpowder. His words made her shudder, for she had no doubt in her mind that Rory would have done just that. "I don't know why your embrace comforts me so much," she said quietly. "You're a stranger."

Rory's hand smoothed her hair, her neck, and pressed gently against the small of her back. "Mayhap 'tis because I'm really no stranger at all, lass."

Kylie turned her face from Rory's shoulder and studied his eyes. Such an odd shade of silver, she wondered if they had always shined such a colour. "I suppose you're not, are you? You've been here all along. I'm the one who's been missing."

In the waning light of day, Rory's teeth gleamed white as he smiled gently down at her. "But you're home now, aye? And no one will ever harm you again. I vow it."

Kylie had not felt such relief, such *release*, since the attack happened. She'd stayed in the hospital, recovering, for nearly two weeks. The gashes in her arms had been deep, the attacker's knife dirty, and she'd fought infection for a long time. Luck was with her though, and not only had her wounds healed without a terrible infection invading, but she'd needed no skin grafts. But it had left her with scars – the sort of scars that people in general just couldn't ignore. She was stared at by children and adults alike, wherever she went.

Rory must have guessed what she was thinking, because he lifted a gloved hand, pulled at the fingers with his teeth, and then took it off. With his hand bare, he used the tip of his finger to trace the long scar on the side of her face, gently, back and forth. "Christ, Kylie, you're powerfully soft," he said. "'Tis a battle scar, a part of you – a part of your life's experiences. 'Tis what has made you such a strong lass." He smiled down at her, but his eyes were steady, intense, and they dropped a fraction, to her mouth, before returning to her eyes. "A warrior." He traced the scar again. "A beautiful warrior."

Kylie felt the heat of a blush creep up her neck and settle into her cheeks, and was grateful for the fading light to cover it up. She studied Rory's profile in the hazy evening, and she had to wonder why it was that modern men had lost that certain something. Was it chivalry? Rory had it by the bucket load, and the fact was . . . he seriously meant what he said. "My grandmother is the only person who ever said I was beautiful." She smiled. "Thank you."

Rory stared, the muscles in his jaws flinched, and his eyes searched her face. The air around them became thick, heavy as the sultry summer night embracing them and, for a moment, Kylie thought he'd kiss her. Electricity all but snapped at the intensity.

She was completely amazed when she discovered how badly she wanted that kiss.

But instead of kissing her, Rory smiled, replaced his glove, and tucked her hand in the crook of his arm. "'Tis high tide now, and the moon is nearly full. Let's walk to the river."

Together, they did. Always a breeze, it rustled through the sawgrass and cat tails, the sound dry and crackly, and so familiar, and with it was carried the pungent scent of the sea. The brackish water below the dock slapped against the pilings, and it reminded Kylie of how much she loved the Vernon, her granny's house, and the life she'd left behind. And beside her walked a man who had been born in Scotland more than 250 years before and then suddenly thrust into another century, another time. Her time. It completely and wholly amazed her.

And he'd been here the whole time. Waiting.

For her.

Never in his live days had Rory been as fulfilled as he was with the modern girl who trustingly walked beside him now. Even with his invisible self, she completed him. He'd waited so long for her to return, with hopes of her finally being able to see him. She had, and now, he never wanted to let her go.

He'd always suspected that would happen.

How difficult it had been to restrain himself – just as it was now, as they walked the dock to the river. It had been centuries since he'd had physical contact with another human being, and even in his previous life, his last two years had been naught but warring. But with Kylie, and her soft skin, pleasing voice, and arousing scent? He'd wanted to kiss her powerfully bad, and almost had. Where his restraint had come from, he didna know. God must have flung it down upon him.

She'd wanted him to kiss her. Even he, a flimsy apparition out of his own time for more than two centuries, could feel it. Their attraction was like another living thing, palpable on the air around them.

He wanted her even now.

The thought of someone touching her, cutting her, as that fool in Atlanta had done, made his insides boil with fury. Had he been alive, he would have hunted the man down and killed him. Slowly.

"You're very quiet," Kylie said as they reached the dock house.

Rory glanced down, and covered her hand with his. "I've just ne'er disliked the night as much as I do right now," he said. And Christ, he meant it. He didna want to leave her side. Her physical side.

"That makes two of us," Kylie said.

Then before Rory knew it, she lifted a hand to his cheek, scrubbed his jaw with the verra soft pads of her fingertips.

"It's just so hard for me to believe that you're so very real," she said, almost a whisper.

Rory stood dead still as he allowed Kylie to explore his features. She lightly grazed his ears, the bridge of his nose, his brows. When she hesitantly slid a finger across his bottom lip, he nearly came undone. He gathered all his strength though and remained steady. It proved to be the most difficult task in all his life – or time-warp life.

"What was it like," she asked, pulling him down to the dock to sit, "the war?" Idly, she lightly fingered the brass buttons on his jacket, the cuffs of his sleeves, the leather of his boots. The hilt of his sword.

He swallowed.

"'Twas sheer hell," Rory said. "Men much younger than myself – mere boys – took to arms and fought for this country." He shook his head. "So many years have passed, and I believe most have forgotten. Those who fought have all died, and their closest relatives have died, as well. The stories have become lost."

Kylie leaned against his shoulder, and Rory thought he'd fall straight into the Vernon. "Not everyone has forgotten," she said softly.

Without warning, she slid her hand to his, pulled off his glove, and inspected his hand. Her slight fingers traced his larger, calloused ones, the thick veins that ran atop it, and the scraped knuckles.

And in the very next instant, the gloaming was over.

Rory's physical body faded with the twilight.

And Kylie simply sat there in the near-darkness, quiet except for her harsh breathing. She swore.

Rory laughed, and watched her. "Dunna fret, lass," he said, although 'twas exactly what he was doing, truth be told. "Tomorrow will bring another gloaming hour. And we shall spend it together."

Rory fascinated her beyond belief, and before she even realized it, he'd put her at ease – made her forget Atlanta and the attack, made her forget the ugly scars it'd left her with. Only the present mattered.

Every day, Kylie spent her time on the verandah, or in the dock house, pouring over the Georgia volumes in search of Rory's fate. Name after name, event after event flashed before her, yet nothing turned up regarding the *Berkshire* or its captives. Although she couldn't see him, he remained by her side and helped her, talked with her. Yet when the gloaming approached, the volumes were set aside and he appeared – as in the flesh as any mortal man – and they'd spend that precious window of time devouring each other's company. Somehow, he'd taught her to feel again.

Sweet Christ, 'twas painful awaiting the gloaming. For over 200 years, he'd searched for someone who would simply listen, and no' run screaming in terror at the sight of an out-of-century man appearing before them, and invisible the next. Now that he'd found such a person, he didna want tae give her up. Her verra presence soothed him, and he craved time by her side. Surprisingly, he'd behaved hi'self. 'Til now.

Without words, he pulled her to a halt. Their eyes locked, his own grey ones to her blue. Her hand flew to the scar on her face, but he gently grasped her fingers, placing them over his heart. Pulling her close, he lowered his head and brushed her lips. The feel of her against him, the softness of her frock and scent of her skin urged him even more. His heart pounded like a wild thing, and when he grazed her tongue with his it took every ounce o' strength he possessed tae remain upright. He threaded his fingers through her silken honey hair, inhaled her very essence, and when her hands crept around his neck and held his mouth tae hers, he devoured her, tasting every inch of her. Breathless, he hovered over her lips. "I never want tae let you go . . ."

Kylie's heart seized at Rory's words. With her eyes open, she swept his bottom lip with her tongue, kissing him slowly, lingering against his skin. She held him tight, as though doing so would prevent him from fading away. He crowded her with his body, wrapped his arms around her and encircled her, consumed her in ways she'd never thought possible. His grey eyes stared down at her, their lips still touching. Strong hands rested against the small of her back, then before either knew it, his presence began to slip, blurring into a faded mist until Kylie stood by the marsh alone. She wrapped her arms around herself and fought the sting in her eyes.

Oh Christ, girl. Please dunna weep. I willna be able tae bear it.

Kylie exhaled. "I never expected to find you. Is this even happening? Is it real?"

His voice brushed the skin of her neck, and she closed her eyes. *Aye, love. 'Tis real enough.*

After a restless night, Kylie awakened, made coffee, and then plunged into the volumes. She asked Rory question after question with little result. Then, almost as if it leaped from the crinkled worn pages, she saw it. Her throat constricted.

What?

"The revolt aboard the *Berkshire*."

Read it tae me?

Drawing a deep breath, Kylie began. "October, 1775. A revolt led by a captured officer of the Revolution ended in a bloodbath. Major Rory MacMillan, followed by a dozen starved and diseased prisoners aboard the prison ship *Berkshire*, overtook several guards in an attempt to man the ship and free its captives. The attempt proved futile. Major MacMillan, accused of being a deserter of the King's army, was shot and thrown into the ship's solitary prison pit, separating him from his men, thus ending the revolt. Somehow, his . . ."

His what, Kylie?

Rory's strained words squeezed her heart. Her voice dropped to a whisper. "His body simply disappeared from the locked prison.

Major Rory MacMillan was never found, seen, or heard of ever again."

The familiar haze began to shimmer before her, and Kylie's eyes grew wide as Rory materialized before her. She jumped up. "What's happening? It's not even four o'clock."

Without words, Rory grabbed her and held her close. His mouth sought hers, then whispered against her lips. "I remember, *mo ghraidh*. A man, another Scottish prisoner, whispered something in Gaelic. A verse. 'Twas just before I was shoved into the pit." He shook his head and studied her. "It somehow sent me forwards in time." His eyes misted. "I didna desert, and I wasna killed."

She stared into his grey eyes. God, she could drown in them. "I believe you."

He kissed her, and it singed her soul. "Christ, *mo ghraidh*," he whispered against her mouth. "The help which I sought so desperately all those years has finally come." He smiled. "Now, I wish I'd never sought it."

They held each other until he began to blur. Tears filled her eyes. "No, Rory. You can't go." She choked back a sob. "Please don't."

"I love you, Kylie Jane Robinson. I believe I always have. Do no' forget that."

The haze faded away, slipping into the late afternoon sun. Tears fell down her cheeks. "Rory?" She looked around, waiting for his answer. "Rory, please." Nothing. Only a wind slipping through the marsh whispered a reply. She tried to swallow, but her throat tightened, burned, refusing to allow it. The air jammed in her lungs. She slid to the cool grass and cried. "God, please give him back . . ."

A few weeks and several cans of paint later, the verandah sparkled white once again. Green, bushy ferns hung down every few feet, and the whirring ceiling fan stirred just enough breezes to keep cool, to keep the fern fronds rustling in the wind.

God, she ached for him.

Closing her eyes, she gave the porch swing a push. She could still see him, smell him, could still hear his voice . . .

Are you awake yet?

Kylie sighed. He sounded so real.

"I said –" two strong hands cupped her face "– are you awake yet?"

She nearly flipped out of the swing. When her vision cleared, she stared into a pair of light grey eyes. She reached out, expecting her hands to pass through, but they didn't. Instead, his hard chest heated beneath her palms. He pulled her close, and she inhaled his clean scent. "Rory." Her words choked from her throat. "How—"

"I don' dare ask questions, *mo ghraidh*." He kissed her hair.

Kylie's eyes drifted shut. "What does that really mean?"

Rory's mouth edged close to hers. "My love."

"You are a miracle," she said on an exhale.

He tilted her face up and claimed her lips. "Love always is, lass." Marsh and magnolia swept across the verandah as they held each other into the gloaming hour . . . and beyond.

A Wish to Build a Dream On

Michelle Willingham

Garrett was completely wrong, Mary Samson told herself, straightening in her seat. *You are not a prude who's incapable of being impulsive.*

Wasn't this impulsive enough? Taking two weeks' vacation from her engineering position to travel to Ireland? She hadn't taken a vacation in three years because . . . well, she'd always been too busy. There were simulations to run, project meetings to attend, and countless emails to answer. She'd prided herself on being dependable; a responsible adult with a good job and a bright future.

It hadn't been enough for Garrett. They'd dated for almost a year before he'd dumped her last Thursday.

"It's just not working, Mary. I need someone more impulsive. Someone who likes to live on the edge."

"I can be more exciting," she'd promised him. *"Spontaneous, even."*

"Mary, the only spontaneous thing you've ever done was buy whole milk instead of two per cent."

And even that had been an accident. Mary's stomach twisted at the memory of their break-up. Her only consolation was that it had been easy. There wasn't another woman; he'd simply been bored. They'd never moved in together, so there was no furniture to move, no locks to change. Not even a single dirty sock left behind. Here one minute, gone the next. Why then, did she feel so awful, as though he'd been her last chance for a real relationship?

"Are you all right?" her seatmate Harriet asked. Besides herself, Harriet was the next youngest member of the tour group. She was seventy-five, widowed and wore her white hair styled in a large pouf. "You don't look well."

"I'm fine. Why do you ask?"

The older woman handed her a pack of tissues. "You look as though you're considering throwing yourself off the bus. Or in front of it."

Mary glanced at their tour guide Neil, who was trying to lead the passengers in a chorus of "Kum Bah Yah". Reaching for a bottle of Motrin, she nodded. "Always a possibility."

Harriet beamed and opened her tote bag, revealing several bottles of alcohol from the last hotel's minibar. "Here. Choose your poison." For herself, the older woman selected a bottle of Jack Daniel's.

Mary doubted if they were supposed to drink while on the tour, but Neil's perky singing was enough to drive anyone to overindulge. She reached for a bottle of Disaronno Amaretto. "*Sláinte.*"

The two tiny bottles clinked together, and Harriet offered a toast. "May the wind at your back always be your own."

Mary choked, coughing at Harriet's remark. The alcohol burned her throat, and she took another swig. It was beginning to mellow her out. "Sorry."

"Did you make a wish then?" Harriet asked.

"No. Should I?" Wishes were for birthday candles and shooting stars. Not for contraband bottles of minibar alcohol.

"Of course. Ireland is a land of magic. You never know when your fondest dream will come true."

Mary was about to add a sarcastic remark when she suddenly glanced at Harriet's face. The stubborn glint in the older woman's eye suggested that she wasn't going to let this one go. "Don't scoff. You can't say you don't believe in something, just because you've never seen it. Even scientists know there are some things which can't be explained."

True enough. "It doesn't mean I expect to see leprechauns hiding in the break room."

"The bastards are more likely to be raiding the Coke machines," Harriet retorted. She took another sip of her whiskey. "I'm speaking of the fairies. You've heard of the Irish superstitions, haven't you?"

"A little." She'd heard tales of babies snatched at birth, changeling tales. Myths of selkies and other fey creatures. "I know you're not supposed to offend them."

The old woman's expression turned darker. "No. You're not." She stared out of the window at the road, which had grown narrower. Hedges lined the left side of the road and, below it, the sea roiled with grey waves and white foam. Harriet rested her chin on her palm, eyeing the wild landscape. Gorse and heather bloomed on the sides of the cliffs while sheep grazed in the grass.

When they reached a series of stone huts on the side of the mountain, the tour bus rolled to a stop. Mary wasn't exactly in the mood to view prehistoric beehive huts, but perhaps the sea air would clear her head.

Harriet stopped her before they got off the bus. "I'll tell you this, Mary Samson. Make a wish, when the time is right. It might come true."

Not wanting to offend her seatmate, Mary nodded. "All right." She didn't know what Harriet was talking about, but if it made the woman feel good to give advice, there wasn't any harm in smiling and going along with it.

The grey skies rolled a fog off the sea, cloaking the Dingle Peninsula in a low mist. It was cooler outside, and Mary buttoned up the pullover sweater she'd bought at the last tour stop. As she trudged up the path, following the guide, Harriet's words came back. *Make a wish, when the time is right.*

Some people would wish for a winning lottery ticket. Maybe a house in Bermuda or a job promotion.

I want a family, she thought. Her parents had been dead for ten years, and there was no one left. No aunts, no uncles. Not even a grandmother. It was loneliness that had made her register for an online dating service. And though her gut had warned her that Garrett wasn't Mr Right, she'd hoped he could be Mr Almost-Right. She had been willing to settle, to mould herself into the woman he wanted. And how pitiful was that?

Stepping into the grass, she sat on a large limestone boulder, watching the sea from her vantage point. The tour group continued on without her, and she rested her hands on the rock, letting her thoughts drift. At her feet, the grass swayed with the gusts of wind.

She realized her tennis shoes were squarely in the middle of a circle of mushrooms. A fairy circle, so the legend went.

Funny. Perhaps that was what Harriet had meant. All right, she was game for anything. Superstitions didn't mean a thing, but why not make that wish?

I wish a man would love the woman I am, not the woman he wants me to be. And I want to have a family.

She looked up and saw the old woman rushing towards her. "No!" Harriet cried out. "What have you done?"

Mary frowned, not understanding. It was just a circle of mushrooms. A common gardening problem, nothing more. But her heart began to quicken with an unnamed fear. "What is it?"

The old woman reached her side. "Get out. Get out, before it's too late."

"I don't know what you're talking about. It's just—"

A blinding migraine seemed to strike out of nowhere. A pulsing, swollen pressure that pressed against her brain.

"Those who step into an empty fairy ring die at a young age," Harriet breathed. "It's forbidden, didn't you know that?"

"Don't be ridiculous." Mary tried to stand up, but a wave of dizziness seemed to pull her down. "It's just a bunch of mushrooms." Probably the amaretto, coming back to haunt her.

Harriet grabbed her hand and pressed something soft into it. "Take this. And whatever you do, don't let go."

It was a piece of brown bread, left over from breakfast. What on earth?

"It's an offering. It might pacify the fey."

A strange music seemed to emanate from the ground, the faint sounds of harp strings. "Do you hear that?" Mary leaned forwards, trying to make sense of it.

Harriet was mumbling under her breath, her hands working upon a strand of rosary beads. Prayers. Mary wanted to smile and tell her not to be silly. It was going to be OK.

But before she could speak, her knees buckled beneath her. She stumbled on to her hands and knees inside the circle. Grass tickled her face, and pressure rose up inside her skull to an unbearable pitch. She gripped her head, but the agony kept building and rising.

A small pop, and she was ripped free of her body, her spirit hovering above the fairy circle.

Some wish, Mary grumbled. She wasn't supposed to die, for God's sake. That was her last thought before her spirit was torn through the fairy circle and across to the other side.

Mary opened her eyes and saw a tiny man, about the length of her forearm, staring at her with an appreciative smirk. He wore clothes that blended into the surrounding grasses, and he propped his elbow against one of the stones. A leprechaun? No, she had to be dreaming.

"You're a fetching one, aren't you?" he remarked. "He's going to like you."

Mary wasn't sure what the little man was talking about, but when she glanced down, she saw that she was completely naked. "Oh, my God." She rolled on to her chest and looked around frantically for her clothes.

"They're not there. You can't exactly bring clothes with you, once you're dead. Or, partly dead, in your case."

"Partly dead?" She scrambled around for some vegetation but only came up with a daffodil or two. And she could just imagine what it would look like to have flowers plastered across her bum.

"Indeed." The man nodded towards the ring of mushrooms, which was nearby. "You made a wish, before you were taken. That's what saved you."

"Somehow, I'm pretty sure that I'm asleep on the tour bus, and I'm going to wake up." Mary glared at the man. "You're probably going to tell me you're a leprechaun and you're looking for your Lucky Charms."

He shrugged. "Not a leprechaun. My name is Kevan, and I am one of the Daoine Sídhe."

The Deena She? Who? Play along, Mary. You're dreaming anyway. What's the harm?

"You wished for someone to love you and for a family." Kevan rubbed his beard, staring at her. "A powerful wish, love is. And it holds the power to save you. You have three days to fall in love and make him love you in return."

"What do you mean *him*?"

"The man you wished for. He'll be arriving shortly. And when the sun rises on the third day, you'll either get your wish . . ."

"Or?"

"Or you'll die, Mary Samson. And this time, it's for ever."

Ireland, 1173

Cian MacCorban was a man who trusted his instincts. Though some would accuse him of being ruled by his dreams, he knew differently. They weren't dreams; they were realities yet to occur. Too often, the visions came upon him without warning. And every last one had come true.

Even the deaths.

That was the cursed part of the Sight. He saw friends, family members, knowing *how* they would die. But not *when*. Never that. He hadn't known that a death was about to happen until it was too late.

His people feared him, and most had abandoned him. His ring fort was falling apart, and he no longer cared. What did it matter, when he was nearly the only one left?

Cian mounted his horse, preparing to ride out. He let the horse lead, opening his mind to the vision he'd seen again last night. A woman's face, her honey-blonde hair cut short to her shoulders. Intelligent grey eyes and an uncertain smile. For so many years, he'd hoped this vision would come true: the woman who was meant for him.

He'd seen the morning sun rising through the circle of standing stones. One day, she would be there. For ten years, he'd ridden out to the circle, hoping to find her. But when he glanced behind him, he sensed that even *she* would not want a man like him. A man cursed with visions of death.

It was easier to be naked in public if you had a tiny waist and a perfectly toned body. Mary had neither of these, and it was her own fault for avoiding the gym. Kevan, the man of the Daoine Sídhe, had vanished some time ago, and she was left trying to decide what to do. She couldn't exactly make clothes out of the grass, and there weren't any palm leaves lying around either.

Before long, she heard hoof beats approaching. Mary dived behind one of the standing stones, trying to hide what she could of her body. A man was on horseback, likely a historical re-enactor, given his simple clothing and the blue cloak fastened with a brooch. His blond hair was unkempt, hanging across his shoulders. His dark blue eyes were tired, like a man who hadn't slept in years.

Though he was tall and handsome, it was the bleakness that held her attention.

When he started to walk towards her, she held out her hand. "Wait! Don't come any closer. I don't have any . . . that is, I'm not wearing – Oh, damn it, just stay where you are."

He startled, as though he were trying to puzzle out her words. "You're real. Not a dream."

She wasn't sure what to say to that. Instead, she pleaded, "I'm in a bit of trouble here. Could you please throw me your cloak?"

Without questioning her, he unfastened his cloak and threw it. It fell slightly short, but Mary eased it towards herself with one foot. Only when she'd covered herself from neck to ankle, did she step out from behind the standing stone.

"Thank you," she said. "I wish I had an explanation for why I'm not wearing any clothes, but the truth is, I'm not sure how I got here. Am I still in Ireland?"

He nodded. "May I come closer to speak with you?"

"I . . . um . . . yes, sure. Oh, and I promise I'll give you back this cloak as soon as I can. I suppose you'll need it for the re-enactment."

His blue eyes narrowed. "The what?"

She stared at him. Utter confusion appeared on his face, as if he didn't know what a re-enactment was. *Don't panic, don't panic. He's just staying in character.*

"I'll give it back to you later," Mary said. "In the meantime, maybe you could help me find my tour group?"

He shook his head slowly. "There is no one here. But if you're needing food and shelter, I can give you that. Perhaps there might be a gown you could borrow."

A gown? She gripped the edges of the cloak together. One minute at a time was all she could handle before going crazy. Was this the man she was supposed to encounter? The one who had to love her before the third day, or she would die?

"I appreciate your help." She walked alongside him towards his horse. "What is your name?"

"I am Cian MacCorban, chief of the MacCorban clan. Or what's left of them."

Mary introduced herself, and Cian reached out to assist her on to his horse. When he swung up behind her, she was startled at his body warmth. Though it was early summer, the weather wasn't as warm as the Florida heat she was used to.

His arms came around her waist to grip the reins, and Mary felt self-conscious at his inadvertent touch. Wasn't this a dream? She'd had vivid dreams before. Surely this was one of them. But the sensation of riding a horse and feeling a man's arms around her was all too real.

It felt safe, being with Cian. Though she knew it wasn't wise to go off with strangers, she didn't have a choice. If she *was* dreaming, then there was no harm in it. And if she *wasn't* dreaming, then she was already half-dead to begin with, and it didn't matter.

"Are you the man I was supposed to meet?" she blurted out. "The one waiting for me?" *Great, Mary. That made a lot of sense. He won't think you're crazy now.*

Instead, his grip tightened around her waist. "I've seen you in my visions for over twenty years, Mary Samson. I've dreamed about you every night, wondering when you would finally be here."

"Oh." She couldn't think of what else to say. It should have felt creepy, like he was a stalker. Instead, there was a strange sense of relief. She'd made her wish, and here he was – the man fate had paired her up with. If he'd been waiting for her for over twenty years, then it shouldn't be so hard to make him fall in love with her, should it?

But she was supposed to love him back. And if she'd learned anything from her relationship with Garrett, it was that love couldn't be forced. It either happened, or it didn't.

She rode in front of Cian for nearly an hour before she saw a ruined fortress ahead. Built upon a small crannog, the ring fort probably housed ten to fifteen people. But as they rode across the bridge and through the gate, her suspicions sharpened. The place was falling apart, with hardly anyone to take care of it. Rotting hides and animal manure gave the place an indescribable odour, one that wasn't at all welcoming. She saw only four other men, and they were all staring at her.

After Cian helped her down, she took in her surroundings. "Is this where you work? Is this a re-enactment village?"

"This is my home." Distaste lined his face, as though he didn't care for it either.

Though her brain warned her not to ask, she couldn't stop herself. "Cian, is this real?"

"What do you mean?"

She swallowed hard, her heart hammering against her chest. "What year is this?"

"It is the Year of Our Lord 1173."

No. No, it wasn't possible. But it *was* as if she'd stepped back in time, into a medieval world where the men wore swords and the women sewed their own clothing. No modern medicine, no cars. No toothbrushes or personal hygiene.

Her brain was screaming. Maybe it was better to just let herself die. After all, surely they had toilets in heaven. She didn't like primitive conditions, and the stone roundhouse certainly qualified as that. She'd never even been camping, for heaven's sake.

Cian adjusted the fire, dropping more peat bricks on top of it. He gestured towards a pile of furs. "I'll be back in a few hours. Make yourself comfortable."

And though she promised herself she wouldn't do anything stupid like pass out or scream, her knees buckled of their own accord, and she found herself crouching on the ground. *Breathe. Just breathe.*

Cian was at her side instantly. "Are you all right, *a chara*?" He sat down, pulling her on to his lap.

She almost laughed. All right? She'd been sent back in time nearly a thousand years and he wanted to know if she was all right? If she recalled her history properly, they burned crazy women at the stake.

You're already dead, her conscience argued. *Well, almost.*

It doesn't mean I want to become a human barbecue.

"I . . . need a moment," she whispered.

His hands moved to the sides of her face, his fingers threading through her hair. "It's softer than I thought it would be," he murmured. "And you're prettier than the woman I saw in my dreams."

She couldn't answer because, at the moment, he was holding her like a cherished possession. As if he couldn't believe she was real. His blue eyes were shadowed, his face haggard. But there was a fierce hope within his expression.

Her pulse quickened as she reached out to his face. What sort of man was he? His face was clean-shaven, unlike his kinsmen.

The bristles on his face were starting to grow smooth. A small scar ridged the edge of his chin up to his lip.

This was a man who had waged battle upon his enemies, a warrior who lived by a different set of rules. And he was staring at her as though she meant everything to him.

"Cian." She said his name, testing it out.

Before she could speak another word, his mouth lowered to hers. Softly, like they were reunited, he kissed her. Beneath the cloak, she shivered, her flesh rising up with unexpected arousal. He wasn't the barbarian she'd expected. No, his kiss was seductive, alluring. She could kiss a man like him all night long.

You might have to do more than that, her conscience warned. Three days was a heartbeat in time, barely enough for anyone to become friends, much less fall in love. But a kiss was a start.

He deepened the kiss, cradling her head as his mouth coaxed and tasted. "I'm still dreaming, aren't I?" He broke free of her, staring at her swollen lips.

Mary clutched the edges of her cloak, not knowing what to say. "It's not such a bad dream." Even if he was a stranger, she felt an unusual connection to him.

A half-cocky smile tipped at his mouth. He released her swiftly. "I'll hunt for our noon meal. In the meantime, you can look about for a gown or some clothes. Ask Brían, if you've a need for anything."

He started to leave, but his gaze suddenly grew distant. For several minutes, he didn't say a word, but stared at the whitewashed interior walls of the roundhouse. It was as though he'd fallen into a hypnotic trance, one where he lost track of the world around him.

Without warning, his hand curled into a fist, and he cursed in Irish. Cian slammed the door open, and Mary followed him outside. "What's the matter?"

He stopped short. Casting a glance behind him, he said, "It's nothing."

Typical man. "You saw something, didn't you?" His earlier admission – that he'd dreamed of her – made her wonder what sort of visions he had.

"I did. And we'll not speak of it again."

Cian kept walking, his stride quickening. Almost as if he couldn't wait to be rid of her.

*   *   *

The vision might well have been a razor blade, from the way it sliced through him, cutting to his heart. Cian had seen flashes of Mary, her eyes warm with an unnamed emotion, her arms welcoming. He'd seen her in his bed, her body flushed from lovemaking.

And he'd seen the moment the light had faded from her eyes.

She'd died in his arms, and the pain of losing her was unlike anything he'd known. Damn it all, he'd just found her. He'd sensed that she was the person he'd been searching for, the other half that would fill up the emptiness he'd lived with for so long.

He was so tired of losing loved ones, of foreseeing their deaths. Not again. It was better to live alone, where he didn't have to endure the visions.

His cousin Logan walked alongside him, his bow ready. "She's the one you told us about, isn't she? Your bride."

"I thought so at first. But I was wrong. She can stay for a few days, until her kin can find her." After that, he'd not see her again.

"But you said –"

"I know what I said," Cian snapped. Since they'd likely scared off any of the game, he didn't bother keeping his voice low. "But I'm not about to let my curse affect her. If she stays, she's going to die."

"It might not be until she's older. Years from now," Logan argued.

"I've already seen it." He closed his eyes, trying to will away the vision. "Perhaps if she leaves, it won't happen quite so soon." In the vision, she'd been cradled in his arms. The sooner he sent her away, the better chance that she would live.

"You've no control over another person's fate, Cian. Only God can decide when a person is ready to die."

"I'm tired of being God's messenger." He shook his head. "Leave me here, Logan. I've a need to be alone."

Cian MacCorban might be living in a medieval pigsty, but Mary didn't plan on enduring it. After exploring the ring fort, she'd found that most of the huts were abandoned. Only Brían remained behind. She'd attempted to speak to him, but he spoke little English. It didn't appear to bother him when she entered each of the dwellings, searching for clothing. With hand signals, she got his permission to take a primitive pair of trousers and a long tunic. She hadn't found gowns of any sort, and was rather happy about it, to be honest. She'd only get the dress dirty.

So, she'd tied the trousers with a belt made of rope and found a pair of gloves. Holding her breath, she began the arduous process of cleaning the ring fort. She ordered Brían to haul off the loads of waste and rotten carcasses. He didn't argue, and she suspected that he secretly agreed with her about the need to make the place more presentable.

What she wouldn't give for some disinfectant right now. She worked hard, scrubbing at a pile of soiled wooden dishes. After that, she swept the small roundhouse and straightened up all of Cian's belongings. She believed in order and cleanliness. Once it was done, she felt calm, a stronger sense of control.

When the afternoon waned into evening, she waited for Cian to return. Her stomach rumbled and she was thirsty, but she wasn't about to drink the pond water. Not without boiling it first, anyway.

Brían spent the remainder of the time sharpening his sword and knives. He was a quiet man, tall and observant. Even so, he didn't think to offer her anything to eat. She wondered if there *was* any food at all. From the deserted huts, it didn't look like it.

By the time Cian returned, Mary was having visions of her own. Hot fudge sundaes and steaming cups of coffee. Large sandwiches stuffed with meat, cheese, lettuce, and tomatoes. Chocolate chip cookies.

She was not, however, envisioning a dead deer slung across the backs of the two men. Wincing, she turned away as they prepared to dress the meat. She'd had venison before and she wasn't a vegetarian, but it didn't mean that she particularly liked to see where her meat came from. Plastic-wrapped packages in the butcher's aisle at the supermarket were just fine by her.

Within another hour, the men had a large piece of meat roasting over an open fire. Cian had avoided her for most of the time, and she wasn't sure why. Only three other men joined them, and she noticed that there were no women and children.

The deserted ring fort had a ghostly aura to it, as though the remaining inhabitants had died. Mary rubbed her arms for warmth, trying not to wonder why everyone was gone.

Cian saw the direction of her gaze, and it was then that he noticed her cleaning efforts. He spoke quietly to Brían, who nodded and pointed back to her. Mary tried to smile, but her mouth wouldn't quite work. Cian's expression didn't exactly look pleased, and suddenly she was reminded of Garrett's complaints.

Why do you always feel the need to clean up after other people? If I put my beer down, you don't have to recycle the bottle right away.

She'd thought she was keeping her apartment clean, making it a pleasant space for both of them. It was easier to clean up along the way, rather than spend hours trying to shovel out a week's worth of living. Efficient and tidy – that was the way she liked it.

But now, she had an Irish warrior staring at her as though she'd riffled through his undergarments. He crossed over to her and handed her a generous portion of venison on one of the wooden plates she'd scoured. The gesture was completely at odds with the grim look on his face.

Mary murmured her thanks and Cian stood in front of her as if trying to choose the right words. She avoided his gaze, afraid she'd overstepped her boundaries. When the seconds shifted into minutes, she broke the silence. "Aren't you going to eat something?"

"In a moment."

She dug into the venison, pretending as though the meat was the most fascinating object on the planet.

"Why?" he asked.

"Why what?"

"Why did you spend hours cleaning this ... place? It means nothing to you." He glanced around as though he expected it to crumble into the ground. And perhaps he wanted it to. The mess she'd tidied had represented months of neglect, like a man who didn't care any more.

But he'd given her shelter and food, and this was a way to repay him. She'd wanted to make herself useful, bringing a little bit of his home back.

"I didn't mean to intrude," she said. "I just thought it might help you." Before he could say a word, she added, "But if you'd rather I put things back, I can. Well, probably not the trash or the animal hides. We burned those, but I could probably—"

He put his hand over her mouth, cutting off her senseless babble. "It was kind of you."

There was a flicker behind his shielded emotions of a grateful man. And just as quickly, it disappeared. He picked at the venison on his own plate, not even attempting conversation. It was as if the man she'd met this morning had gone. Whatever he'd seen in his vision had completely transformed him. He was acting as if she had a dreaded disease and he didn't want to be near her any more. It disconcerted her, reminding her of Garrett's rejection.

Mary needed to lighten the mood, to somehow make him see that she wasn't any threat. "What do you do at night, to entertain each other?"

Cian shrugged. "We're not much for singing or storytelling. Sometimes a game of dice, if we're feeling up to it."

"What about sports?" At his blank look, she amended, "Games with a ball?"

Brían had overheard their conversation and spoke rapidly to Cian. A few moments later, he returned with a round leather ball. It wasn't quite what she'd envisioned, but it might work.

She hefted the ball in one hand. It was slightly larger than a softball, and the weight was manageable. "Want to play?"

His blue eyes turned dark with another meaning, one she hadn't intended. He looked at her as though he wanted to kiss her again and, Lord help her, she wouldn't mind so much. Cian MacCorban was incredibly handsome, and she'd always had a weakness for a sexy knight with a sword. Or, in this case, an Irish chief.

Cian ordered the men to gather round and they each took turns lobbing the ball at a crooked fence post. Each time they missed, they took a swig of mead from a drinking horn. When her own ball fell short, Cian handed over the horn. "Drink."

"No, really, I'm not thirsty."

"It's your penalty, *a stór.* For missing the target." He shot her a wicked smile, and her good sense melted like butter in a hot skillet. His hands curved over hers as he lifted the horn to her mouth. The mead tasted sweeter than she'd expected, but the fermented drink was strong.

"I'd better not miss too often," she said. "Or else I'll be so drunk you'll have to carry me to bed."

His smile deepened, and Mary's face turned bright red at the unintended innuendo. "It would be my honour, *a stór.*"

That was when the cheating began. At first, it seemed unintentional. A light brush against her shoulder when she threw the ball. Then Cian sneezed loudly at the moment she aimed at the target.

Mary wasn't about to let cheaters prosper. No, she stretched her arms up, letting the edge of the man's tunic she wore bare the skin of her shoulder. She stood beside Cian, whispering an innocent question in his ear when he tried to throw the ball.

In the end, her head was buzzing, and she felt like she was standing outside of herself. She'd never been this uninhibited before. It was like being among a group of brothers, who had no qualms about wrestling in front of her or daring her to drink another swallow of mead.

Later that night, Cian dragged her away, sweeping her into his arms. Both of them were laughing, and she found herself feeling better than she had in years. He brought her inside his roundhouse, and she held tightly to his neck.

Perhaps it was her impending death that made her so bold. Lord knew, she wasn't the kind of woman who drank more than a glass of wine or two. And she certainly had never kissed a man within an hour of meeting him.

Cian was holding her body as though she weighed nothing. Slowly, he lowered her to stand in front of him, but she didn't let go of him.

"Why is this place abandoned?" she whispered. "Why are there no women or children?"

The pain returned to his face, the edge of a man who shouldered endless guilt. "They left of their own accord. Because of me."

"What could you possibly have done?" She traced her hand down his jawline, noting the scar upon his chin. This was a man who must have seen the face of death, over and over.

"It isn't what I did. It's what I saw. My curse." He released her and went to the door. "But you needn't trouble yourself over it. I'll send Brían to find your family, and they'll take you home."

"I have no home or family. Not any more." The cold shivers ran through her once again, and she clutched at her elbows. "I don't even know how I got here."

"Or what happened to your clothes?" he said grimly.

"No." It was the only truth she could give him and, right now, she sensed he was going to leave her. "Will you stay with me?" She moved towards him, her knees swaying slightly from all the mead she'd drunk. "I'd rather not be alone tonight."

His expression grew haggard. "I'm going to get you some stones from the fire outside. They will keep this space warm."

You could keep me warm, she almost said. But then that was the mead responding, not her brain.

When he'd left, Mary sank down on the rough pallet, staring up at the thatched ceiling. She hadn't allowed herself to be afraid before. But now, the fear coursed through her veins, filling her up inside. She had never really believed in the supernatural, but now, it seemed her life depended on it. There was no real proof that she would die on the morning of the third day. Then again, she'd watched her body fall lifeless into the fairy circle. She'd been sent back in time nearly a thousand years and had spoken to a man the size of her arm.

You're either going crazy, or this is real.

Cian returned, using the butt of a spear to roll several heated stones into the space. And she knew that if she didn't do something, he was going to leave her. He arranged the stones and stood back.

"Sleep now. In the morning, we'll decide what to do."

When he tried to leave, she blocked the doorway. "Cian, did I do something wrong?"

He rested his hand upon the wall. "No, there's nothing."

There was a look of indecision on his face, as though he wanted a reason to stay, but honour prevented it.

"I had fun tonight," she whispered, touching her hand to his face. "Even if I can't play ball to save my life."

His face furrowed at her phrasing, and she reminded herself to watch the way she spoke.

"It's been a long time since I had a reason to laugh," he admitted. Cian covered her hand with his own. For a long moment, he looked upon her, his gaze searching.

I can be more spontaneous, she thought to herself. Maybe it's time to be impulsive.

Although the engineer inside protested at what she was about to do, playing her life safe had never gotten her anywhere. She had less than two days left, so why not?

Mary stood on her tiptoes, her face nearing Cian's. She moved slowly, giving him every chance to pull away. Instead, his mouth came down upon hers, kissing her like a desperate man. She clung to him, unable to catch her breath. His arms slipped around her waist, lifting beneath the tunic to her bare back. He worshipped her skin with his hands, pulling her tightly against his body.

Too fast. She couldn't stop the rush of feelings, nor rein in her own response. But common sense evaporated in the intensity of his kiss. He threaded his hands through her hair, altering the embrace until he laid her down upon the pallet. She tasted the mead upon his tongue, the intensity of his desire for her. And when at last he broke away, she pleaded, "Stay with me tonight. Don't go."

He cursed, dragging his mouth against her lips for another kiss. "I'll sleep in this hut, to keep you safe. But I swear, I won't dishonour you."

"Please stay. That's all I ask."

He slept on the opposite side of the hut, atop a folded cloak. In the middle of the night, she heard him awaken. The nightmare caught him and he started speaking Irish, his words tangled up with fear. Mary felt her way towards him and knelt down.

"Cian, wake up. It's only a dream."

He reached out and pulled her to him. His body was trembling, and she soothed him, running her hands over his tight muscles. "It's OK. I'm here."

His breathing was unsteady, and at last he seemed to realize where he was. "I wasn't supposed to fall asleep."

"Isn't that what most people do at night?"

"Not me." He sat up, but Mary supported his weight, her arms still around him. "I try not to sleep. Then, when I must, I sleep so hard the dreams don't come."

That explained why his eyes were always so tired. "It's not healthy."

"Neither are my dreams."

"What did you dream of?" He remained silent, and she had a sudden suspicion. "Did you dream of me?"

She rose up on her knees, turning to face him. In the darkness, she couldn't see his face, but she touched his shoulders. "Tell me what you saw."

"Don't you understand?" he whispered. "My dreams come true. All of them have happened, just as I saw them."

"You dreamed of me. You said you'd been waiting twenty years."

He emitted a harsh laugh. "Aye. Twenty years for the worst nightmare of all my days."

He took both of her wrists in his hands. "I saw you dying, just now. I saw you in my arms, the moment the last breath of life left you. Just as I saw the deaths of each of my family and friends. It's why they left. Why they all leave."

"Everyone dies," she said softly. "And whether you see it or not, doesn't make you responsible."

"I can't stop their deaths. Not even yours."

"I know it." She moved closer to him, cupping his face. "I have a curse of my own, Cian. From the Daoine Sídhe. I'm going to die before the sun rises tomorrow morning, so the man said. The difference is, I'm not going to waste my last day wishing I had more time."

She pressed a kiss against his mouth. "I'm going to enjoy every last moment of it." And she had no intention of telling him the rest of the story. There was nothing that would drive a man away faster than for him to feel cornered in a relationship. *Fall in love with me, or I'm going to die.* If that wasn't pressuring a man, she didn't know what was.

Cian didn't question her certainty, but instead lowered his forehead to hers. "Then I won't waste the last hours I have with you, either." He lifted her in his arms and took her back to bed. With his arms around her, she fell asleep once again.

Cian eased off the pallet, letting Mary sleep a little longer. He left her a plate of bread and some venison to break her fast. Though she claimed she knew of her impending death, he wondered if there was a way to prevent it. Tomorrow, before the sun rises, she'd said. He struggled to recall every detail of his vision, but all he could remember was her lying in his arms before she stopped breathing.

She wandered outside, her eyes sleepy. A slight smile tilted her mouth and she held out the plate. "Thank you for the breakfast. Did you want some?"

He was beginning to grow accustomed to her strange speech. Though he suspected there was a great deal about her that he didn't know, he asked no questions. Right now, he didn't want the answers.

"I'm fine."

Mary set the half-eaten plate of food aside. "Well, if you change your mind, it's there." She glanced up at the sky, which was full of clouds. "Doesn't look like I'll have good weather for my last day alive."

He stood up and took her hand. "Don't talk that way."

"Sorry. Didn't mean to be morbid, but I do have a request."

"Name it."

"Will you take me out horseback riding? I'd like to see more of the countryside."

"If that's your wish." He released her hand, intending to see about the horses. Regardless of her prediction, he'd decided to pretend like it was any other day. As though she were a sister or a friend, not the woman he felt so drawn to. He wouldn't let himself fall into the trap of caring for her, not if she was going to die. Best to shield himself from it.

Mary ventured a smile. "I've never been on horseback before. It looks like a beautiful way to see the land."

"It is." He saw her take a step forwards, as though she were about to embrace him. Instead, he moved away, taking the long path towards the stable. He didn't miss the disappointment in her eyes, but it was for the best. It would hurt far less, if he kept himself distant from her.

After he saddled her horse and led her out of the ring fort and across the bridge of the crannog, he stayed at her side. "My family has lived here for a hundred years. The crannog is an artificial island, but it protects us from raiders and wild animals."

He thought she mumbled something about "killer squirrels" but couldn't be sure. When they reached the open fields, Mary turned to him. "Show me how to gallop."

"You said you've never been on a horse before. It's not safe."

"Oh, come on. I want to go faster. How hard can it be?"

"Your backside won't forgive you." But he reached over and lifted her on to the horse in front of him. "It's better if I take you with me." Driving his heels into his stallion's back, he took her across the meadow as fast as he dared. Her hair streamed away from her face, and she gripped the horse's mane tightly. He brought her towards the sea, letting her glimpse the deep blue waters against the harsh cliffs. Then he slowed the horse.

Mary turned to him, and the blinding smile on her face stole his breath. She rested her palm on his cheek and drew him in for a light kiss.

He knew he shouldn't touch her, but he wanted to hold her. She eased her leg until she sat side-saddle, and put her arms around his waist. "That was amazing. Thank you."

She sat against his lap, and he let her remain there, with her head resting against his chest. "I've only known you for a single day, but it feels like longer."

His grip tightened around her, for she was right.

"I'm glad you're here, Cian," she murmured.

His answer was another kiss on her temple. Right now he wanted to take her back home, to keep her at his side for always. But just then, the wind whipped against them, rippling the grasses on the hillside. His gaze was drawn to one of the mounds, and upon it, he saw one of the Daoine Sídhe. The small man stared at them, his gaze threatening.

"That's the man I saw," Mary whispered. "Kevan. He's the one who said I'm going to die before dawn tomorrow."

Cian turned his mount towards the man, but as soon as they reached the foot of the hill, Kevan vanished. "How did you offend him?"

"I stepped into a fairy circle," she admitted. "I thought it was just a ring of mushrooms."

She shivered in his arms. "Take me back, Cian. I need something to take my mind off tomorrow morning."

Cian had gone out searching for blackberries along the edge of the forest when the back of his neck began to prickle.

"Fulfilling her last request, are you?" Kevan interrupted. The tiny man of the Daoine Sídhe had a smug expression on his face.

Cian didn't bother to hide his anger. "She's innocent and never meant to offend. She didn't even know what the circle was."

Kevan laughed. "She didn't tell you how to break the curse, did she?"

Cian stilled, not knowing what the man was speaking of. "No."

"Well now." Kevan rubbed at his beard. "She didn't tell you that love has the power to save her life? I find that interesting."

"I don't want her to die," Cian said, forcing himself to kneel on the ground. If he had to humble himself before a member of the Daoine Sídhe, so be it. Mary's life was worth it. "I will love her, if that's what I'm meant to do."

Kevan laughed. "You can love her all you wish, but it won't save her. Only if she loves you in return, will she live. And it doesn't seem that she feels the same way now, does it?"

The words pricked him like the blackberry thorns. "There's time enough to convince her."

"Her soul will belong to us, Cian MacCorban. In a matter of hours. And there's naught you can do about it."

The remaining hours slid away and the skies opened up a rainstorm that quickly turned the ring fort into mud. Mary struggled to cook the fish Cian had caught earlier, but was afraid she'd made a watery mess of them in the sputtering outdoor fire.

In the end, he brought some of the heated rocks inside the hut and finished cooking the fillets on the hot stones. While they waited for the food to finish, he offered a handful of blackberries he'd found.

"It's early for them, but you said they were your favourite."

She smiled and ate the blackberries, but when Cian joined her, he spat one out. "These are the worst things I've ever tasted."

"Oh, they're not that bad." They were, but it was the thought that counted.

He pushed the bowl away. "I saw Kevan near the forest, when I was picking the berries. He told me more about your curse."

Her face reddened, and she found an excuse to stare at her hands. Couldn't a woman keep any secrets to herself? "What did he tell you?"

"That if we fell in love, you would live."

She drew her knees up to her chest, not meeting his gaze. "We met yesterday, Cian. People don't fall in love that fast. It was never worth trying."

"Not even to save your life?"

She bit her lip to keep back the tears. Did he think she could simply turn feelings on or off with an imaginary switch? She'd done everything she could to make Garrett love her, and nothing had worked. In fact, the harder she'd tried, the more he'd disliked her. And she didn't want Cian to feel that way.

"I don't believe in love at first sight," she said quietly.

He reached out to her hands and pulled her to stand before him. His posture was stiff, and she sensed she was crushing his pride. "Is it . . . that you could never love a man like me?"

"Cian, you don't understand. We come from two different worlds. You're handsome and kind, but we have nothing in common. I didn't tell you the entire truth about me." She took a deep breath, knowing he needed to understand everything. "The reality is, I'm not like you. I'm from the twenty-first century."

The confession hung between them like weighted stones. "When I entered that fairy circle, I died in my own century," Mary continued. "The Daoine Sídhe sent me back in time here, for three days." The bottled-up feelings seemed to overflow and she stared down at the ground. "The reason I know I'm going to die is because I'm already dead. And love can't stop that, no matter what Kevan told you."

He was staring at her, not speaking. No doubt he thought she was insane. *And, here we go with burning a witch at the stake. Nice job, Mary.*

"I don't know what to believe any more," he said. "You're doing everything you can to keep me away."

"I don't want you to be hurt when I'm gone."

He stroked the side of her face, which was now wet with tears. She didn't even realize she'd started crying. "Time cannot change what's here." He laid her hand upon his heart. "But if you won't even try to love me in return . . ." His voice drifted off.

She couldn't answer. The fear of her own death loomed closer. Only hours were left and she couldn't believe that something as simple as love would have power to conquer eternity in the grave.

"I have feelings for you, Cian," she admitted. "But I don't believe that anyone could fall in love in this short a time. I believe that you may care for me, but you don't love me."

"Let me try, *a stór*. Let me show you what I feel."

He laid her down upon the pallet of furs, then kissed her deeply. The touch of his mouth was gentle, trying to soothe away her raw nerves. Mary tried to relax, but his unfamiliar touch kindled up a heat that she couldn't control. He loosened the ties of the tunic, waiting for permission to slide it away.

There was every opportunity to say no. But in his eyes, she saw a hunger, a need to show her what he felt. And though she didn't believe he could possibly love her, she didn't stop him from removing the layers of clothing between them. For tonight, she would reach out for something she wanted.

Cian's body was honed, tightly muscled from years of fighting. She smiled as she traced his warm skin, over his back and down to his tight hips. He trapped her wrists, leaning down upon her, and kissed her. His mouth was demanding, fighting for her response. And when she met his tongue with her own, he filled his palms with her breasts.

He touched her and murmured, "I would die in your place if I could, Mary." Then he lowered his mouth to her breast, teasing her. She grabbed his hair, arching her back as he kissed her stomach and thighs.

"You're the woman I've dreamed of my entire life, Mary Samson." She guided him inside her. "Whether or not you love me in return, I am yours. Now and always." Tenderly, he made love to her, his mouth teasing at her breasts while he joined their bodies together.

"Cian," she whispered, urging him faster. He raised her hips up, her legs locking around his waist. And once he quickened the pace, his body rocking against hers, she felt herself uncoiling, her body straining for release.

Again and again, he drove himself inside her, his body growing harder with each stroke. The dizzying climax swept over her, and she gripped him hard.

When he lay sated upon her, he kissed her lips again. "I don't think I'm going to let you sleep at all this night, Mary Samson."

She could hardly think straight, her body was molten with satisfaction. "I thought men needed time to recover."

"Oh, I will, no doubt of it. But as for you . . ." He ran his tongue down the curve of her breast. "I want you to remember this night."

The sky was grey, and Cian dreaded the coming dawn. True to his word, he'd spent all night with Mary in his bed. She was more passionate than he'd ever imagined, even playful in the positions she'd asked him to try. But shadowing even their most ardent moments was the fear of losing her. He'd opened the door to their hut and wandered outside for a drink of water. Wearing only a pair of trews, he didn't bother with more clothing. No one was here to care.

He studied the ring fort, wishing for a glimpse of the Daoine Sidhe, but there was nothing. He'd even left a piece of bread upon the hearth, an offering for Mary's life.

But no one appeared.

As time went on and she still didn't awaken, he went to her side. When he pulled her into his arms, she gave a sleepy smile then burrowed into his chest. "It's not time to get up yet," she mumbled. "Sleep with me, Cian."

But he couldn't. In his mind he replayed every image from the vision of her death. And he knew, in his heart, that the moment would come soon. She claimed that she had already died, centuries in the future. Though he'd never heard of anyone who had travelled through time, he was a man who believed in magic, for it ruled him.

And when the faintest hints of the morning sun gleamed on the horizon, he went and chose his sharpest knife. He'd fallen in love with Mary Samson and if she couldn't love him back, then he might as well join her in death, giving over his own soul to be with her in the afterlife.

The sunlight cast a reflection off the blade and she opened her eyes at last. "I have never been so tired in all my life. It was worth every minute." She reached up and kissed him, holding him close.

He kissed her back, praying that his vision was wrong. That it wouldn't happen this way. But only seconds later, he felt her skin growing cooler, her hands falling away. Fear entered her eyes, and she looked at him. "It's happening, isn't it? I can feel it."

"Don't," he murmured. "Stay with me. Let me love you."

Then her eyes grew empty, falling shut.

"What's happening?" Mary asked Kevan who was standing before her. "What have you done?"

"I've merely kept my promise," Kevan replied. "Your time is finished now."

"But I do love Cian," she whispered. "I just never believed he would possibly love me back."

The small man's eyes gleamed. "You never told him what you held in your heart, Mary. And now it's too late."

"It's never too late for love," came a female voice. Mary turned and saw Harriet standing before them. Her white hair looked like a snowball, puffed around her face. She wore an olive polyester pants suit and in her hand she held a can of Coke.

"Harriet, what are you doing here?" Mary asked. "Tell me you're not dead, too." She stared at her surroundings, but there was only endless white, blinding her to all else.

"No, but I can't say as I'm alive either. I'm only half-human and I move about when it suits me. You might consider me a fairy godmother of sorts." Harriet's smile widened as if she liked that idea. "And right now, I'm doing what I do best. Forcing the Daoine Sídhe to keep their promises." She tossed the can of Coke at the small man. "Kevan, send her back. All she had to do was win his love and love him in return." Harriet pinned her with a stare. "You do love him, don't you, Mary?"

"Yes."

"And he obviously loves her," Harriet pronounced. "That's all settled then. Kevan, you'll keep your word, and, Mary, you'll have no memories of the twenty-first century any more. We can't have you inventing toilet paper before it's supposed to happen. A slight case of amnesia will do the trick nicely." She waved a hand and the veil between worlds parted.

From behind the veil, Mary saw Cian holding her lifeless body in his arms, his eyes filled with anguish. Then she saw the knife clenched in his hand. The blade gleamed, and Kevan smiled. He'd known Cian's intent.

"Send me back now," she ordered. *Let it not be too late.*

A hand shoved his wrist away before he could plunge the blade into his chest. Cian jerked back when he saw Mary's eyes open, her hands touching his. "Don't!" she begged.

The knife clattered from his fingers, and he gripped her tightly. "My God. I thought you were dead. You weren't breathing. I couldn't hear your heart beating."

Tears poured down Mary's cheeks and she was shaking. "Kevan almost didn't keep his word. But I convinced him of the truth." Drawing back to look into his eyes, she said, "I thought a man like you would never love someone like me. I didn't dare to hope for it. But I love you, Cian. I don't care what your dreams tell you, or how many members of your clan left. I'm staying right here."

He kissed her, thanking God he hadn't taken his own life. To have her back, to hold her in his arms once more, was the greatest gift he'd been given. With every touch, he murmured words of love, promises he would keep.

But then, the world folded into a familiar blur. He stared off into the distance, afraid of the future he would see. Though he tried to keep it at bay, there was no denying the vision before him.

Mary caught his hand, whispering. "What is it? What did you see this time?"

He sent her a shaky smile. "Not death. A blessing." Reaching out to her stomach, he rested it there, imagining his babe already growing inside her. "I dreamed of life."

Her answering smile and understanding filled him up with a happiness he'd never expected. "Our family."

As he led her back inside their home, Mary whispered, "Harriet was right. Wishes can come true."

Time Trails

Colby Hodge

June 29 1886

Texas Ranger Rand Brock nudged the toe of his boot against the swollen mass at the bottom of the wash. He took off his hat and wiped the sweat from his brow before settling it back on his head. It was hot. The kind of hot that made you wonder if hell would be just as bad. Thinking about the heat wasn't making this job any easier.

He'd seen men who'd been in the water a while. Just like cows they would bloat up and then the skin would burst beneath the hot West Texas sun but this . . . it looked as though the body had been chopped up, randomly stuck back together, and then cooked in a pot until it melted into an indistinguishable blob. And that was before it got caught up in the flash flood that carried it down the canyon and left it half buried in the sand.

He dropped down into a squat and gave it a closer look. Unfortunately for Rand, he recognized it, or maybe he should say a part of it. "Hell's sweet heat!" His horse, Joe, twisted its ears at his curse and looked at him curiously.

The face, what was left of it, bore a distinct scar that ran from a missing ear to the corner of its mouth. He jumped back when a scorpion crawled out of the open mouth and quickly scuttered into the rocks that littered the riverbank. Joe pawed the ground behind him and tossed his head as he stretched his lower lip out and waggled it back and forth.

"Go ahead. Laugh it up, Joe." Rand knelt back down to look at the body. "I'm sure Hank thinks it pretty funny." There was no doubt in his mind that he was looking at Hank Miller, who was supposed to be on his way to the Federal Prison in Leavenworth along with two other prisoners. His partner, Tom, was their escort. He'd been on the trail of the entire group after the prison wagon turned up empty and burning at the bottom of a ravine. The driver had been alive, barely, and gasped out something about the attack coming from the sky before he'd died of his wounds, which were as big a mystery as his last words. He had a big round hole in the middle of his chest like someone or something had stuck a red hot poker clean through him.

Since the driver's last words kind of went along with something a copper miner had said after stumbling into town a few days earlier, Rand had centred his search in this particular canyon. The miner reported strange lights at dusk, a boat that floated in the sky, scorpions made from steel and fire arrows. And that was all before he downed a bottle of whiskey.

This was not what he expected to find. Not at all. "What happened to you?" he said to the dead man before him. He took his hat off again and wiped the sweat away. The sun was merciless, the thunderstorms from the night before the forebears of extreme heat as if the lightning he'd watched from his shelter had boiled the air. He looked upstream. Whatever had killed Hank and left this mess had to have occurred up the canyon somewhere.

"Guess there's nothing left to do but bury you, or what's left of you." He went to where Joe browsed among some gorse bushes and yanked the small shovel from his pack. He took his shirt off and hung it over the saddle as he loosened Joe's bit. "Don't get lazy on me." The horse had been his faithful companion for many years. "This is the last trip for you and me. Once this is over and we get back to Laredo I promise it's nothing but sweet grass and fat mares."

Sweat dripped down his chest as he dug a hole far enough back from the river bed to keep Hank from washing out in the next flash flood. Finally he was content with the depth of the hole and went back to where the body lay. Another hour under the hot sun had not helped its condition one bit and Rand looked at it in distaste. Luckily he was wearing gloves and he finally reached down and grabbed the pulpy mass around what he thought could possibly be shoulders and pulled it from the sand.

What came with it made Rand jump back a good ten feet. There was another body. Or was it? What was between them was a twisted heap of . . . something . . . but beneath there was another part of a face.

"Tom!" Rand turned his head and heaved up the contents of his stomach. He wiped his mouth on his arm and covered his bile with some sand before turning once more to look at what was left of Texas Ranger Tom Jacks. Something protruded from his torso, something sharp and shiny, like the blade from a sword. Rand covered his mouth and swallowed hard as he pulled the piece of metal from his friend's body.

It was unlike anything he'd ever seen before – about three feet long and hinged in the middle so that the piece flexed, like a knee or an elbow. Rand moved it up, then down and marvelled at the intricate craftsmanship of whatever it was. The tip of it was as sharp as a razor and sliced open the finger of his glove.

"Tarnation!" He started to fling the part away, then thought better of it and took it over to Joe, wrapped it in a piece of hide and stuffed it in his saddlebag. Then he grabbed the bodies and dragged them over to the hole and rolled them in. He shoved the dirt over the grave, packed it down with the flat side of the shovel and gathered as many rocks as he could find to place over it.

"Damn . . . Tom . . ." He stared upstream for a moment, then back down at the dirt. "I'll find who done this. I swear." Rand pushed the shovel into his pack, swung up on Joe's back without bothering to put on his shirt and rode upstream. He'd had enough of that place.

April 27 2143

Shay McCoy studied the data on the screen as her handler, Topher, quantified the position of the quirks they'd discovered. Time had been fractured by some idiot who did not have a clue what he was dealing with. More of Wiley's work no doubt. The escaped criminal was determined to corner the market on time travel by reinventing the wheel and had left traces of his attempts all over history. This meant she was often cleaning up after him instead of hunting for him. It was her fault he'd escaped and she'd be damned if someone else was going to run him down. It was her case, her problem and she would handle it, or die trying. She could do nothing less since she was a Five-one Captain of the Time Travel Enforcement Agency.

"I need it narrowed down, Topher."

"I'm working on it . . . got it . . . 1886 . . . somewhere in . . . West Texas."

"Please tell me it's not the middle of summer." Shay hated the desert with a passion. Nothing but scorpions, rattlesnakes and dry heat that made it impossible to draw a breath.

"Give me a minute," Topher replied.

Shay shook her head in aggravation. Minutes were valuable, especially when some idiot was screwing around with them. The window for correction was short but luckily the damage in West Texas in the late nineteenth century should be minimal. There weren't that many people around the area in that time, if the data was accurate. It should be. The world's history had been carefully mapped and archived just in case something like this happened.

She checked her supplies while Topher studied the screen. Her armband, which stretched from wrist to elbow, was synchronized with Topher's computer and spewed out data just a millisecond after he relayed it to her. Her weapon, the PR37, was fully charged. It hung on her hip from a belt that also carried a back-up charge, a sanitation bag, a med kit and a pair of goggles. She stuck a small vial of sunscreen into the med kit. No need to take any chances, even though she expected to be back before daybreak.

"Third of June 1886; 10.17 p.m.," Topher said. "I've already ordered a costume set up."

"Not going to need it," Shay said. "It's the middle of nowhere and I'm going in at night. No one will see me. I'll be out in six, well before dawn." She picked up the pack that held enough explosives to implode a small city. "This is all I need right here."

"You're the boss." Topher punched the coordinates into the console.

Shay checked the charge on her weapon. "So they tell me." She stepped on to the transporter and shimmered out of existence.

The sun had just dipped behind the canyon ridge when Rand made camp. The sky was cloudless, with yellows and pinks streaking out from the sunset into the deep violet of the east yet he saw lightning in the north, at the head of the wash.

He made camp behind a large rock that formed a shelter close to the wall of the canyon. He gave Joe a small ration of feed, stripped him down and gave him a good rub before turning him loose to forage along the river bank. Then he shucked his pants and boots and waded into the river. He waded out until the water reached his thighs and shivered, despite the heat that still hung heavy in the air. The vision of whatever had happened to Tom and Hank still hung in his mind and twisted his gut. The bottle of whiskey he carried with him should help with that. He hoped.

"Here's to you, Tom." Rand pointed the bottle towards the sky and took a long draw. He watched as night closed in and stars popped out in a sky as dark as velvet. The full moon hung clear and close enough to touch right over the lip of the canyon. It was a beautiful night, the kind you could only see in West Texas. Looking at the beauty of the night made the horror he'd seen that much more disgusting, and that much more intense.

It was bright enough that he could keep on travelling if he wanted to but he was bone weary from his days on the trail, and knew Joe, who was old, would have to feel just as bad if not worse. Upstream, to the north, he saw the flashes of light that meant another thunderstorm would come in the night yet there wasn't a cloud in the sky. He could only hope that it wouldn't be enough to flood the canyon again and wash another mystery up at his feet.

"I hope I find the son of a bitch who did that to you, Tom." Rand took another draw from the bottle, stuck the cork back in and sunk below the surface. He felt the water gently wash over him and marvelled at the peacefulness of the river, compared to the raging torrent that must have carried his friend downstream. Finally, out of breath, he stood in one powerful motion, slinging water from his head in a big arc. At the same instant, he felt something slam into him, with a white flash of light. Rand staggered back and fell once more beneath the surface of the water.

Shay felt her body falling and spun her arms wildly to catch herself but there was nothing to grab on to. Whatever happened had to have occurred while she was in transit and it had knocked her off course. How far and how much was yet to be determined. She landed face first in the sand and quickly pushed herself up, coughing and gagging as the sand got in her mouth and nose. She instantly realized she was not alone and drew her weapon. A horse stumbled up from the sand and shook itself clean.

Shay quickly checked her arm display. She'd been caught in a time current, the very thing she'd come here to stop. She was off course by nearly a month, too late to stop the beginning of the rift they'd discovered.

It was also bad news for anyone caught in the aftershock of the rip. "Your life just got a lot shorter," she said to the horse that blinked at her as if it were trying to decide if she were real or not. "Sorry," she added. "Wrong place and wrong time for both of us." She checked her display again. She needed to get her bearings and report in. She had six hours before she could jump again, she might as well make good use of her time.

Shay took a moment to look around. Even thought it was dark, the full moon illuminated the area enough to discern landmarks. She was in the middle of a deep canyon that was littered with huge boulders. As long as it didn't rain she should be safe from flash floods. A shallow yet wide river assured her that she would not die of thirst as long as her sanitization kit held out.

"At least I didn't land in the water or on the edge of the cliff." Topher must have seen the rip coming and made sure she had a safe landing, if that was what you could call it. Her med stats would show that she survived but she still needed to check in. T.T.E.A. protocol required that she call him first, just in case there was someone around. In this period of time, the locals didn't take kindly to weird things like time travel. There were plenty of accounts of T.T.E.A. agents being accused of witchcraft, and even one case of an agent dying at the hands of hostiles during the six-hour gap between jumps.

"This is five-one calling base," she said. She touched a finger to her jaw where her link was planted so there was no possibility of losing it. There was also a remote in her arm panel and she tweaked it while she waited for Topher to confirm.

Nothing but static. Since they were in a time before any signals bounced through the atmosphere there had to be some sort of damage, possibly caused by her rough landing. She'd have to wait for Topher to solve it on his end. Her target was still in range so she decided to make for it.

"Better make sure the wolves are at bay." Shay programmed her display for scan. She was confident she could handle anything that came at her with one shot from her PR37 but it was nice to think she wouldn't have to use it. The thought of disrupting the life of anything or anyone in the past was disturbing to her. The horse was already a victim of the rift. She'd hate to think of anyone else falling prey to it.

A blip showed up on her screen. An animal caught drinking at the river? She checked the display and then looked in that direction. The light on her screen showed a significant body mass lying in the river. "Oh no." Shay realized the blip was human and had to be a man by the size of it. She wasn't dressed for interaction. And she certainly didn't want to have to explain who she was and what she was doing here. Still she couldn't go off and leave him to drown.

He'll die soon enough if you don't fix it . . .

This area was supposed to be deserted, populated with nothing but rattlesnakes and scorpions. Sure there was a possibility of a random hunting party but still . . .

She heard him. There was a splash and she turned and looked at the river. Moonlight danced off the surface, giving it a surreal look, as if she were staring at an abstract painting. She caught a movement in her peripheral vision and watched as a man pulled himself up with the help of the rock. It was too late for her to move, too late to hide so she stayed where she was and hoped to hell that he was dazed and confused enough not to ask too many questions. Any other problems that arose could be easily solved with a stun blast from her PR37.

In the exact moment that his eyes found her, Shay realized he was naked. He stood in the moonlight as if he were carved from stone, the only movement the water sluicing down his body, trickling into the grooves and dips that gave sharp definition to his muscular frame. She could not help but watch the water's trail in fascination, from his wide shoulders, over his smooth pectorals, into the ridges of his stomach, before trickling into the V that split his lean hips. After a long moment, in which she forgot to breathe, he moved, his long legs churning through the water.

"What in hell's sweet behind just happened?" His voice was more like a growl and it wakened her from the trance his appearance had placed upon her.

Shay levelled her PR37 straight at him. "Don't take another step."

He barely spared her weapon a glance as he kept on moving. He raised a dark eyebrow. "Are you planning on shooting me with that?"

"Yes I am," Shay said indignantly.

He stopped when he got to her and stood, with his arms crossed, imperious and impervious, dripping, and totally oblivious to the fact that he was naked. He towered over her, intentionally she was sure of it, and stared down at her with eyes that lost their colour in the moonlight. His dark hair was plastered against his forehead and curled over his ears. Once more she felt as if she were looking at a statue that was carved from stone.

"Well?" he asked.

Shay didn't get where she was by being intimidated. She stuck the point of her weapon in the middle of his chest, right in the indentation between his pectoral muscles.

"I could blow a hole clean through you. It would cauterize instantly and give you time to think about what the hell just happened while you lie here and die."

"It wouldn't be any stranger than anything else that's happened to me lately," he snapped and walked away.

Shay stared after him. She'd seen more than her share of weird during her time at the T.T.E.A., but this was the first time anyone had ever been so cavalier about her presence. Especially when she'd had a weapon stuck in his chest.

His very nice chest. She had to admit the view of him walking away was as nice as the one from the front, if not nicer. The man was definitely fit. There wasn't an ounce of fat on him. He was all cowboy . . . long, lean and hard in all the right places.

Get over it . . . Now was not the time to think about how long it had been since she'd been with a man. She had a job to do. "What do you mean by strange?" Shay suddenly realized what he'd said. Did he know something?

He was talking to the horse now, stroking its nose, using soft soothing sounds to calm it. The horse leaned into him. She found his state of undress very annoying for some reason. The guy acted like he was in his bathroom instead of the middle of nowhere. Come to think of it, the middle of nowhere probably *was* his bathroom and would be hers too before too much time passed.

"Oh hell," she said.

"At least that makes some sense." He gave the horse a last comforting pat and walked behind a rock beneath an overhang of the cliff. "Where did you come from?" He pulled on a pair of well-worn jeans.

"I'd rather not say," Shay said. "What did you see?"

"I'd rather not say," he quipped. He walked back to the river and picked up a bottle that lay along the bank. "At least one good thing has happened today," He held up the bottle as if it were a great prize, then removed the cork and took a long drink. He held the bottle out to her as he walked past. "You look like you could use some too."

"Er . . . no thanks." Shay followed him back to the rock and watched in astonishment as he lay down on his back and placed a hat over his face. "What are you doing?"

"Getting some rest. I don't know about you but I've had one hell of a day."

Rand didn't want to admit it to the woman, but he felt as if he'd been ripped in half. At the moment he couldn't care less if she shot him. He spared a glance at her, from beneath his hat. She leaned against the rock with her arms crossed. She wasn't pretty in the usual way; instead she had strong clear features and a quiet confidence that bespoke intelligence and contentment. Her hair was strangely short for a woman. It barely touched her shoulders and framed her face in a riot of curls that gleamed white in the moonlight. Her left arm was covered with some sort of contraption that had tiny coloured lights on it. He couldn't even begin to figure out what that was all about. She was dressed strange too, all in black with thick boots over pants that looked like a second skin, a shirt that looked like his longjohns and a short coat of the softest leather he'd ever seen. If she wanted to draw attention to herself she'd succeeded. The way her pants hugged the lines of her legs made him want to wrap them around his waist in the worst way, even if he did feel like the ass end of an armadillo.

She had to know something about what had happened to Tom. It was the only logical explanation of what she was doing out here. How she'd got here without him seeing her was another story entirely. One he needed to think on for a bit. This was why he'd decided to lie down. He needed to catch his breath after whatever it was had slammed him into the river.

"I'm guessing that you're feeling pretty sick right now. Kind of nauseous and weak?" She dragged the toe of her squared-off boot through the sand.

He was. How would she know that? "Where did you say you were from?"

"I didn't." She looked at the thing on her arm again. Pushed a couple of the lights. Took what looked like a flask from her belt and drank from it. "The question is *when* did I come from."

Just when he was beginning to think the night might make a turn for the better she had to go and get all crazy on him. Luckily his gun was handy. Rand sat up and eased his way around to where he could grab it if need be. Lightning flashed in the distance and he waited for the sound of thunder but none came. The woman looked at it also, then back at her arm.

"OK. I'll bite. *When* are you from?"

"I'm from 2143. That's two hundred and fifty-some years from now if you're counting. That blast that knocked you on your ass was caused by me getting bumped from my destination by whoever is messing around up there." She pointed towards the lightning flashes.

"I'm going to need another drink." He looked for the bottle. She grabbed it off the boulder she leaned against and tossed it to him. "So you didn't plan on landing here?" As if anyone would come to this canyon deliberately. Rand had learned a long time ago that it was best to humour people when they were loco, until you could get the drop on them. The weapon she'd waved around earlier was pretty wicked-looking. He didn't know what it was but he was pretty sure it didn't shoot bullets. That whole thing about cauterization did not sound appealing at all.

"No. My plan was to land about a month before this date. In time to stop it."

"Stop what?"

"The rips in time."

Rand laughed. After everything else that had happened this day it was pretty much all that was left to do. He sat back against the canyon wall and let out a big whoop then took another draw off the bottle after wiping his eyes. "I haven't had a good one like that in a while," he admitted.

"It will more than likely be your last." She crouched down before him. "Still feeling weak?" She took the bottle.

"Yeah. Too much sun." Rand looked her up and down. "And way too much excitement."

She handed him her flask. "Drink this. You're probably dehydrated, and this—" she pitched his bottle away "—isn't helping things."

Rand sniffed the flask, decided that it had to be OK since she'd just drunk from it and it smelled pretty good, kind of fruity like apples and oranges. He took a drink and was amazed at how cool it was going down his throat. His stomach felt immediately settled although he was still weak and wanted nothing more than to stretch out and sleep for days. If only there was a nice soft bed available.

He definitely didn't mind the company at all. Several days in the sack with this woman would be a treat.

"Feel better?"

"A bit." He wondered if there was something alcoholic in the flask. Something that would make him as crazy as she was. Still there had to be an explanation for what he saw, for what happened to Tom, and for every other weird thing that he'd seen and heard lately. Since no one else was forthcoming with explanations he might as well listen to what she had to say. "What's your name?"

"Shay McCoy. Captain Shay McCoy. T.T.E.A. That's the Time Travel Enforcement Agency if you're wondering."

"Yeah ... right. Rand Brock. Captain Rand Brock. Texas Rangers."

"A Texas Ranger? I heard about you."

"About me?"

"No. About the Rangers. You guys were legendary. Still are as a matter of fact. It should please you to know that the Texas Rangers are still alive and kicking in the future."

"Yeah, I was worried about that." Rand took another drink from her flask. "So why are you here again? Something about a 'time rip'?"

She drew a long straight line in the sand. "Time is linear. One long line, year after year, day after day, hour after hour and so on. It all keeps coming, one after the next. But . . ."

"I get a feeling I'm not going to like this *but* . . ."

She nodded. "Someone is here, in this place, messing with time." She drew a hash across the line. "Every time they try to move

through time they rip it. Or maybe 'fracture' is a better word."
She drew a couple more hash marks and then drew lines off them.
"The fractures become their own time lines. Kind of an alternate
reality which messes up our realities in the future."

"You have got to be kidding. How is that even possible?"

"There are lots of things that are possible in the future. Mostly
because of things that are happening now, in your time. You call
it the Industrial Revolution. In the next hundred years there are
unbelievable changes that will happen, including air flight and men
walking on the moon."

Rand straightened at the mention of air flight. The driver said
the attack came from the air. Maybe what she was saying did make
some kind of sense. "And time travel?"

"And time travel. The problem is regulating it. There are those
who think anyone should be able to go anywhere and do whatever
they want."

"Which leads to history being changed which changes the
future."

"Yes. There's a group who think they can change things for the
better. One of them, a guy named Wiley, managed to jump into
time and he's trying to corner the market on time travel by being
the first to invent it. Then he can control it."

"And offer it to the highest bidder."

"Greed is something that's pretty much the same no matter what
time you are in."

"What good is it going to do him in the future if he's back
here?"

"He's hoping to keep it in the family. He can trace his lineage
back pretty far and apparently whoever his ancestor is in this time
was rich, smart and greedy."

Rand rubbed his fingers over his eyes. "You're giving me a
headache."

"It's not me." Shay pointed to the hash marks in the sand.
"You've been split."

"What?"

"There are two of you now. The blast that announced my
arrival? It ripped your time line. So now there are two of you in two
separate – yet parallel – time lines. It's why you feel weak. You're
half of what you were."

Rand staggered to his feet. The sudden movement made him dizzy and he wobbled enough so that he grabbed on to the boulder for support.

"I know it's hard to believe but it's true. You feel horrible because your life just got cut in half. If it happens again, you'll be split again. Another fracture, another parallel time line."

"How do we fix it?"

"Go to the source. So why don't you tell me what it is that you know?"

"About time travel? Nothing. All I've got is a partner and a prisoner who look as if they were melted together like candle wax, a dead driver who said the attack came from the air, and lightning in the sky without thunder." He went to his pack. "And this." He handed Shay the strange piece of metal. "I found this in my partner's body."

"They were using them to experiment on," Shay said.

Rand's stomach turned at the thought. "Bastards." He had no idea what had been done to Tom, but the results of it were enough to make him think that it had to have been horrible for anyone involved. Even to a cold-hearted killer like Hank Miller.

The touch of her hand on his arm was meant to be gentle and soothing but still his body reacted in ways that were far from gentle. Rand looked into her eyes and saw gold flecks over green and a clear calm gaze that gave him no doubt that she was entirely truthful with him.

"Help me stop them," she said.

He was so very tired. Rand let out a sigh and picked up his rig. "Beats getting drunk."

Still no word from Topher. Her display read three hours until she could jump. If she were *able* to jump. She stood on a rock by the river, hoping the added height would give her a better signal. She really needed to get up higher. She needed to see the lie of the land. Rand was convinced that the river held the clue since the bodies had come from somewhere upstream.

The river wasn't much more than a trickle now. It was hard to believe that it had enough power to carry these huge boulders downstream but apparently it had. The lightning was closer now. Daggers of it shot across the sky, right over her head. If she'd had a metal rod, she probably could have pulled it to her. It had to be the source of the time machine. What else could it be?

Shay looked at Rand, who stood at the head of his horse, stroking its neck as he murmured in its ear. The poor beast was done in. Its head hung limply and its body trembled with weakness. It could go no further. They'd run out of room. There was no place to go but up and it looked as if it would be a difficult climb. The walls of the canyon were narrow and the terrain rocky.

"Sorry old man," Rand said. "I promised you sweet grass and fat mares but it looks like I can't come through for you." His voice broke as he touched his forehead to the animal's. "I'm sorry I let you down." He unsaddled the horse and slipped its bridle off.

Shay felt a strange welling in her throat. Where did that come from? She was getting all emotional over a cowboy and his horse. Life was like that. People died. Pets died. It happened all the time.

But how many times did it happen because of some idiot playing around with a time machine? Being in the wrong place at the wrong time totally sucked. The man was just doing his job and his life was ruined.

He pulled his gun from his holster. Was he actually planning on shooting the horse? Shay jumped down from the rock and ran to him just as he put the barrel of his gun against the horse's head. "What are you doing?"

The face he turned on her was tortured, haggard and weary. The effects of the time rip on his body were already showing.

"I can't just leave him here to die. He'd starve. Slowly. And the buzzards would be at him. He deserves better than that. We all do."

"He's your friend?" she asked.

Rand turned away. "Yes."

She rubbed her hand down the face of the horse. Its eyes looked flat and hollow in the moonlight, full of pain. The essence of the horse was gone, leaving nothing behind but a shell that obeyed because that was what it was trained to do. "I'll do it," she said. He started to protest but she stopped him with a look. "My way will be kinder, I promise." She took her med kit from her belt and loaded all twelve tranks into the hypo-gun. She spoke soothing words as she found the pulse in the animal's neck. She quickly shot in the dose and the horse blinked, one time, slowly dropped to its knees and lay down with a heavy sigh.

The ranger looked at her.

"It's like he's going to sleep," she said. "Talk to him. Tell him it's OK to go."

Rand knelt down next to the horse and spoke into its ear as he rubbed down the long arch of its neck. The animal let out its breath and was still. Shay watched as Rand wiped his arm across his eyes and then slowly he stood.

"How long do I have?" he asked. "Before the same thing happens to me."

Shay shrugged. It would be nice if she had an easy answer. "It depends upon your life expectancy. Your horse was already old before the split. Without knowing when and how you die, I can't say." She looked at him. He was all hollows and angles in the moonlight and she still could not tell what colour his eyes were. "You could die in the next five minutes or it could be years. I just don't know."

His laughter sounded bitter and hollow. "Sounds like another typical day." He slung his saddlebags and rifle over his shoulder. "If we're going to get this bastard before I die then we'd best get a move on."

"Well, that explains a lot," Rand said an hour later. They were lying on a ridge overlooking a lake. Dawn was still a few hours away and clouds were moving in, yet the moon cast enough of a reflection across the water to give them a good view of the surrounding area.

A dam lay across the mouth of the river. In the middle of it was a large sluice gate, which was operated with gears and pulleys. Beside it was a building with an open roof. Steam rose from one side of the building and occasionally a flash of light would flare out.

"I don't know exactly what it is it explains but it's got to mean something," he added. He rolled over on his back and threw his arm over his eyes. He felt like he'd been run over after a hard night of drinking. Yet he still felt the clench in his gut every time he looked at Shay.

If he was going to go out, he might as well do it in the arms of a beautiful woman. The hard part would be convincing her to oblige him. Surely any woman that walked around in pants that hugged every muscle of her long legs and the curve of her luscious behind wouldn't mind helping a guy who was about to die.

"I wonder how they got this stuff out here?" It wasn't exactly what he was thinking but still he wondered. The building was pretty big and there'd been no sign of a wagon train, coach, or even a spur off the railroad.

"Probably by airship," she said. "I think it's docked over to the left." She moved her head, still scanning the area. "He's using solar power." She was looking through a pair of binoculars that had the same strange lights on them as the thing on her arm. "The sun heats the water and creates steam. The steam turns the turbines, which turns the platform. I'm betting it's got mirrors all around it. It seems like I remember seeing a drawing of something similar in the archives."

"You can tell all that from looking through those binoculars."

"They're infra-red." She spared him a look. "They can read heat." She handed them to him and he rolled over on his stomach next to her.

He peered through them and sure enough saw bright red spots. "So if the big spots are heat from the steam, then does that make the little spots people?"

"Yes, it does."

"So what are those?" Rand pointed towards the ravine. The glasses showed some smaller red spots that were moving towards their position. He dropped the glasses and peered into the darkness. "Rats?" It was the only logical answer. Still, he had yet to meet a rat that wore spurs.

The noise was getting louder. They could see nothing, but they heard small rocks tumbling down the ravine. The moon was behind the clouds so it was difficult to see. Though without a doubt Rand knew something was there. He'd learned several years ago never to ignore the feeling of being stalked and he drew his gun. Shay dropped her pack and did the same.

"What is it?"

"Since I have to guess, I'm going with some sort of steam-powered guard dogs," Shay said. "Let me take them out."

Rand cocked his pistol. "You're kidding, right?"

She stood and took aim at the ridge. "Nope. You'll make too much noise. They'll know we're up here." Shay fired her gun and a blast of blue light came out of it. It made a buzzing sound, like a swarm of angry bees. He had to admit it was much quieter than his

.45 yet he hated not being able to fight back. Especially since there were more things swarming towards them.

It looked as if the ground was alive and moving. The moon suddenly split a cloud and Rand saw what was stalking them. There had to be a hundred or more, metal scorpions, as big as cats, with hinged legs that moved across the rocks and pincers raised and clacking together. They were looking for targets.

"Don't let them touch you." Shay was blasting as quickly as they came at her.

"Yeah . . . right." Rand slid his pistol into the holster and picked up his rifle. He swung it like a club at the things and they flew apart with the impact. They kept on coming and he was soon breathing hard and his arms ached. Shay kept on firing until her weapon died on her, then all she could do was kick them in Rand's direction and let him finish them off. She danced away from the last one as its claws nipped at her ankles. She bumped into Rand who had just launched one into the canyon and they stumbled backwards. He slammed his rifle into a boulder and the stock cracked. He lost his balance and they both went down. Rand caught her in his arms and twisted so he took the full impact of the fall.

She was sturdy. The impact of their bodies hitting the ground made him grunt and they lay still for a moment as they caught their breath. Shay's body lay on top of his, chest to chest, thigh to thigh, and hip to hip. She was a perfect fit and his body recognized it. He could not help but tighten his hold on her. Her head lay up under his chin and the scent of her tousled curls filled his nostrils. The aroma was unlike anything he'd ever experienced and a vision of blue skies and a grassy meadow bursting with flowers of every colour filled his mind. Was it heaven? If it was it was as close as he ever hoped to get and there was only one thing missing.

"Are you OK?" he asked.

Shay raised her head. Her eyes held the moon in them. She parted her lips to speak but before she could say anything he kissed her. Rand moved his hand into her hair as his lips touched hers, and he was surprised, yet grateful, when her lips moved against his and her hands framed his face. She gasped, enough so that her lips parted, and he took advantage of the opportunity to trace her bottom lip with his tongue. She responded and it felt like a kick in the gut. The feel of her body against his, her hips pressing against him stoked the fire. He rolled her over quickly, and she moved against him. His hand found her breast and she sighed as their tongues caressed.

"Five-one come in. Five-one are you there? Shay!"

Rand raised his head and looked at her in confusion. Her eyes glinted silver in the moonlight before she closed them, her face clenched in frustration, a mirror of his, he was certain.

"What is that?"

She pushed him aside and he rolled, painfully, away.

"It's base," she said. She touched her arm. "This is five-one. Check three."

"Thank God," the voice said. "We thought we'd lost you."

"I hit a bump." She stood up and ran her hand through her hair.

"Yeah. Any side-effects?"

Rand sat up and took a long drink from his canteen as Shay looked down at him. She handed him her flask. "Drink this." She mouthed the words then continued with her conversation. "One. No make that two. One down. One with me."

"You've got a local with you?"

"Affirmative. Status one-oh-one A. Rand Brock. Texas Ranger. Can you verify for me?"

"Affirmative. Rand Brock. Got a date of birth?"

"December 22, 1849." Rand looked at her in confusion as she repeated his birth date back to whoever she was talking too. Why did she need his date of birth?

Instead of answering she held her hand up and walked away. Her voice dropped enough that Rand knew she did not want him to hear any more. Not that it mattered. It wasn't as if anything that happened from here on out would change a thing.

"Topher," Shay said after she stepped away from Rand. She shifted the communication to her headpiece. "I've got the machine in my sights. Can you run some parallels for me? How bad is the rift?"

"As of now there are three. I think we're still safe as far as the time line. There's no effects either way. Not even with your Texas Ranger. Did you get a name on the one who expired?"

"It was a horse."

Topher laughed. Shay looked over her shoulder at Rand who still sat on the ground, sucking back the energy drink from her flask. Hopefully it would keep him going for a while longer. Being split was a bitch. She was surprised he'd been able to keep up. She'd only been with him a few hours but she knew without a doubt that Rand Brock was one hell of a man.

"Hey, to him the horse was important." She'd never forget the look on his face when they put Joe down. Nor would she forget how she felt when he kissed her. The man needed to live.

"Sorry." Topher seemed contrite. "What is your plan?"

"Take this thing out, then come back and keep it from happening."

"Roger to that. Still can't pull you for another eighty-seven minutes."

"That's fine. Got anything on the name yet?"

"Yeah. Rand Brock. Texas Ranger. Went after missing prison transport June 23, 1886. Presumed dead. He was born 1849. Parents divorced 1873. No impact from the rift. I'm guessing that both of his lives expired shortly after the event. It says the body was never found."

"Thanks, Topher." Shay looked at Rand once more. He was staring at his broken rifle. He flung it away in disgust. "Five-one out."

"What do we do now?" Lightning streaked from the building. Shay's hair stood on end and the eerie light turned Rand's dark hair to a strange shade of cobalt blue that matched his eyes.

Shay picked up her pack. "We take it out."

It had been remarkably easy. Just circle the perimeter and place the charges. The only hard part was ducking every time a trail of lightning lit the sky, especially since it seemed to be right over their heads. If there were guards they never saw them and no one stopped them. They were both out of breath when they returned to their overlook and Shay turned on the remote. The explosion shook the canyon. Rand rolled on top of her to shelter her body as debris from the building rained down on top of them. Flames lit the sky and the angles of his face as she turned beneath him. There was another explosion – the airship, most likely – and then silence, except for the crackle of the fire.

His hand smoothed her hair back from her face. "What happens now?"

"I jump back to my time."

"How long do we have until then?"

"About ten minutes, give or take."

"That's not enough."

Shay looked into his eyes. There was pain there, reflected by the flames, but worse, there was loneliness. Loneliness was something she knew. She touched his forehead and pushed back the dark hair that fell across it. There was a streak of dirt on his cheek and she rubbed it off with her thumb. He grinned at her, like they were sharing a private joke.

Except there was no joke. She was leaving in a few short moments. He would be alone, in the middle of nowhere, with no way to get back to civilization and a fat chance of living long enough to make it anywhere in his weakened condition. He would die here. Alone.

"Care to grant a dying man's last wish?" His lips nibbled at hers and her heart swelled inside her chest.

"Oh, what the hell," Shay said. She wrapped her arms around him and kissed him. "Whatever you do, don't let go. I'm pretty sure ten minutes isn't going to be enough."

They were still kissing when they made the jump.

The Walled Garden

Michele Lang

Spring 1988
Columbia College
New York City

He had left me for dead.

I think this is what bothered people the most. That, and the fact he had attacked me in broad daylight, as I had wandered through Riverside Park in September, daydreaming.

The doctors had established that he had only *tried* to choke me to death and had only ripped my clothes, not taken them off completely. So when I returned to school – my freshman year – with a bruised trachea and a battered soul, the other girls couldn't kid themselves that I was somehow at fault. I was just in the wrong place at the wrong time.

What a downer, I know. But in the end, I was just another statistic in a gritty, crime-ridden city. Plenty of my ex-friends tried to rationalize me away, leave me for dead, too. I don't blame them, at least not any more.

But at the time, I survived by staying angry, not by leaving the past to the past. I was used to being the weird kid: Mireya, the Puerto Rican girl from Brooklyn on a prep school scholarship in New England, now on scholarship at a fancy Ivy League school in New York. My mom was a seamstress, never finished high school. I already knew how to make my own way.

I kept to myself, and kept silent, long after the physical harm to my throat had healed for the most part. I slept in my clothes, and I kept the light on for a solid year. My best friend Colleen made me eat, and until I could go back to swallowing pizza and home-made chilli, she cooked me split pea soup. Two years passed, years in which I excelled in my studies but lost myself.

I was OK in the daytime, in the dullness of my routine. But at night, all alone . . .

If it weren't for a man named Jonathan Mellon, my would-be murderer would have won. But Mellon refused to leave me for dead. When it really counted, he stood his ground. And he did it to set me free.

I first encountered Jonathan Mellon at the scene of a different crime, two years after I almost paid for daydreaming in the park with my life. The Columbia campus centres on a quad of buildings, libraries, lecture halls and dorms. But most of the students live in housing off-campus, sprinkled around the iffy neighbourhood of Morningside Heights.

I lived in River Hall, around the corner from the place in Riverside Park where I had almost met my end. The morning I found Mellon at the entrance to River Hall, his antique Mercedes was parked in front – what was left of it, anyway. Some evil bastard had taken a baseball bat to the doors, smashed in the lights and all of the windows, and slashed all four tyres.

I had just returned from my first class of the day, and the street was relatively deserted. Curiosity got the better of me, and I walked around the car to survey the damage. A polite note in the rear window proclaimed: "No Radio, Don't Bother". Spray-painted along the destroyed side of the champagne-coloured car in response: "JUST CHECKING".

I caught the anguish of the young guy, who was about my age, and I winced for him and his murdered car. "That's pretty cold," I muttered, not expecting him to reply or even notice me – by now I had perfected the art of invisibility.

"It certainly is," the man replied, his focus staying steady on the car, the expression on his face pained. He had a faint accent that I couldn't place. "This is my bitchy little sister's car, too. Oh, bother."

His genteel misery troubled me somehow. Guys like him – tall, preppy, golden blond – were not supposed to have problems. They were supposed to live off-campus in their own daddy-purchased apartments, go to the Village to party with The Cars and the Talking Heads, and show up for class just often enough to pass.

"Maybe you should call the cops," I said, my voice husky with disuse. This was the longest conversation I'd voluntarily had with a man in months. "You should report it. I know it's a pain, but at least they'll put your complaint on file."

He turned to face me for the first time. His eyes burned with cold, blue fire, and I could see he was angry as well as in mourning. But his lips remained fixed in a small, careful smile. "This is the third car I've had smashed up like this in this neighbourhood. The police just shrugged and did the paperwork last time. A man's got to choose his battles."

We looked at each other for a long moment, and I suddenly had the strangest feeling that I had met this man before.

The stranger broke the silence with a smile and a nod. "I know you," he said. "You're in my miserable art history survey course, aren't you?"

I felt the jolt all the way down to my shoes. Did he know me for the notorious reasons most people did? I'd heard the whispers trailing after me in the cafeteria, on the quad. Maybe this preppy blueblood moved so far outside my customary circles that he just didn't know about me. The thought gave me hope.

I swallowed hard, turned my attention back to the remains of his car. The intrepid radio hunters had smashed up every car on the block the same way. "Art history," I finally, lamely said. "It's miserable? I like the teacher."

"Oh, her," he said, and laughed uncomfortably. "She's ready to toss me out altogether."

"Really?" Amanda Zee was one of my favourite teachers, just out of graduate school, and passionate about teaching as well as publishing her scholarship. "She doesn't seem like such a hard-ass."

"She's not. I deserve to fail."

I swung back to face him, and for a moment all of the upper west side of New York held its breath. My heart decided not to stop but instead to gallop, and the ragged edges of a familiar panic began to prickle on my arms like phantom brambles, poking into my skin, pulling me down.

There was something uncanny about him, about the deserted

street and the smashed-up cars. He was a rip in my grey, mundane reality, a flash of gold on the cement sidewalk.

I forced myself to smile, though the effort probably looked pretty ghastly. "Sorry about your car," I whispered, and I slipped away into River Hall, my student ID at the ready. The security guard, an ageless mummified Egyptian named Ali, sat silent behind his desk as I streaked by.

But I swear this time I saw Ali smile as I fled from the golden stranger still standing in the street.

He reappeared the next day, like the sun over the horizon. I saw him from far away from my perch at the top of the Low Library steps. A slip of paper he held between his long, aristocratic fingers fluttered in the breeze.

He climbed the steps, his long legs conquering them with no apparent effort. "This is you, isn't it?" he said without preamble, as if he was used to addressing the commoners of the world and commanding them at his will.

I shrugged and went back to studying the textbook open on my lap, hiding the jolt of fear as best I could. A listless breeze crawled up the Low Library stairs and swirled around my ankles – it was a hot spring that year. "Yeah, I was me, last time I checked."

"No. I mean this." And he waved the paper at me.

I flinched. Had he found the newspaper articles about me, what had happened to me? I raised my head, ready to blow him off with a quick, efficient snarl – and saw just in time that's not what the guy had in mind, not at all. He didn't have a newspaper clipping, but my own hand-lettered sign. One that I hadn't even thought of for a year or more.

"You type papers," he said, his voice rising with excitement. "I need help. I'm failing out of school because my typing skills don't exist. Can you type fast?"

My heart started racing again, at the man's close proximity, but also at the prospect of cash. The paper-typing idea was born of desperation in my sophomore year, and before now it had never borne fruit. If anything, I needed money even more than the year before.

"What's your name?" I said. I didn't mean to act rude, but my voice came out husky and rough, like I'd been crying.

"Jonathan Mellon, of the Philadelphia Mellons." He extended a well-tended, manicured hand, and after a moment I took it and shook it. He was all business, and I took refuge in that.

I leaned back on the steps and smiled. "You already know me from class and by my sign. Mireya Rodriguez, of the Brooklyn Rodriguezes." For the first time in I didn't know how long, I started to laugh at this awkward, lovely white boy, slender and earnest as a greyhound. "Our numbers are legion, Mr Mellon."

"Well, ours aren't." His smile widened and, after a moment's hesitation, he sat down next to me, a careful distance away. "I hope you can type fast."

And so began our nefarious partnership.

I didn't mean to re-engineer his papers, not at first. I got out my trusty IBM Selectric, Mami's high school graduation present to me, checked the ribbon to make sure it was nice and fresh. The spring morning thrummed with life, and I propped up my only window with a wooden coat hanger to let in the semi-fresh air from the enclosed courtyard. A single huge gingko tree grew there, and a family of cardinals had made it their improbable refuge. That courtyard was loud – an opera singer lived in the building across from me, and an oboe player liked to practise until midnight during the week. But I loved that courtyard. For two years now, it had kept me connected to the living world.

On that morning in April, I took a first look at the art history paper due the next day. Mellon's handwriting was terrible. Awful. But his writing was even worse. Plenty of ideas, sure, but they choked each other like too many baby birds crushed together in a too-small nest.

"You got five separate papers here, *mi corazon*," I whispered under my breath as I reread his work. "Hm . . . leave this for next time. Switch these paragraphs, fix the spelling over here . . ."

I started typing, slowly at first, but then my fingers took flight with his words. The paper was his, I swear it. All I did was a little judicious tidying.

Mellon was running a D average in art history, but he got a B– on that paper, with an encouraging note from Miss Zee scribbled on the bottom. And he insisted on paying me what he called the "expedited" rate – three dollars a page, instead of my usual one.

And he insisted on paying me for the title page. Plus a "good luck" bonus, whatever that was.

Once, I would have been too proud to take the extra money. I would have thrown back my shoulders, told him I didn't accept bribes, and walked away. But that Mireya was gone forever. And also, I liked eating and the payment from this one paper fed me for almost a week.

But more than that, I enjoyed travelling the labyrinths of his mind, wandering the tangled byways of his thrown-together thoughts until I found the worthy truth hidden at the centre. All I did was cut away some of the strangling undergrowth when he set those thoughts to a particular subject on paper. That was all.

At least that was what I told myself.

The nightmares started up again a week after that. I had thought the creep who'd dragged me into the bushes in Riverside Park two years before was some kind of bogeyman, some phantom of night, nobody who intersected with my daily life.

But I was wrong. About a week after Mellon hired me to type everything he did for school, I found a wadded-up note shoved under my door. The note was from my attacker, and he knew all about me. It contained too many details, things I had left to die in the mud at the bottom of the embankment.

It was folded neatly, the handwriting so prim and proper, pathologically perfect like a machine had formed the letters on the page.

I can guess what you must be thinking. The coincidence is too great – Mellon must have been the attacker. But, no. Even aside from the perfect handwriting, I knew it wasn't Mellon. Mellon smelled clean and sharp, citrus and mint. The bastard who had tried to kill me smelled of blood and meat.

And now my attacker knew where I lived.

The next week I pretty much kept to myself, as I had when I had first returned from the hospital over two years before. My current RA knew all about the new note, but he was worse than useless – he'd looked a little too prurient when he first found out who I was, and now his face lit up with a creepy delight when I showed him the paper and demanded he call the similarly useless campus police.

So I told the creepy RA to warn Ali, and I stayed to myself. The only person who checked in on me was Colleen, my steadfast friend from the old neighbourhood, and she tried to tease me out of my cave. "You're turning into Pariah Carey," she said, laughing maniacally at her horrible pun.

"Well, you're lamer than Duran Duran," I replied, trying my best to sound like my old, pun-impaired self. I knew I wasn't fooling Colleen or anybody else.

"You need to get outside," Colleen said, trying hard to keep up the facade of chummy amusement, like she could chuckle me out of my bunker. But she picked at her cuticles, the way she always did when she worried about me. "You are going to starve to death in here."

Just then the phone rang, shrieked from under the bed, and I leaped to my feet, a sob strangled in my throat. I rearranged the paisley scarf I kept wrapped around my neck, and Colleen's mask slipped to reveal the horrible reality: my oldest friend pitied me. Me. Pity.

I shot her a hurt look as I reached under the bed for the phone. Part of me hid under there, knowing it was going to be my attacker's voice on the phone.

I cleared my throat and answered the phone. "Hello?" I said, my voice rough and hoarse. I held my breath and waited.

It wasn't. It was Mellon. "I need your help, Mireya," he said, his bland, confident voice a little tremulous. "I got hit with a surprise twenty-four-hour paper. Ten pages. I'm dead."

"Don't say that, don't joke like that." I ran a shaky hand through my hair, and Colleen's pity shimmered into curiosity. Good, let her wonder.

"No, I'm not joking." Mellon's voice sounded tinny on my ancient, beat-up Bakelite rotary. "If I fail this class, my father is going to disown me."

My smile was genuine, and it reached past Colleen's worry to the realization that I could help somebody else. I had the goods, and that knowledge felt really wonderful. "You won't fail. I won't let you, Mellon. Come on over."

Colleen slipped away before Mellon arrived, and she was smart enough not to say anything about him. But she leaned against my rickety door, looked me up and down as she got ready to go.

"Watch yourself," was all she said, but her eyes were full of a fear too big to express in words.

I saved Mellon's academic life that night, and half a dozen more times after that. His grades climbed steadily, but not fast enough to cause suspicion. I only edited, never rewrote, so the over-choked ideas still knocked down his grades to an extent. But for the first time in his academic career, Mellon was gunning for the Dean's List.

After he got his first A, we celebrated by going to the West End, a local watering hole with great music and cheap beer – not that I needed to worry because, of course, Mellon insisted on paying. I had written many a paper of my own at the long, unvarnished bar, with a single bottle of Dos Equis to rent the barstool and the background roar to remind me I still existed.

We decided to cap off our beers with dinner. I wolfed down a roast beef sandwich, giving up any ladylike pretences after the first salty, delicious bite. Finally I wasn't hungry. Finally.

I started on the fries and watched Mellon eat his BLT much more slowly. He took a tiny sip of beer, set his glass a little too carefully on the crinkly paper napkin.

"Hey, Mellon, you OK?" I asked, my voice tentative. I didn't like poking at him through his thick layer of reserve. I liked the space between us.

He hesitated, and then his brilliant smile wiped out the shadows lurking in his eyes. "I'm fine, better than. Because you, Mireya, have got the magic touch." He raised his glass to me. "Thank you for that."

I hadn't thought of myself as anywhere in the same universe as good luck for an exceedingly long, dreary time. I nodded at his noble, if wrong, sentiment, and took a sip of beer myself. "I'm not good luck. You wrote those papers yourself. All I do is type them."

His smile broadened, and he leaned back, enjoying our silent complicity. Elvis Costello wailed a sweet, sad song over the crappy sound system, and I finished off the last of the sandwich. Farewell, sandwich. Mellon must have caught my longing for one more bite. He waved for the waitress. "Hello, please favour us with a platter of nachos."

His odd turns of phrase made me snort with laughter. I loved the way laughing felt.

He cocked an eyebrow at me. "And I amuse you how?"

I sensed his hurt feelings under his politesse, and I hastened to reassure him. "No, Mellon, don't worry. I just thought of you ordering bar food in Brooklyn like that. The waitresses I know out there would just stare at you like you were a freaking alien."

We smiled at each other, again complicit in something neither one of us wanted to identify or name. We both knew we would destroy it by speaking of it.

"It is a beautiful night," Mellon said. "Let's go for a walk on campus. I assure you, it's so well lit it looks like day." He leaned back, and I swear he held his breath, as if he knew how risky a walk in the darkness was to me.

At that moment, I knew he knew about what had happened to me in the park. And for once it didn't change anything between us. We both knew what had happened, but for the first time I didn't care.

How I longed to walk again in the moonlight.

The Quad indeed was lit up like a Christmas tree; golden lights strung through the trees glistened like tinsel. A slow, cool breeze wandered along the brick walkways and between the venerable buildings.

We stood together at the wrought-iron gate at Broadway and 116th Street, the entrance to the Columbia Quad. All was Ivy League perfection. But a strange rustle brought us up short. I scanned the flat, manicured walkway until I found the source of the noise. "Jesus," I muttered, but I stood my ground.

A horde of rats scuttled from under the boxwoods across the way, crossing towards the student centre next to Carman Hall.

"How many?" I croaked. My eyelids felt rusty; I blinked hard to focus my vision and to make sure I was really seeing what my brain insisted was there.

"Oh, about twenty-five or so," Mellon said, his voice chipper but a little faint.

He moved closer to me, and I swallowed hard, appreciating his presence. "I've never seen so many all at once," I whispered. "And they're huge."

"Yep. But they seem pretty mellow for rats."

"You kidding me? You ever see that movie *Willard*?"

"What?"

My mind flashed back on a dozen viewings of the horror flick from the 1970s, played on our grainy black-and-white TV at home on countless Sunday afternoons.

My mouth had gone cotton dry by that point. "Never mind."

I reached out and grabbed his hand. His fingers felt smooth and strong and he never flinched, just squeezed my hand in response. The rat horde stopped, and their little rat eyes focused on us, casually assessing whether they could take us.

They scuttled along the pathway, and we were all in complete agreement – they could totally take us, chew us up and leave our skeletons behind on 116th street.

I held my breath, tensed to run. And the leader, an enormous grey rat with protruding teeth, sneezed and licked his nose. A spell was broken and the swarm turned to the sewer grating near the student centre and they poured themselves between the iron bars like furry rat-water.

"Don't think I'll be dining at the student centre any time soon," I said.

Mellon laughed so hard I thought he was going to pass out. "You're good luck, all right," he finally said. "But you're also crazy, Mireya."

"And you just figured this out? Tsk, tsk, Mr Mellon of the Philadelphia Mellons," I murmured. "Only a crazy person . . ."

My voice trailed off, and I didn't finish my thought – only a crazy person would still be at this school after what happened to me. I was crazy enough to insist on staying. But I had lost myself somewhere, and I wasn't about to give up the fight of getting me back. That meant sticking it out here, now, in this place.

Mellon got quiet. "If you're crazy, then I don't want to be sane."

I kept clutching his hand, and he kept holding mine. And my focus slowly shifted from the swarm of rats to the fact that I was holding the hand of a gorgeous blond boy in springtime, under the light of a New York City moon.

We stood there for a while, Mellon's hair all silvery in the shadowy night. "We better get out of here before we end up as rat chow." My voice sounded raspy but coherent.

"Of course. Right as always." Mellon led the way forwards.

The stars danced over our heads in a swirling foxtrot. "Where are we going, Mellon?" It occurred to me I was drunk or high, but no, my mind was as clear and sharp as the night.

When I looked at him, his eyes sparked silver, like his hair. "I want to show you something. Don't be frightened."

Of course a bolt of pure adrenalin shot through me after that, but I swallowed hard and held on to Mellon's hand. "But should I be? Scared, I mean."

He smiled then, a lonely and untamed smile, an expression I never imagined could look so at home on Jonathan Mellon's patrician face. "Yes. You should be scared. But you're crazy enough to come with me anyway. And, Mireya, no matter what happens, I want you to know that's a good thing."

I took a step closer to him, despite the fact his words freaked me out. "Why? If I only . . ."

"If you only nothing." He pulled me along, under the shifting cotton of the clouds racing by on the wind over our heads. "Just come on."

Our steps quickened as we broke into a run across the quad. No one else crossed our path, though a dense cloud of little birds wheeled wildly over our heads.

He pulled me up the stairs of Low Library, past the kneeling Rodin statue, *The Thinker*, to the entrance of the St Paul Chapel. Faint music rose from the depths of the crypt in the basement. The crypt housed a famous student-run club, the Postcrypt, which hosted musicians on Saturday nights.

I followed Mellon down the slippery, slightly damp stone stairs. As we got closer to the wooden door barring our way into the club, I was surprised to see him pass by the little room, nodding at the kilted guy half asleep on a barstool by the doorway.

"Where are you going?"

He lifted his fingers to his lips and shushed me in response, then pointed to a stairway I'd never noticed before, heading still deeper underneath the chapel.

"Down here," he said.

These stairs were made of different stone than the grey granite of St Paul's Chapel – something red and crumbly like brick, but with streaks of pearlescent white flaking into opalene brilliance under Mellon's elegant feet.

I slipped a little – there was no handrail – and Mellon grabbed me by the elbow to steady me. We exchanged a glance in the low, flickering light, and as he leaned to me my heart started to pound so hard it was almost painful.

"Mireya?"

"What?" I whispered, half-tranced by the shadows on the stairs.

"Don't forget to breathe. You're turning blue."

And he smiled, a kind, warm smile to show me he didn't mean to belittle or tease. I smiled back, and for a moment, in a delicious flash of sensation, it was like I'd gone backwards to a Mireya who had never suffered.

And then that light, girlish Mireya vanished once again.

"Steady," Mellon whispered. "The stairs get steeper."

And so they did. The stairs became blocks of cold brass, slippery and worn through in the middle, strangely scarred and dented by something even colder and harder. The air got colder too, and damp.

But not mouldy. At first I took that apple blossom scent for cider, but when I saw the first flower petals on the stairs, I gasped.

That flower smell came from flowers. *Flowers.*

"How far down have we gone?" I asked.

Mellon shrugged, and I realized with a start that he had a lantern in his hand. A lantern, OK, not a flashlight or even a candle.

"I had this stashed at the top of the staircase," he said, anticipating my outburst. "Thought it would be handy."

For the first time, Mellon made me hesitate. I'd trusted him enough to see him alone for weeks now. His reserve and courtesy had reassured me, even as I had avoided all the people except Colleen in my usual circles.

And here we were, far enough away from the world that nobody could hear me scream for help. And Mellon was acting so strangely I hardly recognized him.

My heartbeat raced in my ears, and I felt my pulse pounding in my throat. I wiped my damp palms on the front of my pants, and waited for him to stop.

He did, and raised the lantern high to take a good look at me. "You are afraid." It was a statement, not a question.

"I'm sorry, Mellon. Yes, I am."

He nodded in reply, slowly. "Nobody can get at you here. You're here with me."

His eyes flashed with electricity, and I forced myself to breathe slowly until my heart could follow my mind and calm down. I had, up until this point, found Mellon unthreatening, a safe male presence in a world of predators. But now, in the weird dappled light of his lantern, Mellon looked fierce and powerful. And protective of me.

I was no old-time damsel in distress. But I was happy to place myself under Mellon's protection in this strange, subterranean place.

"We're almost there, Miss Mireya Rodriguez of the Brooklyn Rodriguezes."

He reached for my hand, bent his head over, and reverently kissed my knuckles, his eyes all the while searching out my own.

And that strange flicker of freedom from the past enticed me again. Somewhere down below a different Mireya waited for me. I didn't know her yet, but suddenly I wanted to meet her, very much.

Mellon held my hand, the one that he had kissed, and we picked our way down the last dozen or so stairs. The flowers dotting the surface of the stairs became a veritable snowdrift of white, and the last step was completely carpeted in their strange, fragrant petals.

It was unbelievable. I took a deep breath, rubbed my eyes as if I could rub the illusion of it all away like tears.

We stood together in a brick-walled garden, trellised with climbing roses and wisteria and the strange apple-scented white blossoms blowing over the stairs. It was broad daylight. A low, rhythmic chirp sounded from somewhere inside the boxwoods planted all along the perimeter of the garden's walls.

"Nightingale frogs," Mellon said, his voice low.

I had never heard of nightingale frogs. Have you? Has anyone heard a song like that, anyone who lives on the surface, ignorant of the world branching away from under their feet?

"It's beautiful, so beautiful," was all I dared to say. "Jonathan, thank you so much."

"My father's people are the Mellons of Philadelphia," Mellon said. "My mother's people, well. . ."

His voice trailed away, and I knew better than to ask. Instead, I tilted my head back and looked far overhead, saw diaphanous clouds racing across the sky, a tiny, perfect moon hanging upside down.

It felt like coming home.

I bumped into Colleen a week later at the Hungarian Pastry Shop, where I waited with my tea for Jonathan to appear. She almost passed me by, her chocolate croissant in hand, but then she did a double take and almost dropped her breakfast on the ground.

"Mireya?" Her voice was no more than an incredulous squeak.

I laughed, a deep belly laugh that felt almost as good as sex. "That's me. At least the last time I checked."

"Oh, girl, you look – beautiful."

"Different, you were going to say." Colleen didn't pity me now, oh no. I think I frightened her a little bit, now.

"Where have you been? You don't answer your phone, I knocked on your door only about eleventy billion times ..." Her voice trembled, even though a smile stayed imperfectly pasted on her face.

I emerged from my bemused haze long enough to really see her. "Oh no, you were worried." I reached up and hugged her around the neck, gave her a peck on the cheek. "You are a good friend to me, sweetie. And an old soul."

She pulled back and her eyes narrowed. "You sound like you're saying goodbye. Or like you are zoned out of your ever-loving mind. That Mellon guy isn't some kind of dealer – is he?"

"No way. Just my boss, and he'll be here in a minute if you want to meet him and make sure he's OK."

She took an absent-minded bite of croissant and backed away, looking thoroughly spooked. "I have class in ten minutes. Sorry." She ate the rest of the croissant in two or three bites, swallowed her meal, and evidently made up her mind to speak. "I'm not sure what's going on with you. All I can say is be careful. Remember your limitations."

Her little speech made me laugh again, sadly this time. "Maybe I should be worrying about you. You always told me to trash my illusions and reach for the stars ..."

"Maybe I'm just saying the same thing a different way." And with a final wave of her fingers, Colleen left for class.

Mellon appeared not five minutes after Colleen's parting words of wisdom. "OK, Mellon," I said, glad to leave her worries behind and ready for business. "What have you got for me?"

His smile, as usual, hid a world of secrets. "A philosophy paper."

I glanced down at the handwritten paper he held out for me. The paper's title: "The Walled Garden".

The words brought me up short and I looked up from the crabbed, scrabbly handwriting overflowing the crinkly lined paper. "I thought . . ."

"Don't worry. It's a hypothetical garden."

I smiled back. "I'll take that to mean that our secret is safe. So in that case, I have something for you. Something amazing!"

The dancing cool light in his eyes went dark, and he sank down in the chair next to mine. "You went back there, didn't you? Without me."

"I couldn't resist."

"You went alone." Something new shone in his face, and I read it immediately and with great pleasure – it was admiration, mixed with a flicker of fear.

Mellon: afraid. My pleasure shaded into amazement. I cleared my throat and straightened the pink lace scarf arranged around my neck. "Yes, alone. I've been in worse places alone, believe me."

He nodded. "You brought something back."

"Yes! Good student, you know your teacher well. But you'll never guess what. A map. A . . . map!"

He drew his chair closer to mine, leaned in and whispered, "A map? Of what? And wherever did you find it?"

"I didn't find it, I made it. And it's a map of the world beyond the garden wall."

He drew back with a cry of pain, leaned in and grabbed my shoulders. He gave me a little shake, caught himself doing it, and then almost crushed me in a fierce, all-enveloping hug.

Now there was a reaction I'd never have expected to inspire out of Jonathan Mellon. And here's the strangest thing: I welcomed that hug. Lost myself in it, in fact. And lost and safe in his arms, I considered what a freaking miracle that sense of safety represented.

"You jumped over the wall!" he murmured against the top of my head. I could feel him swallowing hard. "I can't believe I didn't lose you."

"Of course not. I have the world's best sense of direction. And if I know how to do anything, it's to come back no matter what."

I gently disentangled myself from Mellon's embrace, took out the folded-up square of paper I kept in the back pocket of my jeans. Unlike him, I took pains to keep my work neat, and the graph paper had a sketched pathway and careful notes covering both sides.

I leaned in and waved the paper. "Look, the walled garden is in the centre."

I took in the sight of his quick, neat features as he pored over my drawings. While he was distracted, I stole a close-up view of my strange and beautiful new friend's face. And in that moment, tracing the line of his lips and his jaw with my gaze, I realized I could love this man.

It was crazy, classic-Mireya-crazy. But it also made a certain immutable sense. Because I had never known a man like Mellon, one who quietly moved mountains and revealed worlds without saying a word. One who realized that words are jewels, that if you can work magic, there's no need to brag about it.

He poked me gently in the shoulder. "You're daydreaming again. Go ahead."

I smiled up at him, and he wrapped an arm protectively around my shoulder and rubbed at his jaw with his other hand. I watched him take the map and study it, and a slow realization came to a rolling boil in my mind:

He didn't know about any of this. All he knew personally was the garden itself – he had never gone over the top. And that knowledge put the fear into me for the first time.

Why hadn't Mellon gone exploring down below the way I had?

He poked me in the shoulder again. "So what did you find?"

Mellon: impatient. I'd discovered a world of wonders in my friend, as well as in the subterranean world he'd opened to me. "Well, once you climb the trellis and go over, across the brass stairs, there's a cinder path, lined with cactus and these strange purple vines with flowers."

He nodded for me to go on, an odd expression on his face. I took a sip of my now-tepid tea, and leaned against his warm, strong arm. "About fifty feet down – the pathway slopes down – the way forks. I decided to pick right every time, and the path branched about five times."

I indicated each fork in the path with my pinkie, touching his finger as we traced my recorded footfalls together on the page.

"And then . . ." I hesitated. What I was about to say was amazing, unbelievable, and breathtaking – but I could never unsay it. I savoured the silence before words.

Mellon nodded for me to go on. He was ready.

"I came to a door."

He leaned forwards even more. "To another garden."

"Yes."

He wrinkled his forehead, nibbled at his lower lip. "And you jumped the wall and climbed the stairs."

"Yes, Mellon! It was so amazing."

"And what did you discover at the top of the stairs?" His voice sounded dry and precise, like a lawyer doing a routine courtroom cross-examination in a boring town somewhere far, far away from where we lived.

"It was a speakeasy. I came up through the wine cellar, and all these guys in zoot suits sat in a row along the bar. It had a huge polished bar, even bigger than the West End. And there were – showgirls there, too. Wearing flapper dresses and strappy shoes."

"Astonishing. And what else?"

"The barkeeper knew me, Mellon! He nodded and smiled. Offered me a 'whiskey neat, on the house, girlie'!"

Mellon's face went alabaster, like somebody had turned him into a decorative figurine. "You didn't take it. Tell me you didn't drink it!"

I leaned up against the whole side of his lean, warm body and looked up into his face, so close I could have kissed him. But I resisted. I didn't want to steal our first kiss, not in the middle of his panic. "If I did drink it, Mellon, would I have made it back?"

He hugged me again, and I felt a tremor in his fingers, very slight, where his fingertips pressed against my bare arms. "Promise me you won't do that again. Jump the wall, all alone."

"But it was amazing, Mellon. I'm a history major . . . you can just imagine what that was like!"

"No, promise me. As a boy, I swore to my grandfather never to venture past the garden walls. I never imagined you would just go ahead yourself, without telling me first. Mireya, you astonish me."

I drew back, caressed his cheek until his eyes went from wild to merely troubled. "Mellon, I was free. I met myself down in that pathway, you know? I have to go back. I have to. But I want you to come with me."

"It's beautiful, but it's dangerous."

"It's worth it. Come with me!"

When he didn't respond, I gave in to the temptation and ran my fingers through his glorious, thick blond hair. "Come with me. We'll take the left-hand path together. Don't worry . . . your grandfather will never know."

The left-hand path was wonderful in a completely different way, one that Mellon seemed to find less threatening than the dangerous speakeasy with the all-too-knowing barkeep. We found a walled garden after only two branchings of the path, and we emerged to rolling fields high on a bluff overlooking what would someday become Passaic, NJ. I recognized the view – it was the same as the one in my tiny bathroom window.

A single Indian woman with a baby on her breast sat cross-legged, and she nodded as we walked by. It was autumn, full daylight, and the leaves sprinkling down into Mellon's hair were orange, white and blood red with purple streaks. I carefully filled in my map before we returned to the walled garden under the Columbia University chapel.

Over the next few weeks, my hand-drawn map got more complicated looking than the NYC subway map. I redrew it on to a much larger piece of paper, started naming the pathways so I could keep them straight in my mind, but even so, the twining paths and interlocked gardens crowded each other over the smudged page.

What adventures we had underneath the streets of New York City, Mellon and I. I could write a whole book about it, and someday maybe I will. From the days of Peter Stuyvesant to the Revolutionary War, to the Second World War to hazy futures beyond our own lives, Jonathan and I explored a city unfolding in time as well as space. We always came back, sometimes with difficulty but more often with a familiar, homecoming ease. But I always left something of myself behind.

In all these times and places I found a single constant, a central point more changeless than our own walled garden: Jonathan Mellon himself. Steadfast, mysterious, bearer of secret fears he was strong enough to carry alone. And no matter where and when we went, we agreed our favourite place and time was our own.

The day Mellon brought back his first A+ paper, we didn't travel anywhere or anywhen, but stayed the night in my room. I double locked the door and put my desk chair up under the doorknob in the extremely unlikely event that Colleen would stop by – even she had given up on me, and now none of my old friends remained in my life. We ate turkey sandwiches by starlight with the window open, and the oboe player regaled us with something slow, sad and sweet, like Debussy blissed out of his mind on opium.

When I let down the window shade and took the clips out of my hair, the music seeped into my veins. The room was full of shadows; Mellon's face shone like the moon. Mellon unlocked my body and my heart like a garden gate, and his loving caresses were the key.

Afterwards, we lay together on the bed, so close that the twin bed was plenty big enough for the two of us. I sighed and rested my cheek on his narrow, muscular chest, and I revelled in the calm cadence of his heartbeat.

"Why did you talk to me that day out by your beat-up Mercedes, Mellon? It was no accident we met, was it?"

I could feel that Mellon was holding his breath. He exhaled with a slow and ragged sigh, held me even closer. "You have a scent of magic, Mireya. I found you irresistible. Did from the first moment I laid eyes on you."

He rolled me on top of him, arranged my bare limbs to twine all around him like a climbing trellis of roses. "And I intend to never resist you again."

The night passed slowly and with a blooming sweetness. It was the purest, most uncomplicated bliss I have ever known.

Which only made the note nailed to my door all the more horrible when we discovered it the following morning.

The door itself was scored with scratches and deep grooves, and it looked scorched, like someone had tried to burn their way through it as we slept.

The paper pinned under the nail smelled rank, like piss and beer and smoke. It was ground in dirt. It smelled like Riverside Park in late September.

My body went cold as I reached up and ripped it off the door. I forced myself not to flinch as I turned the packet of paper over in my hands and opened it.

A small bundle fell into my open palm, and I heard Mellon mutter a foreign curse under his breath. It was a lock of my hair, matted and burned.

The note itself was written in that uncanny neat handwriting I had seen before, and it said only:

YOU ARE MINE

I handed the note to Jonathan and went back into my room without a single word to say. My fingers ached at their tips, and at every point where they had touched the paper.

"The words are a lie," Jonathan said, his voice clean and clear and strong. "You belong to me. And to yourself."

I sank to my knees and sat by the window facing the courtyard. A flock of starlings chattered noisily in the branches of the gingko tree.

"No, that note tells the truth, sweetheart." The strength flowed out of me and into the floor under my feet. I sank to the ground, curled up on the floor, and covered my face with my hands. Focused on breathing slowly. In, out. Focused on the fact that I still breathed.

Jonathan knelt next to me, still wrapped in my sheet, and his hand traced a soft pattern on my back. "It was true once, perhaps. But not any more."

"But the – bundle." My words were as heavy as rocks in my mouth. I wiped at my eyes and lifted my head so I could look at him, the closed door looming over us like a gigantic tombstone. He was sleek and golden as a young stag in the springtime.

"It is a curse bag, my love. Do you know what that is?"

I swallowed hard. It hurt. "No. But it means I'm not free. All that time underground . . . none of it means anything. He's still got a claim on me."

"I must have called attention to you. It found you because of me." He sat back, let the sheet fall from his shoulders. In the soft light of early morning, the pain in his eyes pierced me, sharper than the rusty nail driven through the paper on my door.

Suddenly, he shook his head, as though he were making up his mind about something important. "No. You will be free, my love. I'll explain as we go. But we have to hurry."

I knew what he meant. Whoever – whatever – had left me this note, he had gone back to hide at the bottom of the stairs under the chapel. I knew it, as surely as I now knew that I loved Jonathan Mellon with all my heart and soul.

Jonathan took an old-fashioned iron key out of a strange little leather fob he had strapped to his belt. He leaped up the stone staircase and fiddled with the enormous locked wooden doors until they silently swung open.

"Who attacked me that day, Jonathan?"

He looked down at me, reached to me with an open hand. "You know the saying, I am certain. 'Ignorance is bliss.'" And with a strange smile, he bowed and escorted me over the threshold and into the hot darkness of the chapel.

We headed at top speed for the back of the chapel, to the stairs leading to the Postcrypt, and I decided to get the truth out of him, before it was too late. "Ignorance is not bliss, though. It's deadly." I half-hurled myself down the stairs after his swift, retreating figure.

He paused at the top of our stairs, his eyes like dark sapphires. "Sometimes things aren't what they seem. And the illusion is more pleasing, it can lead you to your strength better than the naked truth."

"What do you mean?"

He disappeared down the stairs. I followed, clutching at the wall to keep my balance. "What are you trying to tell me? Who are you really? What are you?"

His voice echoed from somewhere down below. "I've known you for a while. As I said, yours is an attractive magic ... I really couldn't help but love you."

"What are you, Mellon?"

The silence was painful. By now I'd come to the huge brass stairs, and I had to slow down so I wouldn't fall. Without Jonathan to hold on to, I had to slide down and, knowing we came to hunt, I had the presence of mind to bring a flashlight instead of a romantic but relatively weak candle or lantern. For the first time, I could see the deep scratches and slashes clawed into the metal.

"Oh my God," I whispered, half to myself.

I reached the bottom of the stairs, and Jonathan waited for me, eyes wide. "Daytime up above is night down here. And at night . . . the creatures of night claim their share of the world."

A low growl rose from beyond the garden's walls.

"Part of what they seek to claim is you. But I won't have it."

He came to me, seared my lips with a final kiss. "What am I, Mireya?" He held me as the growls got closer. I passed him the flashlight, but the darkness engulfed us, thicker than velvet.

He shook his head and laughed. "It doesn't matter any more, what I am. My father fell in love with my mother, a woman from the dark places. The walled garden is mother's domain. The creature that attacked you is likely my mother's creature.

"But all that matters is you, Mireya. I first saw you at the bottom of a ditch in Riverside Park, and you were fighting for your life. I didn't let him get you then, and I won't let him have you now.

"Listen to me, Mireya," Jonathan continued, as the growls rose to a horrible shriek. "I'm going to take care of the monster that attacked you. Very few pure mortals have a magic like yours. It's a rare and beautiful light, my love – but it attracts the darkness, too. Go back up the stairs, quickly."

"But, Jonathan, sweetheart . . ."

"Don't argue. Go. When it's safe, I'll come for you." The shriek grew into a guttural scream. "Go!"

I had never run away from a fight, not in my entire life. But I knew better than to argue with him – after all, I had met that evil beast before, and had barely survived my first encounter. Now, too late, I understood that Mellon alone had stopped it from snuffing me out. The only way to thank him was to try to survive this second time.

I ran back up the stairs as best I could, half blinded by tears and by the loss of the flashlight, and it wasn't until I stopped for air in the middle of the Quad that I realized it . . .

I still had the map, wadded up in my back pocket.

I finished the rest of the school year in a haze, doing what I knew I had to do in a world that had become a faint dream. I picked up my old nemesis, the telephone, and called Colleen for help; my old friend forgave me for my neglect of our friendship without saying a word. She kept my body and soul together somehow, much as she had the first time I had been attacked. But I think she knew I hadn't really made it back this time, and that I wasn't going to stick around for long.

It was the end of school for the year. I packed up my two boxes of earthly possessions and mailed them to my darling grandmother in New Hampshire. My move thus completed, I bequeathed my drooping spider plant to Ali, the ancient security guard, and he smiled and nodded in silent thanks.

My last night, I sat alone on my bare bed, where I had once made love to a creature of starlight and shadows, and I looked out the window, smelled the wild apple-scented fragrance of the night, and knew I was alone, wild and free. Jonathan's gift to me.

The door trembled under the gentlest of knocks.

I turned, and rose. Scooped up my map, walked slowly to the door. And without hesitation, I answered it.

The door opened to a walled garden. And Jonathan.

Catch the Lightning

Madeline Baker

Prologue

The great white stallion sniffed the freshening breeze. The Apache called him a spirit horse; the Cheyenne called him a ghost horse because of his colour. But Relámpago was both, and neither. For hundreds of years, he had wandered the path between the past and the present, saving countless lives, bringing lost souls together.

Ears pricked forwards, he heard a faint call for help carried on the wings of the wind. With a toss of his head, Relámpago descended from his home high in the Chiricahua Mountains.

One

It was 11 a.m. on a rainy Saturday morning in January when Macie Jenkins decided her life was no longer worth living. Her parents and younger sister had died in an automobile accident six months ago. Her best friend in the whole world had married a computer programmer and moved to Japan. Her boyfriend had left her for his secretary. Last month, the collie she'd had ever since she was a little girl had got lost in a thunderstorm and never returned. Last week, she had lost her job due to the ongoing recession. And this morning, she had found her two-year-old goldfish belly up in the tank. It had been the last straw.

With a shake of her head, Macie turned away from the living-room window. Now that the decision was made, she felt a curious sense of peace. How to do it, that was the question? A knife was too messy. She didn't own a gun. Sitting in the garage with the engine running seemed too creepy. Sleeping pills, of course, that was the best way. And how fortuitous that she'd had her prescription refilled yesterday. Tomorrow, she thought, she would do it tomorrow. But today, ah, today she would indulge in all the things she had been avoiding. She would have a big bowl of warm chocolate pudding for breakfast, a Big Mac, fries and a chocolate malt for lunch, pasta and garlic bread for dinner, and a pint of chocolate fudge ice cream for dessert.

While stirring the pudding, she contemplated leaving a suicide note, and decided against it. No one she knew would really care why she had done it; most wouldn't even know she was gone.

When the pudding was cool, she poured all of it into a large bowl, sliced a banana on top, then sat at the kitchen table and savoured every bite. Good thing she was dying tomorrow, she thought with a wry grin, since she'd just shot her diet all to hell.

She spent the next hour finishing the book she was reading, then she cleaned her house from top to bottom. She didn't want whoever found her body to think she lived like a slob.

Lunch was perfect. She lingered over every French fry, even the little crusty ones at the bottom of the bag.

While fixing dinner, she listened to her favourite fifties oldies. When dinner was ready, she lit a fire in the fireplace and ate in the living room. She grinned ruefully as she again savoured every bite. Six months at the gym, wiped out in one day.

By six, the rain had turned into a thunderstorm. Lightning slashed the skies, thunder rocked the heavens, a ferocious wind rattled the windows. She had always loved a storm. What better way to spend her last night than walking in the rain? One thing for certain, she wouldn't have to worry about catching a cold.

After pulling on her favourite sweatshirt and an old pair of cowboy boots, she went outside. For a moment, she just stood there, her face lifted to the skies. Was anyone up there? Was there life after death? Were her parents waiting to greet her on the other side, or was death the end of everything?

She'd know the answer tomorrow. She shoved her hands into the pockets of her jeans and then, with no particular destination in mind, she started walking. It was kind of spooky, walking in the dark. She glanced over her shoulder from time to time, making sure the lights from the house were still in sight.

A flash of lightning split the skies. Macie stared at it. Was that a horse, she thought, startled, and then laughed out loud. "You're losing it, Macie," she muttered, and let out a yelp when her feet suddenly went out from under her and she found herself falling head over heels down a rocky hill.

A shrill cry rose in her throat, ending in a groan as she slammed into a boulder at the foot of the hill.

And then everything went black.

Cold and wet, Macie woke with a groan. For a moment, she simply lay there, her whole body aching. Why was she so sore? she wondered. Then, in a rush, it all came back to her. She'd fallen down the hill at the far end of the property. If she'd had any luck at all, she thought glumly, the fall would have killed her.

With her eyes still closed, she took inventory and decided that, even though she hurt from head to foot, nothing was broken.

With a sigh of relief, she opened her eyes. She frowned when a thick grey mist rose up from the hill in front of her, let out a surprised gasp when a white stallion materialized out of the mist. It was the most beautiful creature she had ever seen. Even in the dull grey light of the overcast day, the stallion's white coat glinted like liquid silver. A thin black scar, shaped like a bolt of lightning, adorned its right flank.

"Hey, boy, what are you doing here?"

There hadn't been any horses in the area since Macie was a little girl. Most of the barns and corrals had been torn down, replaced by RV parking and swimming pools.

At the sound of her voice, the stallion lowered its head and nudged her shoulder.

Taking a deep breath, Macie grabbed hold of the stallion's mane and used it to steady herself as she pulled herself to her feet.

"So, what's your name? Snowball? No. Thunder? No." She ran her fingertips over the scar on the stallion's flank. "Lightning," she murmured. "I'll bet that's your name. And you fell out of the sky, didn't you? Or maybe I'm hallucinating and you're not really here. But I'm going to call you Lightning, just the same."

The stallion's dark, intelligent eyes met hers, almost as if he understood her words.

"You don't know it, horse, but you came along at just the right time. Thanks to you, I won't have to walk up that hill."

Macie didn't know where the stallion had come from, but somehow, she knew that it had been ridden before. She hadn't been on a horse in years, but it was something you never forgot. Grasping the stallion's mane, she swung on to its back, and nudged its flanks with her boot heels. When she clucked softly, the horse turned and walked up the hill.

Macie shivered as the mist grew thicker, darker, until it blanketed the whole area, so thick that she couldn't see a thing. Muttering, "I hope you can see where you're going," she clung to the stallion's mane with both hands.

The mist grew thicker as they climbed steadily upwards. When they reached the top of the hill, the stallion came to a halt and the mist disappeared.

"What the heck?" Macie stared at the scene before her. Where was her house? Her car? The sidewalk? The neighbourhood?

She glanced from right to left. Closed her eyes. Opened them again. The world as she had known it was gone. "I must have hit my head harder than I thought," she muttered. Because everything she knew was gone.

She blinked, and blinked again, but nothing changed. Buildings she had never seen before lined both sides of a dusty street. An odd ringing sound filled the air; it took her a moment to realize it was the sound of a blacksmith's hammer. A number of horses were tethered to hitching posts up and down the street. Women in long dresses and floppy bonnets strolled along the wooden boardwalk accompanied by men in denim pants, leather vests and muddy cowboy boots. Somewhere in the distance, a clock chimed the hour.

A rumbling like thunder sounded behind her. Startled, Macie glanced over her shoulder to see a stagecoach bearing down on her. She jerked hard on the stallion's mane, sneezed as a cloud of dun-coloured dust rose in the coach's wake.

The stage pulled up at the far end of the street. The driver jumped down from the wagon seat. When he opened the door, a half-dozen men and women emerged.

Macie stared at them as they gathered their luggage and disappeared into the hotel. Patting the stallion's shoulder, Macie muttered, "Where the heck are we?"

Two

"Where the heck are we?" Macie repeated when a wagon rumbled past, raising another cloud of dust. "And where the heck is my house?"

The horse, of course, had no answer.

Macie clucked to the stallion and he moved off briskly. She glanced from side to side as she rode down the street, which looked like a set out of every western movie she had ever seen. There were three saloons, a dry goods store, a bootery, a barber shop and a two-storey hotel. The assay office and the post office shared a false-fronted shop. The sheriff's office was located in a red-brick building.

Several men and women stopped to stare at her as she rode past.

It had to be a dream, Macie mused, but if it was, it was the most realistic one she'd ever had. She could feel the breeze on her face, taste the dust. Beyond the last building, there was nothing but open prairie as far as the eye could see. Macie tugged on the stallion's mane in an effort to turn him around, but the horse kept going.

"Whoa, boy," she said, tugging on Lightning's mane again. "I don't want to go out there."

But the stallion didn't stop.

Macie was considering sliding off the horse and walking back to town when Lightning broke into a gallop. With a startled cry, she leaned low over the stallion's neck, her hands clutching his mane, praying all the while that the horse wouldn't step in a prairie dog hole and break its leg. Or her neck.

The horse was incredibly fast. Grass, trees and hills flew by in a blur as he raced across the ground until the town was far behind and there was nothing ahead but tall yellow grass and scattered stands of timber.

Just when she was beginning to think the animal would never stop, it slowed to a trot, then a walk, and came to a halt at the head of a shallow draw.

"About time," she muttered. After taking a couple of deep breaths, she slid off the stallion's back.

And found herself staring into a pair of dark eyes that belonged to a tall, dark man with a gun in his hand, a knife in his belt and a dark red stain spreading over the lower half of his shirt front.

Before she could think, before she could speak, the weapon fell from the man's hand and he pitched forwards to land face down at her feet.

Pressing a hand to her rapidly beating heart, Macie stared at him.

Good Lord, was he dead?

She stood there, staring at him, wondering what to do, even though there was nothing she *could* do. They were miles from town, and even if they weren't, there was no way she could lift him on to the back of the horse. Besides, he really did look like he was dead.

Macie was still debating her next move when the stallion nudged her from behind. She stumbled forwards, landing on her knees beside the man. Reaching out to steady herself, she accidentally hit the dead man's arm.

And he groaned.

Not dead then, she thought. But she still couldn't lift him.

Kneeling there, she noticed a pair of saddlebags, a bedroll and a canteen lying in the dirt behind him. And beyond his gear, the body of a horse.

Heaving a sigh, Macie gained her feet. Maybe he had something in his bags she could use for bandages.

Rummaging inside, she found a box of ammunition, a sack of what looked like beef jerky and a clean shirt. Feeling like Florence Nightingale, Macie rolled the man on to his back, drew his knife from the sheath and cut the shirt into strips.

Taking her lower lip between her teeth, she lifted his bloodstained shirt, and gagged when she saw the bloody furrow in his left side, just above his belt. Had he been shot? She had never seen a gunshot wound before, but that's what it was, she was sure of it. She wiped away the blood, then saw that the bullet hadn't penetrated his flesh, just gouged a deep gash along his side.

Using water from the canteen, she cleaned it up as best she could, then wrapped several strips of cloth around his middle to staunch the blood. When that was done, she sat back on her heels and blew out a sigh. She had done all she could. The rest was up to him.

Macie glanced around, wondering how far they were from town. When she looked back at the man, he was awake and watching her.

"Water." His voice was deep, raspy with pain.

Macie retrieved the canteen, uncapped it, and held it for him.

He drank long and deep, then looked at her through narrowed eyes. "Who the hell are you?"

"I'm the one who just bandaged you up. Who the hell are you?"

His lips twisted in a wry grin. "Ace Bowdry. Excuse me if I don't get up, Miss ...?"

"Jenkins." She cocked her head to the side, studying him. Long dark hair hung past his shoulders. Dark eyes, high cheekbones and skin that was more red than brown. "You're Native American, aren't you?"

"What?"

"Indian. You're Indian, aren't you?"

He nodded. "That a problem for you?"

Macie shrugged. "No, why? Is it a problem for you?"

He groaned softly when he sat up. "Sometimes."

"What happened to you?"

"I got into a disagreement with a fella about the way he played cards."

"You got shot over a card game?"

"Yep. Fella was dealin' off the bottom. When I called him on it, he called me a name I won't repeat in your presence, and then he pulled a gun on me."

"Oh!"

Bowdry nodded. "He nicked me. I killed him, and then I hightailed it out of town."

"What happened to your horse?"

"He took a stray bullet meant for me. He was a game little stud. I didn't know he'd been hit until he dropped out from under me." Bowdry glanced over his shoulder and there was a note of admiration in his voice when he said, "I'm surprised he lasted as long as he did. So," he added, his tone brisk, "what the hell are you doing way out here? And why are you dressed like that?"

Macie glanced down. What was wrong with the way she was dressed? True, her jeans had faded from red to a washed-out pink, her boots were a little run down at the heel and her sweatshirt was a trifle large ... she sighed again. So, she wasn't at her best.

Shrugging, she said, "I wasn't expecting to meet anyone."

"Who's the white-haired guy on the front of your shirt?"

"It's Grumpy. You know, from *Snow White and the Seven Dwarfs*."

Bowdry frowned at her. "Grumpy?"

"Haven't you ever heard of Snow White?" she asked, then realized that, even if he had, Disney's version hadn't been written yet. "Do you live around here?" she asked, changing the subject.

"No, I was just passin' through."

"Is there a town closer than the one I just left?" She glanced up at the sky, which had grown considerably darker in the last few minutes. Dark grey clouds scudded overhead, blanketing the sun and bringing the promise of rain.

"There's a ghost town a few miles from here." He swore softly as he gained his feet, one hand pressed against his side. "I'd be obliged if you'd give me a ride," he said, then whistled softly when he noticed the stallion for the first time. "Is that Relámpago?"

"Who?"

Bowdry shook his head. "It's gotta be. Where'd you get him?"

"I didn't 'get him'. He just showed up at my house yesterday. Is he yours?"

"Nah. That stallion doesn't belong to anyone."

"Maybe it isn't . . . what did you say his name is?"

"Relámpago. It means lightning." Bowdry moved towards the stud, one hand outstretched. "Hey, boy. My great granddaddy told me about you."

"What about him?"

"He's a ghost horse, you know, magic."

"A magic horse?" Macie said with a laugh. "Yeah, right."

"It's true. Legend says he appears to those in need, that he's as swift as lightning, as sure-footed as a mountain goat and as reliable as the sun." Bowdry patted the stallion on the neck. "My people believe if you treat him right, he'll always carry you away from danger."

Macie frowned. Had Relámpago brought her here to save Bowdry? But that was silly. If saving Bowdry had been the horse's mission, wouldn't Relámpago have just come here? There was no reason for the stallion to come to her. She hadn't been in any danger . . . except from herself.

"You all right?" Bowdry asked. "You look a little pale."

"What? Oh, I'm fine."

"Well, whaddya say we get going? We're gonna get mighty wet if we stay here."

After gathering what gear he could carry, Bowdry swung on to the stallion's back. Macie thought he looked a little pale himself when he reached down to offer her a hand up. She couldn't blame him. Even though the wound wasn't serious, it probably hurt like the devil.

Once she was settled behind him, Bowdry clucked to Relámpago and the stallion moved out at a brisk walk. A short time later, the horse broke into an easy lope.

Macie wrapped her arms around Bowdry's middle, careful to avoid the wound in his side. It was rather pleasant, riding behind him. His broad back blocked the wind and made a nice pillow for her head.

Strange, she wasn't more upset about finding herself in the Old West with a complete stranger, one who had recently killed a man. But then, there was no reason to be upset. She was only dreaming, after all.

Three

The ghost town rose up out of the prairie like a mirage, shimmering in the light of the setting sun, only to fade to dull grey as the sun dropped below the horizon.

Macie shivered as Bowdry reined the stallion to a halt in front of a dilapidated building. The sign over the door read THE PALACE HOTEL. She thought it a rather pretentious name for a hotel stuck out in the middle of nowhere.

The town itself was little more than a block long. Judging by the number of saloons, the inhabitants had had quite a taste for whiskey. Besides the saloons and the hotel, the only other businesses were a blacksmith and a barber.

Swinging his leg over the stallion's withers, Bowdry dismounted. Macie slid off the horse's back. "Is it safe to stay here?"

Bowdry shrugged. "I reckon so. I don't see anybody else around, do you?"

"No, but . . ." She shivered as a chill wind blew a tumbleweed down the middle of the dusty street. "It feels, I don't know, eerie."

"Well," Bowdry said with a grin, "it *is* a ghost town."

"Maybe our ghost horse will protect us," Macie muttered.

"Maybe so," Bowdry said, chuckling.

"Shouldn't we tie him up or something?"

Bowdry shook his head. "He's not going anywhere."

Puzzling over his reply, Macie followed Bowdry into the hotel. As was to be expected, the floors were covered with dust, as were the chairs and the registration desk.

The steps creaked as they made their way up the stairs. Bowdry opened the door to the first room they came to.

"I'll take the next room," Macie said, though she wasn't looking forward to being alone with night coming on.

Bowdry shrugged. "Suit yourself, but I've only got one blanket."

Macie stared at him. "I don't suppose you'd let me have it?"

"Sorry, but I'm willing to share."

She stared at him a moment, her thoughts racing. Sleep alone and be cold, or share a bed with a remarkably handsome, sexy man and be warm? It really wasn't much of a choice.

Bowdry stifled a grin as she followed him into the room. She was a pretty thing, slender and not too tall, with a mess of dark brown curls, a sprinkling of freckles across her nose and eyes as blue as the Pacific.

Bowdry obligingly shook the dust from the faded sheet and the lumpy mattress while she swept the floor with an old broom she found in a hallway closet. A stub of a candle provided a bit of light.

Wincing, Bowdry sat on the foot of the bed. Rummaging in his saddlebags, he pulled out two hunks of jerky. He handed one to Macie, then reached into his saddlebags again and pulled out a sack of tobacco and a package of papers. Under Macie's curious gaze, he proceeded to roll and light a cigarette.

"I've never seen anyone do that," she remarked.

"People don't smoke where you come from?"

"The smart ones don't. Smoking's bad for your health, you know."

"Says who?"

"Doctors."

He grunted softly. "Just where do you come from anyway?"

"California."

He arched one brow. "You're a long way from home."

"Longer than you think. Where am I anyway?"

"South Dakota."

"South Dakota! What year is this?"

"Don't you know?"

"Would I ask if I did?"

"It's 1880."

She blinked at him as she tried to absorb that. South Dakota, 1880. Imagine that.

He regarded her curiously a moment, then said, "How is it that you don't know what year it is?"

"You wouldn't believe me if I told you."

"Try me."

"You're bleeding."

Frowning, he glanced down at his side. A bright red stain was spreading over the cloth wrapped around his middle. Jaw clenched, he dropped his cigarette on the floor, stubbed it out with his boot heel. Lifting his shirt tail, he removed the bloody cloth and tossed it aside.

"Here, let me." Using water from his canteen, she pulled a clean strip of cloth from his saddlebag, wet it and washed the wound.

Bowdry held up one hand, staying her when she would have bandaged it again.

She watched in amazement as he chewed a handful of tobacco, then pressed it over the wound.

"OK," he said, "bandage it up."

Muttering, "I hope you know what you're doing," she wrapped the last strip of clean cloth around his waist.

Sitting at the head of the bed, Macie nibbled on the beef jerky. It didn't taste anything like what she was used to back home.

"I don't know about you," Bowdry said when he finished eating, "but I'm tuckered out."

"If that means tired, you're not the only one," Macie admitted. She glanced at the narrow bed, then up at Bowdry. Her stomach quivered when he smiled at her.

With every nerve on edge, she stretched out on the bed, as close to the edge of the mattress as she could get without falling off.

Bowdry chuckled as he stretched out beside her, then covered the two of them with the blanket. "Relax, pretty lady," he murmured as he closed his eyes. "I'm too sore, and too tired, to bother you tonight."

He was snoring before she could come up with a good retort.

Macie doubted she'd get much sleep, lying beside a strange man in a strange bed, but the next thing she knew, it was morning. When she opened her eyes, Bowdry was watching her.

Macie frowned as a rush of colour warmed her cheeks. "What are you staring at?"

He shrugged. "Nothing much else to look at."

At a loss for words, her gaze slid away from his.

"I guess I owe you my thanks," Bowdry mused.

"You're welcome."

"You never told me where you were from."

"Yes, I did."

"Right. California." He grunted softly. "I've been to California a time or two, but I never saw anyone quite like you."

"You just weren't there at the right time," Macie retorted with a grin, and then frowned, wondering how she could make Relámpago take her back to her own time.

"You got a first name?" Bowdry asked.

"Macie."

"That's an odd name for a pretty girl."

"Ace Bowdry is an odd name for an Indian."

"My mother named me after my old man."

"My mother named me after her mother."

Macie's cheeks grew hotter under Bowdry's regard, even as wings of excitement fluttered in the pit of her stomach. There was no denying he was an incredibly handsome man, just as there was no denying that he looked exactly the way she had always pictured the man she would marry, from his long black hair and dark eyes to his tawny skin and six-pack abs. The fact that he was an Indian intrigued her, which prompted her to ask, "What kind of Native Amer– Indian are you?"

"Cheyenne, on my mother's side. White on the other."

"Oh. Are your parents still alive?"

"No."

"I'm sorry."

A muscle throbbed in his jaw.

She was tempted to ask what had happened to them, but the look in his eyes warned her to keep silent.

Pressure on her bladder had her sitting up and glancing around, then chiding herself for expecting to find indoor plumbing in such a primitive place. Murmuring, "Excuse me," she hurried out of the room and out of the hotel.

The stallion whinnied at her as she ducked around the corner of the building and took cover behind a fat bush. If she had to go wandering through time, why couldn't she have travelled to some place with indoor plumbing and toilet paper?

Bowdry was waiting for her in the lobby when she returned to the hotel. "Ready to go?"

"Where are we going?"

"Someplace with food and hot water."

"Sounds good to me. How are you feeling?"

"Like I haven't eaten in a week. Let's go."

It was dark when they reached the town of Whiskey Creek. Macie glanced from side to side as they rode down the street, thinking it looked like a twin to the town they had left behind.

Bowdry reined up in front of the Montecito Hotel. He dismounted, then lifted Macie from the horse's back.

"I could have got down on my own," Macie said, noting the fine lines of pain around his mouth.

"Yeah. Well . . ." He shrugged.

"Shouldn't we tie the horse up?"

Bowdry shook his head. "He won't go anywhere until his reason for being here is done. Let's get something to eat."

Macie followed Bowdry into the hotel dining room, a quick gaze taking it all in – the tables covered in red-and-white checked cloths, the cowboy hats hanging on the rack by the door, the rough attire of most of the occupants.

They found a table near a window and sat across from each other. A harried-looking waitress appeared a few minutes later. Bowdry ordered a steak "and all the trimmin's" and after a moment's hesitation, Macie asked for the same. She wasn't a big meat eater at home but hey, this was 1880. Cows in this day and age probably weren't shot full of hormones.

Bowdry leaned back in his chair, his arms crossed over his chest. "So, I'm still waiting to hear why you don't know what year it is."

"You really want to know? All right, I'll tell you. When I woke up yesterday morning, it was April 8 2009."

"No sh– I mean . . ." He shook his head, and then he frowned. "You're telling the truth, aren't you?"

"I guess you don't believe me. Not that I'd blame you."

"No, I believe you."

"You do?"

"There are stories among my people of medicine men who rode Relámpago through time."

"Really? How did they find their way back?"

"I don't know. Same way they got there, I guess. Why? You in a hurry to go back where you came from?"

Macie thought about it for a moment, then shook her head. "No."

Bowdry leaned forwards. "It's said the only time Relámpago appears to most people is when they're in danger. Were you in danger?"

Macie's gaze slid away from his. How could she tell him she'd been about to commit suicide? Thinking about it now filled her with shame. There were people all over the world who had it much worse than she did. She lived in a free country. She had a nice house, her health, a car, enough food to eat and money in the bank.

"Macie?"

She blew out a breath. He was a stranger to her. They would part ways, and she would never see him again, so what difference did it make what he thought of her?

"It doesn't matter."

"If you say so."

Macie was relieved when the waitress arrived with their meal. She didn't know why she cared what Bowdry thought of her, but she did. "You were the one in danger," Macie said after a time. "Why didn't he appear to you?"

"I don't know," Bowdry said, and then he grinned. "Maybe he brought us together for a reason."

"Yeah? What reason would that be?"

"Well, since you found me, I thought maybe you'd know."

"I don't have a clue."

"Maybe if we spend some time together, we'll find out."

His words, the look in his deep brown eyes, sent a wave of heat spiralling through her. Spending time with Ace Bowdry certainly wouldn't be a hardship in any sense of the word.

After dinner, Bowdry secured two rooms in the hotel, then asked the desk clerk for lots of hot water to be sent up to their rooms as soon as possible.

Macie felt somewhat lost when she entered her room and closed the door, along with an unexpected sense of disappointment that they wouldn't be sharing a room. And a bed. She shook the feeling away. What was she doing here, anyway? Surely whatever fate had sent her here must know she could end her life in this century as easily as her own.

Moving to the window, she pushed the white lace curtain aside and stared at the street below. How was she going to get back home? If she asked Relámpago to take her, would he? There had been times in her life when she felt like she didn't belong, but in this case, it was true. She definitely didn't belong here, and never would. Yet even as she yearned for home, she knew she would be sorry to see the last of Ace Bowdry. There was no denying that she was attracted to him. And he to her.

Maybe Relámpago was more than a time-travelling horse. Maybe he was a matchmaker, as well.

The following morning, bright and early, Bowdry knocked on her door. "You awake in there?"

Scrambling out of bed, Macie wrapped a sheet around her nakedness and opened the door.

Bowdry grinned at her. "You ready for breakfast?"

"Do I look ready?"

"You look ready for something."

The look in his eyes caused a shiver of excitement in the pit of her stomach. With his gaze focused on hers, he backed her into the room and shut the door behind him.

Macie stared up at him, her heart pounding, her lips slightly parted, as he reached for her.

He's going to kiss me. Breathless with anticipation, she closed her eyes.

There was no hesitation in his kiss. His lips were warm and firm, confident without being demanding.

Needing something solid to hang on to, Macie's hands curled over his shoulders as he deepened the kiss. He made a throaty growl when her tongue slid over his lower lip.

Muttering something unintelligible, he backed her towards the bed, lowered her gently to the mattress, and covered her body with his.

"Damn, woman, what are you doing to me?" he asked, his voice gruff.

"What are *you* doing to *me*?" she retorted.

He grinned at her, a wicked gleam in his eyes. "I don't know," he said, stripping her of the sheet, "but whatever it is, let's not stop."

Four

Macie woke abruptly. For a moment, she stared up at the ceiling, unable to recall where she was. And then it all came rushing back. The horse. The journey through time.

And the man. Ah, yes, the man. She turned her head to see him lying asleep beside her. Just looking at Mr Tall, Dark, and Sexy made her toes curl. They had had sex again last night. No, it had been more than sex, but before she fell too much harder, she should probably find out a little more about him. Like, was he married?

The thought sent a cold chill down her spine. Maybe she should have found that out before they tumbled into bed last night.

Slipping carefully out from under the sheets, she pulled on her sweatshirt, stepped into her jeans, pulled on her boots. She had never been one to have casual sex, and although there had been nothing casual about what had happened between them, the thought of facing Bowdry in the light of day had her stomach tied in knots.

The creak of the bed, the rustle of blankets, told her he was awake. She could feel his gaze on her back.

"Goin' somewhere?" he asked.

"I need to . . . ah . . . use the . . ."

"It's under the bed."

Under the bed? Good Lord, did he expect her to use a chamber pot while he watched?

"Give me a minute and you can have some privacy."

There was no mistaking the amusement in his voice. Maybe she was being silly to be so modest after what they had shared last night, but she couldn't help it.

She bit down on her lip, listening as he dressed, remembering all too well how he looked in nothing at all.

Her stomach fluttered wildly when his arms slid around her waist and he kissed the back of her neck. "I need coffee, and lots of it," he said, his breath warm against her cheek. "How about you?"

"You're a man after my own heart, Ace Bowdry," she replied, feeling breathless. "I'm about a quart low."

Murmuring, "I'll meet you downstairs," he kissed her again and left the room.

Later, after eating breakfast in the hotel, Bowdry suggested they buy some new clothes. "You should have a dress," he said. "Something blue, to match your eyes. And I need a new shirt."

She couldn't argue with that. Falling into step beside him, they walked down the boardwalk to the mercantile. Oddly, it never occurred to her to object when he paid for her dress and a few other items she needed. Of course, the fact that she didn't have any money accounted for part of it, but more than that, it seemed as if she had known him for years.

"I've got a place about twenty miles from here," he said. "I haven't worked it in a while, and it's pretty run down, but I've been thinking about fixin' it up, maybe running a few head of cattle." He removed his hat and ran a hand through his hair. "Seein' as how you're new here, that is, if you've got no place else to go . . . hell, woman, I'm askin' you to . . . hell, it's probably too soon, but . . ."

"If you're asking me to come with you," Macie said, smiling up at him, "I'd love to."

"Well, hot damn!" he exclaimed and, lifting her in his arms, he twirled her round and round, oblivious to the startled looks on the faces of people passing by.

After another trip to the mercantile, where they stocked up on blankets, canned goods, coffee, salt, flour, sugar, baking soda and matches, they went to the livery stable where Bowdry bought a horse and a wagon to carry their purchases. He lifted her on to the high spring seat, then swung up beside her. Picking up the reins, he clucked to the horse. Relámpago trotted after them.

Macie's initial burst of excitement faded as they left the town behind. What was she doing here with a man she hardly knew? That thought haunted her in the days that followed.

As Bowdry had said, the place needed work and they spent their days cleaning up the rough four-room cabin. Bowdry made a trip into town and bought a gallon of whitewash and they painted all the rooms, which brightened the place considerably. Macie had never been much of a seamstress, but she bought several yards of gingham and sewed curtains for the windows in the kitchen and the bedroom. She ordered drapes for the living room from a mail-order house in the East. On another trip to town, Bowdry bought a new mattress and pillows for the bed.

At the end of three weeks, the cabin looked a hundred per cent better, and Bowdry went to work repairing the barn and the corrals. Macie helped as best she could, but she'd never been proficient at swinging a hammer and after she smashed her thumb for the third time, Bowdry sent her back to the house to bake a pie.

It wasn't the best-looking apple pie she'd ever seen, but Bowdry praised her efforts.

As their life settled into a routine, Macie grew more and more depressed. She missed going to the movies and shopping at the mall, she missed watching TV, hot running water and her computer. She didn't like doing her laundry in a wash tub over a fire, or cooking on a wood stove. She missed her microwave and frozen food.

They'd been living together just over a month when Bowdry said they needed to talk.

"I can't help noticin' you're not happy here," he said, not quite meeting her eyes. "I know you're probably used to better than this . . ." He cleared his throat. "And I know I'm not much . . ."

"It's not you," she said quickly. And it was true. She loved him more every day they spent together. He was as strong as an ox, yet tender with her, considerate of her needs. She had only to ask for something, and he did his best to get it for her.

"Then I guess you're missing your old life. If you're truly unhappy here, I reckon Relámpago will take you back home, if that's where you're meant to be."

That night, Macie stayed up long after Bowdry had gone to bed. Did she want to go back home? There was nothing for her there. And no reason to take her own life. In spite of what she had lost, she still had a lot to live for. She was young. She was healthy. And she had a man who loved her. But did she want to stay here? Could a woman from the twenty-first century ever be happy living in the past?

She was still mulling the answer to that question when she woke in the morning.

Stepping outside, a blanket wrapped around her shoulders to ward off the chill, she gazed at the land, and at the tall, dark-haired man who was chopping firewood near the barn.

She was about to go back into the house to start breakfast when Relámpago trotted up to the porch. "Hey, boy," she murmured. "What should I do?"

The stallion shook his head, then whinnied softly.

"I've been asking the wrong question, haven't I? The question isn't whether I can be happy here, in the past. The question is, can I be happy in the future without Bowdry? And you know what? The answer is no."

With her decision made, laughter bubbled up inside Macie. Life wouldn't be easy here, but suddenly, it didn't matter. She was here, with Bowdry, and that was where she belonged. In a flash of intuition, she saw herself married to Ace Bowdry, saw them raising half a dozen kids, growing old together, living happily ever after.

Bowdry looked up just then, a smile curving his lips when he saw her. He sank the blade of the axe into a piece of wood, then strode towards her, his dark eyes alight.

"You can go now," she said, giving the stallion a pat on the rump as she hurried towards Bowdry. "I'm home."

Steam

Jean Johnson

"So this house has just been sitting there, waiting for you to come along and inherit it?"

David refrained from nodding, since that would have caused his cell phone to slip from between his shoulder and ear. His hands were busy carefully pulling dust covers from strange pieces of archaic electrical equipment. "Yeah, that's right. I never even met this guy, but Mom and Dad, and even Grandma and Grandpa always swore he was like the family's Secret Santa, for decades. And 'Uncle' David left it to *me* in his will. Said his 'namesake' should be his inheritor. A pity he and his wife ended up disappearing during that hurricane . . ."

"Well, I hope it was a quick end. And all that Victorian chinoiserie will be right up your steampunk alley, bro," Kevin offered not unsympathetically.

"Actually, I'm more Edwardian than Victorian in my chosen era," David countered. He pulled yet another dusty sheet off a chunk of furniture and found a beautiful, wonderfully preserved oak roll-top desk. "Ooh, baby . . ."

"What, a sexy picture of a dame?" his best friend joked.

"Almost that good, bro. A late-nineteenth/early twentieth-century roll-top desk."

"You're sick, man." The tone of his friend's voice was more dismissive than disgusted, so David ignored the insult. "Listen, after you're done drooling over your Edwardian love desk, you wanna hit the pub for a darts game?"

"That's rather tempting," David admitted, gently rifling through the papers pigeon-holed in the desk, some of which were quite old and yellow, while others were a lot newer. A stack of old photographs, sepia with age, drew his attention. He pulled the pictures out, blinking in shock. They were of a beautiful young woman, her curls piled on her head in a Gibson hairstyle and her dress equally turn of the previous century. But her pose was anything *but* the staid, starchy, glassy-eyed stare of someone forced to sit still for several seconds while the photographic plates were exposed.

Instead, she had coyly unbuttoned her waistcoat and blouse and had lifted her breasts out of her corset, displaying them with a small but clearly lecherous smile.

He dropped the phone. Scrambling to catch it even as it fell from his shoulder, David almost crumpled the pictures as well. For a moment, he was all thumbs, juggling cardstock and plastic, until the pictures fluttered on to the desk surface. The disarray displayed more lascivious images, some half-hidden by the photos that had fallen face down. Gaping, David swallowed and lifted his cell phone back to his ear.

"Uh, listen," he stated, interrupting his friend's rambling comments about doing something or other at the proposed bar, "I just found some very important, uh . . . paperwork . . . that I have to . . . examine much more closely. I think it'll take me all night."

"Paperwork?" Kevin asked, his tone dubious.

"Yeah. Paperwork. Very . . . important . . . paper. Work. I'll chat with you later, OK? Bye." Thumbing the red button, he pressed and held it a second time as soon as the phone blipped, letting him know the call was ended. It blipped and buzzed a second time, letting him know it was now turned off. That left him in the privacy of a gadget-crammed attic with a roll-top desk that would have made an antiques collector weep, and some rather outstanding examples of turn-of-the-century pornography.

Writing on the back of some of the "paperwork" caught his eye. In lovely, large loops, a woman – presumably the one in the photograph – had carefully written, "To my B-beloved David, may this image I-inspire you to look deeper into the mysteries of love and life. Yours F-Forever, Elaine.'

Turning it over, he found his breath escaping him. David fumbled the chair out from the desk, shoved aside the dust cloth which had partially snagged on the oak-rail chair and sat down before the last dregs of blood vanished from his head. He arranged each photograph lovingly. *She's probably quite dead by now. These photos are from a hundred years ago. No one lives that long . . .*

He had always been fascinated with the turn of the previous century. When other kids were grumbling about having to take a newspaper route to pay for Walkmans and CDs, he had been dreaming he was a street urchin hawking papers on a city corner in the days of horses and carriages. When they chatted about the latest action movie, he had wanted to talk about the old silent films. And now, here in this house he had inherited, he had found a treasure trove of antique delights.

David had seen turn of the century erotica before, and had found the profusion of ruffles, the crispness of the muslin and the contrast between demure layers and exposed skin incredibly sensual. But those pictures usually had been taken rather impersonally, either for commercial sale – however discreetly underground – or for someone he didn't know. These pictures had been taken for someone he knew. Sort of. And the subject of all these photographs was beautiful. Long, dark hair, gleaming eyes, mischievous smile, little round spectacles perched on her nose in some of the pictures, and every last one of them was provocatively posed.

Those intimate bits of feminine flesh below her slender neck kept drawing his attention. He could easily imagine kissing her lips, her breasts, even the secrets exposed between her thighs. Knowing he had to move on, David reluctantly returned the erotic images to their pigeonhole in the desk. Studying them in depth could wait until after he had finished exploring the rest of the attic.

His fingers brushed against a book. He pulled it out and opened the plain, dark green leather cover to a random page, finding more of the same looping, feminine handwriting inside as on the back of the photos. It seemed to be a personal journal of scientific experiments of some kind. Sorting through to the front page, David found a piece of paper, much whiter and newer than the rest, tucked into the front.

The moment he opened it, he felt the blood rushing out of his face a second time – but not, now, from lust. It was written in *his* handwriting, and was signed with *his* signature, in the spiky loops that weren't quite copperplate.

Dear Me,
I realize you're not going to believe this at first, but it's absolutely

true. Follow all of her instructions, get this machine of hers going again . . . and she'll be yours. Eventually. (Certain courtship rules still apply, of course; take a couple weeks first.) "Compromise" is the key and "equality" the grease for this maiden's lock. Not to mention "S-steam". Don't worry; you'll understand in due time. Um, you might want to burn this note as soon as you know everything is true. Just in case.

David Maddock.

The real David – the one living in the twenty-first century – stared at the note for several long seconds. The chill in the attic penetrated his dazed thoughts. He adjusted the straps of his suspenders for comfort and cracked open the book once more. It wasn't an easy read, either, despite the lyrical quality of the writer's penmanship and her engaging, slightly rambling, almost conversational style; he was a computer programmer by trade, not an electrician, and never mind a physicist.

But the gist of the technical diary was how this woman, Elaine Cuttleridge, had managed to tap into what he guessed were nineteenth-century terminology equivalents of quantum wormhole physics, and powered it all by means of the several lightning rods he had noticed sticking up over the roof earlier; lightning rods which normally channelled all that energy safely down into the ground, but which, when switched over, could power the machinery cluttering up his newly inherited attic, causing its whirling cube of rings to link to itself four-dimensionally.

In other words, she had somehow managed to create a time machine. In his attic. Which he had deeded to himself in his own will . . . under the pseudonym of "Uncle" David Cuttleridge.

Twisting in the chair, David looked around the attic at the half-uncovered equipment. Well, a corner of his mind thought idly, that explains the archaic, accordion-style camera over in the corner. I must have taken these pictures of my . . . wife . . . myself . . .

His wife. For a moment, David felt dizzy with the contradiction between his bodily lusts and his mental quandaries. Shaking it off, he forced himself to concentrate. *If this is all true – if it is – then somehow I have to figure out how to get all of this stuff working again. Because . . . dayamn . . . that is one hot woman. Brilliant body and a brilliant mind, and somehow she ends up all mine? Predestination paradox, here I come! And – wow – how liberal she must have been, to be so willing to pose so naughtily …*

Another thought had him flushing hot and cold with the possibilities. If she *can* create a time machine, then I can go back in time. I can live in the era I've always wanted to visit! Of course, the medicine and the transportation technology levels would suck, he acknowledged, but just think of the possibilities. I could see Caruso perform in person, not just on some rusty, static-filled cylinder recording. I could invest in companies I could look up in the stock market's history books! And best of all, predestination paradox would work in my favour, because I know I'll have succeeded in going back in time …

… No, no, don't rush, he reminded himself, looking at the note he had penned to himself at some point in time. Romance is the key … well, along with compromise and equality. And "S-steam". Or did I mean "esteem"? Well, probably straightforward steam, given those photographs …

Flushing again, this time with excitement of a more cerebral and emotional nature, David hurried to finish uncovering and dusting off every precious piece of equipment in the attic.

Pushing his bowler hat back on his head, David lined up his feet on the floor and lifted the dart in his hand. The noise in the pub swelled for a moment, then quieted again, allowing him to hear the *thwup!* of his dart hitting the dartboard for a fifteen-point score. His teammate and buddy Kevin cheered, clapping him on the shoulder while the other two guys groaned. Turning around to face them, David caught sight of the television over the bar. The sports channel had given way to a weather update.

One of the words on the screen captured his attention: *Thunderstorm.*

"Uh … I gotta go, guys." Glad he had chosen to stick to a flavoured club soda, David grabbed his long brown duster and shrugged into the leather overcoat. He paused to fetch his darts from the board, packing them into their plastic case, and tucked the case in his pocket. "We'll continue this later, right?"

"But … we're winning!" Kevin protested. "And what is *up* with you and bad weather, lately? Ever since you inherited that house on the hill, you've been vanishing into it any time a thunderstorm rolls along!"

"Maybe he's fancying himself as a modern-day Doctor

Frankenstein," one of the other two dart players drawled, then laughed as he picked up his beer.

"Maybe I am." David flashed his friend a grin and a wink. Tugging at the brim of his hat to make sure the wind outside wouldn't sweep it away, David nodded a polite farewell to the three of them and left the bar. The drive home in his truck didn't take long, but the lightning was already flickering in the distance by the time he got out. Hurrying inside, David didn't bother to remove his coat. That storm was approaching fast, and he didn't want to miss a possible lightning strike.

As soon as he reached the attic, he double-checked the batteries of the flashlight on the neatly tidied desk. One of the many notes to himself he had found had concerned the power going out for a few moments. Once he was satisfied he would still have light if the storm overloaded the power grid, he moved to the switch board. They were large, stiff, old-fashioned levers insulated with glass and padded with rubber, and the thought of his Elaine – well, she wasn't *his* just yet – playing with such dangerous equipment made him nervous.

The flare of light and rumble of sound encouraged him to try. Grasping the wooden handles, David pulled each of the four levers down. The arrays of copper wiring, glass tubes, brass fixtures and those strange wire-wrapped hoops forming a sort of oval-sided cage . . . did nothing.

Nothing.

Disappointed, David wondered if he had done everything right. Some of the equipment had been replaced over the years by more modern versions, and he had added a few replacements of his own, mainly of things which had corroded or deteriorated with time. The instructions in Elaine's diary weren't always clear, though the worst parts had been appended in his own handwriting with terminology the twenty-first century man *could* understand. But the machine wasn't working.

It *is* predestination paradox, David reminded himself, staring at the inert machinery. I *know* these things are going to happen, because they already did happen. I—

KERBOOMMMM!

Dazzled by the flare of daylight-bright whiteness, deafened by the window-rattling explosion, David struggled to see and hear. He could feel every hair on his body prickling up at the sheer proximity of all that electricity. Blinking several times, he finally focused on the oval cage and found it glowing with an eerie purplish-white light. That light suddenly stretched inwards to the centre of the rectangular cage, shading from violet to blue, green, gold, red, and crimson where all the streaking lines met in the three-dimensional centre. Then they flared outwards again, opening into a rippling mirage of milk-white light.

It blurred the lines of the machinery visible on the far side, and distorted the voice, too, but not so far that David couldn't tell it belonged to a young woman.

"Oh! Oh, I did it! I actually did it! I've invented a temporal vortex! But . . . to the past or to the future?"

Prompted by all the notes and clues left by his future and past selves, David moved closer and called out to her. "To the future, my lady!"

"Oh! Uh . . . who is this, please?"

"David Maddock. I take it you are Miss Elaine Cuttleridge?"

"Uh, yes. Yes, I am. But I am T-totally surprised you should know my name – unless I'm F-famous in the future?"

Good grief, she even talks like she writes, David thought, amused. She didn't stammer, she *pronounced* the letter, stating it as *eff-famous*. He knew it had been an affectation in some American circles a hundred or so years ago, meant to emphasize a particular word by stating its starting letter as a sort of fancy prefix. *The verbal and print version of italics, back in an era where italic fonts hadn't been differentiated yet* . . . "I'm afraid not, Miss Cuttleridge. It seems I know you because I inherited this house . . . from my time-travelling self, in association with you."

"Oh – oh, that is utterly I-impossible!" she snapped, and the blurry, milk-water oval rippled. A tallish woman dressed in a waistcoat, ruffle-necked blouse, long skirts, and ankle boots, carrying a carpet bag in her hand, stepped through the milky oval. She did so very carefully, making sure to not brush the wire-wrapped oval frames with anything, not even a stray bit of hem. "I'm glad I made the transduction ovals big enough . . . It is I-impossible, Mr Maddock, because *I* am moving into the *future*. I refuse to spend any more time living in the O-outmoded past."

Her long brown curls, swept up at the top but left hanging free in the back, had auburn highlights. Her eyes were hazel green, and her chin was lifted in a stubborn, defiant tilt. Her declaration caught David by surprise, but his mind leaped swiftly through the variables of her claim.

"The future, my dear, is incredibly complex. First of all, you—"

"Don't patronize me!" Elaine snapped, lifting her chin a little higher. "I may be a 'mere' woman, but I am clearly quite intelligent!"

"I am *not* patronizing you. I'm explaining certain facts, of which you need to be aware in order to live in *this* century," David countered patiently. *I can see why I wrote myself a note; she's a real firecracker. Brilliant, beautiful and bearing a chip on her shoulder. A Suffragette as well as a scientist, if I'm not mistaken.* Glancing at the oval behind her, David saw the bluish-white glow beginning to fade. "Look, according to the notes I read, you will have five days in the future before the next thunderstorm rolls through and the machines can be linked again. Between now and then, I will show you the complexities of life in the twenty-first century. But *you* have to promise me to keep an open mind, and not prejudge me, thinking I'll treat you like a nineteenth-century man. I am not one."

Her hazel eyes glittered with wariness. "Go on . . ."

"First of all, you don't have an identity established with the government. If you don't have an identity, you'll find integrating yourself into the future to be very difficult. And if you claim to be from a hundred or so years in the past," David explained patiently, remembering to pick words she would understand, "they'll lock you up in a sanitarium, and throw away the key. I'm sure that's hardly the sort of future life you'd want to lead. Going back into the past – for select periods of time – will allow *both* of us to help establish an identity for you which you can use here and now in the future. But it must be timed and targeted just right.

"I could easily step into the past and establish myself as . . . David Cuttleridge. Or Marvin Melmack. Or James Earl Jones. And no one would gainsay my identity," David pointed out. "The government did not have the ability to gather and process information at the turn of the twentieth century that it has in the twenty-first century, so I could get away with establishing an identity in the past. For you . . . it will be a lot more difficult. Not insurmountable, but hard all the same.

"And there is another reason to go back into the past, and maintain ties to the past. A couple of reasons," David amended.

Setting her carpet bag down, Elaine folded her arms across her breasts. "What reasons?"

Trying hard not to think of her baring her breasts, David outlined his reasons. "First of all, this house needs to be kept intact and in good shape. If you abandon it completely to the future ... who will inherit it, what will they do with it and wouldn't some *stranger* dismantle all of your equipment, utterly ruining your temporal experiment? *Because* I found out all of the information I needed to know to make sure the machine was in working order, I *know* that you – and I myself – went back into the past, and probably did so several times, to ensure the sanctity of this house and its equipment.

"*Another* vitally important reason is funding," David added. This one, he had thought about quite a lot over the last few months, though not quite in these terms. "Maintaining a house for that long is an expensive proposition. Not to mention the funds we'll need to create the illusion that you do actually exist in the government records of this day and age. Money is a serious concern these days, because of inflation rates. A hundred dollars is a lot of money in your day, but in mine, it would barely feed a family of four for a week, if they were frugal."

"I see ... so you're proposing using *your* knowledge of the future to make sound financial investments in the past?" Elaine asked.

"Why not? These investments would benefit both of us," he pointed out. "You'd need my help just to *find* the right information. Yours may be the Industrial Age, but mine is the Information Age, and our methods of storing and retrieving data are quite complex. I could be quite valuable as a partner."

"Why should I trust *you*? Why not someone else?" she asked.

Lightning flashed in the distance ... and the lights in the attic blinked out. David heard her gasp, and moved back a few steps to the desk. Fumbling, he found the flashlight and switched it on, hearing her gasp a second time. "The power has gone out. It'll be back on in just a few minutes. In the meantime, I have a note from you, which is addressed *to* you, to be given to you when the power goes out. Which it has. I suggest you read it."

Playing the light over the pigeonholes, he found the little flat drawer underneath one side and slid it open. He heard her move closer and extracted the wax-sealed letter. Turning, he found her right at his side, her head level with his own. She must have been quite tall for her era, a corner of his mind observed. She was also still quite lovely, even with her face lit from below by the flashlight's reflected glow. For a moment, all he could see were the curves of her lips, which he wanted to kiss.

The lights came back on. Shaking himself mentally, David handed her the envelope. He watched her break open the yellowed packet and read the writing folded within. This close, he could see the blush staining her cheeks and the widening of her eyes. It made him wonder if he should have tried to read the letter himself in spite of its wax seal.

She flipped through the pages, gasped and covered her mouth, then flicked back and reread whatever it was she had written to herself. Twice, she darted a sharp look his way. David kept his expression polite, interested and mildly curious, despite his livid itch to know what her future self had written in the past.

Finally, she folded the slightly yellowed sheets and faced him. "According to this, you and I shall become quite the pair. Leading double lives, and doubled lives. Apparently our lifespans will lengthen and our aging will slow, simply by travelling through the vortex . . . and we will need to carefully note the exact times whenever lightning strikes the house, record it for our future selves and have our future selves send it back into the past. Plus, apparently, I figure out a way to target specific time-storms, if their exact dates and times are known. All except for these first two strikes, when I got my machine started, and when it connected to yours, precisely one hundred stellar revolutions into the future.

"My letter to myself A-also says that . . . well, that you are a sensual lover, a bit of a libertine and an R-rabid E-equalist. Even more so than your contemporaries," Elaine added, lifting her chin a little.

Mindful of his note to himself, David shrugged. "Why shouldn't I be? Actually, if you don't mind a bit of vulgarity, there's a poem I once heard which describes my feelings exactly."

Lifting her brows, Elaine folded her arms across her chest. "Go on . . ."

"'There is no difference 'twixt you and 'twixt me, save that one stands and one sits when we pee'," he recited.

Her mouth twitched. A snort escaped her, evolving a moment later into a giggle. Covering her mouth, she muffled her laughter, then gave up and dropped it, tipping back her head. Pleased he had amused her, David swept her a bow.

"Well, at least you are A-amusing, Mr Maddock," she admitted, dipping him a curtsy. "I think we might be able to get along in the days to come."

"David, please. If I may call you Elaine?" he asked, mindful of the old customs he had read about. "It's the modern way of things."

"Of course," she murmured. Stooping, she picked up her carpet bag. "So. Five days, you said?"

"According to what I've read, yes." A glance at her machinery showed it was now quiescent. Moving to the pillar, David lifted the switches so that any further lightning strikes would be diverted around the old building. "Now, let me show you the rest of the house," David offered, gesturing towards the stairs, "and all the improvements that have been made to modern life since your century."

The only thing good about his entire day was coming home. Otherwise, today had been very much a Monday. All he could think about was relaxing in front of the television with a good old movie. A comedy, maybe even a Charlie Chaplin classic.

Elaine had arrived on a Friday night, which had given him the rest of the weekend to introduce her to things like the radio, television, computer and internet. She had learned quickly. Entering his house, David found her seated on the floor next to the mahogany coffee table . . . with his remote control and DVD player scattered in pieces across its surface, and her face pressed to the top of a binocular microscope she had dug out of the basement.

There went his plans to watch a movie. She didn't even look up, just continued to look through the eyepieces. Covering his face with his hands, David groaned into his palms. He slid off his bowler hat and hung it up on the coat rack, removed his duster, and cleared his throat. She didn't look up.

"Elaine?" he prodded.

One of her hands lifted and fluttered in a vague greeting. At least she wasn't sitting in front of his computer, glassy-eyed from following too many Wiki-article links, or worse, stumbling across the shocking graphics of modern-day pornography. That had been an awkward experience, last night. All he had done was walk away for fifteen minutes, checked on their dinner, only to come back and find her as red as a tomato. No, this time she was calm, composed and the creator of this unexpected electronic clutter and chaos.

"Elaine, why did you dismantle my DVD player and the remote control?" he asked with as much patience as he could muster.

"Because I have an idea about these infra-red wave things, and the laser thing."

"The 'laser thing'," David repeated.

"Yes, as a targeting mechanism. I told myself I would come up with a means of specifically targeting a particular lightning storm, and obviously I did, but I didn't T-tell myself how. So I am investigating how." She paused and lifted her head to look at him, her bun shifting a little on her head with the movement. "Um . . . were these expensive things?"

Biting back another groan, David nodded. "Yes, expensive. More to the point, I have had a difficult day at work, with meetings interrupting my attempts at coding, errors induced by my colleagues, a boss who insists I work overtime next week, and all I wanted to do was come home, drink a beer and watch a movie. Just so I could relax. Only now I can't do that."

"Oh, I can put it back together," Elaine dismissed. Then paused and nibbled her lower lip, looking at the disarray of parts. "I think . . ."

Giving up, David closed his eyes. She wasn't a *messy* house guest; she did make her bed, pick up after herself, and had even offered to wash the dishes – by hand, until he had shown her the dishwasher – but she did do things like this. He heard the floorboards creak and opened his eyes. She had risen and crossed to him, and now gently touched his arm.

"If we prepared for the future, in the past, and made sound investments in the past based on our future knowledge, why not just use that money to buy a new DVD thingy?"

"Because while I inherited the house straight off, 'Uncle' David's bank accounts and stock shares were put into trust until my thirtieth birthday. Or until I married, whichever came first." Hands on his hips, David met her startled gaze. "E-exactly," he stated, using her trick of emphasizing the first letter. "For whatever reason our elder selves decided, the two of us are stuck on a budget until then. I have just had a stressful day from hell, and if I can't watch a movie . . . well, at least I'm going to go have a cold one."

"Erm . . ." Her hazel green gaze turned hesitant. "If you, erm, meant to have alcohol . . ."

Oh, no . . . Giving her a sour look, David asked, "What did you do?"

"Well, I'm a T-totaller, and I didn't like the thought of alcohol in my house – it is still my house, you know!" she added quickly, defensively. "If we're going to associate with each other in the past and the future, it's M-mine, too! So I gave it to your neighbour down the hill. All of it."

He stared at her, then buried his face in his palms again, muffling another, much more frustrated moan. Elaine patted him on the shoulder.

"There, there. You do sound rather stressed. Perhaps if you had a lie-down, and, erm, palpitated yourself? Well, I'm not sure if men actually can palpitate themselves, since it's a female thing, but perhaps there's a variation which can be applied to them?"

Sliding his hands down his face, David stared at her. "Palpitate?"

She blushed, then lifted her chin. "Yes. My mother's doctor told me about it. It's a medical technique used to relieve hysteria and stress in women. Surely you've heard of it in this day and age?"

Hysteria and stress . . . A snippet of learning from his wide-ranging study of the previous turn of the century resurfaced in his brain. *Doctors used to relieve "hysteria" in women by . . . masturbating them.* Flushing with a mixture of embarrassment and arousal, David reminded himself firmly that he was supposed to take a couple weeks at least in courting her first.

"David?" she asked, guileless and clueless, for all of her intellect.

"Uh, yes, men have something similar," he agreed. *Such as what I did after I found the photographs my future self will have taken of you . . .* "Um . . . don't worry about the DVD player. It was a little old, and I suppose I can afford something new. I'm just going to go up to my room and lie down, as you suggested."

With the photographs I took of you to study as I "palpitate" my stress away . . .

"All right, then – I am S-sorry for dismantling your thingy without asking first. I won't do it to anything else without double-checking," she added, her hand still on his arm. Pressing in sympathy, she hesitated, then leaned in and kissed his cheek. "Thank you for putting up with me, David. It's V-very sweet of you."

Yes ... yes, I do believe I feel the need for an attack of "palpitations" coming on, he thought dazedly. He headed for the stairs with a smile, enjoying the lingering impression of her lips on his skin.

Day ten of his first seventeen days in the past, David was longing for air-conditioning. It was a hot, humid summer evening, filled with the drone of insects and only the slightest stirring of the air as a sort of breeze. Although a man of the year Ought-Nine never took off his shirt in front of a lady, Elaine had taken pity on her house guest, permitting him to strip off his upper clothes. The straps of his suspenders chafed a little, but the occasional, rare puff of air felt too good on his naked chest to care.

Plus, she did slant her gaze towards his torso every few paragraphs, immersed though she was in a borrowed future book extolling the virtues of superconductors. David himself was trying to read back issues of the *Chronicle*, but the heat made it hard to concentrate on the articles in the "Local News" section. Part of his reason for reading the paper was his curiosity about how people lived and thought and, well, gossiped about each other. The other part was to make sure that Elaine's name wasn't besmirched by his presence.

So far no one had enquired as to where he was staying – a hazard since Elaine's father was currently overseas lecturing on the newest learnings in electricity to his fellow scientists, leaving her essentially unchaperoned – but he didn't want to take chances with her reputation. The hilltop house was fairly isolated in this age, with no neighbours at the bottom of the hill. They had, however, driven her father's automobile into town a few times already, with David introduced as "a fellow scientist and colleague of Mr Cuttleridge's" to explain his presence and peculiarities. That had come in handy when trying to explain away certain oddities in his speech and demeanour.

He tried to focus on a description of a soirée given by the mayor and his wife up at the county seat, but just couldn't focus. Groaning, he dropped his head on his hands.

"Stressed again?" Elaine asked, looking up from her book, which she had covered in plain brown wrapping paper to disguise its outlandishly bright cover. "Have you palpitated recently?"

He winced again and dropped his head to the table, slumping in his chair. "If I 'palpitate' any more, I'll palpitate myself to pieces." Wiping his forehead on his forearm only smeared the sweat around; it did nothing to remove the damp, sticky feeling. "What I *need* is a shower."

"I'm afraid all we have is a bathtub in this day and age," Elaine reminded him. "But if you mean to bathe, do not look to me to heat up your water. I'll go nowhere near the stove in this B-beastly weather."

"I'd rather have a C-cold bath instead," he muttered. "One more week of this, and then it's back to blessed air conditioning."

Elaine hmphed. "I distinctly recall suggesting that I come to the future again. But no, you insisted you wanted to live in the past. To revel in its lack of amenities. Well, R-revel all you want. It was your own choice."

"It wouldn't be so bad if you at least had a swimming pool," he pointed out, rolling from his forehead on to his cheek so that he could look at her.

Elaine looked up, but not at him. The thoughtful pinch of her brow intrigued him. Nodding slowly to herself, she picked up her book ribbon, marked her spot and set it aside. She nodded sharply and placed her hands on the table. "Up you get. I might not have a formal pool, but there is a small pond down at the bottom of the hill. Down about where that mini-market thing is located in your era. If we take a lantern and a blanket, some towelling cloths and so forth, we can go down there and . . . erm . . ." She paused, blushing. "No, that wouldn't work. You didn't bring a bathing suit, did you?"

It's been a couple of weeks, the devil in the back of his mind whispered. Or maybe it was the one in his trousers. David shook his head slowly. "No, I didn't. But I won't tell if you won't. This *is* a private pond, yes?"

"As private as it gets. The land goes down to the bottom of the hill, where the Attenborough Farm takes over; technically it's a stock-watering pond," she explained, "but the Attenboroughs have been pasturing their cattle on the west side of their property of late. However, there are many bugs to worry about. If you don't wear a proper swimming suit, you'll run the risk of being bitten in unpleasant places."

"Then the bathtub it is," he decided, pushing himself upright. "At least the windows of this house have mosquito netting on them."

"I am not going to heat any water for you," she reminded him tartly as he rose. "Nor am I going to pump it into the heating pails. I'm too warm as it is to work that hard. Though . . . well, a cold bath does sound like it would be L-lovely."

David grinned and flexed his arms. "No worries; I'll draw enough for you, too."

Pumping water for the primitive needs of the household was a better way to exercise than stopping by the gym. It didn't take that long to get the kitchen pump working, nor to carry two buckets at a time up the stairs. The activities of pumping, lifting, climbing and pouring worked his arms, waist and legs. The fourth trip was tiresome, though. The Cuttleridges had spent all of their money on fitting their house with the latest electrical gadgets, not on upgrading the indoor plumbing.

· Even the tank in the water closet had to be filled by bucket every third or so flush, though Elaine had mentioned her father had plans to rework the plumbing upon his return from his latest lecture tour in Europe.

Once the beautiful, nearly new, claw-footed tub had been filled halfway, David stripped off the remainder of his clothes. The water was somewhere between cool and slightly cold, enough of a shock that he sucked in his breath. The contrast to the humid evening heat was too heavenly to resist, however. Settling happily into the tub, he lazily scooped cool water over his chest and shoulders, and splashed some of it up on to his face, scrubbing away the residue of too much perspiration.

Just as he started to feel better, to feel human once again, the bathroom door opened. Startled, David splashed upright, then into a ball, trying to hide his groin from her view. Elaine poked her head around the corner. Her face was redder than the summer heat could account for, and she looked more hesitant than he had ever seen her before. Which wasn't all that hesitant, for after ascertaining eye contact, she stepped fully into the small room.

"Erm. . . I wrote myself a letter – as you may recall – and in it. . ." She hesitated, then reached into the pocket of her skirt and pulled out a small blue square. "Well, it instructed me to take a twenty-dollar bill out of your wallet on the last visit, and to go down to the mini-market to buy some of these. And to bring them back with me to here and now, to be used when you take a cold bath after I suggest you go and palpitate."

Heat suffused his face. It accompanied a tickle in his chest, which turned into a wry laugh. "No *wonder* you keep suggesting I should go and palpitate myself! You lascivious little . . .! Come here," David ordered, grinning and holding out his hand. She approached and handed him the little condom packet, blushing and smiling. Setting it on the shelf built behind the sloped back of the bath, David gestured at her clothes. "Well? Take everything off! You'll want to get nice and cool in here before we start heating things up again in the bedroom. And I did say I'd draw enough water for you, too."

She smiled and blushed, and started unbuttoning her ruffled white blouse. "I feel so N-naughty, doing this. And yet . . . so free. So future-modern."

"Whereas I feel so R-randy, and never so grateful for a lack of air conditioning in my life," David countered, grinning. Uncurling from the last of his protective huddle, he settled against the sloped back of the tub, displaying himself as well as enjoying her half-shy show. *Brains, beauty and boldness, all wrapped up in time-travelling papers and quantum-mechanic strings.*

She paused in her disrobing, catching sight of his erection under the cool caress of water bathing his flushed skin. The look in her eyes was almost the same one he had seen in that first photograph, that small smile with hints of lascivious pride.

Yes, these are definitely *a few of my favourite things* . . .

"Come here, my dear, B-beloved Elaine," David coaxed as she unfastened her skirt and shimmied her hips, helping her lower garments to drop. "Join me in the tub, and, together, we'll make some steam."

Climbing into the tub, Elaine argued, "I'm not so sure that steam should be considered a viable comparison, David. Electricity has so much more potential. Your own era proves my point."

Rolling his eyes, David pulled her down on top of him. "And I say, *steam*."

As their bodies met, his cool and damp from the bathwater, hers warm and sticky with sweat, he silenced her with a thoroughly modern kiss. Not until both of them were once again hot and breathing heavily did he release her.

"All right, I'll concede your point. Steam, it is," Elaine stated, pulling back just long enough to capitulate. She recaptured his lips with another kiss, proving herself as quick a student of passion as she was of everything else. Murmuring against his lips, she slid her hand boldly down his ribs, underneath the waterline. "Lots of lovely S-steam . . ."

Falling in Time

Allie Mackay

One

Precious lass. You're mine, do you hear me?
  I won't – I can't – live without you.
  Lindy Lovejoy, American tourist and expert on all things
Scottish, heard the words in her mind. But they were real enough
to make her heart thump against her ribs. Her breath caught, too,
and her stomach went all fluttery. In fact, if she weren't sitting on
her bed, bolstered by pillows and surrounded by maps and writing
paraphernalia, she was sure she'd melt into a puddle on the plaid-
carpeted floor.
  She did tilt her head and close her eyes, concentrating.
  Her room, surely the tiniest in the entire bed-and-breakfast
inn, was quiet. Darkness came early on autumn nights in
Scotland and if anyone occupied the room next to hers, they
weren't making any noise. Outside, the wind had risen and
fluting gusts whistled round the eaves and soughed down the
narrow road beneath her window. A glance in that direction –
she hadn't yet bothered to close the curtains – showed a steady
rain just beginning to fall.
  But she could still hear the man's voice. Deep, richly burred and
dangerously seductive, his words slid through her like smooth, sun-
warmed honey.
  I'll ne'er let you go, sweetness.

Lindy bit her lip, listening. He'd breathed the endearment as if he were right beside her, his chin grazing her hair and his breath warm against her cheek.

He was definitely a Highlander.

And he spoke with the kind of fill-her-with-shivers Scottish accent she thought of as a verbal orgasm.

Too bad he was a product of her imagination.

Lore MacLaren.

Hero of the Scottish medieval romance she'd been working on for years and that had only been rejected by – she opened her eyes and frowned – every agent and editor in the industry. At least the ones she'd targeted so carefully.

Not that it'd done her any good.

Biting back a curse she was not going to let pass her lips, she tucked her hair behind her ear and willed her character to stop talking to her.

Now wasn't the time for guilty pleasures.

Even if she was sure that having such a hot, realistic, full-bodied hero – a Highland hero, for heaven's sake! – had to be something really special in the super-competitive business of writing and selling romance novels.

Lore MacLaren would have to wait until her vacation was over.

The research trip that – she just knew – was going to result in her big breakthrough into publishing. She plucked at a loose thread on the bed's tartan duvet, almost afraid to acknowledge how much time, money and effort she'd vested in her plans. Anyone even halfway familiar with karma, knew how easy it was to jinx oneself.

But still . . .

Life could seem so unfair.

Some authors hit New York running.

She'd tried that and failed. Doing everything right and following all the rules had gotten her nowhere. Now she was going to take a detour.

If *Heather Aflame* wasn't wowing the powers-that-be, she'd knock them sideways with *The Armchair Enthusiast's Guide to Mythical Scotland*. In lyrical but concise, easy-to-follow language, she'd regale readers with insider tips on everything from how to drive on the left to finding hidden away entrances to Neolithic chambered tombs and other little known sites that most tourists never see.

Aspiring writers and maybe even some published authors would snatch the book off the shelves. Agents and editors would be impressed, hinting that she should pour her knowledge into writing a Scottish romance.

She'd sell Lore at last.

A fantastic two-book deal would be hers. She could then quit her job at Ye Olde Pagan Times, the New Age shop in her hometown of New Hope, Pennsylvania, where she worked such long hours some of the regulars often asked if she slept on a cot in the back room.

She'd never again have to urge someone to buy a sneeze-inducing bundle of bad-vibes-chasing sage.

Or suffer the equally pungent smell of some of the love potions and herbal treatments for masculine sexual dysfunction that were kept in a locked cupboard in one of the shop's darkest corners.

Sweet lass, I need you . . .

Lore's voice came low and husky. Lindy whipped around with a jolt, sure she'd felt his breath on her nape. Soft and warm, it had caressed her skin, making her tingle with desire and awareness. His words, deep and rough-edged, let her know that he wanted her with equal passion. But a quick glance showed that the room loomed empty. As before, nothing stirred except the damp wind outside her window.

She reached again for her pen and notepad, pushing her Scottish hero from her mind.

Sometimes it didn't pay to have such a vivid imagination.

But she was certain her hard work would always be rewarded.

If her *Armchair Enthusiast's Guide* took off, she hoped to someday earn a living by immersing herself in the world she loved best – medieval Scotland, with all its mystery and magic, and where, she knew in her heart, she should have been born if only some cruel quirk of fate hadn't plunked her down in the wrong time and place, leaving her filled with yearning for a life she couldn't have.

But she *could* write books set there.

Once, that is, she made a name for herself as an expert on the must-see Highland hot spots of Celtic mythological fame.

And that wasn't going to happen unless she stopped thinking about her romance novel's hero and paid attention to the task at hand – studying next morning's route to one of the most celebrated places on her two-week tour through Scotland's ancient landscape.

She peered at the Ordnance Survey map that covered most of her bed. The map was a Landranger 9 and detailed every inch of Cape Wrath, the wildest and most remote corner of Scotland. Just seeing all the squares, lines and minuscule place names filled her with anticipation. This was the part of her trip that most excited her. She'd never been to Scotland before, but she'd dreamed of it all her life.

Scotland's far north was where she belonged.

The next day's journey would feel like going home.

Already, she knew each twist and turn of the way. Every curve of the shore road, the slender crescents of golden sand and even the forgotten homesteads, each one little more than a tiny dot on her map.

Looking at them now, her heart skittered. Though nothing thrilled her as much as the special place she'd explore in less than twenty-four hours. Said to be a portal to the Otherworld as well as a favourite haunt of the fey, Smoo Cave would be the highlight of her trip.

She also meant to make it the *pièce de résistance* of her book.

Levering up against the pillows, she pulled the map on to her lap. But before she could trace her finger along the pink-highlighted stretch of road she needed to follow around Loch Eriboll and along the coast to Durness where the cave was located, the wind picked up, slamming one of the shutters against the wall.

Or so she thought until she remembered the window wasn't shuttered.

What if the banging noise had been the sound of her door flying open . . .?

Lindy's heart stopped and the fine hairs on her nape lifted. This part of Scotland wasn't exactly known for crime, but there were always exceptions. So she slowly looked up from the map and slid a cautious glance across the shadowy room.

What she saw took her breath.

A man stood silhouetted against the light from the lamp on the dresser. Tall, kilted and too rock solid to be her imagination, he wore a very real-seeming sword at his hip and had a dark, roguish air about him that made her mouth go dry and did funny things to her stomach.

He looked very much like Lore.

Especially when his mouth curved in a slow, sensual smile and he narrowed his gaze on her, his blue eyes staring with such heat she gulped.

"Ehhh . . ." Lindy's attempt at speech failed pitifully.

The look in the man's eyes became even more provocative, proving he didn't mind. "You err, sweetness." He took a step forwards, the lamplight gilding him. "I am no' called Lore MacLaren. My name is Rogan." He put back his shoulders, standing straighter. "Rogan MacGraith."

"Your name doesn't matter." Lindy jumped to her feet, finding her voice at last. "For all I know, you could be an axe murderer."

She highly doubted it. But drop-dead-gorgeous Highlanders didn't materialize out of thin air regardless of the popularity of paranormal romance. She also doubted they ran around teeny one-blink-and-you're-through-it Sutherland villages wearing great plaids and packing razor-sharp swords.

And she hadn't noticed any medieval re-enactors staying at the Talmine Arms.

Word was the only other tourists were an elderly English couple and two German bikers.

The proprietor had told her so.

Which could only mean . . .

Lindy grabbed a pillow and held it before her. "I don't have any money," she stammered, wishing his searing gaze wasn't so unsettling. "I'm at the end of my trip and—"

"Och, lassie." Mr Medieval was suddenly right in front of her. "If I wanted your coin—" he plucked the pillow from her hands and tossed it aside "—any sillers you might have would already be weighing down my purse."

He grinned and patted a small leather pouch hanging from his sword belt. Then the look on his face turned wicked as he grabbed her and pulled her to him, holding her so tightly that she could hardly breathe.

"I'm that fast, see you?"

"I see you're a mad man."

"Aye, that I am, true enough!" He released her, his gaze absolutely smouldering now. "So mad for you that if you dinnae cease calling me Lore each time I kiss you, I may have to kill an innocent man."

"*Kiss me?*" The absurdity of his words gave Lindy the energy to dart away from him.

He caught her, his big hand gripping her arm, before she'd gone two steps. "You'll no' be denying our passion?" His gaze went meaningfully to the bed and Lindy was horrified to see that it was no longer the narrow, plaid-covered twin bed she'd been sleeping on.

It was a huge richly carved four-poster, its sumptuously embroidered curtains pulled back to reveal a welter of furred throws, tangled sheets and a sea of tasselled cushions piled near the massive headboard.

Lindy blinked.

Rogan MacGraith's grip tightened on her elbow. "You are mine, sweetness. I'll no' be sharing you with any man. Especially no' a fool named Lore."

"Lore doesn't exist." Lindy couldn't take her gaze off the bed. It looked so real. "I made him up. He's fiction. Just like that bed and—"

"And what?" Rogan arched a brow, pulling her to him again. "This perhaps?"

Without warning, he lowered his head and kissed her, taking her lips with all the intimacy of someone who'd kissed, no *plundered* her mouth, many, many times. It was a hard, ravenous kiss, full of breath and tongue. Rogan held her tighter and deepened the kiss. Lindy's pulse raced and her knees almost buckled.

The kiss was much better than any she'd ever written.

In fact, no real man had ever kissed her so masterfully either.

Whoever – or whatever – Rogan MacGraith was, he knew how to curl a woman's toes.

She wound her arms around his neck and leaned into him, not caring about anything but the delicious tingles whipping through her. His shoulder-length hair felt thick and smooth beneath her fingers, almost cool and sleek like the pages of her map. But she ignored that incongruity and concentrated on how wonderfully his tongue swirled and slid so hotly over and around hers. Or so she tried, until running footsteps sounded on the landing outside her room.

Lindy woke at once and peered into darkness. Her heart was pounding and – dear God – she still felt all tingly and roused.

Rogan MacGraith was nowhere to be seen.

And the narrow bed she was lying in wasn't anything as magnificent as the curtained, black-oak monstrosity she'd glimpsed over his shoulder.

It'd all been a dream.

Except, perhaps, the hurrying footsteps she'd heard outside her door.

"Miss Lovejoy!" The innkeeper appeared at her doorway, proving that much. "Have you been disturbed? The storm blew out a window on the landing and—" he glanced over his shoulder, at the shadows behind him "—I'm checking for damage to the rooms. Looks like the gust threw open your door. I'm sorry if your sleep was—"

"I'm fine." Lindy noticed that her Landranger 9 map was still spread across the bedcovers. "I fell asleep studying my map and didn't hear a thing."

"Right, then." The innkeeper looked relieved. "The missus and I will be up a while yet if you'll be needing aught." He gave her a nod, glanced quickly around her room, and was gone, disappearing as quickly as he'd come.

His footsteps faded into the distance, the night wind howled and shook the window glass, and Lindy fought the urge to laugh hysterically.

She'd lied when she'd said she was fine.

She doubted she'd ever be fine again.

Everyone knew characters talked to writers. The stories would be flat if they didn't. Mere ink on the page and so boring that no one would want to read a single word.

It was also true that – sometimes – characters insisted on being named differently.

That, too, was pretty normal.

Stories only came to life once the names were right.

Kissing was something else entirely.

Yet she knew Lore – no, *Rogan MacGraith* – had kissed her. She could still feel his lips moving over hers, the silken glide of his tongue and the firm grip of his hands as he'd held her against him.

She'd even felt the rough weave of his plaid beneath her fingers. And – how could it be? – she'd breathed in his scent, finding the trace of the cold, brisk night that clung to him almost intoxicating.

But he couldn't have been real.

Shaken, Lindy slipped from the bed and went over to the window. The Talmine road lay dark and silent, a narrow band stretching away into empty, rolling moorland. It still rained and curls of mist drifted across the shingled beach not far from the inn. The pier was deserted. No kilted, sword-packing Highlander stood in the blackness of the moon shadows, peering up at her.

The tiny village slept.

She touched a hand to her lips and trembled.

Her mouth was bruised.

Two

Centuries away – the early fourteenth, to be exact – but much closer otherwise, Rogan MacGraith stood in the shadows of his bedchamber and glared at the shutter that had dared to blow open, its loud crack against the tower wall rudely snatching him from a wondrous dream.

"Hellfire and damnation!" He strode across the room and yanked the shutter into place, latching it with much more force than was necessary.

He shoved a hand through his hair, keenly aware of his nakedness.

Not that sleeping unclothed was anything out of the ordinary.

Truth be told, he doubted any man in all broad Scotland would demean himself by wearing nightclothes. Certainly no man at his clan's proud and formidable Castle Daunt.

Highlanders left such softness for Sassenachs.

But this night . . .

Rogan glanced downwards, his scowl deepening. His nude body only revealed how much he burned for the curvaceous, flame-haired vixen he'd just been kissing and was about to sweep into his arms and carry to his bed before the damnable shutter bang had shattered his dream.

"Odin's balls!" He clenched his fists and willed his manly parts to stop aching. When they did, he snatched his plaid off a chair and threw it on, not wanting any remaining vestiges of lust to embarrass him when he stormed down the tower stairs and into his father's hall.

It would cause a great enough stir just disturbing the men's night rest. The saints knew they deserved their sleep. But one of them might have heard the name Lore MacLaren.

If so, he meant to rout the bastard.

A lifetime of searching hadn't produced the temptress who haunted his dreams, but if he could locate the man whose name she cried in passion, he might just find her. Only then would he know peace.

He'd make her his, insisting she wed him.

And if she refused or – saints preserve him – for some reason wasn't able, he'd finally bend to his father's will and accept a suitable bride of his family's choosing.

He just hoped she wouldn't be Euphemia MacNairn, his clan's current favourite.

She was such a wee slip o' womanhood that a man could blink and miss her presence in a room.

But her tongue was sharper than the best-honed sword.

A fault she kept well hidden, though Rogan had no trouble seeing through her false praise and simpering airs. Her eyes, when she thought no one saw her, held a chill colder than the blackest winter night. And – Rogan shuddered – he'd rather guzzle brine than take her to wife, even if her sire was his father's staunchest ally.

At least the thought of her banished the painful throbbing at his loins.

Grateful, Rogan hastened from his bedchamber. But before he reached the stair tower, a dark shape stepped from the shadows, blocking his way.

"Ho, Rogan!" His cousin Gavin's smile was crooked. "Such a scowl! Are you on your way below stairs to announce that the sun willna be rising on the morrow? Or—" he waggled his eyebrows "—have you been dreaming of *her* again?"

"Her?" Rogan pretended innocence.

Gavin laughed. "Unless you cease blethering about the vixen each time you sink into your cups, you cannae think I know naught of her!"

"I ne'er 'sink into my cups'." Rogan tried to push past his cousin, but the lout shot out a hand, seizing his elbow in a vicelike grip.

"Once was enough." Gavin leaned close and winked, clearly amused. "Truth tell—" he flashed a glance over his shoulder and then lowered his voice "—if such a lush piece invaded my dreams, I'd stay abed all my days."

"You'll hold your tongue is what you'll do." Rogan shook free and glared at him. "Lest you wish me to silence it for you?"

He reached for the dirk that should have been tucked beneath his belt, but remembered too late that he'd tossed on his plaid and nothing else.

Gavin caught the gesture all the same.

Unfortunately, it only drew another laugh.

"I but speak the truth." The lout had the gall to clamp a hand on Rogan's shoulder.

"Why are you skulking about in the shadows?" Rogan changed the subject.

"I was ... er, ah ... visiting Maili." Gavin released him and brushed at his plaid. "You might be of a better temper, too, if you'd partake of her services now and then."

"I haven't tumbled a laundress since I grew my first beard." Rogan stepped away from the cold wind blowing through an arrow slit in the stair tower's thick wall. The chill reminded him of the coldness of his empty bed.

He did his best to assume an air of importance. "I have no time for such frivol. Some of us have weightier matters to attend, see you."

"In the middle o' the night?" Gavin looked close to laughter again.

"Snorri's gone missing," Rogan improvised, seizing the first thought that came to his mind.

His dog *was* out and about somewhere.

And considering the beast's age and bad hip, his disappearance from Rogan's bedchamber was troubling. Snorri rarely left Rogan's side. He even shunned his comfortable pallet by the hearth fire to sneak into Rogan's bed, often sleeping sprawled across Rogan's ankles.

It wasn't like the dog to be missing at this late hour.

Though – Rogan was sure – the well-loved scamp had no doubt crept down to the kitchens where he was known to beg meaty bones and other tidbits from Cook and the kitchen laddies.

Even so, if Snorri hadn't returned by morning, he'd launch a search.

"I was just heading out to look for Snorri now." Rogan started forwards again.

He wasn't about to tell Gavin he was on his way to ask his father's men about a man named Lore who, like as not, was as non-existent as his dream vixen.

Even so, he had to know.

"I saw Snorri trotting towards the kitchens as I was leaving Maili's pallet." Gavin's words stopped him.

"Ah, well –" Rogan forced himself not to continue down the stairs "– I'll be returning to my bed then."

He tried not to frown.

He should have known his cousin would somehow twist any excuse he used, making it impossible for him to complete his intended mission.

Proving it, Gavin nodded and folded his arms. He clearly intended to stay where he was until Rogan turned and tromped back up the way he'd come. Damn his cousin for being such a long-nosed bugger of a kinsman.

Rogan felt the loon's stare boring into his back even when he knew the tightly coiled stairs hid his retreat from the other man's view.

He still felt eyes on him when, moments later, he let himself back into his bedchamber. But the gaze he sensed now wasn't his cousin's.

The eyes he knew were watching him were amber.

And they belonged to her.

The dream vixen who now, damn her luscious hide, was apparently no longer content to merely haunt his sleeping hours, but his waking ones as well.

Rogan could feel her everywhere. In his room's darkened corners – the night candles had gutted hours ago and only a few cold embers glimmered in the hearth – and even right before him, tempting and beckoning, although he couldn't see her.

Her presence shimmered in the air.

Rogan stopped where he was, just a few paces from his bed, and tore off his plaid, letting it drop to the rush-strewn floor. He half hoped his nakedness might call her. So he stood still, waiting, challenging the silence. But the only thing that came to him was the smell of rain on the cold breeze slipping in through the shutter slats.

Until the wind seemed to shift, turning even colder. Then, beneath the night's chill, her scent slid into the room, teasing him.

Light and provocative, it was only a tantalizing promise. But just one slight hint of her was enough to fire his need and set him like granite.

She was near.

He knew it in the depths of his soul.

"Damnation." Rogan sank on to the edge of his bed and put his head in his hands.

Don't leave me.

Stay . . . I beg you!

The words – her words – came to him from a distant place. But although the beloved voice was hers, one so engrained on his heart that he'd recognize it anywhere, she spoke in soft lilting tones very different from the speech she used when she talked to him in his dreams.

You will be killed . . .

Rogan jerked, looking up. This time the words were close. No longer far away, her voice was as clear as if she'd spoken at his ear, pleading. And the words, so ominous and dire, had broken on a sob.

"Lass!" Rogan shot to his feet, glancing around, his heart thundering wildly.

How cruel that he didn't even know her name.

But – he could scarce believe it – he *could* see her!

She stood in the far corner, limned by moonlight. And unlike in his dreams, when she usually wore naught but a smile, this time she clutched a deep red cloak about her, holding fast to its voluminous folds as if a great gusting wind blew, chilling her.

Even more surprising, her lovely amber eyes were now deepest blue, glistening tears making them shine and sparkle like sapphires.

And her hair – Rogan stared, disbelieving – was no longer the deep, gleaming russet he knew and loved, but palest flaxen. She wore it in a single heavy braid that swung low, reaching to her shapely hips.

Ragnar . . . She looked right at him, calling him a strange name as she reached a hand towards him.

Rogan stared at her. How odd that she looked so different. And that she called him Ragnar and not Lore.

Frowning, he took a step forwards. But then his blood chilled, stopping him.

He could see the window shutter through her outstretched hand!

Indeed, now that he'd blinked a time or two, he noted that he could look through more than just her hand. The entire length of her – even her richly worked woollen robe – was as insubstantial as a will-o'-the-wisp.

Yet the strange woman was her.

His dream vixen.

He tried to go to her, but his feet wouldn't move. And neither would his lips when he attempted to speak. He could only stand and stare, watching as she faded into the moonlight, disappearing in a swirl of twinkling sparkles that danced on the air, taunting him, before they, too, vanished as if they'd never been.

"Thor's hammer!" Rogan scrubbed a hand over his face.

Even that one cannot help us . . .

The words came on the icy wind still racing past the windows. But even as he wondered if he'd really heard them, the night stilled. All was silent save for the muffled roar of the nearby sea.

Sure now that he was in danger of losing his wits, he strode across the room and thrust his hands into the corner where he'd seen the woman. But, of course, he felt nothing out of the ordinary.

Rogan frowned. He knew he'd seen her. He'd heard her, too.

Yet . . .

The more he tried to make sense of it, the more it tied his mind in knots. It was one thing to have heated dreams of a hot, passionate woman, but this was something else. And perhaps he could also be excused for enjoying their sensual encounters, real or imagined. He was, after all, a red-blooded man with needs and desires that made it impossible to resist such temptation.

But to have her suddenly appear as a see-through woman in his own bedchamber, calling him a different name and then vanishing before his waking eyes, tested even his limits of belief.

And as a MacGraith – hereditary guardians of nearby Smoo Cave, with all its inherent oddities – he'd been born to accept strange happenings.

This night he'd had enough.

So he crossed the room determinedly and climbed into his bed, pulling the sheets and furred coverings over him. The morrow would be soon enough to think on the things he'd seen and heard.

But as soon as he rolled on to his side and tried to sleep, he knew he wasn't alone.

She was in the bed with him.

Naked, warm, and supple as always.

Rogan's eyes snapped open. He couldn't see her – she was lying behind him, her full, round breasts pressing against his back. Equally rousing, she was sliding one sleek thigh up and down his in a slow, sensual glide that would bring any man to his knees.

Rogan groaned. His entire body tightened.

"Don't leave me." She spoke the same words as before. But this time she used the voice he knew.

The voice he loved.

Knowing himself lost, he turned to face her. His heart caught when he saw the want in her amber eyes. She reached for him, trembling as she wound her arms around his neck, clinging to him, begging his kiss.

"Lass—"

"Don't leave me," she pleaded again, just as he slanted his mouth over hers.

His heart pounded and he pulled her close, thrusting his hands in her hair as he kissed her. She opened her lips beneath his, her tongue slipping into his mouth, firing his senses even as he slid his hands from her hair down over her shoulders and to her breasts. He rubbed his thumbs over her nipples, almost losing his seed when they hardened beneath his caress.

"Lass . . ." He broke their kiss, pulling back to look at her. "I don't even know your name."

"But you know *me*." She bracketed his face, dragging him back to her mouth, silencing him with a deeper, more feverish kiss. "I am yours. I have always been yours. And—" she pressed into him, her silken warmth and lush curves taking his breath and blotting out everything in his world but her "—you, my heart, will always be mine."

"Aye, I am," Rogan agreed, believing it.

And then, for the rest of the long night, he knew no more.

Three

"You can be letting me out here, lassie."

Lindy glanced at the tiny black-garbed woman she'd picked up along the roadside shortly after driving out of Talmine village.

Grizzled and ancient-looking yet surprisingly spry, the old woman was leaning forwards to peer through the car's rain-splattered windscreen.

"That be the turn-off I need, up yonder." The woman sat back and rubbed her hands in glee.

Or so the gesture struck Lindy, flashing another glance at her strange passenger.

In fact, if she'd taken a better look before slowing the rental car that morning, she might not have offered the woman a ride. But she'd appeared harmless enough, hobbling along the edge of the road with a woven-wicker shopping basket on her arm. It was just too weird that on such a wet and windy day, the crone's heavy waxed jacket hadn't shown even a few speckles of rain.

And – Lindy really couldn't explain this – the woman's small black boots, jauntily tied with red plaid laces, weren't at all muddied or damp-stained.

But she did have kindly eyes.

Bright blue eyes that twinkled with merriment as Lindy drove past Sutherland's great mist-hung hills and through the dismal morning. And each time Lindy assured her that such wild weather and rugged landscape were the reasons she'd wanted to come to Scotland, her odd companion nodded enthusiastically.

"Och, I know." She trilled agreement, sounding as if she did. "There be some folk what belong here, they do. These hills are in their blood, no matter where they're born. And when that happens, there's naught what can keep them away. No' time nor the span o' the ocean." She bobbed her head again, sagely. "They always return."

They always return.

The old woman's words echoed in Lindy's mind as she scanned the winding road ahead, looking for the turn-off. But all she saw were miles of bleak moorland and the dark, choppy water of Loch Eriboll. Until her passenger grabbed her arm and pointed, indicating a narrow, heather track which could or couldn't be a path leading to a croft house.

"That's it!" The crone's insistence convinced Lindy.

And indeed, as soon as Lindy stopped the car and the old woman clambered out, Lindy spotted a low white croft in the distance. Half-hidden by the shoulder of a hill, the little house was thatched with heather in the old way and appeared to stand very close to the loch.

"I'd be for asking you in for a cup o' tea, but –" the crone turned up her jacket collar against the wind, her eyes bright in the watery sunlight "– you'll be a-wanting to get on to Smoo afore the day gets too long!"

She leaned close, saying something else, but great buffets of wind were rocking the car and the shrieking gale snatched her words away. Lindy only saw the old woman's lips moving. But she caught the almost mischievous wink she gave Lindy just before she stepped back and, turning into the wind, hobbled off down the path to the cottage.

A cottage where – Lindy only registered after starting to drive away – the two deep-set windows shone with flickering candlelight.

Lindy frowned and hit reverse, just to be sure.

Scotland did seem like a land where time stood still, but the last she'd checked, electricity was in use. Even in wild and remote Sutherland.

But when Lindy slowed the car and came to a halt where she'd let out the old woman, the narrow heathery track leading to the croft house was gone.

Lindy blinked.

Then she looked again, even getting out of the car and shading her eyes against the sun that was just beginning to break valiantly through the clouds.

But the track really wasn't there.

Nor was the low-lying croft house, though – the fine hairs on her nape lifted – the shoulder of the hill that had kept part of the cottage from view still ranged distinctively against the backdrop of the loch.

Lindy's heart began to pound and she whirled around, scanning the empty moorland for the old woman. But, of course, she, too, was nowhere to be seen.

Nothing stirred anywhere except a few clumps of scrubby, wind-tossed gorse and several wheeling seabirds, determined to take advantage of the howling gale whistling along the loch shore.

Then the sun dimmed again, once more slipping behind the clouds, and – for one startling moment – Lindy was sure she saw a man standing in the distance, watching her. Tall and broad-shouldered, he stood, unmoving, on a narrow curve of the dark, pebbly strand.

He looked as powerful and forbidding as the wild landscape surrounding him. In fact, Lindy swallowed, everything about him screamed that this was where he belonged. He was as much a part of the big, brooding sky, the sea and the dark, rolling moors as the cold, racing wind that seemed to quicken and chill the longer she watched him.

She could feel his stare.

It was fierce, almost compelling.

Lindy put a hand to her breast, unable to look away. The wind was icy now. It made her eyes tear, but she was afraid to risk blinking. The man hadn't budged a muscle that she could tell, but something about him made her believe that any moment he'd come for her.

He'd move – she just knew – with incredible speed, appearing suddenly before her. And then, before she could even realize what was happening, he'd pull her into his arms and start kissing her.

Or so she thought until the sun peeped out from a low bank of clouds again and she recognized the silhouette for what it was: the stark black outline of a tree. No braw Highland laird readying to stride across the heather and seize her. It was only a tree.

Feeling foolish, she turned back to her rental car and scrambled inside. She gladly turned the key in the ignition and drove away a bit faster than she likely would have done otherwise.

Thinking about how much the man – no, the tree – reminded her of Rogan MacGraith, didn't hurt either.

It also helped that she found the passing scenery almost surreal, as if she'd left the real world and driven straight into the fabric of her dreams.

Whatever the reason, she kept her foot firmly on the gas pedal and knew she was still in the twenty-first century when she spotted a sign for Smoo Cave. The attraction's tiny car park loomed quickly into view. And if she'd still had any doubts about reality, a small blue car, quite old and battered, was parked right in front of the little shop-cum-museum, claiming pride of place and letting her know she wasn't the day's only visitor.

Torn between relief and annoyance, she sat for a moment to collect herself and then climbed out of the car. She had to lean into the wind as she crossed the car park to the well-marked entrance to the cliff path. Incredibly steep steps led down to the cave entrance far below and she surely wasn't the first tourist to worry about the danger of being blown away at some point during the perilous descent.

Och, even auld as I am, I could take thon steps in my sleep.
You've no cause to fash yourself.

The words – spoken in the soft Highland voice of Lindy's earlier car passenger – came from right behind her.

Whirling around, she saw the old woman standing there. She still sported her heavy waxed jacket and the small black boots with red plaid laces. Her wizened face wreathed in a smile when Lindy blinked, her jaw slipping.

"Time's a-wasting, lassie." The crone tilted her head to the side, her blue eyes dancing. "'Tis now or never, lest you wish to miss –"

"I can't believe this is the place you said we couldn't miss!" A heavy-set woman, shaped roughly like a refrigerator and wearing a bright yellow oilskin, loomed into view, bearing down swiftly on the crone.

Except – Lindy's heart stopped – the crone was no longer there. In her place stood a thin, sparsely haired man wearing a wrinkled grey suit made all the more incongruous by his tightly knotted blue tie.

The old woman, if she'd even been there, had vanished into thin air.

But before Lindy could puzzle over what she'd just seen and heard, or hadn't, the overbearing woman gripped the man's elbow and marched him across the car park towards the battered blue car.

"I told you we'd find only wind and rain up here with the heathen Scots!" she scolded, her English accent – one Lindy usually found almost as enchanting as Scottish – losing its charm as the woman ranted at her husband. "Those steps are murderous. Only a fool would risk their neck traipsing down them, rain-slick as they are."

She threw a glance over her shoulder at Lindy, shaking her head before she gave her husband another glare. "Some anniversary trip you planned! We could be in Blackpool now, or Brighton. But no-o-o, you had to drag us up here to the wilds of—"

The slamming of the car doors cut her off, but Lindy could see the woman's jaw still working as she revved the engine. With a puff of smoke, the little blue car chugged away, disappearing down the road and leaving Lindy alone in the wilds of bonny Scotland.

That was what the woman had been about to say, after all.

Though Lindy was sure she'd have left out the bonny part.

More fool she!

Lindy was glad for the sudden peace that descended.

Somewhere a dog barked in the distance. But otherwise, all was silent except for the rhythmic wash of the sea, the wind and the cries of seabirds.

Lindy's heart swelled. This was her idea of heaven.

She turned back to the entrance to the cliff path, thanking the weather gods for such a damp, blustery day. Had the sun been shining and the lovely, remote sea cave baking under a Highland heatwave, there'd surely be people crawling about everywhere, ruining the atmosphere.

Spoiling the otherworldly ambiance she'd travelled so far to enjoy.

Now . . .

She couldn't have wished for a more perfect day.

Eager to plunge right into it, she rolled her shoulders and splayed, then wriggled her fingers, before starting down the narrow steps to the rocky little bay and the cave at the base of the cliff.

Her descent raised the hair at the nape of her neck, made her breathing difficult. She'd only gone a short way when her scalp tingled and, in a momentary flicker, her long flaxen braid swung round from behind her, bouncing against her hip and into her sight. She stopped in her tracks, her blood freezing.

She didn't have long flaxen hair.

And she hadn't even worn braids as a child.

Her hair was auburn and reached just past her shoulders. At the moment, it was caught back by a clip, because of the wind and how much it annoyed her to have the strands fly across her face, whipping into her eyes.

She knuckled her eyes now.

She couldn't have mistaken her hair for a long blonde braid. She'd surely just caught a reflection of the sun glancing off the water. It wasn't a bright day, but there were moments when the cloud cover parted a bit.

Even so . . .

She shivered and rubbed her arms, glad when she again caught the sharp barking of a dog. She liked dogs. And this one's barks lent an air of normalcy to a day that was beginning to turn just a tad too unusual for her liking.

She saw the dog then. And when she did, she knew such a strong rush of relief that she almost laughed out loud at her nervousness.

Huge, grey and scruffy, the dog looked old. He wasn't wearing a collar and a tag either. But he seemed to be enjoying himself as he trotted along the damp shingle, pausing now and then to sniff at tide pools near the dark-yawning entrance to the cave.

Hoping to catch a good picture of him – after all, such a shot would look grand as an accompaniment for her *Armchair Enthusiast's* chapter on Smoo Cave – she dug into her jacket pocket for her digital camera.

Just as she pulled it free, something caught her eye and she glanced around, sure it'd been one of the seabirds she'd seen earlier.

She didn't see any birds, but she did note a heavy bank of thick, roiling mist far out at sea, its drifting, grey mass almost blotting the horizon.

Lindy stared, shivering.

The wind felt icier now. And she was sure her imagination had kicked into overdrive but she'd swear the air smelled different. It seemed tinged with a deeper, brittle kind of cold one might expect to find in Iceland.

It was definitely a crisp, Nordic type of cold.

Lindy frowned.

She could almost taste the snow. She half expected to see little sparkly bits of frost clinging to her jacket sleeves when she looked down to examine them.

But, of course, she saw no such thing.

Yet she did see something extraordinary when she glanced up again.

Three large open-hulled boats were pulled up at the water's edge, their elaborately carved prows and rowing oars proclaiming their identity. Not to mention their square sails, raised and ready, and the colourfully painted shields hanging along the wooden sides.

They were exquisite replicas of Viking longboats.

Lindy stared, eyes rounding.

They looked so real.

The bulky fur-wrapped packages and wooden barrels and crates crammed into the narrow space between their rowing benches looked equally authentic. Clearly provisions, the supply goods indicated that the re-enactors were about to embark on a staged journey and not a warring raid.

Only . . .

Lindy gulped.

The little group of men who came into view just then, striding down the opposite cliff path, didn't look like modern-day men dressed up as Viking re-enactors.

They looked like the real thing.

Worst of all, one of the men near the front, leading the others down the steep cliff side, was *him*. The man she often dreamed of and who she'd named Lore in her romance novel, but now knew to be Rogan MacGraith.

Except – Lindy's heart tripped – when a tall blonde-braided woman in a flowing red cape appeared at the top of the bluff, her hair and her cloak whipped by the wind, Lindy knew that the man she was staring at was named Ragnar.

In that instant, she also knew that she'd once been the woman.

She'd fallen in time, and was reliving a fateful day that had changed her life ever after.

Tears streamed down the woman's face and, even from here, across the cove, Lindy could see how the woman's anguished gaze stayed pinned on the man as he strode purposely down the path, making for the longships.

He was heading to his death, Lindy knew.

She could feel the woman's pain clawing at her heart, ripping her soul.

"No-o-o!" Lindy wasn't sure if she'd yelled, or if the red-cloaked woman on the other cliff top did, but the cry echoed in the cove, causing the men to pause and swing round to stare up at the woman.

Lindy watched her, too, looking on as the woman pressed a fist against her mouth and shook her blonde head as Rogan – no, Ragnar – called something up to her. But whatever it was, the wind took his words and Lindy couldn't hear what he'd said.

Then he turned away again and, for an instant, his gaze caught Lindy's. He froze, shock and recognition flashing across his face before he whipped back around to stare up at the woman on the cliff.

Only she was gone.

And before Lindy could see his reaction, he disappeared, too. His little party of men and the three beached longboats vanished as well, the entire scene erased from view as if none of it had ever been.

Yet Lindy knew it had.

She'd just glimpsed her own past.

"Oh, God!" She started to tremble. The camera slid from her hands, bounced twice, and began clattering away. "Damn!" She grabbed at it, but her foot slipped and she plunged forwards, tumbling down the remaining steps.

Blessedly, they weren't that many, but she slammed painfully on to her knees all the same, flinging out her arms to break a worse fall. Even so, she feared the hard shingle might have cracked her kneecaps. And her hands were definitely bleeding. They hurt badly, burning like fire.

"Oh, God . . ." Shaken, she slumped against a rock just as the dog she'd seen earlier came bounding up to her, barking excitedly and wagging his tail as he scampered close to sniff at her scraped and bloodied knees.

"Snorri!" A man's deep voice called the dog away. "Leave the lass be."

"Oh, God," Lindy gasped again, recognizing the rich burr. "It's you! Lore . . . Rogan!"

And then, just as she glanced up, seeing indeed that it was him, a sea of stars flittered across her vision and the world went black. But not before she felt strong manly arms slide protectively around her. They were familiar arms and so dear, nothing else mattered but knowing that Rogan MacGraith was lifting her, holding her safe.

She'd come home at last.

Wherever – and *whenever* – that might be.

Four

Her hands were bandaged.

And – this is what really woke Lindy – someone was kissing her fingertips.

That same someone was also murmuring Gaelic love words, his breath soft and warm against her skin. Lindy's heart skittered and she opened her eyes, looking into the face she'd loved forever. She knew that now, the surety of it filling her with a completeness, a sense of rightness and contentment, such as she'd never known.

At least not in the twenty-first century life she'd left behind.

That she was now somewhere else was clear.

The evidence was all around her. But most of all, she felt it inside her. She'd been returned to a place and time she belonged, it was like nowhere else. If she had any doubt – which she didn't – the love shining in Rogan MacGraith's eyes as he sat beside her on the huge medieval four-poster bed, told her everything she needed to know.

The important things, anyway.

Such as how much she meant to him and how glad he was to see her.

That his dog – the one she'd seen below the cliffs, when she'd fallen – stood beside the bed wagging his tail and looking at her with adoration was another boon.

She was definitely welcome here.

The dog edged forwards to nudge her with his nose, proving it.

His master grinned, the sight warming her to her toes.

"Precious lass." Rogan's voice, so deep and deliciously burred, was even more seductive than in her dreams. "I would spare you every hurt, but if you had to fall down the cliff to come to me, then—" he kissed her hands again "—I thank the gods for the misstep that brought you into my arms.

"And now that I have you—" he reached to smooth the hair back from her face "—I would know your name at last."

"Lindy." She didn't want to speak. It was bliss just to listen to his beautiful voice. "My name is Lindy. Lindy Lovejoy."

"Lindy." He made her name sound like a song. "'Tis a fitting name for one who fills my heart with such gladness. Sakes, lass—" he took her face between his hands, kissing her soundly "—when I saw you fall, I thought I'd lost you. To have you so close, within touching distance and then . . ." Rather than finish, he pulled her hard against him, almost crushing her in his arms. "You are mine, Lindy. Now that you're here, I will never let you go."

Lindy almost swooned. "You won't have to. I'm here now and I'm not going anywhere."

She hoped that was true.

It was so hard to believe he really was holding her. Running his hands through her hair, touching her face, and – oh, joy! – kissing her.

She wasn't dreaming.

This was real.

And – she suddenly realized – with the exception of the linen bandaging wrapped around her hands, she wasn't wearing anything. She was naked. Though, proving medieval gallantry, someone had taken care to cover her with a soft furred throw and a lustrous welter of silken, richly embroidered sheets. She was also leaning back against a sea of plumped pillows.

Her comfort clearly mattered.

But her clothes . . .

They were definitely gone.

As if he'd read her thoughts, a slow, dangerously sexy smile curved Rogan's mouth. "You couldn't stay garbed as you were. I had to—"

"You undressed me?" She blinked. The notion both excited and embarrassed her.

"You'll no' deny I've done so before?" His smile reached his eyes, the effect positively wicked. "Many times, it's been, aye, if I were to count."

"I know that." She spoke the truth. He'd undressed her a thousand times, in her dreams and fantasies. In the pages of her umpteen times rejected romance novel. And, she now suspected, he'd also done so in other lifetimes such as a Viking.

She tightened her arms around his neck, half afraid he'd disappear. "What I don't understand is how I came to be here. How did you find me?"

He glanced at his dog. "Truth to tell, it was Snorri. He'd gone missing and when I went searching for him, I heard his barks and followed, knowing he'd be at the cave. I reached the strand just in time to see you falling."

"You didn't see me before?"

"Oh, aye." He grinned. "In my dreams, nigh every night, if you'd hear how it was."

He patted his dog's head, scratching the beast's ears. "You can ask Snorri. We keep no secrets from each other. He knows how I've pined for you."

"That's not what I meant." Lindy hesitated, aware of the heat staining her cheeks. "I know we've shared dreams. But there's more. I'm certain –" this was so hard to say "– we've shared past lives. That we've always been together, but this time something went wrong. I was born in the wrong place. Somewhere distant and far from here and impossible to reach you, until—"

"The cave brought you back to me." He made it sound so easy. So plausible.

Lindy frowned. "Smoo Cave? So it really is a kind of time portal? An entrance to other realms as all the lore and legend claims?"

She so wanted to believe.

Rogan was nodding as if he did. "I canna say if the cave is a time portal. Though, after seeing your clothes, I'll own they did no' come from any world that I know." He stood and started pacing. "That's why I left them in the cave. There are cracks and crevices so deep that no man can retrieve anything that is thrown into them. And—" he came back to the bed, once more sitting on its edge "—strange as Smoo is known to be, I couldn't allow my kinsmen to see such raiments. Your shoes alone would have caused too many questions. That is why I stripped you." His gaze flashed the length of her, the look in his eyes burning her as if he could see her nakedness right through the thickness of the furred covering and bed sheets.

"And you're not curious yourself?" Lindy had to ask.

His gaze burned even hotter. "All I care about, sweet, is having you with me."

Taking her in his arms again, he kissed her thoroughly, leaving her breathless when he pulled away. "You could have come to me draped in seaweed or glittering from head to toe in twinkly starlight and it wouldn't have made a difference. I only want you."

"But –"

He pressed a finger to her lips. "There are no buts in my world, Lindy-lass. Though I will tell you that, as a MacGraith, I slipped into this life knowing that there are things we canna ever hope to explain.

"MacGraiths are the hereditary guardians of Smoo Cave. Since time was, we have been here at Castle Daunt, watching always to ensure that nothing passes in or out of the cave without our knowledge."

Lindy stared at him. "So you're fairies?" The plots of countless paranormal romance novels came to mind. "Immortals guarding the entrance to—"

"Guarding, aye, but we're no' immortal." He laughed, grinning again. "We're flesh-and-blood men, as rock solid as any other man." His smile turned wicked again and he pulled her back into his arms, holding her close. "You should know how solid I am, Lindy-sweet."

She flushed, knowing indeed.

His *solidness* was very apparent, though neither one of them had yet acknowledged the obvious.

It was one thing to be naked together and burn up the sheets in a dream. Being naked in his arms *for real* was both a wildly exhilarating thought and flat out terrifying.

And not alarming without reason.

Trying to be discreet, Lindy cast an assessing glance at her well-covered body. The sad fact was that, although Rogan was undoubtedly passionately in love with her in fantasy form, the *real* Lindy Lovejoy might just be packing a few pounds more than the dream edition.

Sure that was true, her cheeks flamed brighter.

How sad that her love of fish and chips had kept pace with her around Scotland.

Not to mention haggis with neeps and tatties.

Or steak and ale pie.

Lindy frowned, wondering if she could just stay hidden beneath the covers forever.

A notion that brought another, equally disturbing thought. How could she think in terms of eternity when she might only be here a nano-second? She'd spent too many hours working at Ye Olde Pagan Times not to be well versed in the ins and outs of all things supernatural.

Her manifestation in Rogan's time had surely upset the balance in her own world.

Something somewhere wasn't right.

It was kind of like plucking a thread from a knitted sweater. No matter how carefully you pulled, a hole appeared.

"Oh, God." Dread tightened her chest and heat burned her eyes, blurring the richly appointed room and all its lush, oh-so-real medieval trappings.

Rogan sprang off the bed. "What is it?" His gaze flew to her injured hands. "Are you in pain? Did I tie the bandages too tight?"

Snorri barked, sharing his master's concern.

"Or—" Rogan jerked a glance at the door "—shall I call for the clan hen wife? Perhaps you hurt yourself worse than we know. You might be in need of—"

"No." Lindy stood, careful to snatch a pillow and hold it strategically. "I'm fine, really. It's just that—"

"Here—" Rogan swirled a plaid around her shoulders "—I'll no' have you taking a chill." He strode across the room and yanked the shutters tight, dusting his hands as he turned back to her.

But not before Lindy caught a look at the view. A cold drizzle was falling and she'd seen mist, lots of drifting curtains of mist. But she'd also seen endless rolling moorland and dark, rugged hills. A vast wilderness that stretched as far as the eye could see. It was also a landscape covered with thick woods.

The Scotland she'd left hadn't been anywhere near as forested.

Needing to be sure of what she'd seen, she gripped Rogan's borrowed plaid more tightly about her and went to the window, opening the shutters he'd just closed.

She hadn't been mistaken. She really was looking out at medieval Scotland.

And if the scenery wasn't proof enough, the deep silence was. Only a world truly empty of everything modern could be so still.

And the *texture* of the air! Even with the damp gusting wind and all the mist, everywhere she looked, the world seemed filled with light and colour in ways she'd never have believed possible. Almost like an uncut jewel, sparkling in its purity.

Lindy gulped, her heart splitting. It was as if she'd stepped inside her own story.

She so wanted to stay here.

"Just *what*, lass?" Rogan's arms went around from behind and he pulled her back against his chest. "Tell me what's troubling you."

Lindy bit her lip. She was *not* going to cry. "I . . . it's just that—"

"Ho, Rogan!" The door flew open and a young man burst into the room. Big, hairy and kilted, he looked like he'd just stepped off the set of *Rob Roy* or *Braveheart*. But for all his fierce appearance, the slack-jawed, owl-eyed stare he gave Lindy made him much less intimidating.

"It's herself!" He raised an arm, pointing. "Your dream vixen! You've described her so often, I'd know her anywhere."

"You're forgetting your manners." Rogan scowled at him. "MacGraiths know better than to gawk at women, whoe'er they might be. This loon, if you're curious—" Rogan glanced at Lindy "—is my cousin, Gavin."

"My lady." Gavin bobbed his head, the crookedness of his smile revealing a chipped tooth.

The introduction made, Rogan crossed the room in three swift strides and took the younger man by the elbow, turning him back towards the door. "Away with you now and hold your flapping tongue."

"I canna. Your da sent me up here with grim tidings." Gavin broke free and swatted at his mussed sleeve. "One o' the men just hastened in from Smoo. Lady Euphemia was walking along the cliffs above the cave and before he could call out a warning—" he paused, throwing a look at Lindy "—she slipped into one o' the sinkholes. He swears he saw her go down and even heard her scream, but when he ran over to the edge o' the crevice and peered in, she disappeared."

Lindy gasped.

Rogan slid an arm around her, drawing her near. "The tide washes in and out of the sinkholes. Have men searched the beach? Or, if there's no sign of her there, have they taken out boats? She could have been washed out to sea and might be in the water around the cliffs."

"To be sure they've done all that, but they won't be finding her." Gavin sounded convinced. "She's gone, sure as I'm standing here."

"No one can be sure until a thorough search is made." Rogan started steering his cousin out the door again. "Others have fallen into the sinkholes only to be found later, wandering the moors, as well you know."

"Did you no' hear me, man?" Gavin thrust his jaw. "I said she disappeared when the guard peered o'er the edge, into the sinkhole. He saw her right enough and then, like mist before the sun, she vanished!"

"And how ale-headed was the guard, eh?" Rogan shoved his cousin out the door and slammed it behind him, this time sliding the drawbar in place.

"I'm sorry, lass." He turned to Lindy, reaching for her. "Dinna let Gavin's blethering—"

"I don't think he was." Lindy moved away, thinking again of sweaters and pulled threads. "That woman's disappearance will be my fault. I came here and, as is the way with such things, someone had to be sent forward to my time." She paused, leaning against a table. Guilt swept her. "It's because of me that an innocent—"

"Euphemia MacNairn lost her innocence the morning she awoke and discovered she had breasts." Long strides brought Rogan to where she stood. He braced his hands on either side of her, caging her against the table. "I regret speaking poorly of her if she truly has come to harm. But you need to know, as you'll hear it soon enough, that she was my clan's choice for my bride. I resisted because—" he leaned close and kissed her, slow and deep "—I knew you'd come to me someday, somehow.

"And—" he straightened, his expression solemn "—because Lady Euphemia was the last female I'd have wed, regardless. There's no' a laird or kitchen laddie in these parts, save o' this clan, that she hasn't bedded."

"But—"

"I told you, Lindy-lass, no buts."

"Even so—"

"None o' those either." Rogan shook his head. "Truth is, Lady Euphemia has been trysting with a shepherd who has a cottage in the next glen. She has to pass by Smoo Cave on her way to meet him." He stepped closer and cupped Lindy's chin, lifting her face to his. "That'll be what she was about. A pity if she fell into one of the sinkholes. But she should have thought of the danger thereabouts before she traipsed across those cliffs.

"Now—" he set his hands on her shoulders, looking down at her "—I'd hear what was fashing you before Gavin came bursting in here."

Lindy glanced aside. She still believed the MacNairn woman had been sent forward in time. And if so . . .

"I don't want to be responsible for someone else's misery." There, she'd blurted the only honourable thing she could say.

Rogan lifted a brow. "If Lady Euphemia has replaced you where'er it was you hail from, sweetness, I promise you, she'll no' be unhappy. Such females know well how to fend for themselves."

"Then . . ." Lindy considered.

"Do you want to stay with me?" Rogan's arms were around her again, pulling her close.

So near that she could feel him pressing against her.

"You know I want that – to stay with you." She leaned into him, unable to resist.

"Then do." He swept her up into his arms, carrying her across the room. "Stay here and be my wife."

"I will." She didn't care that the plaid fell from her shoulders as he lowered her to the bed. As for her few extra pounds, the smouldering look in Rogan's eyes said he didn't see them.

Oh, yes, she'd marry him.

In her heart, she already *was* his wife.

She didn't want to dwell on it too deeply, for fear of jinxing herself, but she believed that, after losing him in their Viking life, whatever powers watched over souls had now reunited them.

For a moment, she wondered if such gods or their helpers might wear small black boots, carefully tied with red plaid laces. The thought made her smile. Seeing as she was here, she supposed it was possible.

It was just a shame she'd not be able to put her experiences in a romance novel. She was sure that if she could, her book would be a bestseller. But then Rogan was throwing off his plaid and stretching out on the bed beside her, and she no longer cared.

And as she opened her arms to him, pulling him down to her, she knew she'd never feel the urge to read or write a Scottish medieval romance again.

After all, why should she?

As of this moment, she was living one.

Future Date

A. J. Menden

1

Surely I'm stuck in a time warp, Ella thought. That's the only logical explanation. Time can't be moving this slowly.

She looked across the dinner table to her companion, and he gave her a too big smile, one that showed rows of crooked, yellow teeth with a bit of salad stuck between two of them. Ella suppressed a groan of dismay. No, it was no time warp that had her in its clutches. It was only another blind date from hell.

"Soulmate, my ass," she muttered under her breath. There was no way this man was her mystical other half, the one she should be bonded to for life.

No matter what the New-Age-y online dating website claimed.

This was the latest in a long line of dating websites and agencies Ella had visited, and it was definitely going to be the last. She had only started visiting the self-proclaimed matchmakers of the new millennium since her mother began nagging her about finding a boyfriend. As a kindergarten teacher, she didn't meet many single men, and the few that she did didn't interest her. That was the problem; Ella never met a man who she wanted a second date with.

This latest prospect, Bachelor Number Three from the Soulmate Agency, was definitely not getting a second date. For one thing, his table manners were not much better than any of her students, and they were five years old, not thirty-five. As soon as the salad had arrived, she knew it wasn't going to be pretty. He had already started chewing on the ice in his drink, a habit that set her teeth on edge, and, sure enough, he was the type to smack his lips when he chewed.

Bad table manners might be something Ella could overlook in the right guy. Maybe no one had taught him any better growing up, and it was something that could be fixed with a gentle reminder. But his personality was no better than his manners.

"Don't see how you do it every day," he was saying as he cut into his steak, causing blood to flow out all over the plate, making her stomach turn.

"I'm sorry?" she said, trying to draw her eyes away from the gore in front of her. She liked red meat as much as the next person, but just something a little less likely to "moo" during the meal.

"Trapped in a room with twenty screaming and whining brats all day long, five days a week, with no break. You must have nerves of steel."

"You don't like children?"

"They're OK as long as I don't have to deal with them for long."

Ella blinked. "Your profile said you were the divorced father of two."

"Yep. My ex-wife was the one that wanted them. Don't get me wrong, I love my kids," he rushed on to say quickly, as if he could sense her outrage and wanted to cut it off at the pass. "But I never really saw myself ever having kids. It was something she wanted and I did it for her. I see 'em every other weekend and by Sunday I'm completely stressed out and ready to drop them back at their mom's. Don't all of those kids drive you nuts?"

"Sometimes, but that's true with any job," Ella said, wondering why Serena hadn't called her yet. She was incredibly glad she had insisted on meeting her date at the restaurant and had her own means of escape. After the date with the guy who turned out to be married and was looking for a little thrill on the side, she and her best friend had devised a method for getting her out of bad dates. Serena would call halfway through the meal. If Ella was having a good time, she would remember she accidentally left her cell phone on and turn it off. If she wasn't, she could answer and get out of there.

So far, Ella had never accidentally left her cell phone on.

The waiter came by to check on them and Ella waved away any mention of dessert. "I'm going to have to call it an early evening," she said with an apologetic smile to her date. "Papers to grade, you know how it is."

"In kindergarten?" He frowned.

"They have tests and homework too," she said gently. "Just the check, please," she said to the waiter. "Separate."

Her date shook his head. "Stay and at least have an after-dinner drink."

"No, it's a school night," she said. "I have to get up early."

"Well, this was a waste of time and money." He crossed his arms across his chest and sulked, a position she saw almost daily. But not from a grown man.

"Excuse me?" She looked around for the waiter, hoping to see him rushing towards them so she could leave.

"Get dressed up; shell out money for an expensive dinner like this just to get the brush off. I'm surprised you didn't have a friend call you with a fake emergency halfway through, like a lot of women do."

"First dates are all about seeing whether or not you are compatible," Ella said in the soothing voice she usually reserved for a child about to have a temper tantrum. "I'm afraid we're just not compatible."

"God damn waste of time." He grimaced.

"Then I suggest you stop dating so you don't waste any more of it," she said as the waiter walked up with the bill. "Have a good evening." She paid her half plus a generous tip for the waiter (Bachelor Number Three was definitely giving off non-tipper vibes) and made her escape.

Just as she stepped outside, her phone went off. With a sigh, she answered.

"Oh, my God, Ella, you've got to get over here! Your cat/dog/bird/hamster died!"

"Yeah, thanks for calling," she said. "You're about thirty minutes too late. I'm already getting in the car and leaving him behind."

"But Bachelor Number Three was going to be your soulmate," Serena said with a dramatic flair. "The website said so."

"Yeah, well, I'm done with internet dating. And agency dating. And every other dating. Just dating in general."

"You always say that and then you always try it again. You're an incurable romantic."

"Or an incurable masochist."

"Why don't you come over? There's an 'I Love the 1980s' marathon on television and a bottle of wine in my refrigerator that is just begging to be drunk."

"That's the point. I don't want to get drunk, I just want to go home and soak in the bathtub in peace."

"Your mother's going to be calling to see how the date went and she'll be disappointed that there aren't going to be grandchildren in the future anytime soon."

Ella sighed. "OK, I'm coming over. But only one glass of wine and since dining with Bachelor Number Three killed my appetite, I'm bringing over burgers."

"My hero."

Two

After one too many episodes about the glories of the 1980s, and a glass of wine following an overly greasy hamburger and French fries, Ella was feeling half-sick. Especially when she saw what Serena was doing.

"I told you I'm not doing internet dating any more."

"See, the problem is you've just hit the wrong websites," Serena was saying in the enthusiastic tone she got after a few glasses of wine. "There's plenty of fish in the sea, you just have to be fishing in the right ocean."

"I think you're mixing metaphors there."

"Whatever. What about this one?" Serena clicked on a website that showed smiling, happy couples. One website looked pretty much like the other, and Ella had to think for a moment.

"Tried it. Kept getting guys who wanted to 'hook up'."

"What about this one?"

Another website, another group of smiling people. "Sent the guy who wanted to discuss cultural elitism all night."

"What does that mean?"

"I have no idea."

"There's got to be something out there . . ." Serena scrolled down. Then, with a big smile on her face, she clicked a link. "Got it."

Ella peered over her shoulder. "Future Date? You're right, that is something pretty out there."

"This is just too funny; they've definitely latched on to a new marketing scheme." Serena clicked on the "About" page. "Listen to this: 'Welcome to Future Date! Do you feel like you've dated all the single men in your area? What about in your time? At Future Date, we connect available, single men from the future with women from the past.'"

"What?" Ella looked closer. "They're not serious."

"Of course they're not! What, did you think Soulmate Agency was being serious when they promised to connect you with your metaphysical other half? It's a marketing ploy, a gimmick. Oh, it gets better, listen to this," she continued, scrolling up. "'Each match is based on compatibility – mental, physical and biological. We run a thorough background check on each interested party to weed out any possible blood-relative connection.'"

"Thank God, because I didn't want to chance a paradox," Ella said sarcastically. "But how could they claim that anyway? There are possible variables for any decision. I could have married Bachelor Number Three tonight and had a great-great-great grandson who's trolling this website as we speak in one future."

"But you didn't."

"But who's to say I didn't in that future?" Ella pointed out.

"But in order for you to meet Mr Future Date and live happily ever after with him, you didn't have kids with anyone other than him, so that negates the possibility that you're his great-great-great grandmother or whatever from an alternate future. I think. Stop it. You're making my head hurt. The real point is they do a background check on everyone, which is good, because that way you know you're not dating a convicted sex offender or something. They just dress it up in silly sci-fi nonsense."

"I don't know, Serena," Ella said. "Who would sign up for something like this?"

"Someone else who gets the joke and just wants to have fun and meet someone new. They probably just connect people out of different time zones or something. That's the 'future' bit." Serena was already clicking the "Sign Up Now!" button.

"I don't know if I want a long-distance relationship."

"Oh, relax. They're not asking you to travel into the future for him. He comes to you." Serena winked. "Now, you were born in Warren, right?"

"No, absolutely not." Ella shook her head. "I'm not doing this. I'm not getting set up on another blind date, this one is practically guaranteed to be bad."

"You don't know that . . ."

"It's a website that's set up like a bad science-fiction movie. And I'm not that into science fiction. And there's always the possibility I'll get someone who's serious about it and really believes they are a time traveler . . . No." She shook her head again for emphasis. "I'm not doing it."

Serena pouted. "Fine, be that way. Don't meet the future hunk of your dreams."

"If you're that into it, you do it."

"Maybe I will."

"And on that note, I'm going home." Ella stood up and put her coat on. "I'll see you at school tomorrow."

"When your mom calls, tell her I said hi."

"I'll tell her you tried to set me up with H.G. Wells." And with that parting note, Ella shut the door behind her and stepped back out into the cold evening.

Going over to her car, she glanced down as she was putting her key into the lock and groaned. She must have run over some glass or something because her front tyre was flat. Swearing under her breath, she kicked the tyre in frustration. "The end to a perfect day."

"Something wrong?" A voice asked from the kerb.

She turned to see a man in a heavy jacket and baseball cap standing there. She couldn't make out the details of his face in the dark, but he didn't seem like an axe murderer. Then again, do axe murderers ever seem like axe murderers?

"Oh, just a flat tyre," she said, gesturing to the car. "I was going to call someone."

"Don't you have a spare?"

"In the trunk, but the jack always sticks . . . It's OK, really. I'm just going to call someone." She got out her cell phone to illustrate that point so he would go away.

"No, don't do that. I'll change it for you, no problem."

"You don't have to do that."

"I told you, it's no problem. Look, I know you don't know me – I'm some random guy that just walked up on the street. So just get out the tyre and the jack and put them on the ground and then I'll come over there and change it and you stand over here. That way I'm never too close to you."

Ella's face coloured. "I didn't mean to imply I thought you were some sort of maniac."

"You're just being cautious. I understand. Can't trust Good Samaritans these days. Ready?"

She did as he requested and, within a few minutes, he had the old tyre off and the new one on again.

"Thanks for this," she said, stepping a bit closer to him. She could see a hint of smile and a glimmer of blue eyes before he ducked his head.

"Like I said, no problem. I'll see you around." He turned and abruptly walked off in the opposite direction, leaving her to get in the car and leave the incident behind her.

Three

Ella had forgotten all about the evening at Serena's by the end of the week, caught up in preparing for the kindergarten class play and the day-to-day drama that was teaching a bunch of five- and six-year-olds how to read, write and count. All thoughts of dating, let alone dating men who purported to be from the future, went completely out of her head until Serena walked up to her after dismissal one day and said, "You're going to hate me."

Ella finished saying goodbye to her last student and made sure the little girl made it safely on to the bus to go home for the day before turning to her friend. "What did you get me into now? It's not the PTO carnival, is it? Did you volunteer me to run the cotton candy booth again?"

"Would I do that?"

"Yes, and I'll come home covered in sticky glop like last time! Why can't you volunteer me to do something easy, like the fishing game?"

"Well, it's not cotton candy and it's not the fishing game. It's nothing to do with the carnival or school at all."

"Oh, God . . ."

"Remember that dating website we were checking out?"

"*You* were checking it out, not *me*," Ella retorted and then her face fell. "Oh, no."

Serena nodded.

"You didn't!"

"I did. I signed you up."

"After I told you not to!" Ella smacked her on the arm with the clipboard she was carrying.

"Ow! I'm telling the principal!"

"You do that and I'll tell him you're impersonating me online for the purposes of dating. I won't even get detention monitor duty." Ella sighed. "Why'd you do that?"

"There were some pretty hot guys on that website. I was checking out some of the profiles."

"Serena, that's just the bait they use to hook you in. Take my name off the site right now, there's no way I'm paying for that."

"You don't have to pay, it's a free site. It's like a social networking site, just dating."

"With people supposedly from the future."

"That too. But you've already got a bunch of potential matches and some of them have already sent you invitations to chat. There are some pretty hot ones on your list. I'm half tempted to sign up myself."

"You should have." Ella shook her head. "And 'chats'?"

"Yeah, they send you a list of people you would be compatible with and then you can read their profiles. If you think they're someone you'd like to get to know better, you can request a chat. If they accept, you can instant message each other on the website. And if they're not interested, you can't message them again. It's a good system actually, so you don't keep getting requests from losers you're not interested in. I've already picked out some of the better prospects for you."

"You're too kind."

Curiosity was working its way into Ella despite her many reservations. "Hot guys, huh?"

Serena nodded with a smile. "Really hot."

"And they requested to talk to me?"

"Sure did."

"You didn't put up someone else's picture on my profile or claim I'm a celebrity or something?"

"Nope. You're a schoolteacher who would enjoy a quiet evening at home with a special someone, and the collected works of William Shakespeare."

"And the future guys?"

"Actually, none of them seem to be buying into the site's sci-fi stuff, either. They're just talking about being law professors or enjoying writing poetry. The usual dating website stuff. No one's talking about fighting the glow-worms from planet Neptune or anything crazy like that." Serena grinned at her. "Come on. You know you want to at least take a peek at who's interested."

They snuck back to Serena's classroom and fired up her computer.

"The firewall better let me through ... ah, success!" Serena crowed as she got back to the website and entered Ella's info on the log-in page. "I set you up a separate email address so all of your Future Date emails go through there. I didn't figure you wanted to use the school's address for that."

"And you figured I wouldn't find out as fast."

"That too. Now, I wrote down your log-in information. You know, in case you were interested." She gave Ella an innocent smile and passed her a slip of paper. "You can access your information either through the links the website sends you in the emails or on the actual site." She clicked a page labelled "Requests". "And here are the guys that are interested." She moved so Ella could sit down and scroll through.

Ella clicked through the requests, each with the picture of a smiling, handsome man next to it. If you clicked on the picture, it brought up each man's profile page. Ella followed the links. There was a college professor, an artist, a professional athlete, a dentist, a therapist, a car salesman, a banker, a mechanic, a ranch hand, a police officer and a journalist interested in her. They all ranged in age from twenty-five to forty, single and divorced, with hometowns listed all over the country.

"A lot better fish than any usual website, huh?" Serena said, pointing out a few of her favourites. "And your profile's been up less than a week. Their system's still computing matches."

"Why are all of these hot guys single? And wanting to talk to me?" Ella shook her head. "It's got to be a scam. It's probably to get money out of desperate women looking for love."

"So don't send them money. Just talk to him. Or him." Serena pointed at two different profiles. "Or him."

"No, if I'd talk to anyone on this crazy website, it'd be . . ." Ella scrolled over and clicked on one of the profiles. "Him." It was a picture of a man with close-cropped dark hair and serious blue eyes, with what looked like a park in the background of the photo.

Serena gave the picture a second glance. "Him? Why?"

"I like his smile. It's honest. He's not smirking like he knows he's all that and he's not trying to do the shy thing. He just . . . is. He didn't take the picture at home off of a web cam or cell phone or something and he didn't pose for the picture like a prima donna. It looks like it's one snapped by a friend or something." She scrolled down to read more of the profile. "He's thirty-one, he's a journalist, he has a pet dog named Bandit, a niece and a nephew he loves to spoil and he's looking for a serious relationship. He also enjoys reading classic literature but isn't above going to see the latest blockbuster movie or reading a best-selling mystery. He's also been known to read a torrid romance or two."

"It says 'torrid'?"

"It says torrid."

"He sounds perfect!" Serena looked over her shoulder. "Oh wait. No, he's not. He's got a major flaw."

"What's that, other than being on this website?"

"His name is Herman."

Ella laughed. "So his name's Herman, so what?"

"That sounds like a grandfather's name, Herman. That's so old-fashioned."

"Maybe the name's come back in vogue in the future," Ella said with mirth.

"Maybe. But I can't see you walking down the aisle in your gorgeous wedding dress carrying a bouquet of a dozen long-stemmed roses, that you hand off to me as you take his hands in your trembling ones, and then breathlessly say, 'I, Ella, take you, Herman.'"

Ella laughed again. "Well, maybe it's a family name."

"Maybe."

"Maybe he has a nickname he goes by."

"Maybe you should accept his request and find out."

Ella looked back at the screen at the photo of a man with a smile that made her feel safe for some reason. He just looked like a nice guy, one who called his mother every week, didn't move too fast on a date, and was kind to animals and children.

"Maybe I should," she said, and clicked accept before she could think twice.

Four

Ella's curiosity continued to get the better of her. She stayed away from the computer long enough to watch a few television programmes while she sat on her couch, eating a microwave frozen dinner. But the siren song of the computer, and whether or not the good-looking man with the nice smile had replied to her yet, made her finally dig out her laptop and fire it up. While it was loading, she noticed her hands were shaking and her stomach had butterflies.

"What is wrong with you?" she muttered, mad at herself for acting like a teenager instead of a grown woman. She went to the homepage of the website, logged in and was immediately met with a chat bar and one message.

Glad you decided to accept my request. It's nice to meet you, Ella.

She bit her lip and typed, *It's nice to meet you, too, Herman. Or do you have a nickname you go by?*

She didn't expect an immediate reply and was surprised to see one.

No, just Herman. I know, Herman's not a popular name, but I'm bringing it back in style!

She laughed at that. *My name didn't get popular until well after I was out of high school, so I've lived with an unusual name too. I don't usually do internet chats, so I'm probably bad at it.*

You're fine, he replied. *Just like making small talk anywhere else. I just finished up covering a city council meeting, so trust me, anything you say will be the most wildly interesting thing I've heard all day.*

She laughed again, already starting to feel comfortable. *I helped small children paint a set for a school play. I think more paint ended up on the floor and on their smocks than on the set.*

And what play are they doing?

Three Little Pigs. *It's a musical.*

Of course it is. I wouldn't expect anything less.

I wrote it.

Seriously? That's neat. I was always into theatre growing up and when I went off to college, I originally wanted to write plays. Not musicals about pigs necessarily, but I wouldn't have ruled it out either. Alas, I've turned my creative talents to reporting about government woes. I thought it would pay better and I wanted a steady job.

As long as there are kids, there's going to be a need for teachers. I love what I do, but the lure of a steady job appealed to me too, I have to admit, she replied. *That and having summers off.*

They still do that?

She blinked. That was the first time he had worded anything that sounded remotely like he believed the future thing. Cautiously she typed, *Well, I know a lot of school systems have gone to year-round school, but ours hasn't yet. Our buildings are so old, they need a lot of work done, or no one would be able to concentrate in the heat of summer.*

Who can? I know I can barely pay attention to my work when it's a nice day out. I just sit and stare out the window and watch the traffic pass by until my boss asks me what I'm working on. It's nice to have to go out on assignment just to have an excuse to be outside instead of in an office all day.

I try to make excuses to take the kids outside, too, she typed. *For nature walks. We've been raising tadpoles and then releasing them at the pond near the school.*

Wish I had a cool teacher like you. My teachers were all stuffy old men that didn't want to be bothered to do anything active.

They continued to chat back and forth about their respective childhood school memories and best/worst teachers until Ella realized it was almost midnight.

I've got to get up in the morning!

Sorry. I forget not everyone is a night owl like me.

It's not your fault. I just lost track of time.

That's a good thing, right?

She smiled. *I think so.*

Great. Because I was having a good time, too. Want to chat again tomorrow?

She took a deep breath. Did she want to? Yes. Should she? She didn't know. This was a screwy website, and while he seemed like a normal, sane individual, you never knew who you were really talking to online. He could be some creepy old guy with no teeth for all she really knew.

Screw it. She typed, *Sure. Have fun interviewing councilmen tomorrow.*

Have fun with the play. Be sure to tell me if the pigs escape the big bad wolf and live to sing another day.

As she signed off, Ella noticed something strange about Herman's messages. All of the messages were time and date-stamped, like a lot of email messages. Hers all had the proper date.

His were all dated the next day.

"Like he's emailing from the future," she scoffed out loud. Shaking her head and reminding herself of different time zones, she turned off her computer.

But not the nagging feeling in the back of her mind.

Five

Ella paced back and forth outside of the restaurant nervously. "This is crazy," she hissed into her cell phone. "What am I doing here? I don't know this guy."

"You've been online chatting with this guy every night for the past two weeks," Serena said on the other end. "You're having dinner, not marrying him. Talking to someone online for two weeks is knowing them enough for dinner."

"If he is who he says he is."

"A journalist from the future?"

"Ha, ha. He's never actually said he was from the future, you know."

"He probably assumes you know that, since the website advertises it."

"Be serious! You know what I mean. He could turn out to be a sex predator or something."

"They do background checks, remember. He's not a sex predator. And if he turns out to be something other than who he says he is, you can just leave and never talk to him again. But if he is who he says he is and he travelled all the way from . . . where did he say he was from?"

"He didn't. When he suggested meeting, I suggested meeting somewhere in between our two locations and he just said to pick the time, date, and place and he'd be there."

"Maybe he's homeless."

"Homeless guys have computer access?"

"Everyone has computer access, hon."

"Arrgh!" Ella growled in frustration. "Why am I standing outside in the cold having this ridiculous conversation with you?"

"I have no idea. Get in there and meet him already! Call me later and let me know how it goes. I want details!"

Ella disconnected, stowed her phone in her purse and took a deep breath, smoothing out an invisible wrinkle in her dress. This was it. She was finally going to meet Herman, who liked coffee but not tea, loved action movies and had never seen an episode of *Grey's Anatomy*, and who agreed with her that Duke Ellington was not only the greatest jazz musician, but the greatest musician ever, period.

Ella gave her name to the maître d' at the door, who whisked her to a table towards the back of the restaurant where a very familiar-looking man sat, looking just as nervous as she felt. "Thank God it's actually him," she whispered under her breath.

Seeing her approach, he smiled and stood up, revealing a tuxedo shirt, jacket and tie with jeans. Her smile quavered slightly. So he had offbeat fashion sense, so what? At least he didn't show up for her date with food-stained clothes or cut-off jean shorts, which two of her previous dates had done.

"You're even lovelier in person," he said, taking her hand in his for an awkward shake, and then giving her an even more awkward kiss on the cheek. His voice was warm and comfortable, with a hint of familiarity.

"Thank you. It's so nice to finally meet you in person," she said, taking the seat he held out for her.

"So I've been dying to ask, did you solve the case of the missing lunches?" he asked as they looked over the menu.

She laughed, thinking of the student she had told him about. "Yes. Apparently he didn't like what his mom was packing for him in the morning, so he kept 'losing' them at school in order to have hot lunch instead. He'd been throwing away the lunches in the boys' restroom before school or giving them to other kids."

"You've got to admire that kind of ingenuity," he said with a dazzling smile and the two of them lapsed into easy conversation that lasted throughout the meal.

Ella was enjoying herself, enjoying the ease with which she related to him, as if he was an old friend. It was almost inconceivable that they had never met face to face until today, and even more strange to think they'd met on some kooky website, which was just what she was about to say to him until he interrupted her with a guilty look, saying, "I've been avoiding the subject, but I think we need to talk about the future."

She blinked. "The future of us? We just met."

"No. I mean, yes, we probably should talk about that too, but no, I meant the future. I need to explain to you about the website."

"Oh, that." She waved her hand. "I know it's silly. My friend and I were just being crazy one night and joined up. Was it a similar thing with you too?"

"I figured as much, which is why I've been avoiding the subject. I don't want to upset you, but we can't build on a relationship when the whole truth isn't out there." He took a deep breath. "This is the thing. It's true. I am from the future."

Ella stared at him, her heart dropping into her stomach. Her worst fears were coming true. He was crazy.

"In the decade in which I was born, there was a huge overpopulation problem on Earth. The government finally had to declare a limit on births."

So crazy. "That's not possible," she said gently. "The government couldn't do that. They couldn't take away people's rights like that."

"They can and they did. They were concerned the planet couldn't sustain the amount of people being born, so families could only carry one child to term. And when given the choice, many families wanted a boy over a girl. So boys were overwhelmingly carried to term over girls."

Even though she didn't believe a word of this, she was horrified at the story. "Any child is a blessing, why would they care?"

He shrugged. "I'm definitely not saying it was right. Because, now, the male population outnumbers the female overwhelmingly. The birth rates have dropped dramatically because there aren't enough women to, pardon the expression, go around. Now the governments of the world are concerned that there aren't going to be enough workers in the future to sustain society. They've still kept the limit on births, but they've stopped allowing any scans for the sex of unborn babies so people have to take what nature gives them."

Ella shook her head. "That is a crazy story."

He continued. "We've perfected time travel. It was originally a way for the very wealthy to vacation, so long as they follow specific rules so as not to upset the time line, and only for a specific amount of time. See?" He showed her his watch, a complicated-looking thing that seemed to combine a cell phone, watch and computer in one and was, indeed, timing something. "It's a lot easier to manipulate emails to go back in time than it is to send people. It was decided to set up the website as a way for men to find wives in the past."

Her mouth dropped open. "What, like a mail-order bride?"

He looked sheepish. "I guess you could say that."

Ella snapped up her bag, on her feet in an instant. "I knew this was a mistake. I knew it. From the moment I saw that website."

He got up too. "Ella, wait, please!"

"Not only are you crazy enough to believe the site hype, you make up this insane, and might I add *sexist*, story to go along with it! Don't try to contact me again." She hurried past the waiters, who were trying to hide the fact that they were watching, out the door and into the parking lot.

"Wait, Ella, I can prove it!"

"Yeah, right."

"There's going to be a freak blizzard tonight. You're going to be snowed in over the next couple of days. School's going to be cancelled."

Ella stopped short, keys out and ready to get into the car. "You can't know that."

"I read the article last night because I had a feeling you wouldn't believe me."

"Whatever. Just don't contact me again."

"If you decide you believe me, *you* contact *me*."

"Don't be expecting it." Ella got into her car and drove away, leaving Herman behind in her rear-view mirror.

Six

Ella woke up before her alarm clock went off, something she rarely did. Blinking, she realized it was because the light coming in from her window was extremely bright. Had she slept in? She checked the alarm clock again, but it still read 7 a.m. Feeling as if every nerve in her body was on alert, she walked over to the window and brushed aside the curtain to look out.

There was snow everywhere; catching the sunlight and reflecting it back brightly. School was definitely cancelled.

Ella was trembling. Before she had gone to bed last night, she had checked the weather report, and there had been no chance of snow whatsoever.

"There's no way he could have known that when the television meteorologists didn't," she whispered. "No way."

She hurried over to her computer, went immediately to the website and typed.

How did you do that?

As usual she got an immediate response. *It made headlines. I told you I read the article. Do you believe me now?*

I believe something is going on, she replied.

What's it going to take for you to believe me?

Take me back to your place.

Pardon me?

I want to see the future.

You can't. That's part of the rules. Unless you're permanently moving to the future, I can't bring you here. Too much risk of you finding out what companies to invest in, becoming a multi-millionaire and somehow messing up the time stream.

Then I'm not going to believe you. It was some weird coincidence . . .

He didn't respond for a while, and then came back with – *I could take you into the past.*

She stared at the screen. Surely she hadn't read it right.

As long as we don't visit the past during your lifetime, where you could alter something about your own life, I could take you. For an hour or so. It's expensive enough, me travelling back to see you. Time travel costs really go up when you take a passenger.

Oh, of course. Stupid travel agents! she quipped, while still numb with shock.

So name a time period and we'll go. For an hour or so.

Any time?

Any time.

Ella sighed. Why not go all out? *Then I want to go swing dancing. I learned how to dance about five years ago. I want to go to the Cotton Club. But more importantly, I want to go hear Duke Ellington perform "It Don't Mean a Thing If It Ain't Got That Swing".*

Sounds great. Let's go.

Right now?

You doing anything else today?

And before she knew it, Ella was standing outside in the massive amounts of snow, in a fake fur coat and slinky silk dress, shivering while people attempted to shovel their driveways and kids playing in the snow gave her weird looks.

She waved merrily at one of the kids giving her a questioning look and in an eye blink Herman was standing there in front of her, dressed in a suit and fedora.

She gasped and stumbled back. "How did you do that?"

He held up his wristwatch. "Time travel, remember?"

She looked around, seeing no car he could have come from. Indeed, the snow surrounding him was clear of footprints. She shivered again, and not from the cold.

"You look lovely, but you're not going to be able to swing dance in that."

"It was the only thing in my closet that looks remotely like something out of the 1930s. If I have to sit and listen to Duke Ellington, I'll do that too."

"Are you ready?" He took a matching watch out of his pocket and checked the time.

"Does it hurt?" she asked as he slipped the watch on her.

"It's extremely cold in one sharp instant. And then you blink, and you're there. Now, according to our guidelines, I have to tell you that you cannot say or do anything that is going to seriously impact the future. You talk with as few people as possible. Think of it as bird watching or going on safari. You watch the people interacting and try to stay out of their way."

She nodded and he took her hand, then pressed a button on the watch. And in an eye blink, a terrible coldness settled over her.

The next thing she knew, they were standing in the back of a crowded room, the gorgeous sounds of jazz and people laughing mixing with the haze of cigarette smoke that filled the room.

"Oh, my God." Ella looked around. Everywhere people were dressed like something out of one of her grandparents' picture albums. "We're in the Cotton Club." She pushed past the crowd to get a good view of the band performing in the crowded club and gasped. "Oh, my God!" She pointed to the stage. "It's Duke Ellington!"

Herman was smiling. "I can see that."

"They're playing 'Sophisticated Lady'!"

"I can hear that."

"Oh, my God!" She threw her arms around him and hugged him. "This is the best date I've ever been on!"

He laughed. "Does this mean you believe me?"

"Either this is real or I'm hallucinating with you."

"It's real, all right. Now –" he held out an arm to her "– want to dance?"

They spent the next forty-five minutes dancing to every song Ella's dress would allow and sitting out at a table nearby for the others, enjoying the music and just basking in the presence of the band.

"Our time's about to run out," Herman said to her.

"Oh, no!" Ella said with dismay. "And he hasn't played it yet."

"I'll be right back."

Ella watched in awe as he skirted around the dancing couples and went up to where the band was performing. Her mouth fell open as Herman talked to the famous musician himself, pointing back to where she was sitting. He smiled, nodded, and then turned back to the band as Herman walked back to her. The first notes of her song rang out.

"How did you do that?"

"I told him I'd travelled from far away to impress a girl," he said with a wink. "And playing this song might help my chances."

"Chances for what?"

He didn't say a word as he led her out on to the dance floor again. Even as they danced to the upbeat song, Ella knew one thing – she was falling for him, big time. "I'm glad you brought me here," she said over the music.

"Me too," he said. "I'm glad you finally believe me. Ella. I know we're moving fast, but I have to tell you something – I'm falling in love with you."

She felt her face flush. "I think I'm falling in love with you too."

And then, he leaned forwards and gave her the warmest, sweetest kiss in all of time, in front of all of the patrons of the Cotton Club and Duke Ellington. They were still kissing even as the ice cold of time travel took them away in an eye blink.

They broke off the kiss shyly and took in their new surroundings. "We're back already?" Ella asked, disappointed as she looked around to find herself in the snow once again outside her house.

"The travel lasts for only an hour, remember? I got a few bonus minutes to allow for time to come get you. It came with the package deal."

"Naturally," she said in shock.

"Listen, Ella," he said. "I'm afraid I've got to tell you something else. Something important."

"More important than being from the future?"

"I told you before, time travel is pretty expensive. And I'm just a journalist. We don't get paid much, even in the future." He ran a hand through his hair. "I can't afford to keep coming back to see you."

Her heart plummeted into her stomach, and she was surprised to realize how much the loss of him would affect her. "What? So we can't keep seeing each other any more? I thought that was the whole point of this, to find someone in the past."

"It is and I did. I met you, Ella." He took her hands in his. "Like I said before, I know we're moving really fast and I know you barely know me, but I also know that there's no other woman in all of time that I want to be with. Love at first sight might be a cliché, but I think in this case, it's also true. I'm asking you to go to the future with me."

"You said I couldn't go to the future."

"I said you couldn't go to the future for a visit. But you could go to the future permanently." He squeezed her hand. "With me. We wouldn't have to get married right away; I wouldn't ask you to do that. We can wait until you get acclimatized in the new time period."

She was stunned at what he was asking. "I'd have to leave everything and everyone I know behind. For ever!"

"Not for ever, we could save up so you could come back for visits, like on holidays or something. And you could email them, as I said before; emails are easier to send back in time than people."

"They'd just think I disappeared on them!"

"Tell them you're joining the Peace Corps or something."

She shook her head. "I don't think I can. I don't think I can give up everything I have and everyone I know for someone that I just met." She met his eyes. "Herman, I think I am falling in love with you, but how do I know it will last?"

"How do you know with anyone?"

"And this is only the second time I've met you," she said. "Shouldn't you have at least three dates before you commit to something big like this?"

"Well, we've met three times actually."

"No, we haven't."

"I wasn't sure if you'd agree to go on this date, so the other night I borrowed money off of my dad to do one last grand gesture. I went back to the night you signed up for the account on Future Date and met you in person."

Her mouth fell open. "W-What?"

"I thought I'd do something romantic, like meet you with flowers after the bad date you were telling me about, the one with the guy who didn't like kids. You never mentioned the name of the restaurant though; you only said you went to your friend Serena's where she signed you up on the dating site. So I found her address online and met you outside of her apartment."

"No, you didn't."

"You had a flat tyre."

She gasped, staring at him in recognition. "Oh, my God! That was you!"

He nodded. "I was going to try to use that as proof of the time travel. I realized afterwards that didn't really prove anything about time travel, only that I met you before. So—" he shrugged sheepishly "—we've met before."

"I don't think changing a tyre counts as a date," she said with a wry smile.

"It should." He looked at her, his eyes so hopeful. "So, will you go to the future with me?"

Ella couldn't believe she was even considering this. She had never done a crazy thing in her life before signing on to that website. She had always been the good girl and played it safe. Had anyone ever said that she'd be standing in the snow after having been on a date to see Duke Ellington in the 1930s, contemplating marrying a guy that she just met face to face a few days ago, she would have laughed.

Instead, she smiled.

"Yes," she said. "I will."

Author Biographies

Madeline Baker
New York Times and *USA Today* bestselling author. Also writes as
Amanda Ashley.
www.MadelineBaker.net

Sandy Blair
Award-winning author of Scotland-set historical romances.
www.sandyblair.net

Gwyn Cready
RITA-award-winning author of *Tumbling Through Time*, *Seducing
Mr Darcy* and, coming April 2010, *Flirting With Forever*.
www.cready.com

Autumn Dawn
Author of *No Words Alone* and *When Sparks Fly, both* from
Dorchester.
autumndawnbooks.com

Colby Hodge
Award winning author of the Oasis series and *Twist*. Also known
as Cindy Holby.
www.cindyholby.com

Jean Johnson
New York Times bestselling author of the Sons of Destiny series.
www.JeanJohnson.net

Michele Lang
Author of the upcoming Lady Lazarus historical fantasy series.
www.michelelang.com

Holly Lisle
Author of *Talyn*, *Hawkspar* and thirty other novels in the fantasy, SF, paranormal suspense and young-adult fantasy genres.
www.hollylisle.com

Allie Mackay
National bestselling author of light, Scottish-set paranormals. Allie Mackay is the pseudonym for Sue-Ellen Welfonder, *USA Today* bestselling author of Scottish medievals, including her popular MacKenzies of Kintail series.
www.alliemackay.com

Sara Mackenzie
Writes paranormal romance for Avon, and also historical romance as Sara Bennett.
www.saramackenzie.com

Michelle Maddox
Author of the futuristic romantic thriller, *Countdown*, as well as several paranormal romance and young adult fantasy novels (writing as Michelle Rowen).
www.michellemaddox.com

Margo Maguire
The author of seventeen historical novels, including the Warrior time-travel series from Avon. Writing in both the medieval and Regency eras, her books have been translated into more than fifteen different languages.

Maureen McGowan
Debut author of sexy paranormal romance and women's fiction.
www.maureenmcgowan.com

A.J. Menden
She has never travelled in time, but does enjoy big band music.

Author of the Elite Hands of Justice series. The first in the series, *Phenomenal Girl 5*, was nominated for a Reviewers' Choice award from *Romantic Times* magazine and the second, *Tekgrrl*, was chosen as a Top Pick by *Romantic Times* magazine.
www.ajmenden.com

Cindy Miles
Cindy Miles is the national bestselling author of the ghostly paranormal Knights series.
www.cindy-miles.com

Sandra Newgent
A debut author who thrives on romance and adventure, she's even cycled around the USA in the name of love. She writes paranormal, time travel, romantic adventure and historical romance. *Every love has its time*.

Patti O'Shea
Nationally bestselling author and winner of numerous writing awards, her books have appeared on the Barnes & Noble, Waldenbooks and Borders bestseller lists. Currently, she's working on the Light Warrior series about a society of magic users that protects humans from demons and monsters.
www.pattioshea.com

Patrice Sarath
Author of the popular *Gordath Wood* and the Red Gold Bridge fantasy series.
www.patricesarath.com

Michelle Willingham
Internationally published author of the Irish medieval MacEgan Brothers series.
www.michellewillingham.com